I0653975

WE CAME ALL THIS WAY

A Novel

MIKE HEPPNER

Thought Catalog Books / Prospecta Press
Brooklyn, NY

Published by Thought Catalog Books, a division of The Thought & Expression Co., Williamsburg, Brooklyn. Founded in 2010, Thought Catalog is a website and imprint dedicated to your ideas and stories. We publish fiction and non-fiction from emerging and established writers across all genres. For general information and submissions: manuscripts@thoughtcatalog.com.

Second edition, 2017

ISBN: 978-1-945796-58-6

Printed and bound in the United States.

10 9 8 7 6 5 4 3 2 1

ALSO BY THE AUTHOR

The Egg Code
Pike's Folly
The Man Talking Project
Nada
This Can Be Easy or Hard

PRAISE FOR MIKE HEPPNER

We Came All This Way...

"Well-written and intriguing." – Kirkus Reviews

"One hell of a good book! Funny and sad—and fiercely original—with a raucous cast of characters who are both flawed and yet perfectly rendered."
— Will Ferguson, author of 419 and 2012 Giller Prize winner

The Egg Code...

"In this impressive debut novel, Heppner tackles his complex subject with a sure hand, creating a story that heartbreakingly displays the eternal frailties of human nature." – BookPage

Pike's Folly...

"Heppner's prose is ax sharp, and he fells a great many American demons in putting forth his haunting and redemptive vision of New England's past and present." – Publishers Weekly

This Can Be Easy or Hard...

*"This collection of short stories murders everything but the undeniable throb of life and love." — Zaron Burnett III, author of How Do I Survive This Sh*t?*

I. WHAT I DID IN OHIO AND MICHIGAN

CHAPTER ONE

Welcome to nowhere.

We are a loose collection of individuals who have made a choice and come to this place. Some of us are related by blood, others by circumstance. Our numbers were once thirty-eight and now they are ten.

We live on a manmade island located fourteen nautical miles off the coast of Newfoundland. Our President is Wallis Crim, 34, born and raised in Milner, Ohio. My name is Roseanne Okerfeldt, President Crim's personal assistant. I'm also his sister. I'm thirty-one, separated, with four children. The twins, Mary and Connor, live with their father along with their older brother Vance in Grand Rapids, Michigan. Star has chosen to stay with us on the island. Other full-time residents are as follows:

Dr. Emmanuelle Snow, 35, medical advisor and Head of Surgery. Dr. Snow also has an eight-month-old son, Sander, who was born on the island.

Dr. Clement Snow, 73, technical advisor.

Charity Blaise, DDS, 41, Head of Dentistry and Dr. Clement Snow's second wife.

Stephanie ("Steffi") Blaise, 12, child of Dr. Blaise's first marriage.

Neil Laporte, c. 40, cook and fisherman.

Gavin Baptiste, 48, Head of Security.

Together we are citizens of the Independent Island Nation of "Mobility," which is also the name of a wheelchair manufacturer in Moline, Illinois.

The island was built four years ago, in 2010, under the direction of Dr. Clement Snow. It has since survived two fires, yearly storms, an attack by pirates, and countless power outages. We call it an island but it's really a semi-submersible platform with room for eighty people on three decks. Much of the platform was salvaged from a retired Danish oil rig that Dr. Snow purchased at auction. Among other crimes, the Canadian government has accused us of using the island for illegal offshore drilling, but this has been proven false.

Nowadays the island stands three-quarters vacant, and to save power we've sealed off the bottom deck. Star has her own room facing the mainland; on clear days she can see the lighthouse at Cape Spear through her binoculars. We spend most of our time indoors, though in the summer we sometimes go topside to sunbathe on the helipad. The island's sophisticated on-board communications system permits us to intercept radio and television programs from around the globe, which makes us feel less isolated.

Days tend to follow a routine. Our cook, Neil Laporte, leaves at dawn on Mandy One to catch our dinner. Sometimes he takes Dr. Blaise's daughter, Steffi, who's keen on fishing. Our security task force, headed by (and now consisting entirely of) Gavin Baptiste, makes three daily patrols around the perimeter of the island in Mandy Two. Unless someone needs a filling replaced or a crown re-glued, Dr. Blaise looks after her elderly husband, Dr. Clement Snow, who's lately shown signs of decline.

When she's not taking care of her son, Dr. Snow's daughter Emmanuelle ("Mandy") presides over the medical wing on Deck

Two. Mandy has the biggest job on the island but also seems to do the least amount of work. She'll probably be the next of us to leave.

Then there's my brother—President Crim, I should say. Getting around has always been hard for him, so it's my job to make his life easier. I bring him his lunch, his dinner, his paperwork, his change of clothes. I help him in and out of bed, prepare his baths. I try to be a good sister.

It's a tough life out here, though rewarding. Only Sealand in the North Sea rivals Mobility in terms of worldwide public interest. We've been featured on the Discovery Channel, 60 Minutes, and CBC Radio, and our online store logs hundreds of transactions each month, selling Mobility T-shirts, shot glasses, bookmarks, key chains, and other such collectibles. But along with fame comes hardship. As a group we've been laughed at, persecuted. Dr. Clement Snow can't set foot in Canada, and I'm still considered a fugitive in the United States. Mobility isn't only my home, you see. It's also my prison.

CHAPTER TWO

I was fifteen the year Wallis came home for Christmas break and introduced us to Mandy Snow. Imagine it's 1998 and your older brother's off to college for the first time. You've finally got the whole downstairs to yourself. If you're like me, you like to stay up late listening to your headphones and smoking with your bedroom window cracked open. Cigarette of choice, American Spirit. You store your CDs in a shoebox under your bed, all the discs scratched and stuck in the wrong jewel cases: The Cure mixed up with Oasis and Third Eye Blind. Until recently, you haven't thought of boys as anything special, but now you can't think about anything else. You stare at them in class, keep an eye out for them at lunch, dream about them in bed. You get off on their smell, their bad penmanship. You're nothing like the little kid you were a year ago.

Wallis wasn't due in from Penn until the 25th, so my mom and I spent an hour on Christmas Eve getting the house wheelchair-ready again. My brother was ten in 1990 when he broke his spine falling out of Mrs. Deaver's station wagon on his way to a scout trip. The backseat had been crammed with too many kids and someone had forgotten to pull the door all the way shut. After the accident, my parents had a special toilet installed in the downstairs bathroom with grab bars on the sides so he could push himself up. They also widened the doors to his closet and invested in a new bed with side rails and an adjustable mattress. The ramp to the front door was fun to slide down in the winter.

Dad left the house after dinner for Christmas Eve services, and I wasted no time switching off the holiday music in the living room. My dad was the only one of us who still went to church. Every Sunday he walked or drove the six blocks from our house in Milner to the Good Shepherd Lutheran Church, which I passed on my way to school. The building was stone and traditional but had a modern annex that looked out of place. When I was younger my friends and I rode our bikes in the parking lot, and Gretchen Clearwater once broke her collarbone doing a stunt off the steps to the thrift shop.

Mom swept into the room with two glasses of wine. "Don't tell your father," she said, handing me one.

I sipped and pretended to look disgusted. "That's a very expensive chardonnay," she said. Mom was a silvery beauty with a hard chin and wrinkles that she covered with makeup. She was six years older than my dad—they'd had us late.

"It's great. I'm just not used to it," I said. My regular drink in those days was Jim Beam and Coke. I wasn't a very good kid growing up. I started sneaking drinks in my early teens, smoked behind Kroger with my friends Erin and Jill after school, and swiped the occasional twenty from my mom's desk. Petty delinquent stuff. I wasn't much better as a student. School bored me, though I did well enough in every subject except art. My art teacher said I took her assignments "too literally," whatever that meant. Ask me to draw something and I'll draw it. I can't promise it'll look like much.

I took another sip, then one last quickie and placed the glass on the coffee table. Under my sweater I wore the heart-shaped pendant that my boyfriend Brian had given me for our first Christmas together.

Mom pushed some pillows aside and dropped next to me on the couch. "What happened to the music?" she asked. I gagged. "Some of it's nice," she said.

"Mom, I've been listening to Christmas music since September." I had an after school job at the Pier 1 Imports in Montclair where we played the same dozen Christmas carols all day while unwrapping the holiday décor in the back room. It wasn't too awful. One of the assistant managers, Dean, went to Montclair Community College and scored us beer after work. Always the same joke: "Hey, Dean, can you pick us up a case of Pabst?" "Yeah, if you blow me." No one ever blew him.

At Pier 1 we wore blue aprons over our jeans and hoodie sweatshirts, and we'd park our used Honda hatchbacks out in back by the dumpsters. I just had my permit, so either my dad would drop me or I'd ride in with Erin. I spent my paycheck on incense and things for my room: a rag rug, a woven tapestry from Portugal. The full-timers were guys who'd gone to schools like Milner ten years ago and found themselves still in the neighborhood. One guy, Steve, had a Ford GT that ate up most of his salary. We made out once before I met Brian.

Other than Pier 1, my only job was babysitting. I wasn't naturally good around kids, though I took care of the Hodges girls on Friday nights. I could handle the diapers and putting Aggie and Kate down in their cribs, but I always had to force myself to keep them entertained with books and games and stuffed animals. I never imagined having a kid, let alone four. If you'd asked me what I'd be doing at age thirty, I would've said, "Making money, hopefully." Not a lot, but enough to travel three or four times a year. I'd probably be married to some guy. We'd have a condo in Westlake and go to concerts. Maybe I'd have my own business, something I could do out of the house. I wasn't particularly ambitious. I guess I just wanted to coast.

"What did Brian get you for Christmas?" Mom asked, and I showed her the pendant. "Very pretty. Is it silver or white gold? Remember, silver tarnishes. If it's white gold, you should get it rhodium plated every two years."

I tuned her out. Brian and I had only been together for three months, and we'd just started holding hands in public. Not a good topic for family discussion. Brian was half-Korean, which I thought was cool. He had floppy black hair that hung in his eyes and soft kissy lips. I liked how he looked at me, his eyes giving me all the attention in the world.

Earlier that afternoon I'd led him to a rusty old bench near the edge of Hayes Park. Most kids had already left town for the holidays, and Brian was heading out in an hour to visit his aunt and uncle in Columbus. From where we sat we could see clear down the sledding hill to the frozen pond below. Little kids were sledding and wiping out at the bottom while their parents looked cold.

I handed him his bag of presents. The stuff from Pier 1 was a joke, some markdown soaps and bath beads I got with my discount. I'd gone to Macy's for his big gift.

"I've never worn cologne before," he said.

"Put it on." I opened the box and spritzed him behind

the ear. The cologne brought out the pine smell of the woods.

"Mm. I may need to attack you," I said, nuzzling his throat. We hadn't had sex yet—we were innocent in that sense—but I had my eye on the 31st. I wanted to ring in the new year with champagne and condoms.

He laughed and squirmed away. "Aw, you're tickling me, dude."

It was his turn, so he took a jewelry box out of his pocket. I wondered how much he'd spent, if he'd borrowed the money from his parents. He couldn't have made more than seven bucks an hour bagging groceries at the Kroger downtown.

He opened the box. The necklace was one of those Shared Heart pendants from Zales—ninety-nine dollars plus a free box of chocolates.

"I didn't know what to pick," he said.

"It's perfect. Can you put it on me?"

He tried but his thumbs were no good, so I put it on myself. We kissed some, and I let him run his hands over my chest.

"So. Columbus. That sucks," I said. His head was buried between my breasts, his face in my sweater.

"It's my mom's side of the family. My cousins are cool. They live a mile away from this huge state prison, and every now and then someone gets out and they have to lock down the neighborhood. Rapists and murderers and shit. You'd never know—it's a real nice place. There's a Borders and a Gap and a Sports Authority."

Brian and I didn't really know much about each other. I knew that his favorite jacket was from Eastern Mountain Sports and his first concert was Kenny Chesney and we'd both had Mr. Dale last year for American History. Mr.

Dale made us sit in alphabetical order—Brian's last name was Young and mine was Crim—so we didn't see much of each other. Brian spoke more in class than I did. He raised his hand a lot, and Mr. Dale only called on him when he couldn't get an answer out of anyone else.

We weren't rich kids at Milner High. Most of our parents were teachers or small business owners or had jobs working for Sperry Steel. We were working-class Democrats. We lived in nice ranch houses and inherited our parents' old cars for our sixteenth birthdays. I knew for a fact that at least half of us were having sex by tenth grade. The school itself was built in the fifties—single-story, pretty non-descript except for the breezeway connecting the west wing with the science building. Our principal was an out-lesbian named Mrs. Carter, and everyone acted like it was no big deal. I would describe Milner as basically moderate, politically speaking. We liked Clinton. Kids listened to hip-hop and smoked weed and still managed to put in a clean appearance on school-pictures day.

"I'm glad the necklace fits. I went to Montclair Gardens. I thought I'd run into you there," said Brian. Montclair Gardens was the shopping mall across the street from the Pier 1 where I worked. Erin and I liked to dash across the four-lane highway during our break and have lunch in the food court. The mall was one of those huge, four-story plazas with a fountain and a marble concourse. Montclair kids and Milner kids hung out in the parking lot by the Cineplex. A good half of the stores catered to teenagers—they sold our clothes and played our music—but the mall cops had an attitude about us. The only troublemakers lived in Montclair—they shoplifted at Pier 1 all the time and there was nothing you could do about it unless they practically waved the incense or votive candles in front of you. Stealing's easy, if you want to know the truth.

Mom had another look at my necklace, nearly choking me in the process. "I think it's probably white gold. Sometimes it's hard to tell. White gold isn't actually white, did you know that? It's got a surface plating that makes it look white. Those earrings your father bought for me in Taos are white gold. Let's see…" She pulled tighter on the necklace. "Yep, that's gold—see where it says '10K'?"

"Mom, I don't care," I said.

"I'm sure you don't, but it's good to know the difference. You can rub the plating right off if you use silver polish on a piece of white gold."

"I'm not stupid. I know how to take care of things." I twisted and squirmed until she finally let go. "I don't care if it's silver or gold or how much it'll be worth in ten years. It's just a necklace. Stop ruining it for me."

We both sipped our wine.

An hour or so later my father came back from church. Hearing the front door open, Mom called across the house, "Boots off."

"Got it," he said over the thump-thump of his knocking the snow off his boots. She leaned over the sofa and spread the window blinds. "I wonder if it's still coming down."

Dad appeared in the living room in his stocking feet. His cheeks looked red and hard from huffing around in the cold.

"Good service?" Mom asked.

"Not bad," he said.

"Do you feel spiritually enlightened?"

He chuckled gamely. "What I feel like is a glass of sherry. You?"

She gulped back the rest of her wine and handed him her glass. "What was the sermon about?" she asked as he went out to get their drinks.

"Just what you'd expect. We went over some passages from Luke. *And then we all held hands and sang a song.* Where's the sherry?"

"Bottom shelf. Was it crowded?"

"Not too bad. Most people go earlier in the day. Pastor Bob asked after you."

"He did? Did he say, 'Where's your sinner wife and daughter?'"

"Hardly. No, Bob's not like that."

Dad returned with two small pours of sherry, gave one to Mom, then took his regular seat near the fireplace. The bottoms of his blue socks were damp, and he still had some snow in his hair.

"Before you get too comfortable," Mom said, "the fire."

He laughed to himself. "You always say that. 'Before you get too comfortable' right after I sit down. Oh boy..." Moving like an old man, he pushed out of his seat and threw another log onto the fire. "It's a complicated procedure, I know."

"Did you really hold hands in church?" I asked.

"Your father's kidding, dear. He's being a wit. *A card.* Roseanne and I were just talking about Brian," she said. Dad looked at her uncomprehendingly. "Brian, the boy she's been dating?"

"Ah, yes. I knew there was a boy, I just didn't remember the name," he said.

"He bought her a necklace for Christmas. Show your father the necklace."

Mom drove me crazy when she got like this. I dutifully held up the white gold pendant, gave it a silent two-count, and shoved it back under my sweater.

"He didn't see it, Roseanne. Get up and really show it to him."

"I saw it fine. Dazzling. Sounds like a serious relationship," Dad said in his *Masterpiece Theatre* voice. He and I laughed; Mom didn't.

"Define serious," I said.

"Serious, as in lasting more than three weeks," Mom said. She rose to bring my empty wine glass into the kitchen, showing it to my father as she passed. "You weren't supposed to see this."

"Then don't show it to me, Jess. If I'm not supposed to see it, don't wave it right under my nose." Cupboards banged in the kitchen, and he asked, "What are you doing?"

"I'm looking for the *biscotti!*"

"That's fine, just don't break everything while you're at it."

"Can you guys not be assholes to each other for one night?" I suggested. No one listened. Mom stormed back with the biscotti and enough cocktail napkins for a block party.

We had an early night, and I stole an extra glass of wine before going to bed. My parents never marked the bottles or kept the booze locked up. It was almost like they wanted me to drink it.

Dad left the next morning to fetch Wallis at the bus station in Montclair, and I took my hot chocolate onto the deck to wait for them. The snow had drifted and the yard looked dirty. We'd always had plenty of room to run around when Wallis and I were little, though I was the one who usually got hurt. At six I broke my jaw tumbling out of the big maple between our house and Mr. Leeland's. Another time I stepped on a steel rake in my bare feet and had to get a tetanus shot. Wallis was supposed to keep an eye on me, but I guess he didn't do a very good job.

I went back inside, and a few minutes later our van pulled up. "Who's next to Dad?" I asked, joining Mom at the dining room window.

A shape—not a Christmas present or a piece of luggage but a person with a head and shoulders and two arms—sat in the passenger seat. Definitely not my brother—he couldn't ride up front. Through the windshield I made out a slim face and long, straight hair: a girl, older than me, maybe even older than Wallis—and tall; her head loomed over my father's.

"Wallis didn't mention anything. I wasn't expecting another guest. We've barely enough roast as it is," Mom said.

"I think it's a girl," I said as we hurried to the door, and my mother, pulling it open, called with forced cheer, "Merry Christmas!"

The cold swept into the house, so we shut the door and shuffled down the icy path. Swaying to keep her balance, Mom said, "Phil, you forgot to sand the walk."

Dad stood next to the van. "The bag's in the door, Jess. You're welcome to do it yourself."

The girl had already stepped down, and she looked past us to the house. She was, as I say, enormous, at least six feet tall, and wore blue mirrored sunglasses. I wondered if she played basketball.

Dad introduced her. "This is Mandy, Wallis' friend," he said neutrally.

"Hello, Mandy. It's nice to meet you. Do you live in

Milner?" Mom asked. I knew she was hoping Mandy's next stop would be Christmas at home with her own family.

Mandy shook her head, still watching the house. She seemed to have a thought about it, though I couldn't tell if it was good or bad.

"Mandy's from Canada. She's down here on a... what did you call it?" Dad asked.

"A merit scholarship," Mandy said.

Wallis banged on the window, and Mom said, "Forget something?"

"No, I didn't forget," Dad said, sliding open the side panel. Wallis had on the same brown corduroy jacket he'd worn home for Thanksgiving. I could imagine him up at Penn wearing it everyday to class.

"Hey you," I said.

"Hey back. Someone want to get me out of here?" Wallis asked.

Dad unfastened the safety belts holding Wallis' chair in place and pulled down the ramp. To our surprise, Mandy got in front and helped Wallis out of the van. She handled the wheelchair like she'd done it before.

"I'm in the way. I'll get the door," Mom said. Mandy didn't have any bags, just a red backpack that she wore over one arm.

With Mom in the lead, we trooped up the path to our house. My parents chose the steps while Mandy, Wallis, and I took the long way up the ramp. Once inside, Wallis parked himself in the living room next to the Christmas tree. We'd stacked all the presents high against one wall to make room for his chair.

"I tried calling but I couldn't get service on my phone. Mandy got stuck. She was going to stay at the dorm, but we found out we all had to vacate for the holidays," he said.

Mandy kept her sunglasses on, her hands jammed in the pockets of her ski vest.

"Well, that's quite all right. We have plenty of room at the table." Mom's smile crystallized. "How long will the dorm be closed?"

"Through New Year's, but don't worry. I'm heading down to L.A. tomorrow. I just need a place to crash for the night," Mandy said, finally removing her sunglasses and clipping them to the collar of her vest.

"You're not spending the holidays with your family? Or maybe they're in L.A. I'm sorry, I'm asking too many questions," Mom said.

"Mom's in Ottawa, Dad's out east. It's too much of a hassle," Mandy said.

"And you don't want to pick just one, I understand. Well, sit and take off your jacket. Wallis, would you and Mandy like some eggnog before we open our presents?"

They said yes, so I went into the kitchen to help Mom with the drinks while Dad kept Wallis and Mandy company in the living room. Mom was quiet as she portioned out the glasses.

"She's going to be bored watching us open presents for two hours. Can I have some Bacardi in mine?" I asked.

"Most certainly not."

"Why not? You let me have wine last night."

"Night time is one thing, Roseanne. It's Christmas morning."

I watched her top off the other glasses with spiced rum, concentrating on getting each pour just right. "And why does what's-her-name get to have some?" I asked.

"Because she's older, and she's our guest. Here, don't just stand there. Help me carry these."

We brought the drinks into the living room. Mandy grabbed two and handed one to Wallis.

"I feel silly in my robe. Let me go upstairs and throw on some real clothes," Mom said.

"It's fine, Mom. No one cares," Wallis said.

"Really, it'll just take a second. It's almost nine, anyway." Leaving her eggnog on the coffee table, she clutched her robe around her neck and slipped out of the room. We spent an awkward moment sipping our drinks.

"Where do you live in Canada? I've just been to Toronto," I said finally.

Mandy smirked. "Not *Niagara Falls*? Whenever I tell Americans I'm from Canada, they all think Niagara Falls."

I slouched back, feeling insulted. "No, I've never been to Niagara Falls. I don't even know what's there."

"Well, there's a *waterfall*, for one thing. Every few years someone goes over in a kayak and gets themselves killed. And there's a bridge with traffic that always backs up from New York. What else... gift stores, fine Canadian dining."

"What's Canadian dining?" Dad asked.

"Oh, let's see... twenty-four hour breakfast is a big thing. We like our steaks well done. Ginger beef, beans and toast. Chinese smorgasbord."

I gazed over at the presents to avoid making eye contact with her. I didn't want to open my gifts in front of Mandy. I didn't want her to know anything about me, what I liked, my taste in clothes.

Mom eventually returned in blue jeans and a thick red sweater. She'd had some time to pull herself together, and her speech sounded rehearsed.

"Now Mandy, on Christmas we like to open our presents in the morning, then Roseanne and I will do some baking in the afternoon, and we'll all sit down for dinner around five. I hope a roast is okay."

"I'll eat anything." Mandy swept back her hair, her arms and legs sprawled across the sofa. I'd changed my mind about her playing basketball. If I had to guess, I'd say she pitched softball—she had the same captain-of-the-team cockiness that Gail Bolander, our star pitcher at Milner, had. She even looked like Gail—pretty and hard at the same time.

"As long as it's not dorm food," Wallis said.

"Are you kidding? I love dorm food. You should try the veggie stew at McClelland. They only make it on Thursdays."

I sat on my hands. "So... you guys eat together and stuff?"

Mandy gave me a withering look. "Wallis is a hermit. He only leaves his room to go to class."

"Really? I don't like that." Mom nipped at her drink. "Wallis, is this true? You should be getting out more often. That's part of the college experience."

"It's not the part I'm interested in," he said.

"Wallis is a classic academic. He's like my father. Half the time he doesn't know what day it is. He wears ties to class. He answers questions without raising his hand," Mandy said.

This wasn't going over big with my mom, I could tell. "Well, you certainly know a lot about my son. Are you an Econ major as well?"

Mandy laughed at the apparent dumbness of this. Frost continued to accumulate on my mother's nose and chin.

"Uh, no. I'm auditing a calc class. That's how we know

each other. It's purely extracurricular. Actually I'm a double-major, Bio and Poli Sci. The Poli Sci's to please my father."

"Impressive," said my dad.

Mom reluctantly admitted that it was. "You must not have any time to enjoy the city."

"Philly? That's okay, I'll pass. West Philly's a dump," Mandy said.

I looked at my watch. Somehow only ten minutes had elapsed since we'd sat down.

We opened our presents—my parents got me tickets to see *Fame – the Musical*—and by noon we'd all run out of things to say to Wallis' new friend. I spent some time in my room putting away my Christmas gifts before helping Mom in the kitchen frost the traditional Christmas cake. Wallis and Mandy were watching TV in his room; it sounded like a *Star Wars* movie, judging from the music.

Mom whispered, "I'll try to do better at dinner. She's actually a perfectly pleasant girl. I'm sure she's just nervous and feels awkward about being around a group of strangers."

"She's not pleasant at all. She thinks she's so great because she's from a foreign country. Just because you're smart and cool and from—Ontario or Ottawa or wherever—doesn't mean you're better than everyone else," I said, still seething from Mandy's crack about Niagara Falls.

Mom set down her frosting knife and gave the cake a quarter-turn. I didn't know why we associated baking with Christmas. Because Mom and I weren't religious, we had no real traditions to fall back on, just the ones we'd invented ourselves.

"It's hard for me. I can't quite tell if they're dating.

Wallis has never really had a girlfriend before. Believe me, I want him to be happy, and there's no reason he shouldn't have fun, but…" She looked up from the cake. "He's in a wheelchair, for God's sake. Think of it from the girl's perspective."

By the time we'd finished decorating the cake, the *Star Wars* movie was over and Mandy was in the kitchen looking for a glass of water. "It's for Wallis," she said.

"You don't have to wait on him, you know. Wallis can get his own glass, and I can fill it for him. We keep everything in these bottom cupboards," Mom said.

Mandy took a glass out of the cupboard and filled it with tap water. No "thank you" or anything. "I like your house, Mrs. Crim," she said to the window over the sink. Even that sounded like a put-down.

At dinner my father asked Mandy if she had any family other than her parents in Canada. Mom hadn't said much all night, and she sat with her chair half-turned toward the kitchen.

"I had an uncle but he died. My dad's sister is still alive but we never see each other," Mandy said.

"So it's not a close family," Dad said.

"Close enough. I see my dad once or twice a year. Mom's busy with her consulting service. My parents trust me. They don't need to keep an eye on me all the time."

Mom jumped up. "Shit, I forgot the creamed onions. Keep eating, keep talking."

While she was out of the room, Mandy turned to Wallis, raised an eyebrow, and said in an arch tone, "*She forgot the creamed onions.*"

Mom came back with another steaming plate for the table, and we carried on with dinner, Dad asking his usual polite questions and Mom and I sulking at opposite ends of the table. Dessert was a relief, and I wolfed my last bites of cake and ice cream as I brought my plate to the sink.

Venting on the phone that night, I complained to Brian, "God, what a jerk. I could barely last through dinner. I've been in my room for two hours with the door closed. I think everyone's gone to bed. Wallis might still be up. I wish I was there with you."

Brian and his family had gone to Dave & Buster's after dinner to play video-games while the adults hung out at the bar. I could hear the din of the arcade over Brian's cell phone, kids screeching, games buzzing and chirping and shooting out tokens.

"My cousins are playing Dance Dance Revolution. They've got a crowd of girls watching them. My cousin Tay rules at DDR. He's been battling these Casian lame-o's all night. My ears are *totally ringing*! I wanted to chill out in the mall for a few minutes but they wouldn't let me bring my pop."

I rolled over in bed and looked at the clock on my nightstand. "Isn't the mall closed on Christmas?" I asked.

"The concourse is open but the stores are closed. We were here last night too. Tay bought some pants at American Eagle. Oh, and there's a Benetton! I was psyched. The chick on register was a bitch to my cousin, though. She yelled at him for trying on a pair of jeans. She was like, 'Nice work folding those jeans, dude.'"

Sometimes I wondered if I liked Brian enough to have sex with him. He seemed really young; he'd seen *Dr. Dolittle* with Eddie Murphy six times that summer and his favorite group was Spice Girls. Erin had told me the first time wasn't that great anyway. Her first had been with a senior named Dave Connors. They'd done it in his parents' shower, but Erin was drunk and only remembered a dull ache between her legs the next morning.

The room breathed quiet when I got off the phone. I had some incense burning on my dresser and it smelled like Pier 1.

Tired of hanging out in bed, I got up and eased open the door. Wallis called to me from his room across the hall.

"What's up?" I asked.

The lights were off, and he was lying in bed. "Shut the door and let's talk," he said.

The room was pitch black with the door closed, so I turned on a lamp. Seeing the trapeze bar over his pillow always gave me the chills. Wallis used it to pull himself up in the morning, but to me it looked like something wicked and spindly watching over him.

"Where's your buddy?" I asked, taking another step into the room.

"Crashed out on the couch."

I pulled up a rocking chair and wrapped my arms around myself. Wallis' room ran a few degrees cooler than the rest of the house. It was like the cold spot in the swimming pool.

"Mandy doesn't seem very nice," I said.

"Oh? When wasn't she nice?"

"When I asked where she lived and she made that crack about Niagara Falls. *That* time. And then when Dad sang Christmas songs like he does every year and she just sat there looking sarcastic."

"Give her a chance. She's really a genius, you know. You think *I'm* smart, I'm nothing. And she's been to more countries than everyone we know combined. She's been to Israel, she's been to China... she's been to the *Galapagos Islands*."

"Where are the Galapagos Islands?"

"They're in the middle of the Pacific Ocean, near South America. You know, Darwin? That's where Darwin wrote *The Origin of Species*. Evolution. Mandy went with her parents before they split up."

The more he praised Mandy, the more I disliked her. "Why did they split up?"

"Her dad had an affair with one of his students. He used to teach at the University of Ottawa. Linguistics. He's French-Canadian. A Canuck." He smiled at the word, as if he'd just discovered it.

"He did it with a student? That's gross. And how do you know she's really been to all those places? She might be a compulsive liar," I said, hoping.

"Unlikely. I've seen the pictures of her in Jerusalem standing at the Wailing Wall—have you heard of the Wailing Wall? It's where Jews go to deliver their prayers to God."

"Is Mandy Jewish?"

"No. You don't have to be Jewish to visit the Wailing Wall. It's not like Mecca." He read my blank face. "Mecca's in Saudi Arabia. You can't go there unless you're Muslim."

"That's dumb." My eyes went to the TV and the *Star Wars* box lying on the VHS machine. "Were you guys really watching TV in here or were you making out?"

"No, we're not like that."

"You're allowed to have a girlfriend, Wallis. You're in college. Mom's right—you should be getting out and having fun."

"I am. My kind of fun."

"Your kind of fun doesn't count," I said, reaching over to look at the *Star Wars* box. The description on the back made the film sound colossally stupid. I tossed it across the room. "Darth Vader's lame," I said.

Before I could go back to my room, Wallis asked, "How's your boyfriend?"

"He's nice. He gave me this necklace, see?" I showed him the heart pendant from Zales, which I'd kept on over my pajamas.

"Aw, how sweet," Wallis said.

"He *is*."

"How serious are you guys?"

"Me and Brian? I don't know. We've 'gone public,' so..." He laughed, and I asked, "What?"

"Nothing. I just forgot how kids talk in high school. 'Gone public.'"

I wanted to kick his bed. "It's not like you're suddenly so old, Wallis. You're only eighteen. And how old is Mandy?"

"Nineteen. Just turned."

"Well she *acts* like she's eleven. Brian's *way* more mature and he's young for his grade."

"I'm sure he is. Just be careful. You don't want to wind up like Katie Eisencroft."

Katie Eisencroft was a classmate of Wallis' who'd married a guy from Montclair right after graduation—got pregnant, the usual—and now lived in her in-laws' basement. I had no intention of winding up like her.

"Don't worry about it," I said, switching off the lamp.

"Hey—"

I bent forward in the darkness and kissed his warm forehead. "Merry Christmas. I hate Mandy. Sleep tight."

CHAPTER THREE

The subject of sex came up a few days later at work. I was talking to one of the older stock boys, Devon. Devon was always giving me advice during our lunch breaks. He knew I smoked pot, so he told me about a friend from college who'd taken a hit off a joint without realizing it was laced with PCP and wound up in a mental hospital for two weeks. Message: be careful. He also asked a lot of questions about Brian—what sports he played, where we went on our dates, etc. I could've said the most absurd bullshit and he would've nodded understandingly and said, "That's cool." But we liked hanging out and had fun ripping on the customers and complaining about the crappy wicker furniture the company pushed on us every week.

"What's too young, anyway—thirteen, fourteen?" I asked. We were in the tiny break room near the store's back entrance. The room was big enough for a small counter, two stools, and a wall of lockers where employees kept their purses and lunches. A bulletin board over the counter posted the week's shift schedule, a list of promotional items for December, and various memos from the home office. Someone had taken a pink ballpoint to one of the memos and scribbled:

I ENJOY WORKING FOR PIER 1 IMPORTS. IT IS SUPER KEEN.

"It depends," Devon said. "I mean, historically… if you were around in, like, caveman times, you'd only live to thirty—that's in the wild. Not even caveman times—as recently as five hundred or a thousand years ago. So people were having kids when they were twelve or thirteen. That's why guys are most sexually… what's the word?"

"Active?" I suggested, stealing one of his curly fries.

"Yeah—or something—when they're in their teens."

One of the managers stuck her head in to ask when we were going back on shift. "We've still got ten minutes left," Devon said.

The manager frowned at the clock above the lunch counter. "When did you take your break?" she asked.

"Twenty minutes ago. Therefore."

The manager ducked out of the room, and I gave Devon a high five. I looked forward to reaching the age when I could talk back to grownups. I still felt intimidated by most adults. Everyone over thirty was either a teacher or a parent.

Brian and I went out that night after work. His mother dropped us off at the Cineplex where we saw a dumb comedy featuring a hodgepodge of SNL veterans and a talking goat. We made out the whole time, alternating between kissing and gazing vacantly at the screen.

The mall was closed when the movie let out so we walked around the concourse and past the stores with their gates down. The fountain in the middle of the atrium was switched off, and the same security guard told us twice to be out by ten.

Pausing by the fountain, I whispered to Brian, "Tonight?"

"No way, dude. Where would we go? My mom'll be here any minute. Besides, I don't have anything."

I dropped his hand. The trick in buying condoms was finding a place where no one knew you or your parents, which wasn't easy when you didn't have a car. A girl couldn't buy them without looking like a slut, and guys were clueless about the whole thing: so many different brands to choose from, not to mention the various styles, ribbed, lubricated, extra-sensitive. It was harder than buying beer.

"Don't worry about it. I'll borrow some from my cousins," he said.

"No borrowing, please. There's a CVS in Westlake. Just ride your bike."

"My mom gets her crazy pills there. I'll figure it out."

We agreed to meet on New Year's Eve at the south gate to Hayes Park. After that, we didn't have any plans. Somehow reality would alter at the stroke of midnight and conjure a world where Brian and I could have sex.

I spent an hour on New Year's Eve trying to make myself pretty. I didn't normally wear much makeup, just lip gloss and eyeliner, never any mascara or blush. I didn't like wasting a lot of time on my hair so I usually just tied it back. That night I added an opal barrette from my mom's jewelry box and slipped out the back door.

By the time I reached the park, my legs were cold and my feet were aching from walking the five blocks in heels. I'd snuck out on my own; my parents had their own New Year's party to go to, and Wallis was home studying for the winter term at Penn, which started up in a few days.

Brian stood with his friends by the tall cast-iron gates.

I recognized Jeremy Owens, who did the Friday PA announcements, and Paul Slade, who carried the biggest, most over-stuffed backpack in tenth grade. I didn't really know either of them.

Brian peeled away from his friends and met me inside the gates where families had staked out places on the lawn to watch the fireworks.

"Looking good, dude," he said. He wore baggy jeans, bright white sneakers with the laces untied, and a Bengals jacket. We lived closer to Cleveland but the Browns had been bad for so long that everyone rooted for Cinci.

I held his arm as we continued along the edge of the lawn. Brian showed me the inside of his jacket pocket, and I pulled out a box of Trojans.

"Don't flash it around," he said.

"I'm not. Why Trojans?"

"That's what they had. I had to do it quick—people were looking."

The top of the box read, "America's #1 Condom, Trusted For Over 70 Years." I didn't even know condoms existed seventy years ago.

"You steal it or something?" I asked.

"No, I didn't steal it. Cost $3.99. The cashier lady put her hands all over it. I'm like, just put it in the bag! She's holding onto it, checking the price." I laughed. "It took her five minutes to ring it up. I'm standing there, the lady behind me's setting her shit on the counter, shampoo and hairspray and a bottle of wine. I fuckin' wanted to die. Then the cashier says, 'Happy New Year.'"

"She probably thought you were cute," I said. The condoms came three to a pack. I suppose at Costco you could buy them by the pallet. Some guy would drive up in a forklift and dump them into the back of your truck, enough to get you through college.

Across the lawn a family with two young kids ran around with sparklers. It didn't seem long ago that Wallis and I played with fireworks on New Year's Eve. Dad would fill an empty coffee can with an inch or two of water, and we'd douse our sparklers once they'd burned down. I liked the hissing sound of the glowing tip hitting the water and the snaky trail of smoke that slithered over the lip of the can.

We stopped where the lawn sloped to the pond, and I checked my watch: half past ten.

"Where to now?" I asked. I didn't want to return the way we came, past Jeremy and his buddies. Most guys Brian's age didn't know how to talk to girls. Paul Slade was one of those fourteen-year-old boys who made farting noises by cupping his right hand under his left armpit and flapping his left arm like a chicken. Try it—it works.

"I guess we could just walk around," Brian said, pulling away.

I stayed put. "Hey. We don't need to do this."

"No, I wanna. Let's just get away from all these people."

We left the park through the back entrance where a couple of seniors were smoking pot. One of them, Will Harris, played drums in a Rush tribute band with two other stoners.

"Where are you guys going?" he asked lewdly.

Brian stopped. "Just *goin'*."

Will, in his cackling doper glee, said, "Gonna get *laid*, yeah. I hear yuh, man."

Brian looked pissed but I held him back. "Don't mind

them," I said, "they're baked. Happy New Year, guys. Any gigs coming up?"

Will's forehead constricted as he sucked on his joint. He hadn't planned on doing this much talking. "February 7th, yo. Or it might be the 8th. Gotta look at my..." Cough. "*Date*book."

With no destination in mind, we left Will and continued toward the town center. Cops slid by, maybe one out of every ten cars, looking for drunk drivers.

Brian said, "Assholes like Will make me mad."

I found his hand in the sleeve of his jacket. "I guess it doesn't bother me. I've seen my share of creeps. People were assholes to my brother when he was at Milner and he never let it get to him."

"What would they say?"

"Oh...'wheelchair, tardo, cripple.' Stupid stuff."

We reached a commercial block where a row of shops stood closed for the night. Here my friends and I would spend our weekly allowances at Au Bon Pain and Caribou Coffee and TCBY.

"I wish we had a car," I said, staring down the block. The only sign of life was a station wagon pulling out of the First Federal's drive-thru ATM.

"I wish we were older, like eighteen," Brian said.

"What would be different if we were eighteen?"

"Everything. We wouldn't have to sneak around. I'd have a car, like a jeep or something, and we could drive down to Kentucky."

"What's in Kentucky?" We'd walked as far as Au Bon Pain, where the chairs were up on tables. I wondered which was worse, working at Au Bon Pain or Pier 1.

"The drinking age is different, I think—or maybe it's not. There's way more woods and shit, and they've got stores that don't even exist up here... like, *totally* different grocery stores, totally different restaurants, and the signs on the highway are totally different too. And my cousin says the kids only have to go to school 180 days a year, which rules."

"That *does* rule. Hey, do you know why stores and restaurants leave their lights on at night? So you can see when someone's trying to break in."

We strolled past the Talbots where my mom bought her cable v-neck sweaters and stretch trousers and wool pencil skirts. I suddenly felt silly. I wanted to go home and eat through a tub of Rocky Road with my brother.

We stopped at the ATM with its green lit-up panels and flashing buttons. The screen read, 'Happy New Year from your friends at First Federal.'

"Do you have a credit card?" Brian asked.

"Yeah, right. Don't you need to be an adult?"

"Probably. Another thing we can't do."

He stabbed at a few random buttons but the message on the screen didn't change. "Happy New Year to you, too," he said.

The wind blew around my legs, and I stood behind him to get out of the chill.

Peering up and down the street, he said, "Well, what now? My place is out. Yours?"

Wallis, I thought. "Out. Hey, I'm kind of tired anyway. I might not even make it to midnight."

He looked disappointed but didn't push it. A car drove up to use the ATM, and we dashed out of the way. The old man behind the wheel glared at us through his windshield, and I felt naked in my bare legs and stilettos.

Brian reached for my hand. He didn't know what to do with me next.

CHAPTER FOUR

Wallis returned to Penn the same week I went back to school. None of my New Year's resolutions lasted the month of January. I drank, smoked, fought with my mother on a near-daily basis. I guess I didn't care about much of anything. I didn't even care when Brian lost interest and dumped me in March. I spent the rest of the school year and most of the next wearing baggy clothes and walking around with a permanent slouch. I didn't want to be a girl anymore. Girls annoyed me—I hated the way they smelled, how they hugged each other all the time, the whole fake scene. But guys weren't much better.

By senior year, I was openly smoking around the house. Mom made me take my cigarettes outside, and I had to wash my hands before touching any of the furniture. My drinking was out of control, and I even got a week's suspension for showing up to class with Captain Morgan on my breath. My grades, which had once been in the top ten percentile, had sunk to Cs and Ds.

Four months before graduation, Principal Carter called me into her office. You couldn't talk to me in those days; I just slumped in her cracked leather chair and stared at her penny loafers.

"What are you doing for college?" she asked.

"Dunno. Probably go to MCC. I might just keep working at Pier 1," I said. My boss at Pier 1 had promised I could move up to full-time after graduation. The job included benefits plus two weeks paid holiday. Unlike Principal Carter, he didn't care if I slammed shots at ten in the morning.

She asked what I got paid at Pier 1, and I told her. "That's barely minimum wage," she said.

"Whatever," I muttered, glancing away as she read my transcript on her desk. I didn't want to see the look on her face.

"You used to be good at math. What happened?" she asked.

"Mr. Wheeler didn't like me," I said. The calendar on the wall was a picture of bright red tomatoes sitting in a produce crate.

"Okay, that was last year. It says you're getting a C minus in Ms. Peters' class."

"She goes too slow. The class is boring. It's the same stupid stuff we did last semester."

"I know that's not true, Roseanne. What do you think I do around here? I approve the curriculum for every teacher in this building."

I stopped listening to her. A nice lady, but she was wasting her time with me.

A few weeks later, I woke up one Sunday feeling bored and decided to go to church with my father. Mom must've been nagging me at home: church wasn't normally on my agenda. Church sucked, just like school sucked. You could say I was anti-social.

It was a nice spring day, so we walked. The church bells were already ringing when we got there—I'd made him late. Past the front steps and vestibule, we continued into the main part of the church where a choir sang and the altar boys lit the candles near the cross. I wondered if they liked doing it or if their parents made them.

We slipped into a pew at the back, and Dad opened his hymnal. His singing voice was rough and limited to about two notes. I didn't sing; instead I watched the altar boys finish their work and bow to the cross behind the communion rail.

After another song and some Bible readings, Pastor Bob delivered his sermon. The congregation chuckled at his joke about the new President. I was surprised—I didn't think you could laugh in church. Then he talked about some recent earthquake in Central America and how we should always keep our problems in perspective. It was a good sermon—not religious at all, and I don't think he mentioned Jesus once. It was more like someone just talking to you about life.

Two old guys sent the offering tray around, and I smoothed a dollar against my leg. It was my change from the pack of smokes I'd bought the night before. I'd gone out after work with some of the guys from Pier 1. They were just about the only friends I still had. Maggie Hanson was twenty-four and a transfer from the store in Avon. She had a three-year-old son and drove a big black truck. I liked her okay. Frank Tanner sometimes went bowling with us on Saturdays. Frank managed the stockroom; he was bald, forty, and had worked at Pier 1 since the mid-eighties. A lot of laughs.

Mom was on the phone with Wallis when Dad and I got home, and she passed the receiver to me without saying hello or even asking where I'd been. I took it into my room and closed the door, kicking off my church shoes and flopping onto the bed. We gabbed for a few minutes.

"Hey," I said, "I was thinking of coming up next weekend. Shit's pretty dull down here. Mom's being a bitch and I've got Senioritis big time. Is that cool?"

"Sorry, sis, I can't. Mandy and I are flying up to spend a few days with her dad in Canada. We're leaving Thursday after class and we'll be back on Tuesday."

My hopes sank. I hadn't seen Mandy in two years, and Wallis rarely mentioned her over the phone. From what little I'd heard, her social life didn't seem to involve him. The word he used was "colleagues." Wallis had colleagues and I had people I knew from school.

"Why are you going all the way up there? Why can't her dad just visit her at Penn?" I asked.

"Dr. Snow's busy. Besides, I want to see his lab. I guess he's got this crazy place that looks like a glass box and it's right near the ocean."

Canada sounded icy and faraway. People in Canada wore bulky parkas with fur-lined hoods. They had French-sounding names like "Yves" and "Denis."

"Aren't plane tickets expensive?" I asked.

"Dr. Snow's paying for it."

Mom shouted at me from the hallway to help with the laundry, but I ignored her. "He must be pretty rich," I said.

"He is. Mandy's grandfather was Lieutenant Governor of Ontario in the fifties. Her great-grandfather ran the University of Toronto. There's oil in her family too."

I had nothing to say, my local gossip paling in comparison. *Hey, Wallis, remember Ken Duffy from middle school? He's working at the Taco Bell on Route 6.*

"Sorry to disappoint you. You can come up the weekend after next," he said.

"I don't want to come up then. That's like *two weeks*

from now. I'll be dead by then. Everyone hates me here. Mom hates me."

"Dad doesn't hate you."

"No, but Mom does. Mom objectively, factually *hates* me. She yells at me for everything. She yelled at me because I left a candy wrapper in the car last night. *A candy wrapper*, Wallis. It's not like the car's so pristine. She's had that stupid wire sculpture-whatever-the-fuck-it-is in the back seat for three months."

Mom banged on the door again, and I told him I'd call him back.

As it happened, I didn't make it out to Penn that year. Every weekend I worked extra hours at Pier 1. We had a promotion on summer picnic-ware—parti-colored wine glasses and citronella candles and paper lanterns to hang over the patio. Another sales associate and I were talking about finding an apartment after graduation. We'd looked at a few places in Montclair; there weren't many rentals in Milner, which was out of my price range anyway. It kind of bummed me out that I couldn't afford to live in my own hometown.

Wallis came down for my graduation in June. He'd bought me a dictionary and a gift card to Barnes & Noble. I laughed when he gave them to me in my room.

"Me no speak English," I said, setting the wrapping paper on my bed.

"That's not just any dictionary. It's the OED."

"It's got better words in it?" I asked, kissing his forehead.

"You're a pretty good writer. Maybe you'll keep doing that." The dictionary was huge, weighed about twenty pounds, and came in a leather slipcase. The words were so tiny that you literally needed a magnifying glass to read them.

My school held its graduation indoors because of the rain. There wasn't quite enough room in the gym for all two hundred of us and our families, so some had to stand. I'd gotten stoned a half-hour before the ceremony. Assistant Principal Fitzwilliam looked like a Hobbit. The Valedictorian's speech was just some kid talking.

Mom cried when I showed her my diploma. She put her hand around my neck and pulled me in for a kiss. "Jeez, ma, it's only a piece of paper," I said.

I hadn't been invited to any graduation parties, so Mom made reservations for the four of us at some frou-frou French place in Westlake. I was mostly quiet during dinner. I'd smoked some more pot that afternoon and felt like I was holding a tennis ball in my mouth.

Dad asked Wallis about his summer plans. By now Wallis led a more-or-less independent existence from the rest of us. He didn't even need to pester Mom and Dad for money since his academic scholarship paid for most of his expenses.

"Will you be working at the library again this year?" Dad asked.

"No, I've got a new internship. It's up north," said Wallis.

Mom drew her napkin into her lap. "Where up north? When's this? And how long will you be gone?"

"A couple months. It's Dr. Clement Snow—you know, Mandy's dad. He talked to my department chair. We're doing research on Baffin Island in eastern Canada. It's really fascinating. The Inuit live in these small communities—there's no currency, just barter economies that have been in place for hundreds of years. We might even write a paper together."

"You and this Dr. Snow?" Dad asked.

"Yeah. He's mostly interested in the linguistic variations from settlement to settlement, of course."

Dad laughed and stirred at his food. "I understand none of this," he said.

"Is it safe? Will you have everything you need?" Mom asked, her hand traveling from her lap to her wine.

"Dr. Snow will take care of me," Wallis said. His worry-free smile infuriated me. I wanted to grab him by his tie and shake him.

"Wallis, you know very well *your* needs aren't the same as everyone else's. You can't just run off to the middle of Canada—the middle of some *island*—without your medicine, your doctors' support, without going to therapy once a week," Mom said.

The tennis ball popped out. "Everyone? Hello? I graduated high school today? Why don't we talk about that?" I whined.

"No one's ignoring you, Roseanne. We're all very proud of you. I think we'd feel a little better if we had a clearer sense of what you wanted to do with your life other than drink and do drugs and work at Pier 1 Imports," Mom said.

Somehow we survived the rest of dinner, and I went straight to bed when we got home. Some graduation, I thought. I should be out partying. People should be buying me drinks and telling me how great I am.

Wallis returned to Penn in the morning. I had to be at work at one, which depressed me. Yesterday I was a high school student who worked part-time in a store. Now I just worked part-time in a store.

Rolling out of bed, I stopped at my desk on the way to my closet and glanced at the dictionary Wallis had given me. It seemed to expect something of me, but I didn't know what.

Summer that year didn't feel like summer. Other kids suddenly looked older to me, the rare times I saw them around town. Guys with scruff, guys with full beards. Girls who'd bump into me at Walgreens, squint, and then remember me. They all seemed so serious about their lives. They were going to Kent State to study business, or Case Western for computers. Kids who'd been total jokes just weeks ago now had their shit together.

After weeks of unpacking shelf stock at Pier 1, I finally switched to full-time and went in on a lease with a girl from the store, Lisa Grey. Lisa was twenty-two and had a steady boyfriend who lived in another town. We didn't have much to talk about, apart from work. She was the kind of girl who usually closed her door as soon as she went into her room.

One night at the end of summer, Lisa and I sat around the living room of our apartment in Montclair drinking Zima and talking about going out.

"It's strange," I said, lying back on Lisa's sofa. Most of the furniture was hers—the entertainment center, the floor lamps from Target, the wine rack where we stored our bottles of discount chardonnay. "I used to hate school, but now I kind of miss it. Not having to study and take tests, but learning things. Some of it was interesting."

"Take some classes then," said Lisa. She'd been working toward her degree online. Sunday mornings I'd see her at the dining table wearing her glasses and staring at her laptop.

"Yeah, like I have time for *that*. Besides, my grades

sucked. I probably couldn't even get into a crappy state school," I said.

"My older sister Natalie didn't do well in high school either, but she spent a year in community college, got her grades up, and now she's finishing her Bachelor's. And they've got night classes too, so you can fit it in around work."

"Pier 1 can suck my *ass*," I said, getting up to grab another Zima from the kitchen. When I got back, I asked, "Do any cute guys go to community college?"

"Rosie, there are cute guys *everywhere*," she insisted. It was easy for her to say, not being single like me—single, eighteen, and still a virgin.

"They don't shop at Pier 1. The only guys who shop at Pier 1 are designers, and they're all-"

"*Gay-ay.*"

I gave her a Zima and kept one for myself. I'd been lapping her all night. "I need to stop drinking these," I said.

That week I made the decision to enroll at Montclair Community College. In exchange for getting Mondays and Wednesdays off, I agreed to work every Friday and Saturday night. The store closed at nine, and I could usually have the drawers counted and the lights off by nine-thirty.

I settled on two classes, English and accounting. I figured English would be easy and accounting would look good on my transcript. The campus was a fifteen-minute walk from home but I always drove it. I didn't want anyone thinking I didn't have a car.

Montclair Community College was ninety-percent parking lot, the glass and cement buildings resembling an office complex. My first day I saw two men having a fistfight out by the athletic field. Graffiti covered the concrete entrance to my building, and I made a mental note to buy mace.

My accounting instructor was an older woman, Mrs. Snell, who carried a big bag and wore running shoes to class. The class was small, just eight people including myself, and I was the youngest by far. The cutest guy was a middle-aged man named Robert who also happened to be blind. I couldn't imagine doing it with a blind person, at least not my first time.

Robert asked me questions during our break. My answers delighted him. You live around here? How nice. And you work at Pier 1? Wonderful. He didn't have a cane or a seeing-eye dog, so maybe he wasn't completely blind.

English class met down the hall, and our teacher was Walter Brice, a man with wild curly black hair and tortoiseshell glasses. For our first assignment we wrote about our childhood home from the perspective of a stranger. We had twenty minutes, and Walter Brice spent the time in the hall checking his phone messages. I scribbled out a page in my spiral-bound notebook. Looking it over, I liked what I wrote. It was funny—Wallis would probably get a kick out of it—and had a nice, natural flow.

When Walter Brice called for volunteers, I raised my hand.

"'The House Where I Grew Up: a Memoir,'" I read. "Here's the deck where my brother and I used to hang from the railing and drop onto my father's shoulders. I remember one time-"

"...stop you for a sec. Can anyone tell me the problem with the first sentence?" Walter Brice asked the class.

A hand shot up—some guy, some stupid fucking

burnout prick from Montclair. "It's not from a stranger's perspective," he said.

"Good. Let's hear yours," Walter Brice said.

The prick from Montclair read his story while I stared at my notebook, seething. When he was done, I raised my hand again. "What was so great about that? Mine was good too. You didn't let me finish."

"Would you like to finish?" Walter Brice asked.

"Not now. I just want to know why you think his was better than mine."

"It's not a matter of better or worse..." he said, checking his class list, "Roseanne, but maybe you can answer your own question. Think about the assignment. Think about your opening sentence and think about Pedro's. Do you see any difference?"

I hated questions like that—questions that weren't really questions. They always made me feel dumb.

"My house is nicer than his," I said.

My roommate laughed when I got home and gave her the full report: two lame classes and not a worthwhile guy in either one. Pouring myself some wine, I said, "Now I remember why I don't like school. I should do like you and take classes online, but then I'll never meet anybody, and if I never meet anybody..."

I blocked my mouth with a swig of wine. My own words embarrassed me. Most girls went to school because they wanted to learn about life, not just troll for sex. That was my big motivation: to join the world of sexually active adults. I was tired of sex being such a mystery. I knew what it looked like—I knew about penises and vaginas and getting wet and getting hard, and I knew that guys thought about it once every eight seconds (which was basically like thinking about it all the time), but I didn't know what made people so crazy for it. What kept them coming back for more.

"What do you do when guys hit on you?" Lisa asked after we'd been drinking awhile. I'd seen her chat with men before. She had a way of being nice and seeming interested without promising too much.

"Usually I get nervous and start talking about how much I hate my job."

She smiled. "It sounds like you're too hard on yourself. Look, I didn't meet Dave until I was twenty. It takes time."

"Was he your first?" I asked.

"Not exactly, but… essentially, yes. The first that mattered. Hey, I've got an idea," she said, reaching for her cell phone.

"What are you doing?"

"Let me call Dave. Maybe he knows someone. He works with a guy named Randall—sweet guy, cute, good job. I don't think he's seeing anyone."

I begged, "No, please, just… forget it. How old is he?"

"Randall? Probably Dave's age—twenty-six, twenty-seven."

"*No.* Lisa, I'm way too young. He'd never want to go out with me."

She was already speed-dialing her boyfriend. "Roseanne. He's a guy. You're not too young."

Dave picked up, and within minutes she was describing me to him over the phone. "Her name's Roseanne, but everyone calls her Rosie. Sure, she's pretty—she's *beautiful.* She's smart and fun and…hold on. How old are you?" she asked.

"Eighteen. Almost nineteen," I peeped.

"Old enough. Anyway, call Randall and let's work out

a double date. I'm assuming he's not still obsessed with Vicki."

When she hung up, I asked, "Who's Vicki? I don't want to go out with this person if he's going to be talking about some other chick all night."

"Oh, he won't. He's not that kind of guy. Besides, he hasn't seen her since she moved to Minneapolis, and that was six months ago."

Dave called back almost instantly to say he'd spoken to Randall, who'd sounded interested in me. Lisa looked pleased with herself when she got off the phone.

"How interested could he possibly be? It couldn't have been more than a two minute phone conversation," I said.

"Roseanne, please. We're all going out next Tuesday. Besides, you can learn a lot about someone in two minutes."

I wondered if that was true. How much could a person learn about me in two minutes? Customers who saw me working at Pier 1, strangers, generally kept their thoughts to themselves. Guys rushed in and asked to use the bathroom. Old ladies seemed mistrustful of me—they frowned and took their change. They didn't beam at me like they did at the other girls.

The next Tuesday Lisa and I drove in her car to meet Dave and his friend at The Melting Pot in Fairview Park. The Melting Pot was a chain of upscale fondue eateries. I'd been to one for my mom's fiftieth birthday. As we parked, Dave called to explain that he and Randall were stuck at work and running twenty minutes late.

"I'm sure there's a bar. Let's have a drink," I said. I'd paid good money for a fake I.D. that got me served just about everywhere.

Once inside, we found the bar and ordered two nine-dollar glasses of white wine. "Cheers, girlfriend. You look good," Lisa said.

I took a big sip of my drink. "I haven't been on a date in ages. I'm nervous."

"You'll do fine. It's not an audition. It's a Tuesday night out with friends."

We waited another fifteen minutes before Dave called again to say they'd just gotten on the highway.

Lisa folded up her phone. "Let's go ahead and grab a table."

"I might as well order another of these since we're here," I said.

I ordered a second glass and told the bartender to transfer the bill. Carrying my drink and my nearly empty purse, I followed Lisa and the hostess into the dark catacomb of the restaurant. I was feeling the wine, and when we sat down I asked the hostess to bring us some bread.

"You okay?" Lisa asked.

"Just starving," I said. I figured I'd order one more glass to go with dinner and that was it.

We heard voices winding their way to our table, and I gripped my cushion as the two guys appeared, one tall and skinny and the other slightly meatier with uncombed brown hair and rosy lips. They wore business shirts and ties, and the heavier one had on an I.D. tag from a place called Technology Solutions. *David Rasmussen*, it said.

Dave sat next to Lisa, who laughed and pulled off his name-tag. "After five, babe," she said.

Randall waited to be introduced. "Oh," Lisa said, "Randy, this is my roommate, Roseanne."

I shook his hand, which was cool and smooth like glass. I liked his long face and dimpled chin, the shadow on his cheeks after working all day, his short haircut and straight teeth. He was a good head taller than me, which I also liked, and his shirt was clean and pressed as if he'd just put it on.

My first, I thought.

"Rosie," I said, sliding over to make room.

"Nice meeting you." He had a big, deep voice, the kind that belonged outdoors. I imagined he liked camping and mountain climbing.

"Sorry we're late. Coreen called a meeting at four-thirty, and I got stuck on the phone with Ken in shipping. I'm Dave, by the way," Lisa's boyfriend said, shaking my hand. His grip was firmer than Randall's, and his skin was warm and soft. I liked Randall's better.

With all four of us seated, the guys ordered their drinks—a draft beer for Randall, an apple martini for Dave. Our waitress described the various menu options, choices of cooking styles, the different cheese fondues you could get for the table. Then she left, and Dave launched into a long and tiresome monologue about his day. He wasn't what I'd pictured. Given my sense of Lisa, I'd expected cuter, quieter, less of a dork.

Randall asked if I liked fondue.

"I haven't had it in a long time. I don't go out to eat much. It's so expensive," I said.

"You think it's expensive? No, it's not that bad," he said.

"I guess not."

"You can make your own fondue too. I used to have a fondue pot, but, uh…" He laughed. "*She* got it."

The drinks came, and Dave placed our order. I was so hungry that the wine hurt my stomach. The hostess had forgot our bread, and I didn't want to be a nag and ask again.

The first course was a cheese fondue, which the waitress prepared table-side. As she stirred the ingredients, she asked me, "Did you go to Fairview High? I swear you look familiar."

"No, I'm not from around here," I said, though Milner and Fairview played each other at football once a year.

"I remember now—my friend Tina has a sister who looks just like you. She graduated in '97. She's the sweetest kid... and can *draw*? Phew. That girl's an artist. Anyway, I'll leave you with this," she said, turning the heat down under the pot.

Randall was telling us about his parents' summer cabin on Lake Ontario. "It's right on the water. Basement floods once or twice a year. Nice place. Neighbor's a total psycho, though. We called the cops on him last summer. Oh yeah! He was burning leaves on his lawn, drinking beer with one hand and spraying lighter fluid with the other. He's one of those inbred trailer trash types that lives year-round in Oswego County."

"Is that the guy who told your brother he'd kill him if he parked his truck in front of his house again?" Dave asked, dipping a piece of cauliflower into the fondue pot.

"Yeah, but I put a stop to that," Randall said. He wasn't the type to brag, which made me like him even more. "Dude's harmless. You just don't want to stare over the fence."

"It sounds nice... I guess," Lisa said.

"Y'all come up some weekend when it's warmer. We'll take the boat out."

Dave flagged down the waitress and motioned for another round of drinks. "Rosie, what do you do for fun?" he asked.

I felt stupid being around so many older people. "I

dunno... party, mostly. Sometimes I like to stay home and read. I'm going to school," I added hopefully.

Randall asked, "What are you studying?"

I wished I could've said something impressive like Pre-Med or Pre-Law. "Just general subjects. I'm sorry, I'm not much of a scholar."

"That's okay," he laughed sweetly.

"My brother thinks I'm a good writer, so... maybe I'll try that."

"What sort of writing? I like Stephen King. I like books about crazy people who flip out. I have this problem where I can't say the name of a book I've read or a film I've seen without giving a synopsis of the entire plot. For example, what's the name of a book?" Randall asked.

I couldn't think of one. So many books—millions? *Billions?* I couldn't think of a single one.

"Or a movie," he prompted.

"*Gladiator, Cast Away, Perfect Storm,* c'mon, c'mon... 'smatter with you people?" Dave rattled off.

Randall proceeded to tell us the entire story of *Cast Away,* even recreating some of the sound effects. I chose to find this sexy and hilarious, and before I knew it I'd finished my third glass of wine with hardly a bite of food, which was too bad because the waitress had taken away the first course and was setting up the broth for our entrée.

Dave pointed. "Rosie. 'nother wine?"

I nodded yes. I'd reached the stage where I knew the night would end with me finishing off the last glass in bed, hopefully Randall's.

"Wow, look at all this food. I haven't eaten since I left the house this morning," Randall said.

"No lunch? Aw, why?" I asked.

Dave and Randall exchanged a look. My eyes went to Lisa, who stared back. "What?" I asked.

"Nothing."

"You're smiling."

"I'm not," she said.

Before leaving to get our drinks, the waitress told us to let the broth come to a low simmer.

"Hey, let's eat," I said.

"You gotta *wait*, Roseanne. It's not ready," Lisa said.

"No, I know, I'm just... I'm saying let's get *ready* to eat. Like, get our stuff together. And then it'll *be* ready. What looks good to you?" I asked, leaning into Randall.

"All of it, the steak, the chicken," he said. Again, that look.

"You *guys*. You guys are up to something," I smiled, pointing from Dave to Randall.

No one spoke as we watched the broth steam in the pot. More drinks appeared—at some point the waitress had turned into a ghost.

"God, it's taking a long time. Let's turn this sucker up," I said, looking under the table for the temperature control.

"Rosie, just leave it. I'm sure it's fine," said Lisa.

"We can probably start eating," Randall said.

"Nah, it needs to be hotter. Here." I found the temperature dial and adjusted it from two to five. "There, I turned it up one."

"Not too hot," warned Lisa.

"No, but it's gotta be hot enough to cook the food. See, it's not even boiling yet."

"It's not supposed to boil. It's supposed to *simmer*, that's what the lady said."

Dave meowed and chuckled into his drink. I must've been quite a sight. My cheeks tend to get red when I've had too much to drink, and my eyes have trouble focusing. I get loud too. But at the time all I cared about was eating and moving the date along so that Randall would like me and wouldn't get bored and would want to see me again.

"Here we go," I said as bubbles popped on the surface of the broth.

"Good, turn it down. We don't want it to splatter," Lisa said.

"Chill, girl, it ain't gonna splatter. It's only on five, see? It goes all the way up to eight." I surveyed the assortment of raw meats and vegetables, stabbing away with my fondue fork. "Is this chicken or pork? I never can tell," I asked Randall, who reared back.

"Jesus, Roseanne," Lisa said, "you almost poked Randall's eye out."

"I did? No, I didn't. I just don't know if this is chicken or pork."

"I think it's pork," Randall said.

"He says it's pork. See, I *knew* it was. I gotta trust my instincts." No one else had gone ahead, so I stuck my fork in the pot. There was a sound like something crispy exploding. I let go of the fork and gave a soft little scream. The whole pot sizzled.

"Ho!" Dave said, bolting out of his seat. Lisa ordered, "Turn it down! Turn it down!"

I looked over to see if Randall was laughing, but he'd covered his face with his hands.

"You all right, buddy?" Dave asked.

"Got me right in the fucking eye."

Dave turned off the pot and the sizzling stopped. Both guys stood, Randall still covering his eye. I felt maybe a half-notch more sober.

"I'm sorry, I didn't know it was so hot," I said.

"Let's go to the john," Dave grumbled as he led Randall away. Where Randall had been sitting, now there was only a crumpled cloth napkin and a little impress in the cushion. *Randall's butt.*

"Roseanne, how drunk are you? How many wines have you had? I've only had two. I never would've set you up with Randall if I knew you were going to get drunk like this," Lisa said.

"All right, I won't have any more." I took my fork out of the pot and cut into the meat. It still hadn't cooked through. "Think he hates me?"

"What do *you* think? You get sloppy drunk, you almost poke his eye out with a fork… I'm *so* fucking embarrassed right now."

"Let's just start over, then… when the guys get back. I'll be good. I won't have any more wine. You can have what's left in my glass," I said, nearly spilling it as I tried handing it to her.

"I don't want it. I don't want your goddamn-"

The waitress returned, and Lisa explained what had happened. "Oh, you don't want to touch the dials. Don't touch anything. You can get really hurt. People *have* gotten hurt. You can get first-degree burns—first or third, whichever's the worst. I've seen it happen," the waitress said.

She brought us a new pot and restarted it on two. By the time the guys returned, the broth was simmering as before.

"Are you okay?" Lisa asked.

Randall hesitated before taking his seat. His face looked fine, though some water had got on his shirt. "Yeah. It was more startling than anything else," he said.

"I'm *so* sorry. She brought us another pot. I won't touch it again," I said.

"It's okay," he said.

"Helps to follow instructions," Dave muttered.

"I know, I'm stupid. I'm not used to this kind of fondue. She brought us another pot, though."

"You said that already. Can we eat now?" Dave asked, snatching a fork.

"Come on, Rosie, eat. No one's mad," Lisa said.

I meekly stuck a piece of beef on the end of my fork and slipped it into the broth. As our food cooked, Randall said, "The bathrooms in this place are really nice. I remember when this was a P.F. Chang's."

"Yeah, I *miss* P.F. Chang's. I thought that would've done really well out here," Lisa said.

"Too close to the Benihana," said Dave.

"Benihana's Japanese, dude," said Randall.

Dave, Randall and Lisa continued to reminisce about the stores and restaurants that used to be on the strip: Chi-Chi's, Big Boy, Magic Pan. Their nostalgia seemed to predate mine by decades. All the while I kept my eyes on the pot. I didn't want to make things worse by saying something foolish.

"I think mine's ready," Lisa said, reaching for her fork.

I'm not sure exactly what happened next. I wasn't thinking clearly, and the room was still spinning at a steep lean. Somehow I knocked into Randall's fondue fork, and it sprang out of the pot. Dave freaked, Lisa freaked. The piece of lobster tail that Randall had been cooking sprayed hot broth up into his face and lap, where it landed. Shrieks, screams, looks of terror.

"Rosie, what are you doing?" Lisa cried.

Randall jumped out of his seat, an oily stain on his pants. I went for the stain with my napkin.

"No no no," he said, dancing away as the waitress came over.

"Get some towels," Dave barked at her. "Dude, your pants..."

"Fucking *shit*," said Randall, really in pain this time.

"Goddamn, and it had to be the lobster," Dave said. I leaned over to retrieve the lobster tail from the middle of the floor. "Leave it! Don't touch anything. Sit there in your goddamn seat and don't move."

I took my hand back. The whole night seemed to be happening to someone else.

The waitress returned with a dishtowel. I thought I heard her say, "Oo, crotch shot," but probably not.

Randall pressed the towel against the stain. "Don't forget your face," Dave said.

"This first," Randall muttered.

"Hurts?"

"Like a bitch."

"Let's get this food wrapped and call it a night," Dave told Lisa, who looked stunned.

"I don't think it'll keep," I offered.

"And *I* think you're a nut. You *definitely* shouldn't be drinking. Good work, Leece," Dave said. I started to cry.

"Don't be mean to her. She made a mistake," Lisa said.

"Two mistakes in two minutes—that's good enough for me. Can we get the bill?" he asked the waitress.

"Randall, I'm..." I began.

"It's okay," he grunted as he wiped off his face. Except for the huge stain on his khakis, he looked more or less all right.

"I thought your fork was going to fall into the pot, and I... I reached for it."

"Oh, Rosie, shut up. That doesn't make any sense," Lisa said quietly. The music in the background was "Cat's in the Cradle" by Harry Chapin or "You Make Me Feel Like Dancing" by Leo Sayer or "Raspberry Beret" by Prince and The Revolution.

Later in the car, she said, "You know, I've wanted to say this before but I didn't think we were close enough as friends, but I'm going to say it now. You've got a *big* drinking problem, Roseanne. You drink too much and you smoke too much pot, and it's going to cost you relationships-" A car cut us off on the highway, and she gave it the finger. "Fucking asshole! It's going to cost you relationships, and no one's going to want to go on a second date with you... and it'll speed up your aging too! Seriously—all that pot and wine and hard liquor? It's bad for your skin and your hair will fall out and people will think you're forty when you're twenty-five."

I leaned against the window and closed my eyes. Like I said, you really couldn't talk to me in those days.

That same year I turned nineteen. Because Lisa and I weren't socializing much, I started going out by myself. Probably not a good idea—but hey, I survived. I drank a lot of crap wine and ate a lot of bar snacks and talked to men about sports and their cars and what they did for work. Then one night I wound up in a place called Geronimo's and let an older, divorced guy named Martin take me home.

Martin worked for an airline company and owned the right half of a duplex. We hooked up that one time and that was it. He had a magazine subscription to *Men's Journal* and kept the back issues in a basket by the john.

Potpourri in the bathroom to impress the ladies. He wore his wife-beater T-shirt as we fucked on the sectional in his living room; the dog, an old Collie, banished to the kitchen. His eyes watered as he stared at my tits. I was the best thing that had happened to him all month.

What was it like? It was okay. I liked the fact that I was finally *doing* it. I liked seeing his response to me. His eyes became vague and rangy, as if he didn't know which part of me to look at next. That felt good, being admired like that. I liked how I could give him a hard-on just by taking off my bra. I liked holding his balls and being naked in front of him and how he kept telling me how fucking hot I was. The sex itself mainly hurt. I was concerned about the condom not working and had a hard time letting go. I'd never seen a man have an orgasm, not even in a movie, and that was interesting. I liked the idea that whatever was happening to him had something to do with me. The look on his face said, *I want to say this girl's name and I can't remember it.* His cheeks turned red, his eyes shut and his cock pulsed and I knew he was shooting it and for a second I just lay still and watched. I might've even half-felt something toward him then. I think I wound up disappointing him, though. Maybe I wasn't animated enough, didn't suck his dick. Who knows? The fuck I care now.

I took two more classes the next semester, another accounting class and an elective called "History of Western Religion," which I took to please my dad. Accounting was dull as expected; I had Mrs. Snell again and sweet blind Robert in my section, and the three of us felt like a team. Not much to report there. But in Religion I met Josh.

CHAPTER FIVE

Josh, Josh, Josh. What can I tell you about Josh Okerfeldt, my husband of eleven years and the father of my children? Josh grew up in Byron Center, Michigan, a small town just south of Grand Rapids. He'd been studying at the theological seminary in Ashland. He wasn't a regular at MCC, but his school let him out of his cage two nights a week to take classes. I didn't know any of that at first, of course. My mind was on other things.

After Martin, I was intent on making up for lost time. I'm neither proud nor ashamed of this phase in my life. It's just what happened for a few months there. The floodgates just opened. I slept with a lot of guys, maybe a new one every weekend. If you were a male between seventeen and, oh, forty-five, and you were cute and clean and brushed your teeth after every meal and we ran into each other at Scooter's or Exotica, you probably would've scored that night. You would've had fun too. Let's just say I was a quick learn—not that I didn't have my standards. You had to wear a condom (unless you didn't have one, and then you just had to be careful and promise to pull out in time). You had to shower first if you wanted a blowjob, and you had to give me five seconds warning when you were going to come. If I got nervous or scared or just suddenly changed my mind, you had to leave without calling me a bitch. And *goddamn* it, if nothing else—the name's Roseanne, not *Roxanne*.

Josh and I didn't talk much early on in the semester. Once or twice we chatted before class, and I picked up some of his background. His father was a Lutheran minister and his mom sold craftwork online. The last movie he'd seen was *Titanic*. In the theater. When it first came out. Josh had pretty brown eyes and dark curly hair that I couldn't stop looking at, but I told myself to leave him alone. He deserved better than me.

One day a guy came into Pier 1. He looked familiar, and not in a good way. He was dressed sloppily in ripped jeans and a yellow flannel shirt. He had a possessive, assuming smile that spoke of privilege and an overabundance of self-confidence. But it was the tattoo I remembered from Exotica—a blue salamander chasing down the side of his neck.

I tried sneaking off behind the tableware section, but he caught up with me. Lisa, Frank, and the rest of my coworkers were on the other end of the store. It was two in the afternoon, a time when the number of customers was small and we usually priced stock. For maybe the first time in my life, I wished I had someone to wait on.

"Hey... Roxanne, right?" the guy said, popping off his purple sunglasses. His eyes looked hung-over. He was one of those twenty-two-year-old guys from Montclair who lived at home and did crystal meth and drank Grey Goose on their parents' Gold Card. I couldn't remember if we'd actually fucked.

I pointed at my name-tag. "Close," I said.

He seemed not to notice. "I haven't seen you around 'the place' lately."

"Yeah, well, I've been there. And my name's not Roxanne, it's Rosie." I began refolding a stack of table linens in the hopes he'd go away.

He came closer to where I could smell his warm skin. "I didn't know you worked here. That's cool. I always liked this place. It's real clean and shit. I need to pick up some incense. I'm all out of sandalwood."

I pointed to the Candles & Fragrance section but he said, "Can you show me?"

I rolled my eyes and led him over to the wall of incense. Before I could sneak away, he got behind me and pressed me against the rack. "What the fuck are you doing?" I said.

"You look nice in an apron," he whispered, nipping at my ear.

I pushed him off. "Beat it or I'll get my manager," I said.

He grabbed my elbow. I didn't want to make a scene, so I stayed. "Hey, I'm sorry. I just... I thought we were cool," he said.

"Well we're not. I don't know you and I don't appreciate you bothering me here."

He smiled. He seemed like such an obvious creep in the harsh light of day. "You know me. You know my dick in your ass," he said.

I would've slapped him if I wasn't at work. My throat hurt, and it was all I could do not to let him see me cry. "Just get your stuff and leave," I said, storming back to the cash registers.

There was no one else to help ring customers, so I did it myself. "Three dollars and seventeen cents," I said, not looking at him as he counted out his change. I gave him his purchase without a bag.

"Bye-bye, *Rosie*," he said, strutting out to his jeep.

To the surprise of my coworkers, I ran back to the

bathroom, locked the door, and threw up. It'd been a while since I'd seen myself through someone else's eyes, and I didn't like it.

That night I cornered Josh in the hall right after class. I knew I was being silly. I was nothing to him, just a dumb girl who never raised her hand except to ask about tests and homework. But it felt worth the risk. I needed some other kind of human company.

"Would you like to have coffee with me?" I asked.

I'd caught him speechless. We'd been discussing the Old Testament, and he'd disagreed with Professor Hofvander about the authorship of one of the Psalms.

"When?" he asked.

"Now. I know a place. You can follow me in your car."

I led him out to the parking lot and gave him directions to Monty's in case we got separated. Josh drove a blue hatchback with silver duct tape holding together one of the side view mirrors. I watched him behind me. He held his head steady and drove with both hands on the wheel. He must've thought I was crazy. All the way I blasted my Eminem CD to psych myself up.

Monty's was an all-night diner five minutes from my apartment. I'd puked in their bathroom a few times. The food wasn't great but it was the only place nearby that wasn't a bar.

We took a booth with a view of the state highway, a long strip of fast food joints and car washes that eventually led to my parents' neighborhood. We ordered coffees, and I got a plate of fries.

"The gyros here is really good. Do you like gyros? It's like a wrap, but it's got lamb and tomato and onion and this special sauce, I don't know the name of it. It's Greek," I said.

"I've been to Greece," he said, rubbing his eyes under his glasses.

"You've been to Greece? Then you've probably had gyros."

"I was eight. I went with my parents. We went to Greece, Turkey, Israel, Egypt. I don't remember much of it."

"I hear the club scene in Greece is pretty intense. You can drop acid and... but you were with your parents—and you were eight."

I told myself to shut up. I didn't want to sound like a skank.

Unfortunately Josh didn't pick up the conversational slack, so I asked him what he thought of our professor. Here he became more animated.

"He's approaching the Bible from a scholarly point-of-view, which I appreciate. In the Church we don't always keep the scripture in a historical context. That's why I wanted to take this class. I'm mainly interested in the Bible as a cultural document."

"So you don't, like... want to be a priest or anything?" I asked.

"God, no. Church twice a week is enough for me."

We sat with our coffees and listened to the jukebox.

"My dad goes to church. He's not into it like you. I think he likes getting out of the house and having his own friends," I said.

"What church does he belong to?"

"Lutheran," I said. I didn't know much about the place other than that they believed in Jesus and the water from the drinking fountain tasted like shit.

"Missouri Synod?"

"Missouri? No, it's right here in Ohio."

He laughed. "Missouri Synod is the name of the denomination. They're huge around here. My family's Evangelical, but I've got a bunch of friends in the Missouri. We went to a retreat in Colorado last spring."

Part of me couldn't believe I wasn't out chugging Rum and Cokes with my pals at Exotica. "So what do you do at these church retreats? Do you, like, read the Bible and stuff?"

He slid deeper into the booth and put one leg up on the cushion. "No, Roseanne, we don't. I mean, we *do*, but we also have cookouts and go skiing, and some of us even went into Denver for a Nuggets game. You can take classes if you'd like, but they're optional. The only mandatory event is the rally at the end of the week."

"What happens there?" I asked, envisioning thousands of well-groomed boys and girls in matching khakis and golf shirts gathered in a sports stadium pumping their fists and shouting, "We love you, Jesus!"

"Last year they had a Christian rock group and a modern dance ensemble from Japan, and people took pictures and traded emails with each other, and there was a benediction from the camp leader, and then we all went back to our rooms to pack."

"Sounds like a blast," I said.

"It was okay. Things can get a little doctrinaire sometimes. *Dogmatic*, you know. I don't like to argue with loudmouths."

"Oh, me neither. I hate loudmouths… though I suppose I shouldn't hate anyone."

"Why not? You can hate people."

This surprised me, coming from a nice guy like him. "I… can?"

"Sure. I hate the girl who brings her needlepoint to our class."

"You mean Doris?" Relieved laughter. "Yeah, I kind of hate her too."

I risked making deep eye contact, which Josh returned. I'd never been with a guy who wore glasses before. Contacts, maybe—I wouldn't know.

We finished our coffees and said goodbye in the parking lot. No kiss, but I didn't expect one. I liked the idea of having to work for it. Starting my car, I ejected the Eminem CD and put it back in its case.

Lisa was on the phone with Dave when I got home. I wanted to tell someone about Josh but didn't know who to call. I didn't have any girlfriends and the guys I knew were all bad news.

School met again on Thursday, and I came stumbling in ten minutes late. A customer at Pier 1 had kept me an hour past the end of my shift helping her choose window treatments. All day I'd been thinking about Josh.

After class he found me by the door where I was putting away my notebook. "Thought you weren't going to make it," he said.

"Oh, hi. Yeah, well, no." I laughed, stared, laughed again. He'd been wearing a blue shirt earlier that week, now a red one. I wondered how many showers he'd had since our last class, how many times he'd been naked—not just half-undressed but fully nude. "I had to work and then… I had to change out of my work clothes. You know how it is."

"Long day."

"I usually get my second wind right about now. I'm kind of a night owl. You?"

"Sometimes. I've got class at nine in the morning, so I can't stay out late these days."

"Oh." We were the only two left in the room. Professor Hofvander had forgotten his attendance book. "Nine o'clock—that sucks. Whoop!" I covered my mouth. "I shouldn't say sucks."

"It's all right. I won't evaporate." He zipped up his jacket as the last sound of students departing faded down the hall. "What was the name of the place we went to last time?" he asked.

"Mm? Oh, for coffee—Monty's. Did you like it?"

"Not bad. Would it be boring if we went there again?"

It took me a second to realize he was asking me out. "Sure, let's do Monty's. I love that place. My boy Gerald works in the kitchen. He can hook us up with some freebies."

We followed each other in our cars back to the diner, where the regular crowd of old men sat at the counter tucking into their steak 'n eggs. A guy I half-knew bobbed his head at me. Josh and I found our usual booth and stared at the menus until the waitress came around. He ordered the gyros.

"It's your fault if I don't like it," he said as the waitress put down his food. I'd only ordered a coffee for myself. Women can get full sometimes just watching men eat.

"I've been thinking about what you said last time," I said, "about church retreats and how you don't only pray and talk about God. I guess I never really gave the church thing a fair chance. It sounds okay, though—if it's just people getting together and having a good-"

"Personally I don't think the Church is for everybody," he said.

"You... don't?"

"My father would disagree. I went through a phase where I felt like I had to minister to everyone. I even tried organizing a Bible study group at my public school. The other kids called me 'Jesus-freak Josh.' The group only lasted a few months. I realized I was just annoying people and giving them a bad impression of the Church. So I cooled it."

"That must've been hard," I offered, not knowing what else to say.

He set aside his food. "Why are you interested in this?"

"What do you mean? Do you not like talking about it?"

"You're not religious, are you?"

I wondered how he knew. I remembered what Lisa had said about drinking and smoking, how it affected your appearance. Partying every night probably didn't help, either.

"I'm a little religious. I believe in God—I think," I said.

"You think or you know?"

"I think. I'm not sure. I *want* to believe in God."

"Why do you want to believe in God?"

"Oh, the usual—scared of going to hell, that sort of thing."

"But if you don't believe in God, then you don't believe in hell."

"True." I took a deep breath, which turned into a nervous laugh. "You're talking to the wrong girl, Josh."

"How so?"

I wanted to tell him what a bad person I was—how I'd let some guy fuck me in the men's room at the Chalice in exchange for a bump of cocaine; how I'd been stealing money from my mom's purse since I was thirteen. But I didn't want him giving up on me yet.

As often happens when I'm being evasive, I wound up

talking about Wallis—the accident, the months of recovery, the time I did a bad job helping him stand in the bathtub and he slipped and fractured his tibia. I told him about the day Wallis fell out of Mrs. Deaver's station wagon and bounced off the front fender of a 1988 Pontiac Sunbird being driven by a thirty-nine-year-old woman from Elyria (who still wrote us every year), how he was in a coma for three days and how I slept in my mom's lap in the emergency room, waiting for news. The TV in the ER played soap operas with the sound down, the characters raging at each other in cafes and ski lodges, and all the commercials were for laundry detergent. For a week I practically lived on candy bars from the hospital vending machine, Hershey's with Almonds.

"Makes it hard to believe in anything after that, I'm sure," Josh said.

I felt close to him then.

We made love that night. It was a little spontaneous—Lisa was staying with Dave, and I invited him back to watch TV at my place. We got about halfway through *Trading Spaces* before switching to the bedroom. At the time I couldn't have told you with absolute certainty that I hadn't picked up some horrible disease from one of the guys at Scooter's. I guess I just wanted to pretend all those months hadn't happened, that Josh was my first.

We slept naked and made love again in the morning before he had to leave for school. I brewed coffee, sang to myself, thumped around the kitchen in my T-shirt and underwear. I felt like a good little wife.

We spent a long time saying goodbye in the driveway. "See you Tuesday?" he asked as he climbed into his car. His schoolbooks were in the passenger seat.

"Not before that? No, you've got work to do. Just call me when you get a chance," I said. He backed down the driveway, waited conscientiously for another car to pass, then slowly pulled out.

We continued seeing each other every Tuesday and Thursday after class, though he usually drove back to his dorm without staying the night. I didn't mind. I didn't even care if we had sex. By that point I'd stopped using drugs and only drank socially (as opposed to alone in my bedroom until I passed out).

I was at my parents' house for dinner one Sunday night when I finally told them about Josh. I'd turned up fifteen minutes late, so the food was a little cold.

"He even goes to church," I said, thinking it would impress them, especially my dad.

Dad smiled faintly. "Point in his favor," he said, then went back to eating his chicken.

"Your brother called. He's not coming home for another month. Maybe when he does, you'll be able to join us for dinner," Mom said. Her voice expected nothing of me.

Dad said, "He's signed on for another internship with Dr. Snow. They're going to Iceland-"

"Greenland," Mom said.

"That's right. Greenland. I can't keep it straight."

"He's going to Greenland for a whole year because this Dr. Snow can't sit still for more than two days at a time, though from what I understand he's older than me and he's in trouble from the Canadian government—did Wallis tell you this?—for not paying his taxes two years in a row... and now he wants to go to Greenland, which has got to be the least hospitable place in the world. *This* is better than grad school at MIT? How does he expect

Wallis to survive in that kind of climate with no medical care, no contact with the outside world except the Internet and shortwave radio…"

"He handled himself well last time," Dad said.

"Last time *what*."

"When he went to northern Canada with Dr. Snow."

I kept my head down, wishing I'd stayed home. Mom had always picked fights with Dad, but she'd gotten worse since I'd moved out, and *he'd* gotten worse at sticking up for himself.

"That was a different situation, Phil—three months, not an entire year. And they were still in Canada, so there was *some* sort of infrastructure in case Wallis got in trouble. Greenland's not even a real country. It belongs to someone else… Denmark, I think. So if Wallis gets an infection or worse, they'll probably airlift him to Denmark. Anyone know what the hospitals are like in Denmark?"

I couldn't stand it anymore. Their bickering had nothing to do with me, which made it even worse. I was mad that Wallis hadn't told me about Greenland. I was mad that my parents weren't more proud of my brother's accomplishments. And I was mad that I'd met a great guy and no one cared.

I called Josh on my way home. "Can you come up? I know it's late. I just need to be held tonight," I said, crying in the car. It was a three-day weekend and Lisa and Dave were off to some fabulous place for the holiday. Josh and I had talked about going on a trip but it seemed a little soon. He hadn't even mentioned me to his parents.

He agreed, and an hour later I met him at the door wearing a purple nightgown I'd ordered from Victoria's

Secret. I pulled him in by the wrist, kissed him, and said, "I love you."

He laughed as I kissed his cheek, his lips, his neck and chin. He hadn't shaved, and I loved it. "I forgot to lock my car," he said.

"Leave it." Seeing him made me cry again—happy tears this time. I wanted to lose myself in him, to give up my life for his. It wasn't so much to give up anyway.

We went into my room where I put on an Usher CD. Shrugging off my nightie, I held myself against his rough blue jeans and corduroy work shirt. *Wow*, he said as I fumbled with his belt. My room was just large enough for a double bed with no box spring, a chipped dresser, and a low bench under the window where I smoked when I couldn't sleep. The thin blue drapes that came with the apartment moved even with the window closed, and the eggshell light from the street lamp never went away.

I helped him off with his clothes, and we stood next to the bed kissing, holding and touching each other, Josh biting gently at my neck as I dandled his balls, so much like perfect little grapes. My life independent from him didn't matter anymore—other people didn't matter. I looked forward to closing the book on poor Rosie Crim forever.

We'd made love about twenty times since we'd met, and in those weeks we'd gotten good at having sex without a condom. Though he hadn't said so, I had the feeling that Josh thought of birth control as a sin; but that might've only been my stupid imagination. It didn't matter to me: I'd committed to being monogamous—it thrilled me to think of my body as belonging to him—and though we'd come close, we'd never had an "accident." Yet every time he pulled away, I couldn't help but feel disappointed. It was a silly thought, I know, but I was nineteen and searching for a destiny, and this felt like it.

We'd been at it for some time when I knew he was getting close. He was always silent in bed until the very end, when he'd swallow hard and make a warning sound deep in his throat. Sometimes he'd call my name, sometimes just "oh." Then he'd be quiet again, and we'd watch his penis slump and wither in stages like a tired child.

Tonight I wanted more. Josh's thrusts became focused and violent, and I felt my body disperse. I was a fuel meant to be consumed—a spark whose only purpose was to inspire another life.

Josh swallowed. I put my hands on his waist and whispered for him to come inside me. My voice triggered his response. His "oh" escaped a second early and his eyes blinked wide open. It was like he'd surprised himself.

Later, both of us dazed and not touching in bed, he asked, "That was okay, right?"

"Mm, great," I said, sliding my hand across his chest.

He felt for his glasses and put them on. "What just happened, I mean. You're going to be okay, right?"

"I'm fine, honey. It's not my time of the month." Technically it was, but I'd never been pregnant, and I suppose I stupidly figured I was safe.

I should explain what I was thinking at the time. I certainly didn't want a baby, and it was not my intention to trick Josh. I was feeling weak and needy, and I wanted him to make love to me as if we were already married and settled enough to have kids. I wanted the *feeling* of that, without the actual consequences.

I reached for my one remaining vice, my cigarettes. "Still smoking?" he said.

"This is my first all day. I don't have to if you don't want."

"No, it's fine," he said. He'd been about to say something else.

I lit up, took a puff, and blew the smoke toward the door. Josh was quiet, so I gave him a little poke. "Hey. I love you."

He rolled toward me. "I'm just worried, that's all. I wasn't thinking. I should've been more careful."

"Josh, baby, sweetie, you didn't do anything wrong. It was beautiful. Thank you for sharing it with me." He didn't look convinced. "And the chances of me getting pregnant are about a million to one. Trust me. It's not worth worrying about."

He smiled uncertainly, and I set down my cigarette. For the first time in over a month I felt like smoking a joint. "Good," he said, "because you know what happens if you're wrong."

"What's that?" I asked, curling up next to him.

He laughed. "Oh lord, Ro, you really don't know anything, do you?"

We continued seeing each other after that, our sex life improving by the week. He would turn up at my door after his last class and start taking off my clothes in the living room. It was nice but a little scary at the same time. I felt like I'd done something bad to him, thrown a switch inside his brain.

"I don't know what it is, but I can't get enough of you these days," he'd say.

Giving myself to him, I'd think, *poor baby. I know what it is.*

I was ten weeks pregnant when I finally told him. I'd been putting it off, but I knew I'd start showing soon enough. Josh listened with a mixture of shock and resignation. I figured we'd split the abortion fifty/fifty. I'd always heard the guy traditionally paid (unless he was an asshole), but I felt bad for causing this mess. Besides, Josh didn't have a job and I did. His little bit of money came from his parents.

"I made some phone calls, and there's a place open on Saturdays. If you'd just come with me, that would be nice," I said. We were at Monty's, a sentimental choice.

He frowned. "What place?"

I dug in my purse for the scrap on which I'd copied the name of the women's health clinic in Fairview Park. The one in Montclair would've been more convenient but I didn't want to run the risk of bumping into anyone I knew.

I showed him the address. "I think I know where it is. It's right by the highway."

He took the scrap, read it, and set it next to his fork. "I don't know, Ro. That seems like a big step."

"Having a baby is a big step too," I said, snatching back the address.

"True, but my mom was only in her early twenties when she had me. My parents figured it out."

I didn't know Josh's parents but I knew where they lived and how they spent their Sundays, and I could only imagine. "I'm not in my early twenties. I'm nineteen."

"Yeah, but nine months from now... you'll be twenty."

"Seven months until the baby, which means we can't wait around forever. Most places only give you up to twenty-four weeks and then it's too late."

If all this sounds terrible of me, please remember that I was scared and angry with myself and afraid of losing Josh. I'd fucked up everything else in my life and didn't want to spoil this too. If we could just start over, I knew we wouldn't make the same mistake twice and I could learn to be a better girlfriend and maybe even a good wife when the time was right.

"Don't you want a baby, Ro?" he asked.

"Someday. Not now!" I had to keep myself from yelling in Monty's, which was unusually crowded for nine o'clock on a Tuesday night.

"But it's a human life. A little person."

I whipped out my smokes. "This isn't some 'church' thing, is it?"

"What do you mean?"

"Look, I know your dad's a minister and you grew up in western Michigan where there's probably a pro-life sign on every front lawn, but I thought you were different."

"Different how?"

"Different from all those crazy people who think women should be slaves and baby-making machines and who hate anyone who isn't white-conservative-Christian. I thought you were cooler than that."

He looked hurt, so I backed off a little. If he'd said one more word about "little human lives," I would've told him to stuff it and walked out. It was his own damn fault for getting involved with a train wreck like me. But instead he took my hand and said, "It's your body. Whatever you decide."

And that was how Josh saved Star.

I didn't know how to break the news to my parents, so the first person I told was Wallis. He was in town to say goodbye to a few people before leaving for Greenland. I honestly had no idea what he'd say—if he'd laugh or get angry or even care.

His first question was, "Is it a boy or girl?"

"Oh, it's way too early to tell. We won't know for another couple months," I said.

We were sitting in front of my apartment building where I'd brought my cigarettes. Spring had arrived, though we'd had one last burst of winter weather the night before. I shuddered to think how huge I'd be the next time it snowed.

"Do you have a preference?" he asked.

"I don't know. I'm not even sure I want either."

"Who's forcing you?"

"No one," I admitted. Josh had proposed to me that week. There wasn't time to plan a big wedding, which was fine with me. I'd be too embarrassed to meet his friends and extended family under the circumstances.

"Sometimes I get jazzed thinking about it," I said, "but then I say to myself, 'Roseanne, you're so young. You haven't done anything with your life yet.' What's my biggest accomplishment? Graduating high school?"

"That's a big accomplishment," Wallis said. He was trying to be nice, but I wasn't in the mood for it.

"Come on, Wallis. Everyone graduates high school. You can't *not* graduate high school. They rig it like that."

We'd exhausted my news, so I asked about his trip. We both did better when he spoke and I listened.

He told me his itinerary: New York to Reykjavík, then traveling by small plane from Reykjavík to some place called Kangerlussuaq. About a thousand potential disasters right there. "And why are you going again?" I asked.

"Research, sis. No one's done a study of modern-day Greenland before. It's not all frozen wasteland. Their capital city has an actual urban center and a college and a year-round population of twenty thousand. Dr. Snow and

I will have access to their archives, power facilities, local government. By the time we get back we'll have enough material together for a paper, maybe a whole book," he said.

"Good for you, I guess. Just be safe. I'm quitting these, by the way," I said, remembering my cigarettes.

I told my parents a week later. I'd thought—stupidly—my mom would be more understanding as a fellow female, so I went to her first. Big mistake.

"Oh, for God's sake, Roseanne—and you're keeping it? *Why* on earth? Do you honestly think you're capable of looking after a child?" she asked.

"It's a human being, Mom. A little life," I said, quoting Saint Josh.

"And I suppose you think you're proving a point of some kind. Or maybe you're getting back at me for something. I sincerely hope you've stopped using drugs."

"Yes, Mom. I don't even drink anymore, which you would've noticed if you'd ever paid attention."

"And the smoking?"

"I'm working on it. Look, I know I'm still young and it seems crazy, but maybe this is what I'm supposed to do with my life—be a good mom. Is that such a bad thing? I'm not smart like Wallis, I don't have this 'great future' ahead of me."

"You've always been smart and you've always had tremendous potential but you're *lazy* and you make excuses and this is another one—an excuse. You let a boy get you in trouble and now you think you've had some eye-opening revelation. It's so predictable, Roseanne—the whole thing. I could've seen this coming years ago. And by the way, don't ask Daddy and me for a lot of money because we can barely cover our expenses as it is."

I told my father that night. It was hard.

Meanwhile Josh had the task of informing his own parents. I suppose it's different for guys—less shame involved. Still, I'm sure it wasn't easy.

"They were a little stunned at first. Obviously they want to meet you," he said when we were in bed that night.

I'd only driven through Michigan when I was little. Pretty much the only thing I knew about it was that the people were conservative and the football team sucked.

"I feel so awful. I hate myself," I said.

"Don't. Ssh." He kissed my neck, and I put out my cigarette. "Here's some good news. They offered to let us stay with them for a few months to help save on expenses."

"In Grand Rapids? That's a long way from here."

"Byron Center, actually. It's not so far—maybe five hours."

"But what about your school?"

"There's a theological center near my folks. Ashland will let me transfer credits. At the most I'll have to make up another semester."

I started to cry, and he asked what was wrong. "I've ruined your life," I said.

"No, you haven't. Think about all that's happening, Ro. We're having a baby! And *no* the timing isn't great but if it's God's will, I consider it a blessing." He touched my cheek, and I flinched. "What?" he asked.

"My head hurts. Are you shouting all of a sudden? I feel like you're being really loud right now."

"I'm not-"

"*That.* That kills. My head is pounding."

His hand settled back under the covers, and he rolled away. The silence came as a relief. Feeling my stomach, I wondered what the fetus looked like, whether it had a face and eyes and distinct fingers. I'd deliberately avoided reading any books about pregnancy or doing research online. I was still at the stage where I could pretend this wasn't happening.

God's will. What did it even mean? It sounded like code for something.

I poked Josh, and he stirred. "What?"

"Do they have a Pier 1 in Grand Rapids?" I asked.

CHAPTER SIX

We moved in with Josh's parents when I was six months pregnant. I'd given my notice to my manager at Pier 1, who agreed to put in a good word for me at the store in Michigan. My coworkers threw me a going-away party at Chili's where Maggie Hanson and Frank Tanner had beer and nachos and I had to settle for a club soda. I wasn't supposed to be drinking anyway. I was underage.

Josh drove us to his parents' house in his blue hatchback, the trunk and back seat crammed with the few things we couldn't part with, mostly Josh's books. Maggie had given me some of her old maternity clothes, which took up my half of the trunk.

Crossing the border into Michigan, I said, "Looks about the same as Ohio. Same trees, same clouds, same sky."

Josh said, "Try to be more cheerful. My mom will think something's wrong."

"Oh, nothing's wrong. What could possibly be wrong?" Brown grass wept on the side of the highway, and we passed a billboard for a retail outlet that only sold different varieties of beef jerky. You could get spicy beef jerky, teriyaki beef jerky... all kinds of beef jerky.

"Scary," I said, watching the sign blow past. "I am

cheerful, I just thought Michigan would look more different."

"More different."

"Yeah. I thought there'd be mountains and stuff. Aren't there mountains in Michigan?"

"Mountains? No. The U.P.'s pretty rocky."

"What's the U.P.?"

"The Upper Peninsula. You know—the Upper Peninsula and the Lower Peninsula? Geography?"

I laughed. "Fuck you, man, I don't know that shit. I told you, I fucked around in high school. Too bad for you, you got a dumb girlfriend."

"You're not dumb. And definitely don't talk that way when we get there."

I cracked the window and lit a cigarette. Feeling his eyes on me, I said, "It's an addiction. I'm trying."

After another hour of speeding past road kill—enormous dead animals, full-grown deer—we hit Grand Rapids. I had Josh pull over at a gas station so I could pee. At least Grand Rapids looked like a city—not huge but a few tall buildings and a built-up riverfront. I brightened a little. I could see us renting a cool apartment on the water in walking distance from shops and restaurants and places to go for a drink and dessert, just me and Josh—and the baby, of course.

"Is there a lot to do in Grand Rapids?" I asked.

"There's the Gerald Ford museum. That's sorta fun, once. A lot of colleges too—Aquinas, Grace Bible."

We left the highway and took a straight state road across a flat terrain. It looked more like Kansas than Michigan, though I knew Kansas only from the movies.

"Okay?" Josh asked.

I wiped my eyes. "Dandy," I said.

A mile or so off the highway we encountered our first "Abortion Stops a Beating Heart" sign, this one stuck in the middle of a cornfield. Some of the paper had torn off and the metal frame had rusted. "I know, I know," I said.

Past a Meijer store, then another long stretch of emptiness, we turned into an isolated enclave of ranch houses and gravel drives. It wasn't like Ohio where one town blended into the next, and if you made your way far enough north, you'd eventually wind up in Cleveland. Here you had your house and twenty others like it, and that was it. You had to take it on trust that the rest of the world existed.

"You hate it," he said.

We parked in front of a beige ranch with a truck in the driveway and a net-less basketball hoop over the garage. A hand waved from inside the house.

"There's Mom," Josh said. Josh's mother, I thought. My future mother-in-law. Pam.

He hurried around the car to help me out. I'd gotten big over the past few weeks, though Maggie had assured me this was nothing compared to the last trimester. I couldn't sleep on my stomach anymore, and my hands and feet tingled.

Pam opened the door, kissed her son, then went right to me with a hug. She was smiling and crying at the same time, and I was surprised to find that so was I.

"Welcome, Roxanne," she said. Pam Okerfeldt was a cheerful-looking woman in her mid-forties with a hard, bony face and her orange hair cut short.

"Roseanne," I said, quickly adding, "but that's okay. People call me Roxanne all the time."

Guys I fucked in the parking lot behind Scooter's. Guys

who laughed and didn't apologize when they came in my hair.

"I'll get it right," she said, ushering us into a step-down living room and settling me into a recliner. The room felt comfortable and oppressive at the same time. Pet hair covered the floral-print sofa, and I recognized the coffee table: Verona, regularly $199, on clearance for $179.99. She'd bought it at Pier 1.

"Would you like something to drink?" she asked.

I felt like I'd been swallowing dust all afternoon. "Thank you," I said.

"Iced tea?"

"Perfect."

She went to the kitchen, and Josh said, "I'll get the rest of the bags from the car."

"They can wait for now, can't they?" I asked.

"Nah, I like to get it done," he said, popping back outside.

Alone in the room, I noticed a longhaired gray cat standing motionless at the foot of the couch, staring at me. It had a silver tag around its neck and a hostile bearing. "Hi, sweetie," I said, and it blinked.

When Pam returned with my drink, I asked, "What's its name?"

"Gravy. Gravy Gallagher. She's very old. Josh picked her out at the pound when he was six."

She pulled a lint roller from her housecoat and cleaned the cat hair off the couch before sitting down. The cat hadn't moved, and I wondered if it'd somehow died with its eyes still open.

"I know this must be awkward for you, Roseanne, but Terry and I have been looking forward to meeting you. We both think you're doing the right thing."

I thanked her. What else could I say?

"Josh, leave them. Sit here with me and Roseanne," Pam said as he returned with another round of bags.

He stashed the bags in the hall and joined us, bringing the cat back to life with a scratch under its chin. "Gravy's still plugging along," he said.

"We had to take her to the vet. She had a tumor on her leg but they biopsied it and it came back negative," Pam said.

"God's blessings," he said, and she agreed, "God's blessings."

It was all I could do not to run out the door screaming. The house felt small, and I could hear settling noises in the other rooms.

"Roseanne, Josh tells me you grew up in Ohio," Pam said as I drank my iced tea. "I've only been there to visit Josh at school. We won't miss the long drive. I know Terry won't, which reminds me—Josh, your father will be home soon. He's meeting with a parishioner."

Josh glanced at me in passing. I felt like I'd sat down in someone's favorite chair.

My hormones surged, and I started crying again. Pam rushed toward me.

"I'm sorry, Mrs. Okerfeldt," I said.

"What about, dear?"

I hid my face in the crook of my arm. "Because I don't deserve this—you being nice to me, and Josh... and everyone's miserable and it's all because of me!"

"Oh, no... no one's miserable, and no one's mad at you," she said, stroking my hair.

"My mom is," I blabbed.

"I'm sure she's just upset. She doesn't want you getting

hurt. Every mother loves her children and wants what's best for them."

"Mine doesn't. You don't know my mother. She doesn't ever want to see me again." Without thinking, I wiped my eyes and nose on her shirt.

"She'll be here for the wedding, won't she? Both of your parents. You're all welcome to stay here. You and Josh can have Josh's old room in the basement and your parents can sleep on the fold-out."

I couldn't picture it happening but thanked her anyway. My eyes ached from crying.

Pam showed us to our basement room with its pull-up tile floor and wood-paneled walls. Laundry rumbled nearby, and I could smell bleach, mildew, tools in storage. The room itself seemed part of the punishment.

After she left us to get settled, I sank back onto Josh's bed. "I can't believe we get to sleep in the same room," I said.

"Come on, my parents aren't that conservative. Besides, we're as good as married." He dropped next to me and put his arm around my stomach. The baby moved; I felt it more lying down.

"So… this is where you grew up. This is where you slept when you were a kid. Interesting," I said.

"I moved down here when I was twelve. Before that I had a smaller room upstairs. I guess that's where we'll put the baby."

"Uh, no. We'll put the baby in our room, which will be big enough and not in a basement because we won't be here, we'll be in our own place."

"That's what I meant—eventually. It just might be easier to stick around for a few weeks and take advantage of my mom's help. Think about it, Ro. It'll give us time to find jobs and a place to live."

Josh had decided on working full-time until I went back to Pier 1; school for him would have to wait another semester. As for me, I didn't have any more higher education in mind, just work and baby, work and baby.

"Phew, there's so much to do," I said. The laundry paused before restarting. "Your mom's nice. I expected her to hate me."

"Why would you expect that?"

"Why not? Who wants to be a grandma at her age?"

"Maybe she does. She loves taking care of kids. She used to run the daycare at my dad's church."

He kissed me on the nose, then went upstairs to use the bathroom, leaving me alone in his old room. It wasn't such a bad place, really. At least the small windows near the ceiling let in a fair amount of light. I didn't like being so close to the laundry, and I hoped Pam wasn't one of those women who always had a load going.

The room preserved some of Josh's not-so-distant past: a picture of him in a white confirmation robe (his hair longer, straighter, the glasses different), a team banner from WMU, ticket stubs (the Kalamazoo Symphony Orchestra, Brooks & Dunn), a hanging cross made from big strips of woven grass. A more recent picture of his family stood on the dresser. Pam looked exactly the same—she even had on the same shirt—and Josh beamed a rare smile. I assumed the other man in the picture was his father. He looked like a Lutheran minister—big head, broad chest, a gum-chewing grin. His hand pressed down on Josh's shoulder.

I heard steps overhead and two male voices in conversation. The deeper one scared me.

Josh called down, "Ro, my dad's here."

Partly as a stalling tactic, I took my mirror out of my purse and fixed my makeup. I don't know why I wanted to look pretty for Josh's father. Dumb instinct, I guess.

The Okerfeldts were sitting in the kitchen when I joined them. "Dad, this is Roseanne," Josh said.

Reverend Okerfeldt got up and bolted toward me. He had a reddish face, as if his job involved working outside in the wind and sun. Instead of shaking my hand (as my father did when he met Josh), he drew his arms around me and pulled me close. He smelled clean and seemed to give off more heat than the ordinary person.

"Roseanne. You're welcome in our house," he said, stepping back to get a better look.

"Thank you, uh... Reverend," I peeped.

"Call me Terry. I'm sorry I couldn't be here sooner but we're dealing with a number of crises at work. I'll need to go out again after dinner." Spying the bump under my shirt, he asked, "Would it be all right if I touched it?"

I hesitated. I couldn't tell him no, though I didn't like anyone touching my belly, not even Josh. It made me feel like public property. "Of course," I said.

His hand flowed over my stomach like a warm liquid. It was a gentle touch, respectful. I didn't mind it. "Can you feel it kick?" he asked.

"Sometimes," I said. He looked older close up, maybe fifty. His slicked-back hair showed a pale scalp underneath.

"They haven't asked the doctor if it's a boy or a girl," said Pam, working at the stove.

"Good, keep it a surprise. No preferences here. Either way, it's a gift from God." Terry found a stool for me at the breakfast counter. A newspaper lay spread open to the sports section, and a half-empty cup of coffee looked like it'd been sitting there all day.

"Now, Roseanne," Pam said, "I don't know what you like to eat, but I'm making a chicken casserole."

"That's fine," I said. The thought of chicken casserole nauseated me, but I owed it to them to be a good sport.

"We're meat eaters here, speaking of which—Josh, Freddie Dahlstrom keeps asking when you want to go hunting with him up in Alpena," Terry said.

"No time soon," Josh said. He sounded disappointed.

"You hunt?" I asked.

He smiled blandly. "I have hunted."

Terry said, "Everyone hunts around these parts. We're rednecks, I know. Pam and I used to have a side business processing deer, but it got to be too much. We made burgers, sausages. Josh, remember that four point buck you tagged behind the house?" The family laughed. "Josh was about twelve at the time. It's rare that you get a deer to venture this close to civilization unless it's winter, which it was. He'd only been out hunting with me once or twice, but he knew how to load the Remington. Got off a good clean shot. It took some explaining once the police came 'round."

More laughter from Pam and Josh. I wondered where the gun was, if they kept it locked up. "I've never even been fishing before," I said.

"What do you do for fun?" Terry asked. Everyone stared—even Pam stopped cooking and turned her back to the stove.

Well, Terry—is it too soon to call you Dad?—until recently I liked to drink until two in the morning and have standing-up sex with guys from Shaker Heights.

"I knit," I said. It wasn't such a lie. At least I could sew on a button.

We had an early dinner while it was still light out. Before we ate, the Okerfeldts lowered their heads in prayer. I set my fork down and gamely folded my hands in my lap.

Terry finished his prayer by saying, "And Lord, though these two young people face hardship and uncertainty, let them know that they have the love and support of their family, of their community, and of you, Lord, in whose name we pray."

Josh and Pam said, "Amen," and I whispered it too.

"Why do you have to go back to work tonight?" Josh asked after the last plate had been passed.

Terry ate quickly, knife in one hand and fork in the other. "We're moving the library and church archives into the new wing, and we don't have anyone with any knowhow or organizational sense."

"I'll do it," Josh suggested.

"You will?"

"Pay me and I'll do it. It's that or go back to Florsheim, and I really don't want to work for Ben Hadley again."

Terry raised his head. "You're gonna want to see the place first. It's a big job."

"I'll ride in with you."

Nothing more was said about it, and they went back to their food. I silently panicked. We'd only been there a few hours, and already I felt abandoned.

I helped clear the dishes after dinner. Twice Pam asked me to sit and rest, but I refused. I wanted to do my part like a normal person.

"Who cooks in your family?" she asked as we set the rinsed plates in the dishwasher. The Okerfeldts' dishwasher was the old-fashioned kind with a locking lever and buttons that clicked when you pressed them. No timers, no special settings—just on and off.

"No one, really. It's rare that we even eat together."

"Big family or small?"

"Small. One brother, older." I didn't tell her about Wallis being in a wheelchair. We'd get around to it soon enough.

"Terry and I wanted more children but… it wasn't to be." Rinsing the soapsuds from her hands, she said, "Now you and Josh will have to make those decisions for yourselves."

Her tone was different. For the first time, she sounded like she hated me a little.

Josh and his father left for church, and Pam suggested we sit in the living room. I'd been feeling sick to my stomach, and sweating too. Checking my watch, I realized what it was: I hadn't had a cigarette in over six hours.

"Mrs. Okerfeldt, you and your husband have been so nice to me, and-"

"Pam, please," she said, holding her crochet in her lap.

"Okay. Pam. And I want to thank you for dinner and for letting us stay in your home, but…" I tried not to cry. "There's something I haven't told you, and it's that I've been trying for six months—a year, really—to quit smoking… I know it's awful, and I've cut it way down—I'm not as bad as I was before I got pregnant. And I am going to stop. It's just a gradual process, and maybe it's because I'm nervous about coming here today, but I really need to go outside for five minutes and have a cigarette. It's a problem and I'm taking it seriously, and the first thing I'm going to do tomorrow is find a drug store and pick up some nicotine gum, but I wanted to let you know because this is your house, and you've been so kind to me and Josh."

She set aside her crochet. "Roseanne, thank you for being truthful with me, and I can appreciate the difficulties in overcoming an addiction. I used to smoke before I had Josh, and if you weren't carrying a child, I'd say fine. But under the circumstances, I'm going to have to object. The child's health is too important. You should know that I'm here and I care, and if there's anything I can do to help you through this, all you have to do is ask."

I smiled until my face ached. Of all the possible reactions I'd expected, a flat-out "No" wasn't one of them. I thought people stopped saying "No" to you once you got to be an adult.

"I can go down the street if you'd like," I said, hoping she'd see the absurdity in making me walk all the way down the block just for a quick smoke.

"No, Roseanne, now... I don't want to fight about it. You're a free person and no one can make you do anything. That's why God gave us freewill. You're free to engage in dangerous behavior despite the harm it causes others. But my husband and I have been very patient during this whole process, and if you'd like that to continue—and I'm reasonably certain you'll need our help once this baby is born—you need to be more respectful of our wishes."

I hated her. She was fine before, but now I couldn't stand her. I hated her for being so patient and good, and I hated the fact that she was right—I did need her.

I let Josh have it when he came home. "This isn't going to work, hon. Your mother has to understand that quitting smoking isn't that easy. It's not just a matter of saying a few 'Hail Marys' and hoping for the best."

"Lutherans don't say 'Hail Mary,'" he said, untying his shoes at the foot of our bed.

I kicked him. "Fuck you. I hate this. I want to go home."

He put his hand on my leg, which I jerked away. "Hey, listen to this. Dad's decided to pay me twelve dollars an hour to catalog the new archives. There might even be a permanent position for me at the church if it works out."

"As what? Your daddy's sidekick?" I snapped.

"No, as church librarian. I'd be able to help with research, order materials. It's a good job for someone like me."

I didn't know what to say. Short of carrying the Okerfeldt family genes, I had no idea what I was doing there. "Good for you. That's very good news... for you." I closed my eyes and shut down for the night.

The next morning I woke to a grinding sound over my head—someone pushing a lawnmower in the backyard.

Josh and I were married a month later at his father's church. My parents relented and drove up for the ceremony. They'd wanted to stay at the Radisson downtown but Terry and Pam insisted on putting them up.

Pam made us a home cooked meal the night before the wedding. I hadn't seen my mom and dad in weeks. Mom kept a stiff neck and a straight back coming into the house. Dad had on the same light blue suit he'd worn to my graduation.

At dinner, Mom said, "I wish Wallis could've joined us, but it would've been too hard for him to make the trip."

Pam asked, "Wallis is your firstborn?"

Mom nodded hesitantly. "Firstborn" wasn't a word we used at home. It sounded Biblical.

She explained, "He's on a research study in Greenland.

It can be difficult for him to get around. Wallis is a…"
Here it comes, I thought. "…a Special Needs child. 'Child'—he's not a child anymore."

I hated when she described Wallis as "Special Needs." To me Special Needs meant retarded. It didn't mean breaking your spine at age ten.

Pam looked surprised, though I'd told her all this before. I gripped Josh's knee as my mother spoke at length about Wallis' accident, how he'd needed fourteen surgeries to correct the damage to his spine and how she'd had to take out a new mortgage on the house while we waited for the insurance money to come in. Terry and Pam listened gravely, interjecting moans of sympathy like respondents in church.

"Such a horrible thing. That must've been very hard on all of you," Pam said.

"Oh, no… Rosie was the hard one," Mom said, pointing at me.

"Thanks," I said.

"I'm just kidding, dear."

I snatched a roll from the breadbasket and tore into it with my teeth. The cat farted.

"So I guess this is our 'rehearsal dinner,'" Josh said.

After dessert we relocated to the living room. Josh wanted to hear music; he'd been in his room for fifteen minutes looking for a CD to bring up.

"I take Aleve for muscle pain," Pam was saying. "Tylenol for headaches and fever. I take Advil when I've got a cold, Bayer for cramps, and Excedrin for nasal congestion."

"I can't take aspirin. Wallis can't either. Phil takes aspirin, don't you, Phil?" Mom asked my dad.

"Mm? Sure. All the time. I take aspirin instead of

Tylenol," Dad said. Terry cupped his hand around his mouth and booed.

Josh came up from the basement with some CDs. He'd changed into his T-shirt and pajama bottoms.

"What music you got there, pal?" Terry asked. Josh held up a Paul Simon CD. "Don't know it. What else? Don't know it. What else? Don't know it."

Our parents seemed to get along overall, judging by the time everyone went to bed. No one mentioned politics or religion. I don't think anyone even mentioned the baby. By the next morning, Mom and Pam were helping each other make breakfast while the dads loaded the cars with cups and paper plates and other things for the reception.

We had about forty people at our wedding, and except for my parents, Josh, and the Okerfeldts, I knew none of them. The ceremony itself felt vaguely shotgun. Pregnant bride? Check. Embarrassed guests? Check. Terry struggled back tears as he married us, his comments expressing defensive pride in his son. Bible quotes and expansive observations about the State of the Family seemed apropos of some grander occasion.

After the service we drifted down to the church basement for our reception. Altogether I think we spent about seven hundred bucks on food and drinks. The linoleum-and-card-table theme was my idea (joke).

Josh took me aside and showed me the library where he'd been cataloguing his father's collection of articles and books. Half were still in boxes; dozens, maybe hundreds. It must've been nice to get away for a few hours each day—just him and his books and the quiet of the church on a Tuesday afternoon.

"Are you happy?" he asked as I browsed the reference volumes on his worktable. I wondered what was so hard about alphabetizing a bunch of books and putting them on shelves. I could do that.

"You'll feel better once the baby's born. It's a lot to handle all at once," he said.

"It sure as fuck is. Oop." I bit my lip. "I shouldn't say that in church."

My parents were nice and paid for us to stay the night at a fancy hotel in Grand Rapids. Josh went out to get the car while I sat in the reception area with my mother. We'd hardly spoken since that morning. I'd taken off my wedding dress and looked more like myself in my extra-large T-shirt and maternity pants.

"I'm sorry all this happened," I said, sensing it'd be a while before we saw each other again. She and Dad were driving back to Ohio the next morning.

She put her hand on mine. Mom wasn't much of a crier. Physical things made her cry—cutting her finger in the kitchen, dropping a heavy box on her foot. Rarely anything as vague as disappointment.

"It's okay, dear. You're doing the best you can. And Josh is a decent person." She kissed my hair, which I'd shaken down from its bun. "Have fun tonight. I think you're allowed one glass of champagne."

Josh and I spent our wedding night watching the city skyline from our room on the twenty-third floor of the Amway Grand Plaza. I left the TV on mute, feeling more relaxed with something on in the background. We couldn't have sex but I gave him a hand job in front of the window. It was what it was.

Later in bed, I asked, "Do you remember that old movie, *The Towering Inferno*? Every single famous actor from the sixties and seventies was in it. I always think of that movie when I'm in a tall building like this. Although this isn't so tall. Tall for Grand Rapids, I guess." Josh was asleep; his nose sounded stuffed up. "Are we swaying? It feels like it. Maybe I have an ear infection. I remember getting stuck in a traffic jam on our way to Canada, and the Ambassador Bridge started swaying. Scared the shit out of me."

He turned over. Light from the TV flashed on the ceiling. The building wasn't swaying. Everything was perfectly still.

CHAPTER SEVEN

It hurt like hell.

CHAPTER EIGHT

I was high on pain meds when we brought Sarah home. (Her nickname, Star, would come later.) For a week I had a hard time moving around, so Pam put her down for her naps. Pam and I worked well together, and I got weepy when I thought about how much I owed her.

"Raising a child is group work," she said as Star slept in the bassinet near my bed. I still had my breasts hanging out after feeding her. The first thing you lose is your self-consciousness.

"Who helped you with Josh?" I asked. Both Josh and his father were at the church, leaving behind this cloister of women.

"Not his father, I can tell you. The Okerfeldt men tend to be hands-off when it comes to babies. I don't think Terry took a real interest in Josh until he was six or seven. I had my mother, my older sister Carol, my younger sister Bea. Fortunately Josh was an easy baby. Sarah seems easy too."

We looked over at the bassinet, the same one I'd use a year later with Vance. I didn't like what Pam had said about the Okerfeldt men. Maybe it was a generational thing. Josh seemed like a natural father to me. He'd been helpful during the delivery and wasn't reluctant to change diapers or comfort Star in the middle of the night.

"I hope she inherits my father's disposition. I'm more like my mom. I guess I cried a lot when I was little," I said.

"All babies cry. You just have to find a quiet place inside yourself and ride it out." Pam rose from her chair and pulled the bed sheets over my chest. "I'll take her upstairs if she gets cranky," she said, leaving me alone with the baby.

I think I slept a total of three hours that whole first month. My cervix ached, and I lasted about ten seconds the first time Josh and I tried having sex. Gradually the pain stopped—being able to drink wine again helped—and I turned my attention to getting back into shape. Pam seemed content to watch the baby, so I'd go out for thirty-minute jogs around the neighborhood. I wanted to feel my age again. (Twenty, in case you've lost track.)

After three months, I decided to go back to work. The Pier 1 in Grand Rapids hired me as a part-time manager on the basis of my old boss' recommendation. I suppose I could've exercised more imagination in finding a job, but my brain was baked and I wanted to slip into something easy.

My new coworkers treated me like some sort of odd celebrity, given that I'd worked at two different Pier 1's in two different states. The new store was larger than the first but otherwise featured the same smells, the same aprons, and the same three k.d. lang songs playing in the background.

"We got robbed once," another manager told me during one of my first shifts. Her name was Doreen and she gelled her hair. "At gun point. I wasn't working. I was on vacation. I was in Dallas for vacation. My boyfriend lives in Dallas—lived in Dallas. Now he lives in Maryland and he's not my boyfriend no more."

I tried guessing her age. She looked about twenty-five but seemed so much younger than me. "Did they ever catch this person?" I asked.

"Nope. No security cameras. That one's a fake," she said, pointing at the camera above the store's entrance. "He told everyone to go into the stockroom and lie face-down on the floor. Girls were crying. Then he made Jasmine open the safe and take out the bank deposit. Got away with eight hundred dollars."

She grinned wildly at a customer passing through the door. Out in the parking lot a man with a Big Gulp spat Pepsi-colored ice at the pavement.

"I think you'll like it here. We get good customers, nice people, most of 'em. I'd like to work at another Pier 1 someday. Yeah," she said wistfully. "Not two at once, not at the same time. Just when I'm ready to move on."

That afternoon I helped a retarded man buy votive candles.

When I called home during my break, Pam said, "Sarah's good. She's crying for her mama."

"She is? No, she's not," I said.

"Yes, she is. Not all the time. She has her moments."

I smiled at one of my coworkers and waited for him to leave the break room.

"Is she actually saying the word 'Mama' or is she just crying? Because if she's just crying then she's not 'crying for her mama.' That's something different."

Pam was silent.

That night I brought up the subject of apartment hunting with Josh. I only worked Mondays, Thursdays, and Fridays, which left the weekend and most of my afternoons free.

"Today's paper had lots of places in our price range—it must be the right time of year. I circled a few. Is Grandville nice? I keep reading about Grandville." We were in bed, and I nudged him with my hip. "Hon? What do you think about looking for a place this weekend? We can take Sarah along if your mom doesn't want to sit with her."

"Maybe. I guess it doesn't hurt to know what's out there," he said.

"We gotta move out of your parents' house sometime. Now that I'm working and you're working... we should have decent references between the two of us."

He switched on the lamp beside the bed. My eyes went to the WMU banner over his dresser. "See, the thing is, I was hoping to go back to school—you know, like we'd planned. I've still got three semesters left, so a lot of that money's going to go to tuition. It might be tight for a year—unless you wanted to work full-time, but then I don't know what we're going to do about the baby. My mom can't do everything."

"She's not doing everything," I said. Between the two of us, Pam and I split baby duties roughly fifty-fifty; maybe sixty-forty, now that I was back to work.

"No, I know... come on, Ro, it's late," he said irritably.

"So what do we do, wait another year while you finish up school? In this basement?"

"I realize it's not ideal."

"No, it's not. I've got to go up and down those stairs every time Sarah wakes up. You don't know what it's like being stuck here all day. You're the one who gets to leave every morning at seven o'clock, God knows why."

"Because Dad leaves at seven, and it's when I get most of my work done. At least here you've got company. You'd be alone if we lived in an apartment."

"Josh, dear, your mother and I have absolutely run out of things to say to each other—not that she isn't the sweetest woman, and not that I'm not entirely grateful for all the help she's been. I'm beyond grateful. I'm so grateful I want to kill myself."

He snapped off the light. For several minutes I watched the WMU banner slowly emerge from the dark. The room still felt like a guy's to me. The sheets were rough and solid colored, the furniture dark and sturdy. It lacked a woman's touch—and yet there I was.

We apologized to each other the next morning and snuck out to dinner that night while Terry and Pam sat with the kid. Josh drove us to an Applebee's or a Friday's or an Olive Garden—cheap eats. Hockey on the TV. Try the jalapeño poppers! I had three wines and a salad as Josh nursed his tall beer. Then we went home, said good night to the Okerfeldts, and quietly made love in the basement. It was nice; a lot of kissing and hand-holding, just the way a girl likes it. We even slept naked, which we hadn't done in a long time.

Three weeks later I found out I was pregnant again.

Still keeping track? Yep, twenty-one that August.

The big fuck-up was telling his parents. Well, I didn't tell: Josh told his mom, who blabbed it to his dad, who subsequently informed the congregants of the Trinity Lutheran Evangelical Church of Byron Center, Michigan. If I'd wanted an abortion—and I wasn't sure I did—I'd have the whole goddamn town looking over my shoulder.

The only person (other than my mother, obviously) who was less than thrilled with the idea was Pam. With

Star taking up all her time and most of mine, I'm sure she saw more work for her on the horizon.

One day when we were home with the baby, she lit into me. "You know, some women would be a little more careful, especially when they're barely in their twenties and already have a child and their husband is struggling to make ends meet."

"Josh doesn't like condoms," I said, wanting to shock her. I wanted her to call me a slut and chuck me out of the house.

"Use your brain! He's a man, Rosie. I know he's my son, but for God's sake..." She held a fist to her mouth. Sarah was asleep in the next room. "It's up to you to take control of your own situation. If you don't want to do something, don't do it!"

"I don't know what you people want from me. I've done okay, haven't I? I haven't been neglectful. Either I'm at work or I'm taking care of Sarah. I'm not out drinking and partying and having a good time."

Pam just stared. The Okerfeldts had a tendency to shut down in the middle of a fight.

"Why are you looking at me like that? Why do you hate me so much?" I asked.

"I don't hate you, Roseanne, I just-" Her eyes shifted. "I hear Sarah."

"I'll get her."

"Don't bother." She moved but I stood in her way.

"She's my goddamn daughter and I will handle it," I said.

Star had gone back to sleep by the time I reached her crib, but I stayed behind to watch over her. It felt like night inside the dark nursery, a calm, cool night in the shrinking days of late summer. I knew I had to get her away from Pam, even if it meant working extra hours. I might be able to swing rent if I went up to full-time. But if I worked full-time, there'd be no one to take care of the baby. All of my money would go to paying a sitter. It was either work or stay at home—I couldn't do both... without Pam. I was stuck.

See what happens to silly girls like me?

That fall Josh got his wish and returned to school, though he still worked for his father three days a week. Studying always came first, which I understood. A degree meant a better-earning job in the future and a better life for all of us. So while I changed diapers, Josh read books. While Josh went to classes, I shelved kitchen accessories at Pier 1.

One night I happened to glance through his school books and noticed one I hadn't seen before. It was called *A History of Contemporary American Film*, and it included full color photos from movies like *The Godfather* and *Do the Right Thing*. I asked him what class it was for.

"Oh, I had to take an elective, so I chose a film course. It's pretty interesting. Last week we saw *The Color Purple*. We also watched a bunch of cartoons from the fifties. I've got a paper due on Thursday," he said.

I don't know why hearing about the class annoyed me, but it did. Watching movies sounded too much like having fun out of the house. But I kept my mouth shut.

I was already seven months pregnant with Vance when Wallis swung into town for a visit. I hadn't seen him in over two years, and I nearly cried when I picked him up at the airport.

"Hey... hey... hello to you too," he said as I kissed his cheek, his forehead, even his glasses. He was the first off the plane, and I thanked the stewardess who'd escorted him into the terminal.

"Weren't you supposed to have that kid a long time ago?" he asked, eyeing my baby bump. I raised two fingers. "Oh. Is that a good thing?"

I wiggled both fingers to show indecision. "It's a thing. Good God, Wallis, I'm glad to see you."

The other passengers were coming off, so we got out of the way. I'd borrowed the church's van with its wheelchair elevator to pick him up. He'd made a special trip just to see me, a rare treat. Since returning from Greenland, he'd been to Paris, Copenhagen, Beijing, and Johannesburg, attending conferences on economics with Dr. Snow. I envied his life, even if I didn't quite understand it.

Josh and the Okerfeldts were waiting at the door when we drove up to the house. I smiled bravely through the windshield. I liked having Wallis with me. At least I didn't feel so badly outnumbered.

Once inside, we continued into the living room where Pam had cleared some of the furniture. Star still couldn't walk, so I carried her in to say hi.

"Ah, here's the poop-machine," Wallis said.

I put her down on the floor, and she crawled over to Wallis' chair. "Who do you think she looks like?" I asked as we sat around the coffee table.

"She looks like her own little person," he said. Star tugged on his pant leg, and he let her have one of his fingers.

"I think she looks like Terry's sister, Gwen. Terry, weren't you saying she looked like Gwen? Gwen has the same thin nose." Pam offered a tray of cheese and crackers to Wallis, who shook his head. "Wallis—now that's such an interesting name. But it's not spelled W-A-L-A-C-E, like George Wallace. How did your parents decide on that?" she asked.

"I think they pulled it out of a hat," Wallis said.

"George Wallace had two 'l's. W-A-L-L-A-C-E. You said one," said Terry.

"I did? Well I meant to say two." She turned back to Wallis. "And Rosie tells us you're a scientist. What kind of research do you do?"

"I'm not really a scientist. I trained as an economist with an interest in social anthropology. I study people, basically," Wallis said.

"People," Terry repeated, as if the word concealed suspicious activity.

"The way people behave in small groups, in isolation... how economies and systems of trade develop out of local conditions. It's... academic stuff."

Terry and Pam laughed nervously. Meanwhile Josh sat at the far end of the couch, holding one of his school books in his lap.

Pam served us her usual chicken casserole for dinner. She had a fairly limited range as a cook. Most nights we ate hearty white foods on thick plates bought at Target.

After a quiet meal, I went downstairs to pull the extra sheets out of the dryer. I told Josh, who'd followed me down, "I'll listen out for Sarah. I'm sleeping on the hide-a-bed with Wallis tonight."

"Why?" he asked.

"He might need my help if he has to use the bathroom in the middle of the night. Don't worry, we won't say mean things about you," I promised, starting up the steps with the sheets and pillowcases.

"Why would you say mean things about me? What did I do?"

I touched his cheek. He looked tiny in the dark of the basement, like a bespectacled mole. "Oh, nothing, hon. I'm just kidding. Remember—jokes, laughter, ha-ha?"

Wallis was looking out the living room window when I got upstairs. He didn't notice me at first. Instead he sat rock-like and immobile with his back to the room.

"Great view, huh?" I said. The tree in the front yard threw its haggard branches at the window. It was the kind of tree that would've scared me when I was little.

"Your neighbor across the street's playing air-guitar," he said.

I joined him at the window. I'd spoken to the Okerfeldts' neighbor a few times. Rarely about much: the weather, the price of things. I once saw him hurrying from his house to his truck with tears running down his face. Never found out what had happened.

"I think it's air-bass. Look how he's holding his hand," I said.

"Ah, yes, I see. He's plucking instead of strumming." Wallis yawned. "Your mother-in-law makes good chicken casserole. They're nice people."

"You think?"

"Sure, why not? They're okay."

I made the bed as he unpacked his nightclothes. Pam crept in to turn up the thermostat and snuck away in her slippers.

Once we were settled in bed, he said, "I'll visit again soon, I promise. Dr. Snow's scaling back his travel plans. We're focused on getting this Greenland book together. We might have a publisher interested in Chicago. It's a university press but Dr. Snow knows the editor."

"Sounds exciting. You're lucky. I want to do that."

"Do what?"

"What you do. I want to write a book about Greenland. I want to see my name on a book cover. I want to 'scale back my travel plans.'"

He laughed at the ceiling. "You're funny."

"I do. I want to have travel plans, then scale them back."

"You should be a stand-up comedian. You could be one of those angry women who makes jokes about oral sex and camping and cleaning up baby vomit."

I covered his mouth with my hand to stop him from talking.

Wallis stayed another day before flying back to Canada. I cried at the airport. I wanted to go with him.

"Come up to St. John's sometime," he said, holding his boarding pass against his chest as if someone had thrown it at him.

I laughed. "Yeah, right."

We kissed, and I watched him pass through security. He had to wait in a special line for passengers with disabilities, and I wondered why his wheelchair didn't set off the alarm.

Back to reality, I worked all the way up to my thirty-sixth week. Because Vance was a breech baby, we scheduled a c-section with my Ob-Gyn. My doctor was a stern black woman with a colorful knit headscarf that she kept in place with a brass clip. Her favorite word was "vagina," which she pronounced like a succulent Italian dessert: vagina, *vagina*.

Recovering from my c-section was a bitch, even worse than natural childbirth. The only adult I had any steady contact with was Pam, who rarely let me near the baby. "You're too frail," she'd say, or, "You don't want to burst your stitches." I didn't argue—I felt like a baby myself: helpless, cold, and weak.

Some women will tell you two babies are easier than one: those women are liars. Vance cried all the time—shrieked, really—and only calmed down when Pam held him. As opposed to Star, who at least had my squinty stoner eyes, I saw nothing of myself in Vance. I felt like a surrogate mom. The baby didn't love me, didn't like my singing or my stories. He hit, he screamed, he kicked. From the Okerfeldts I received help but no sympathy. I stopped breastfeeding when Vance's teeth came in early, and Pam even judged me for that.

Motherhood was a tunnel for me, dark and cold and never-ending. It had its rewarding moments, sure, but mostly I remember being exhausted all the time. My skeleton ached and my mind wasn't sharp. I'd given up on being a "good mother," whatever that meant. No, being a good mom required a calm bearing and perspective that I didn't have. Everything was react, react, react.

On the phone with my mother one night, I asked, "When does it get easier? Someone told me six is a nice age. Is it? What was I like when I was six?"

Kitchen clanging in the background. "I just dropped a can of soup on my foot," she said.

"Sarah's still only two. Does that mean it's going to be hard like this for the next four years, or does it gradually get better? Is three a little better than two and then four a little better than three?"

"It never gets easier. You'll worry about your children for the rest of your life. One day you'll be old like me, and your daughter will be asking these same questions on the phone while you're trying to make dinner."

I looked at my watch: six o'clock. I hadn't eaten all day.

"Okay, fine, I'll let you go. But did I tell you what Sarah said last week? 'Damn it.' I think she said damn it."

"Are you sure? 'Damn it' can sound like a lot of different things."

"Like what? 'Spam it?' 'Ram it?' No, I know what she said. I couldn't believe my ears. I've been really good about not cursing. I've wanted to plenty of times, believe me."

Mom wasn't very good at giving advice. I couldn't imagine her as a parent of young children. Long hair and soft milky breasts—not her style. But obviously she'd survived it somehow.

I hung up and checked on Star in her play pen. She had a plastic drumstick in one hand and a little toy frying pan in the other, and she hit the pan with gleeful malice, a banging disco rhythm. It wasn't random noise—you could almost dance to it. So maybe she liked music. I wondered if that was a good thing or a bad thing. Why would it be a bad thing?

"Slam it!" she said. Ham it! Bam it!

Kids were scary mysteries to me. Not good mysteries, like unopened Christmas presents. Scary mysteries, like black holes. I felt like I'd lost control of my life. Self-recriminations rained down on me: I should've stayed in school. I should've made Josh use a condom. I should've gone on the pill, side effects be damned. I should've taken myself more seriously. But there I was, a mother of two, and a slave in my own house. I didn't even feel like a real mom. What would I say to Star when she was a teenager and looked to me for advice? Don't wind up like me? That was about the only nugget I had to offer. But you can't say that to a kid.

More and more I began to feel like everyone would be better off if I just went away.

By the time Star was old enough to walk steady and say more than a hundred words, I'd take her into the city and stroll with her along the riverfront, leaving Vance at home with Pam. We'd talk about what it was like to have a brother—I'd do most of the talking, of course, but Star seemed to enjoy my company. It felt good to know I wasn't such an inept parent that she didn't want to hang out with me.

One fall when Star was not quite four, I brought her to Burton Woods and watched her dive into thick piles of brown leaves the color of men's wallets. The other mothers in the park looked younger, healthier, more successful than me.

"Mommy, what happens when car blows up?" she asked. This was Star's favorite topic—what would happen if things exploded or fell down or got crushed.

"Then you don't have a car anymore," I said.

She was making snow angels in the leaves. "What happens when dinosaur go bang?"

"Then you got a dead dinosaur. Hey, do you want to get ice cream or is it too cold for ice cream?"

I still had twenty bucks in my purse, enough for a treat. If I split town that day, I'd have about sixteen hundred dollars in savings, plus the car.

We left the park and found an ice cream place still serving in late September. Star's waffle cone was about the size of her torso.

I let her finish her ice cream in the car and drove out of the city. For an hour we headed east. Signs announced exits for Battle Creek and Lansing, and a Led Zeppelin CD played through twice. Then a mileage sign gave the distance to Detroit and I panicked. When we got home late, I told Josh that we'd been in traffic and my cell phone had died.

By the start of the new year, Josh and I had finally saved up enough money to rent a house closer to the city, and three days a week I left Star and Vance off with Pam and drove in to work. I'd pretty much cleaned up my act since high school: no more cigarettes, far less drinking, and I'd never cheated on Josh—not that I didn't have my chances. There were the regulars at Pier 1, guys who worked in the city and dropped in once a week to flirt and leave disappointed. I guess I was still pretty enough.

I was also pregnant for the third and last time. Unlike before, we'd actually been trying to conceive. Josh wanted a third child now that he'd finished college and was back to working full-time for his dad. I figured I could manage one last push as long as he promised to get it snipped afterward.

Twins, though: fuck. We didn't find out until the twentieth week, after we'd already told Josh's parents and the rest of greater Grand Rapids. Apparently the second fetus had been hiding behind the first—thanks, Connor. Somehow I could get my mind around three kids, but four sounded like a fleet. I felt like one of those moms from pioneer days who pumped out one kid after another to help on the farm.

Josh could tell I wasn't happy, so for Christmas he bought me a gift certificate to take a creative writing class at the adult education center downtown. "When am I supposed to do this?" I asked.

"It's only three months. I'll put the kids to bed on Thursdays," he said.

"It's not the class, it's the homework. I don't have time to write."

"Kids take naps. You'll figure it out."

I put the gift certificate back in its envelope and looked down at myself. I was sure I'd be the only pregnant woman in class. Everyone would expect me to write about having kids and the joys of motherhood and all that bullshit.

I was nervous my first day. I hadn't been in a classroom in years, and that experience wasn't the best. My instructor was a disappointingly ordinary woman named Dorothy Boxton (I'd wanted her to be grand and eccentric and different from everyone else) who'd written a novel called *Tea Leaves* about a woman (yes, named "Tea") who opens an antique store in El Paso and gets raped by a seven-foot-tall furnace repairman. I'd read it the week before class, and even though it wasn't very good (maybe I just wasn't in the mood) I brought my copy for her to sign.

Dorothy's first words to me were, "When's it due?" Then, "Boy or girl?"

"Both," I said. Sympathetic groans from the rest of the class. I wanted to say, What the fuck are you groaning about?

We didn't do much writing our first class, just went around the room and talked about our likes and dislikes, what authors we'd read. Except for *Tea Leaves*, I hadn't read a book that wasn't mostly pictures of talking foxes since Star was born. The other students intimidated me. One was working on her third novel (the other two "weren't available in bookstores," whatever that meant); another wrote restaurant reviews for *The Grand Rapids*

Press. I wanted to ask him if the new Italian place on Grandville Avenue was worth trying.

When it was my turn, Dorothy asked why I'd taken the class. "My husband doesn't think I have enough to do," I said. No one laughed, so I added, "I'm kidding."

For our first exercise, Dorothy had us write about the most important person in our lives. Most people wrote about their parents, teachers, best friends from college. I chose Wallis. When Dorothy asked me to read, I laughed and covered my page.

"I don't like what I wrote. It's better if I just tell you about him," I said.

"You don't want to read?" she asked. She sounded disappointed, so I gave in.

"Okay. 'My brother Wallis.' That's not the title, that's just... never mind. 'My brother Wallis is only twenty-eight years old and already he's been to more countries than you can shake a stick at. He lives in Canada where he studies Eskimos and other people who live in cold climates. At least I think that's what he does—Wallis is too smart for me and a lot of the time I don't understand what he is saying. But I love him because he is my brother and because I'm so proud of him. Also my brother has been in a wheelchair since he was ten. Still, he never complains or even talks about it—think about that the next time you're sitting around feeling sorry for yourself and whining like an asshole."

Not my best work, I know.

"He sounds like an amazing person," said Dorothy.

"I can really hear your emotions coming through," said one of the students.

"Canada's nice," said another. I just smiled.

I was still revved up when I got home from class, and I kept Josh awake talking about it in bed.

"I got this idea for a story on my way home. Wanna hear it?" I asked. Josh's lumpy shape mumbled in the dark. "Okay, it's supposed to be funny, so don't take it too seriously. The idea's not funny, but it'll be funny when I write it."

"Just tell it," he said.

"I'm still working out the details, but what if I wrote a story about your parents—they're not really your parents, I'd give them different names like Ken and Janice or Paul and Nancy, and he's a pastor at a Lutheran church way out in the sticks and she's a stay-at-home mom who runs her own business selling discount fireworks online."

"My mom?"

"She's not your mom—forget I even said that. They're just these two people, Ken and Nancy, okay? And one day Nancy's at Family Fare buying a Duraflame Colorlog for the fireplace—the whole thing is so clear in my mind's eye—and a flatbed truck crashes into the grocery store and kills Nancy..."

"Vance is up."

"Yeah, and the rest of the story is about how Ken copes with the death of his wife and eventually realizes he doesn't want to be a preacher anymore so he quits his job and sells the house and buys a boat named John Lennon: Imagine and sails down to the Gulf of Mexico where he has a heart attack and dies while masturbating in the shower. What do you think?"

"Mm."

"There might be a little epilogue after that. I think I'll get started while the idea's still fresh. Hey, I think Vance is crying—you wanna get that?"

All week I worked on the story whenever I had a chance—during breaks at work, while the kids were napping, even in the bath with a pad of paper balanced on my knee. It was the first thing I'd really done for myself in years, and I felt proud when I passed around nine copies of the entire fifty-three page manuscript at the next class.

"Wow," Dorothy said, thumbing through the pages, "looks like an epic."

"You misspelled 'highfalutin,'" said the woman novelist.

"I won't have time to read all this," complained the restaurant critic.

We discussed the story a week later. Most of the students liked the grocery store scene, though the woman novelist thought I should've made it an armored van instead of a flatbed truck. Whatever. Dorothy had special praise for how I handled Nancy's death and confessed that she actually cried when Ken tucked his wedding ring into his wife's casket. I didn't believe her—these people get paid to say nice things—but by the end of class I felt lighter than air.

The next week I came across an unfamiliar word in a classmate's story and looked it up in my dictionary. I loved that big old book. The letters on the spine were gold and stood out in the dark. You could drop it on the floor from waist-high and shake the whole house.

For the first time I noticed an inscription on the front page. It read: "To Roseanne—You never know when you might need this. W."

Now, I'm not a crier. I've probably told you about every time I've cried, minus the usual screaming and tantrum throwing as a baby. But that day, seeing what Wallis had written to his undeserving sister—Wallis, who'd always believed in me, despite the drugs and booze and bad choices—what can I say. I cried.

The first four weeks of class were a thrill, but by the second month I'd fallen behind. I didn't have the brain for writing, nor the time. One Thursday I took Dorothy aside after class and told her I had to drop out.

"Par for the course," I said, dabbing my eyes with a Kleenex.

"Dear, why are you sad? You're about to give birth to twins. It's one of the great blessings in a woman's life."

I wondered at this but didn't say anything. "Maybe I'll take your class again, if you're still teaching here in ten years."

"Oh God, I hope not," she said, and we shared an awkward moment in the hall.

Another maternity leave followed, then another long stretch in the hospital. Josh slept on a mat next to my bed while Vance and Star stayed with their grandparents. All night I listened to women in other rooms screaming in childbirth. I wondered why it had to be painful, what the point was. And then you're supposed to feel happy and change their diapers and feed them morning, noon and night. Of course you can't complain, because if you complain, that makes you a bad woman. Some blessing.

The twins, Mary and Connor, popped out around seven in the morning. I kept the TV on in the delivery room and tried focusing on *The Today Show*. Matt Lauer led off with a story about Obama, then Al Roker did the weather, followed by an ad for Crisco cooking oil, another ad for Mercedes, and a preview for *Dateline*. More Matt Lauer, this time talking to a black woman in pumps and a bumblebee colored blazer. She looked like a politician from Texas.

Josh and the doctor told me to push, and I imagined Matt Lauer being hungry and crying and no one giving him any food.

After the twins were wheeled up to the ICU, Josh asked through his surgical mask if I needed anything. "Get me a Twix bar from downstairs," I said.

I had the room to myself that night. Mary and Connor slept in the nursery while Josh stayed home with the kids. With Motrin and Percocet came an invitation to relax. The pain was a subway rumbling well under my feet. I thought about my body, points of contact where the cool bed sheet touched my skin. My feet were in Kansas, my knees in Southern Illinois, my left hand two hours ahead of my right. I was in a spa. I could eat whenever I wanted. If I pushed *that* button, a woman would ride the elevator up from the kitchen and bring me a cup of yellow soup.

I came home two days later to barely-controlled chaos: pots banging, mail stacked on the armchair, a bag of trash waiting by the door. Instantly things were expected of me. I remember a hard stretch of weeks, being up constantly with the twins, never leaving the house, not even bothering to put on real clothes—what for? Pier 1 called several times to ask when I was coming back, and eventually I had to quit: no time, not even for a crappy three-day-a-week job selling drink coasters from Guatemala at a quarter a pop.

One night after visiting his parents, Josh asked what was wrong. "Oh, nothing," I said, my usual response. We were driving home in Josh's SUV, our six-month-old twins asleep in the middle seats, Star and Vance dozing all the way in the back. "I feel guilty watching your mother with the kids. She's done so much more for them than me."

"That's not true," he said.

"It is. Sometimes I think Vance thinks she's his real mom and I'm just some old nanny who puts him to bed."

"He clearly doesn't think that."

Poor guy, your wife's leaving and you don't even know it.

The mail was waiting for us when we got home. A medium-sized package looked like a coat I'd ordered, so I tossed it onto the couch. The twins went straight to bed, and we spent some time giving the older two baths and winding them down with stories. Star sat on my lap and Vance sat on Josh's.

"Dada? Why is the chipmunk sad?" Vance asked, tapping a picture in the storybook.

Josh quickly turned the page. "He's not sad. He's just thinking."

"But why is he thinking?"

"Because he likes to."

"And it's not a chipmunk, it's a squirrel," Star added.

Once the kids were down for the night, I poured myself a glass of wine and went back to the mail. The package felt more like a book than clothes. I smiled at the return address.

"Wallis sent me something. It feels like a present," I said.

Josh poured his own glass of wine. "Oh, that's nice. That reminds me, I still need to get my mom something else for her birthday. I feel like we're short this year."

He took his wine back to his office, and I waited until he was gone before opening the package. The book inside might've been five hundred or a thousand pages. The text looked dense—there were charts, a picture of a steel shed on a glacier. The caption under the picture read, "An observation shed in southern Greenland; author in foreground."

Wallis' book. I knew he'd been working on a book with Dr. Snow, but I guess I'd forgotten about it. Good for him, I thought. At least one of us had done something with our lives. At least when I died I'd be able to say my brother had written a book. My parents would be proud, too. Maybe Wallis writing a book would make up for me being such a nothing.

I flipped back and double-checked the name on the front cover: *Greenland, a Modern Nation,* by Dr. Clement Snow. No "and Wallis Crim"—not on the jacket, not on the inside cover. I couldn't believe it.

Wallis had included a note: "See page 685."

I turned to the page and found, along with a list of other acknowledgments, Wallis' name second to last, right before "Dr. Emmanuelle Snow"—Mandy. Snow's daughter.

My throat tightened. I wanted to throw the book across the room.

———

What happened next is probably the reason you're reading this book. Contrary to what you've heard, it was never my intention to abandon my children. As far as I'm concerned, they abandoned me. Kids can do that, you know. They're just little people with minds and wills of their own. No, long before the police and immigration got involved and everyone lawyered-up, my original plan was simply to drive north, bring Wallis back home to Ohio, divorce Josh, and sort things out with the kids.

Shared custody or whatever. My main focus was on my brother's well-being. Canada wasn't a healthy place for Wallis. He needed to get away from those people.

It took a few days to get my affairs in order before I crept out in the middle of the night, first leaving a note for Josh. I said I'd be in touch soon, that my brother was in trouble and needed my help. I told him not to worry, I'd always be a part of his life and would do all I could to assist with the kids. It didn't seem like enough—the note looked so paltry, just a few lines on a torn-out sheet of loose-leaf—but I couldn't think of anything else to say, so I signed, "Love, Ro," and left it on his desk.

Remember: this is what happens when you're feeling stressed and tired and alone and your in-laws despise you and your husband considers you a burden and you're in your mid-twenties but feel thirty years older and you have to drive an hour to find a liquor store open on Sundays. Maybe it wouldn't bother you but it bothered me.

I was sneaking down the hall when a noise stopped me. Star was standing in her brown-and-pink striped pajamas. She looked at my suitcase.

"Where are you going?" she asked.

I raised a finger to my lips. "Mommy's taking a trip. Go back to bed, okay?"

"How long are you gonna be gone?"

She seemed to glow in the dark, like the only bright thing in the universe. She was all I could see. "I don't know. Not long. You won't even have time to miss me."

"Can I come?"

I hesitated. I hadn't considered taking her along. I'd always figured the kids would be happier without me. "You want to?" I asked.

The light from her wavered across my face. She looked like a little star.

Fortunately we'd thought to get her a passport—I'd always meant to bring the kids up to Canada for a visit, just not like this. We went to her room and packed a few things. I pretended we were playing a funny trick on Daddy so she wouldn't worry or ask the wrong questions. Once we had her suitcase together, we tiptoed outside and climbed into the old hatchback. I winced as the engine started.

"Shit," I said, covering my mouth. Star giggled. "Yeah, Mommy swore. Wait here. I forgot something."

I hurried back across the yard, slipped the house key into the lock, and turned it quietly. The living room was still and dark, black-blue. I saw lampshades, the murk of the fireplace. The sound of the kids breathing blew hot inside my ears. Back to Josh's office, I took a pen and added to the note, "Sarah's with me."

Grabbed my dictionary. Ran.

II. WHAT I DID IN CANADA

CHAPTER NINE

They're on their way to Canada. Five boys, four in back and one sitting next to Gail Deaver who has agreed to drive the boys six hours to the Pinery campground on the Ontario side of Lake Huron. The boys are ten and eleven. They all go to the same school except for Chris Hooper who lives in Westlake. Mark Deaver is not sitting up front with his mother; he and Gail got into a fight that morning over whether Mark could wear his brand new Air Jordan Vs with his scout uniform, and now Mark wants to sit as far away from his mother as possible. He glowers between Chris Hooper to his right and Wallis Crim pressed up against the door to his left. Among other things—hyperthyroidism, bad skin—Chris suffers from Class I obesity and is some thirty pounds over his ideal weight. Nicknames include "Chris Pooper," "Chris Piss," "Giant Tub of Shit," "The Biggest Piece of Poo on the Planet," and "Waste."

They're just leaving Milner, and Gail is having a hard time maintaining the signal to her favorite classic rock station. "You Ain't Seen Nothing Yet" by Bachman-Turner Overdrive keeps bumping into some wacko ranting about the Bush tax increase. They're on a state road that connects towns like Milner and Montclair and Westlake to the Ohio Turnpike: speed limit thirty-five, traffic signals every six or seven blocks, Pizza Hut, McDonald's, Kentucky Fried Chicken, Best Buy, Kmart, T.J.

Maxx. *They pass a Cineplex playing* RoboCop 2, Days of Thunder, *and* Total Recall. *The boys have been out of school for three weeks. In that time, Mark Deaver lost a front tooth falling off his bike, Ron Steidley spent a week in the Ozarks with his family, and Wallis Crim finished* The Lord of the Rings. *Wallis wants to read the* Dune *books this summer and Mark hopes to visit his older brother who now lives in Tokyo. No one knows Jared Singh's plans. Jared's a quiet kid. He sits to Chris' right and stares through the car window. He'd like to get some fresh air—Jared sometimes gets sick in cars—but the switch for the automatic window is broken in back and he feels weird asking Mrs. Deaver to do it.*

As the car continues toward the highway, the boys discuss who's cooler, Schwarzenegger or Bruce Willis. Mark Deaver says Bruce Willis is cooler because he kicks ass. Ron Steidley argues from the front seat that Mark's point is moot since both Schwarzenegger and Bruce Willis kick ass. There is evidence of this: we have the films to prove it. Gail wishes the boys would stop saying "ass." Wallis Crim prefers Schwarzenegger because he can do funny movies as well as action movies. Chris Hooper says "I'll be back" in a faux-Austrian accent and no one laughs.

The boys are looking forward to the camporee, though no one will admit it. Camporees are officially gay. Everyone sleeps in the same big musty tent, and dinner is SpaghettiOs cooked straight from the can. Mark Deaver got busted last year for singing "Me So Horny" at Campfire Expressions. You're only supposed to sing approved-of folk classics like "If I Had a Hammer" and "Puff the Magic Dragon," and for punishment he had to sit out flag football semi-finals and help Mr. Andriotakis clean out his car. For Wallis the highlight of last year's camporee was standing on the edge of a sandy cliff overlooking Lake Huron at sunset. A long flight of wooden steps ran down from the cliff to the beach, and the bow of a small shipwreck poked out of the water fifty yards from shore. Most of the other boys went to the beach to look at the wreck, but Wallis stayed on the cliff and watched the sun bleed down into the water.

They're passing an Arby's, and Mark and Chris want to stop for roast beef sandwiches. Ron tells Chris he's fat enough and could probably live for a year on the fat stored in his ass cheeks. Chris tells Ron to go take a flying dump as Ron grins at his Game Boy. Mark says Chris should be happy he's so fat because his blubber would protect him from injury if he ever got in a plane crash or fell down a flight of steps, and if he was on a sinking ship his fat would act like a floatation device and also make it difficult for sharks to eat him, and in the event of a nuclear war he could hide out in a bomb shelter and, like Ron said, live off his ass cheeks until the radiation died down and then emerge from his shelter and be the only person living on earth, which would rule hard. Chris is getting angry. He says you can't live off your ass cheeks, stupid. He says it doesn't work that way. Mark says, Is that what you learned in Fat School? Gail tells all of them to shut up. She orders Mark to apologize to Chris, who is crying. Mark says sorry-not real fast and Gail insists on a real apology. This time he says "sorry" in his regular speaking voice but "not" immediately soft after, and Gail gives up. Arby's is a block away in the rear view mirror. She can just barely make out "Any Way You Want It" by Journey along with the whack job yammering on about Bush.

Green highway signs call Gail over to the far right lane. There's a smell coming from the backseat. It hits Mark first, then Jared and the others. It smells like the worst bathroom of all time, like pee and poop all at once. It smells like the inside of a cat's butthole—like way up where the poo gets made. Mark buries his face under the neck of his shirt and lurches away from Chris.

Wha'? Chris says—I didn't do it!

Dude, Chris completely farted! Mark screams into his shirt. On the other side of Chris, Jared Singh is bucking in his seat. He looks like he's been sprayed with pesticide. Ron gazes back, appalled. He feels fortunate not to be stuck next to the fat boy.

I didn't do it! Chris protests, his dumpling cheeks blushing murderously. Wallis frowns at the other three in the backseat. From where he sits, the smell has dissipated. It's not worth reacting to anymore.

But Mark isn't done yet. He stops thrashing around long enough to assess the air quality before howling, Dude, did you diarrhea? You did! Chris totally diarrhea'd in his pants!

Jared is practically doing pelvic thrusts. There are only two seat-belts in the back and neither Wallis nor Jared are belted in.

I didn't diarrhea! Don't be a fag-boy, fag-boy, Chris whines.

Gail makes soft protests behind the wheel. She's got her eyes out for the onramp a few hundred yards ahead. Bad Ohio drivers zoom at and around her. They're like darts, a flurry of arrows.

Did you just poo? Is there poo in your pants? Did you just load up your pants? I can't believe it. I can't believe you would do that. I can't believe you would take a massive gooey dump in your pants like that, Mark says, going on and on at great speed like an inquisitor. Ron and Jared groan and laugh. The smell is gone but Mark won't look up from his shirt.

Chris tries pulling down Mark's shirt but Mark flails away, shrieking, Don't touch me with your poo-hands, asshole!

Dude, that smell is nasty, Jared says. Jared's parents are from New Delhi and he speaks American slang with a fruity Indian accent.

I don't smell anything, Wallis says finally. He's tired of Mark beating up on Chris. People fart, that's what they do, and it's just a part of being alive. Besides, "diarrhea'd" isn't even a real word.

Thinking they're on the same side, Mark says to Wallis, That's because the poo smell is so strong that your nose has shut down, like, temporarily. Like to protect itself. Mom, open the windows before the smell comes back!

Gail is trying to ignore her son. They've got a long drive ahead of them, followed by three days of being trapped in the mud and mosquitoes with two-dozen pre-adolescent boys. Most of the other chaperones are married men, bulky guys with jobs in Public Works who yell at the kids things like "Look alive!" during flag football and whose spouses are wisely doing something else with their weekends. Gail comes along to keep an eye on Mark.

Mark pokes his mother. It almost makes her jerk the wheel.

Ma, open the windows, it stinks so bad back here!

Mark, stop it and be nicer to your friend, she says.

He's not my friend! Seriously, I think he farted again. I think he can't stop farting. I think there's something really wrong with him that he can't stop farting like this!

Dude, I'm not farting! I didn't even fart once, says Chris.

Mark asks his mother again to roll down the windows, but she tells him no, the air conditioning is on and she doesn't want to lose all this cold air.

He sinks back into his seat. For a moment he looks about to give up. The onramp is in sight: smooth-moving traffic heading north.

Then he tells Jared to roll down his window.

I tried, it won't work. There's too much farting back here, Jared says. It's like Gandhi saying it.

Mark turns to Wallis. Try yours, he says.

Wallis catches sight of Mrs. Deaver in her rear view mirror. He wants her to think well of him. Especially around his peers, he feels impatient to join the world of adults.

But your mom, he says.

Mark reaches across to paw at the power window switch.

Just open it, he says.

Mark, it doesn't even smell anymore. Just relax. Maybe we drove past a skunk or something.

Skunks smell different from farts, says Mark.

Mark makes another grab at the switch. He's right, skunks do smell different from farts. It's the last time he'll be right about anything in his life.

Wallis tries pushing Mark off but Mark is bigger and stronger and has more invested in winning. There's a scuffle with both boys jabbing and throwing elbows. It's almost like tickling. You can imagine one boy laughing and the other joining in, then a third boy saying, Hey, check out that Ferrari! and a fourth adding, That's not a Ferrari, that's a Lamborghini, then all four boys talking at once about sports cars and merit badges and Joe Montana and Married… with Children, *laughing and sparring and generally tolerating each other all the way to Canada.*

CHAPTER TEN

I must've looked guilty. Maybe it was the pile of clothes in the backseat or the disheveled five-year-old sleeping next to me. It might've been my hands shaking as I gave our passports to the border guard in Windsor. "Coffee," I explained.

The guard frowned and chewed her gum. She didn't like me. It was just after eight in the morning—we'd probably come at either the start or end of her shift.

"You're not drinking coffee," she observed as she brought our passports into her booth.

I glanced down and saw that both of our drink holders were empty. Damn. "Oh, I meant earlier. We stopped at McDonald's for breakfast."

"Long drive?"

I grinned noncommittally, wondering if it aroused more suspicion to leave my sunglasses on or suddenly take them off.

"Where are you coming from?" asked the woman, holding our passports above a scanner. A blue bar of light moved across the passports and back again.

"Grand Ra-"

"Can you take off your dark glasses?"

"Oh, sure." I slapped them away. "Grand Rapids, Michigan."

"You drove all night?"

"Yep." The planet turned. "Fewer cars on the road."

"And what's your purpose in visiting Canada?"

"Oh, my br-"

"Can you wake the little girl please?"

I nudged Star. "My brother lives here. We're visiting my brother. Sarah, honey? You need to sit up. This nice lady has some questions."

Star blinked and reeled in her seat. The guard asked her to state her name, first and last.

"Sarah Okerfeldt," Star said.

"Same last name as mine," I said. I felt the line of cars waiting behind us. A station wagon pulled out of the neighboring lane and drove ahead, unconcerned, its back window filled to the roof with luggage and kids' toys and a cooler.

"Your brother lives in Canada? Is your brother a Canadian citizen?" the guard asked.

I paused—I honestly didn't know. "I don't think so. I'm pretty sure he has a work permit. I mean, he's lived in Canada for," I added it up, "six years. But he's American."

"Where in Canada?"

"St. John's. That's east of here, right?"

The woman stared. Our passports still sat on top of the scanner, one next to the other, pages splayed. "Yes, St. John's in Newfoundland is east of Ontario," she said.

I fielded another series of questions before she finally waved us on. I almost drove off without retrieving our passports.

Grateful, relieved, I found the major highway and pointed us east toward Toronto. It took several minutes to adjust to the kilometer signs and the preponderance of Ontario license plates on the road.

"So... Canada. How do you like being in your first foreign country?" I asked.

Star examined the passport photo we'd taken of her at the post office when she was three. She looked nothing like she did then, moon-faced and chubby. Now her face was thin, the bones showing, like mine. I'd aged her.

"What's 'foreign?'" she asked.

"Oh, you know... like France is a foreign country, Greece is a foreign country. Somewhere that's not the United States."

The highway cut a perfectly straight line across browning fields of grass on either side. A single oil derrick ram-rodded the ground.

"It's okay," Star said.

"Just okay? It's not 'oo-wow-fabulous-exciting?'"

An overpass crossed the highway a mile ahead. It seemed stationary. To our right we passed a small county airport. Two-seater planes drove and parked on the tarmac like compact cars with wings.

"Mommy?"

I swallowed. She's going to ask about her father. She's going to ask why her father and brothers and sister aren't here and I'm going to have to tell her.

"What's up?" My voice was sawdust.

"Don't you like Daddy anymore?"

The overpass still hadn't budged. Canadian radio was a haughty-sounding woman discussing home heating prices between bursts of classical music.

"What are you talking about? Of course I like Daddy. I *love* Daddy. Why do you ask?" I said.

She didn't answer, but the question told me enough.

"Hey, let's play a game. Let's play the Canada game," I said.

"What's the Canada game?"

"The Canada game is where you say something Canadian and I say something Canadian and we just keep going until we can't think of anything Canadian anymore."

Star chewed her lip. The game didn't make any sense to her. She didn't know anything about Canada. The farthest she'd been from home was her grandparents' place in Ohio.

"Here, it's easy. I'll go first. Let's see...ice hockey is Canadian. I mean, that's obvious, so no points for that. Ice hockey and Niagara Falls, and the Olympics are in Canada next year, and Neil Young is from Canada—he did that song, 'Cinnamon Girl.' Your daddy has the album." The overpass wasn't in front of us anymore; we must've passed it. "Other things... lots of mountains in Canada—not this part, obviously. And their flag has a big red leaf on it and they've always been our friends and some of them speak French and some speak English and the ones that speak French speak a different *kind* of French... Quebecois they call it. Good, now you go."

Star didn't feel like playing so I gave up trying to entertain her. Instead we focused on the radio. Every other station was a news channel. I'd heard that Canadians in general cared more about the news than Americans. Even the commercials tended to be straightforward, fact-based, to the point.

Around noon I checked my cell phone to find six messages, all from Josh. I didn't listen, just turned it back off and kept driving.

"Hey, Sarah, what are you going to do when you see

your uncle Wallis? Are you going to hug and kiss him and jump in his lap?"

"I don't know," she said. She'd only met Wallis twice, the last when she was three. It was summer and we'd had a barbecue in Pam and Terry's backyard. Pam had just received a phone call that a friend of hers from high school had died in a car accident, and it spoiled the afternoon.

Star and I drove through a section of farmland that smelled keenly of manure. I hardly knew where we were going. I had the return address on the package Wallis had sent from St. John's and that was it.

By late afternoon we were both starving, so I pulled off the highway and found a strip of restaurants and hotels. Some of the restaurants looked familiar—Chili's, McDonald's, T.G.I. Friday's—while others didn't.

"Swiss Chalet—let's try that one. See how the locals live," I said, steering us into the parking lot.

As we walked across the lot, I searched through the money in my purse. I had ten hundred-dollar-bills, another five hundred in twenties, plus my checkbook with three checks left, all of them rubber. I didn't want to use my MasterCard for obvious reasons. With any luck we'd be in St. John's in another day or two and I could ask my brother for a loan.

A young girl in a brown dress and brown sneakers sat us at a table by the window. I asked if she took American money.

"Yes, but you should get it exchanged at your hotel. The rate is really bad," she said.

"I thought the dollar was strong in Canada," I said.

"Not anymore."

She left us with the menus, and I asked Star, "What sounds good? I can read it to you."

Her finger traced a word. "What's P-E-...?"

I looked at her menu. "Perogies. Oh, they're good! They're like little potato dumplings. You've never had perogies?" I wasn't surprised. Josh and I had raised her on a fairly basic Midwestern diet—pot roast once a week, spaghetti and meatballs, breaded pork chops. We weren't particularly innovative as parents. For books we gave her *Ramona* and *Clifford, the Big Red Dog* and watched *Happy Feet* and *Finding Nemo* on DVD. "Order them. It'll be a new experience. We're going to have all sorts of new experiences together. I've never stayed at an Econo Lodge. There's one down the road. Let's stay there tonight."

The waitress returned, and I ordered perogies and the quarter chicken dinner to share. The perogies came out lukewarm and soaked in butter, but we tore into them, grunting and swooning over our food. I thought about ordering a second helping but decided to save our cash. The Econo Lodge would probably cost at least a hundred bucks.

"So what's your favorite thing we've done so far?" I asked as we waited for our chicken.

"We haven't done anything yet," Star said.

"What do you mean we haven't done anything? We've done tons of things. We've driven something like-" I made up a number. "-six hundred miles. We've been to two countries if you count where we started. We've heard Oasis twice on the radio. That's something."

Star's lips shone with melted butter. "Can we call Daddy tonight?" she asked.

I sipped my pop. "Nn—wipe your mouth, you've got

butter on your mouth," I said, leaning at her with a napkin. "Mm? Call Daddy? Sure, of course we can call Daddy. Of course we can. I know his number—heh." Star wiped off her lips; I almost threw my pop into her lap just to see what would happen. "Look, here comes our food. Let's finish our dinners and then we'll get a room someplace and we'll call Daddy. You can take a nice warm soaky bath and I'll talk to him first and then you can talk to him. Sound like a plan?"

We ate our chicken in near silence, and I eavesdropped on the conversation in the booth behind us—two women talking, one of them very angry and hurt and no longer speaking to some person named Oliver.

After dinner we checked into the Econo Lodge up the street. I paid cash and signed in as "Lisa Taylor" from Albany. Our room overlooked a Tim Hortons and a BP gas station. I found their green and white and steady lights oddly reassuring.

When she saw our room, Star asked, "Mommy, can we sleep in the same bed?"

The room had two beds on either side of a nightstand. The lamp was stained and torn; it looked like someone had thrown coffee at it.

"Yeah, let's take the one by the wall—I like that one better. But we're not going to bed now, silly! You're going to have your bath then I'm going to have one too, then we're gonna watch a whole bunch of TV."

I got her started with her bath and snuck back out into the bedroom to call Josh. I had no idea what he'd say when he picked up. I'd been wrong not to at least call him earlier in the afternoon. If he wanted to yell at me for that, fine.

He answered on the first ring. "Where are you? I've been trying to reach you all day."

"I'm not sure. We're in Canada somewhere. I think we're still in Ontario. We haven't heard anyone speaking French yet," I said.

"That's craziness. That's insane."

"No, it's not."

"It's not? What is it, then?"

"It's not crazy. Look, we're in Canada and we're driving. No big deal. We're not actually driving right now. We've stopped for the night. Sarah's taking a bath."

"Is she safe?"

"Of course she's safe. What do you think? I'm her mom, she's with me."

Silence on the phone. My body ached from driving all day. I resented the energy it took to hold the receiver up to my ear.

"What did you tell your parents?" I asked finally.

"What could I tell them? I said that you and Sarah had gone to visit your brother and you'd be back in two days."

"Two days! It's going to take that long just to drive across Quebec. Canada's a big frigging country. It's like driving from Detroit to… I don't know. I don't know where things are."

I heard splashing in the other room. I'd only recently stopped giving Star her baths. She liked to paddle around and pretend the tub was a swimming pool.

"Listen," I said, "don't say anything weird to Sarah. I need her to be chill."

He agreed reluctantly. His voice sounded older, scratchy, the vocal cords dried out. I'd aged him too.

At the open door to the bathroom, I asked, "Honey? You want to talk to Daddy?"

I handed her the phone and sat on the toilet as she talked to her father. Her bath toys swam in a circle around her. She mainly spoke in one-word sentences, careful with her answers.

When she got off the phone, I walked on my knees to the bath and splashed my hands in the tub. "We've got a lot of driving tomorrow. Are you ready to be my co-pilot?" She nodded vigorously. "Good. We're a team now. We've got to work together. You can be my chief navigator."

"What's a chief navigator?" she asked, making hash out of the big word.

I pulled one of the bath toys out of the water. "It means if Mommy gets lost or doesn't know what she's doing, you have to step in and show me what I'm doing wrong. It's a big job—think you can handle it?"

She nodded, more seriously this time.

Finished with her bath, we toweled her off and tucked her into her pajamas. Star had recently graduated to big person pajamas, the kind without any feet. I installed her in front of the TV and dashed off for a quick shower. When I got out, Star was watching a program about CIA interrogation techniques. A man struggled and screamed as two others held him down and poured water over his head.

I swooped in to change the channel. "Oh, why are you watching that? That's a bad thing to watch. Let's find something a little more pleasant." The other channels weren't much better: a 9/11 documentary, a show about a couple desperately clinging to each other as floodwaters swept through their home, a computer animation tracing the path of the bullet passing through JFK's head. Finally

I settled on a rerun of *The Golden Girls* and got into bed with Star.

"This was a very famous program when I was a little girl. Most of these actresses are dead now. But I remember when this was popular and my mother liked watching it on Friday nights." On the screen Estelle Getty hobbled across the Golden Girls' famous lanai. "See her, the really old one? She's actually the same age as the other actresses on the show but she played the mom."

Star held me as the light from the BP station pierced the drapes. Cars rolled up with their radios blasting, guys and girls just a few years younger than me, looking for a good time. Scaring up some fun. The bar at T.G.I. Friday's probably drew a crowd on Thursday and Friday nights. I remember being one of those girls. You'd put on your tightest jeans and a tank top, find a stool by the Keno machines, and wait for someone to buy you a drink.

The next day Star and I drove into Quebec Province. The temperature seemed to drop ten degrees over night. I was angry with myself for not packing more of Star's sweaters. I'd loaded her up with two pairs of jeans, a half-dozen T-shirts, and a fistful of underwear. For me, I'd packed for a two-week trip. I'd even taken a nice dress, God knows why. It wasn't like we were going out to a fancy dinner.

Just west of Montreal I stopped at a clothing outlet to pick up some warmer things. The signs over the aisles were in French, and I could hear it spoken all around. Little kids, kids Star's age, speaking French! They all sounded like prodigies. *Les Vestes de Filles* led us to girls' jackets, and I grabbed a hooded parka off the discount rack.

"Mommy, can I get this one?" Star asked, holding up a fuchsia snow jacket with fake fur trim.

I caught the price tag on the sleeve. "Nope. That's too much. Let's go."

"But I *really* wanna-"

"No. No whining."

I pushed our cart up to the checkout and asked the cashier if she spoke English. She stared back as if I'd said something horribly stupid and obvious.

"We're going to Newfoundland—do you know where that is? I wonder if you can tell me how to get to St. John's in Newfoundland," I said.

After conferring with her manager in French—one word sounded like "parmesan"—the cashier said, "You have to take the... ferry? From Halifax."

A ferry sounded expensive. I asked if there was another way.

"No, because otherwise..." She drew a wide arc in the air with her fingernail. The arc meant a long trip by land that took us hundreds of miles off course.

The manager scribbled down some directions on a piece of receipt paper, and we left. A cold, stiff wind blew straight down on us in the parking lot. I ripped off the tags so Star could wear her new jacket.

"This doesn't fit me," she complained.

"The sleeves are a little long. You'll grow into it," I said, smuggling her into the car.

By the end of the day we'd reached a small town north of the Maine border. We'd had chips in the car for lunch so I splurged and took us to what looked like a nice restaurant. The sign out front was a carving of a brown fish.

"I bet this place has an *amazing* salad bar," I said as we

went in. Star was doing the thing kids do when they're tired and pretend they can't walk. I pulled her along.

The restaurant smelled of roast beef. I hadn't expected the four-piece jazz band parked near the fireplace. A handwritten sign by the hostess stand read, "This is *not* the Wagon Wheel Inn mentioned in the September 14 issue of the *Standard-Ledger*!!!"

The jazz band was just finishing up their set when we took our seats. The music was too loud for the small room, and some of the other diners looked noticeably pained, fingers in ears. An old man at the table next to ours chewed his roast chicken mournfully, jaw moving slowly, watery eyes focused on nothing.

The band stopped, leaving a wake of dazed silence. It was like an eighteen-wheeler had finally pulled away after idling outside for an hour.

"I don't get jazz music. Like, what's the point? Yeah, yeah, you can play, whatever." I touched Star's hand. "That doesn't mean you can't enjoy it. I want you to. Don't listen to me."

I hadn't had a drink in three days so I ordered a glass of wine. I hardly drank anymore. Before I met Josh, I didn't even know what a wine stopper was—like, why not just finish the bottle?—but nowadays a jumbo bottle of Glen Ellen might last a week.

The waitress brought my wine and Star's ginger ale. I asked Star if she wanted a sip.

"Just a little one. It's strong, particularly if you've never had it," I said.

She put her lips to the glass and made a face. "Don't like it?" I asked.

"It's yucky," she said.

"It's not yucky, you're just too young—which is a good

thing. I'm *glad* you don't like it. Stay away from this stuff. The longer you wait, the better. I'm sure you'll drink eventually—it's in your blood."

She looked alarmed. "What is?"

"Drinking certain alcoholic beverages. It's not *literally* in your blood, honey, that's not what I meant. I mean you're, uh…" No simple word for it. "You're genetically inclined… your granddad likes wine—my father. And my mom too." I'd lost her, so I read out loud from the menu. "They have fish 'n' chips—you like fish 'n' chips. Why don't you get the fish 'n' chips and I'll get a salad and we can share."

Our food came as the band was gearing up for their next set. The diners stirred anxiously, and the old man with the chicken actually cupped his hand and called out, "No!"

I used the loud music as a cover to order a second glass of wine. I needed a little something to take the edge off. We'd be on the ferry by this time tomorrow, which meant being that much closer to Wallis.

For their second number the band played an old-timey, jump-up-and-dance song that failed to excite the room. Pretty much all you heard were the drummer's cymbals. The music, the loudness of it, actually drained the flavor out of our food. It was like you couldn't hear and taste at the same time.

I took Star's hand. "Hey, you wanna dance?"

Her eyes widened. She'd made an art project out of her two pieces of battered perch. "I can't," she said.

"I can't either but I feel bad—they're playing and no one's dancing."

I threw down my napkin and led her to a small clearing between tables. The band took notice and aimed their instruments at us, readjusting the angle of spray. Hot alien sunshine blared from the bell of the leader's saxophone. The upright bassist heaved and attacked his strings with an almost sexual, eager-to-please intensity.

"Star, do this!" I said, approximating the Twist. Our dancing post-dated the music by a good thirty years but I didn't care. I *wanted* to look stupid. The corniness was the point.

Star wasn't dancing so much as mirroring what I did. Men and women looked over their shoulders at the two of us marching and head-banging to swing music. We were cute, sort of. We were annoying.

The song ended, and the bandleader asked people to give us a hand. Strained applause played us back to our seats. My legs were sweating.

"You're a good dancer. Maybe you'll be a dancer when you grow up. That'd be okay. Maybe you'll join some famous ballet company and perform at the Olympics. Maybe you'll even have a dance class of your own and wear paisley scarves and people will call you 'Madame.' Would you like that?" I asked. Star nibbled her food.

We finished eating, drove a mile down the road to our hotel, and stayed up for another hour watching the pine trees blow outside our window. Their skirts moved from side to side like excited girls at a birthday party.

"Aren't the trees pretty, Star? They're different from the ones back home. I don't like the trees in Michigan. I don't *dislike* them—they're okay. They're trees. But I guess I like pine trees better than the other kind. They're more spindly. And they smell good too."

Star tucked her knees under her nightgown. "Do trees breathe like people do?"

"Sure, everything breathes. It's different with trees than

with people. People breathe in oxygen and exhale carbon dioxide, and trees do the opposite. It's called co-existing. Isn't that clever? Isn't God smart?"

The room's electric baseboard heaters made a brittle ticking noise. I turned out the light.

We woke early to make the final push to the ferry landing at North Sydney. I'd read online that the ferry left just before midnight and arrived in a town called Port aux Basques at seven the next morning. After that we'd have another full day of driving across the island to reach my brother in St. John's.

The drive wasn't easy. We were the only car on the road for long stretches of time, and I had to chew gum to keep from falling asleep. The sky was overcast, the color of wet newspaper. Minutes would pass between highway exits, then whole quarter-hours. The only thing we could get on the radio was a man talking about how to build your own solar-heated house. I drove with both hands on the wheel.

"I hope we hit a gas station soon. Not literally 'hit,' not plow into one. But we're almost out of gas. I should've brought an emergency tank. I didn't think it would be so desolate out here."

Star was biting her fingernails, a habit she'd picked up from me.

"Iley," I said, "we should discuss what to do if something unexpected happens, like the car breaks down or we run out of gas. I mean… this is really the middle of nowhere."

A huge bird sailed over the road. It had a long bill and tail feathers and flew with a purpose.

"Star? You listening? I'm serious. What would we do? Let's say we ran out of gas right now. Boom, the car stops and we're stuck. What would be the first thing you'd do?"

She didn't answer. "I'd panic, to be honest. First I'd panic, then I'd cry, then I'd wait for something to magically happen and then... I don't know. I guess I'd call your father."

We didn't have to worry about it much longer: signs for a Petro-Canada popped up soon enough. The station shared a parking lot with a diner and a convenience store. I paid forty American dollars for a full tank of gas and told Star to pick out some snacks for the road. The woman behind the register looked like a female version of Jimmy Page.

"Are we in Nova Scotia yet? We're trying to reach North Sydney. Is it close?" I asked.

The woman answered in English but I couldn't understand her thick accent. She stood in a booth that was filled with cigarettes and encased in bulletproof glass.

Back on the road, Star asked why her uncle Wallis lived so far away.

"Why? Because that's where he works. Uncle Wallis has a very special job—you can't just do it anywhere. It's not like Mommy when Mommy worked at Pier 1. They have Pier 1's all over—there's probably a Pier 1 in Hong Kong and New Zealand and maybe even the middle of the Sahara Desert."

"No, there's not," she laughed. The car felt sturdier with a full tank, lower to the ground.

"Maybe not *that*, but Hong Kong and New Zealand, I bet. You can live wherever and still get a job at Pier 1. But that's because there's nothing special about it. There's nothing *wrong* with it either—you do what you gotta do—but it's not special like your uncle's job. So that's why he lives far away, because he's special."

Star put a Cracker Jack into her mouth.

We reached the ferry landing at eight, and our tickets took one of my last hundred-dollar-bills. We left the car in the loading area and walked a block for a late dinner. The town was small and the only place open was a seafood shack on the water. Seagulls strutted in the parking lot and the ground was covered with broken shells. After a quick bite we returned to the landing to wait for the cars to load. Star huddled inside her new jacket as we hung out by the docks.

"How come it smells so bad?" she asked, poking at the water with a stick.

"That's the ocean. There's salt in the water. Though I suppose this isn't technically the ocean—it's probably a bay or an inlet or something."

"Why is there salt in the water?"

"I don't know, Star—that's just the way it is. We'll ask your uncle when we get there. He'll be able to tell you everything."

By eleven o'clock the cars were loaded and we'd claimed a couple of seats in a semi-private compartment on the top deck. A small snack bar served the usual chips and hot dogs, but you could also buy little bottles of generic "white wine" and twelve-ounce plastic cups of keg beer once we'd pulled out of port. I bought a beer and brought it back to our cabin. I wanted to drink and watch the moon tremble over black water.

As I nursed my beer, I told Star, "You're going to see so many things, kid… have so many new experiences. This is just the start. It's the world, Star. *This* is the world." She was asleep. "Byron Center is not the world. Grand Rapids is not the world. They're *part* of the world, sure, just like China's part of the world and Japan and India and all those great countries. All those places to visit and get to know. And that's what I want for you because you're my daughter and I love you and I'd do anything to offer you the best life possible, and it's just *not* possible suffocating in that house seven days a week... and maybe once a year we drive north to Traverse City and go to the sand dunes. That's all great, but there's more. There's *this*."

It was still dark out when the ferry pulled into Port aux Basques. I woke Star and bustled her downstairs to the car deck. The air was bitter cold, and my thin windbreaker only seemed to make it worse. Along with fifty or so cars, we filed down a ramp and onto dry land where I got directions from the visitors center. The town was sturdy and not quite awake. All the buildings looked like sheds.

"It reminds me of England, not that I've been there. England or Wales. *The English countryside*," I said in my fake-Cockney accent. The cars ahead and behind us on the winding town road were all from the ferry. We were like members of a touring group who couldn't get away from each other.

We stopped for breakfast at a place called Corner Brook where I had two enormous sunny-side up eggs—the yolks were like yellow drink coasters—and a salty slab of bacon. Star only wanted Frosted Flakes. The diner's countertops were the color of mint-chocolate-chip ice cream, and ours was the only car in the lot that wasn't a truck. One truck looked particularly old and had wood slats in the bed for hauling livestock.

"Lots of farmers around here, I'll bet. That's a hard job—important too. I can't think of too many jobs more important than that. Firemen, policemen... doctors. I guess every job is important."

Star poked at her cereal. "Mommy? What color is Daddy's hair?"

"What do you mean? You know what color—it's brown. Or maybe you mean what kind of brown. Is that what you mean? I would say that it's very dark, dark brown, almost black."

"What about Grandpa Terry?"

"Grandpa Terry's hair is mostly gray. You know the answers to these questions, Star. Grandma Pam's hair is reddish-orange, and she dyes it."

Star put down her spoon. I reached across the table, took the salt, and moved it to the other side of the pepper shaker. The empty napkin dispenser had a spot of rust on it.

I pushed the speed limit all morning and afternoon, wanting to make good time on the last stretch. This part of Canada was hilly and most of the trees had already lost their leaves. We crossed small ponds and ice-bright rivers that fed the larger body of water sometimes visible to our left. Every twenty minutes or so we'd pass another small town consisting mostly of trailers and tin sheds, the kind of temporary shelter you'd sometimes see near construction sites. Star found the rugged landscape exciting. She sat on the edge of her seat, bouncing and straining at her safety belt as she pressed her hand against the window.

"Mommy, I saw a bear!" she cried.

I nearly swerved the car. "You did? Shit—I mean shoot, wow, that's crazy. Bears are afraid of people, though. Maybe it wasn't a bear."

"It *was*. It was big and had black fur," she insisted.

"That could be any number of things. Maybe it was just a really big duck."

She stared out the window, still dreaming of bears. I marveled at her imagination. Star had a stuffed animal back home that she called Mr. Stomachache. A walrus. Mr. Stomachache was allergic to everything. He also went to counseling for anger management issues. His wife was a bison.

By early evening we began to see signs for St. John's. I hoped Wallis had a bath at his place—Star and I both needed one.

"This looks like a decent-sized town," I said as the city came into view. We hadn't seen anything larger than a hamlet in nearly two days. "It looks like there's things to do. It's not some hick-y little Podunk hole-in-the-wall... is what I mean. There's *stuff* here."

I nearly got into three accidents gawking at the sights as we pulled into town. St. John's had a bustling waterfront with big red and black freighters parked at the docks and modern glass office buildings standing shoulder-to-shoulder with restaurants, shops, and one quaint little pub after another. Despite the cold, window-shoppers crowded the streets, flowing in and out of the many boutiques and used record stores. One place sold handmade soaps, another gourmet cookware. A banner over the main street advertised a pub-crawl that night.

"Mommy, why are you crying?" Star asked.

I wiped my eyes. "Oh, I'm just so happy we're finally here... and that you're getting a chance to experience all this. See? This is what happens when you make an effort to see the world. Look at that—look!" I pointed out a man in jeans and a long flannel shirt walking past our car. "That guy has a tattoo on his face. On his *face*, Star. Can you imagine what'd happen to him back home? They'd run him out of town. They'd stuff him into a van and drive him up north and *shoot* him and leave him in a ditch. But here…?" I watched in my rear view mirror as the man swung into a bar. "Here he's embraced. He's *welcomed.* This is the difference between the U.S. and Canada."

I dearly wanted to join the pub-crawl but knew we had more important things to do. Once out of the congested downtown, I pulled into a BP station and dug out the package with Wallis' return address on it. The cashier inside the station looked impressed by the address and pointed us up the road.

"Great town you've got here," I said. Even from a few blocks away, we could still hear sounds from the party on the water. The cashier looked dubious, and I said, "No. Don't spoil it for me. Don't tell me you've got the highest number of stabbings per capita or something. Let me have my dream."

Star and I got back in the car and began a long climb through a hilly and dark part of town. The homes were spread out; some were modest, little more than ordinary ranch houses set back in the woods, while others were great stone fortresses that looked like they'd been put there two hundred years ago. Then the houses stopped and we continued along a stretch of woods that broke here and there to reveal the harbor below.

Pulling over, I flicked on the cabin light and consulted the address. Wallis' handwriting wasn't the best; the '9' easily could've been a '7.' The road didn't look promising, only trees and a dark hovering mist.

We inched ahead, my right foot on the gas pedal and my left on the brake. Finally Star spotted a light. A driveway picked up where the road dead-ended, and I followed its curving path some hundred yards to a clearing where an imposing glass house stood. Two houses, really—a larger and a smaller connected by an open walkway that straddled a pond and a sedate waterfall.

I killed the headlights and drove the last few feet to a gravel lot in front of the house. The air thrummed: I heard the splash of the falls, nighttime insects singing to each other in the trees, the distant kettledrum roar of the open sea.

"We're here," I said.

Star gaped at the house. She'd never seen anything like it before, and neither had I. It was gigantic, ten times the size of Terry and Pam's ranch back in Michigan. One vast room on the first floor had a red leather couch and a fire going in the stone fireplace. Steel, pancake-flat light fixtures hung at different heights from the tall ceiling. In another room a woman reclined in bed and read a magazine.

We quietly got out of the car and tiptoed across the gravel, taking the slate path around the pond and falls.

"I feel weird ringing the bell," I whispered.

Star jogged ahead, and a fanfare of security lights bore down on us. The lights bleached the color out of her jacket. We froze, and for the first time I noticed a number of people sitting and standing around the red leather couch. They saw us too: an older man, tall, with a white beard and black mustache, wearing a black turtleneck and a glinting medallion; a middle-aged woman in a shiny green housecoat; a little girl, maybe seven, reading a book on the couch; two men, both bearded and muscular, in black tank tops; and one other person—my brother. He sat on the couch with the little girl's feet in his lap, his wheelchair parked nearby, his mouth formed in an 'o' of surprise.

The older man and the woman in the housecoat

conferred as the two men in tank tops drew up next to them. Then Wallis spoke and the rest stopped talking. They all looked now. I raised my hand and said, "Hi."

CHAPTER ELEVEN

A half-hour later, Star was watching TV in the depths of the Snow complex as I listened to Dr. Clement Snow explain the history of the Beothuk, the natives who'd settled on the island of Newfoundland before the Europeans arrived in the Fifteenth Century.

"They weren't a terribly social people. They lived in small villages, rarely more than a few dozen inhabitants. Not much is known about the language—the tribe's been extinct for nearly two hundred years. Avoided the Europeans, even avoided most other tribes, the Mi'kmaq and Inuit. It's why they died out, really. No one got along with them. Without access to trade, they lacked the proper resources for survival. Their self-sufficiency was misguided, if ahead of its time."

Dr. Snow had been lecturing without pause since I'd arrived. I'd been given wine and a plate of food as I sat inside the great room at a long table carved from a single piece of polished wood. With us were Dr. Snow's wife, Charity (the woman in the green housecoat), and Wallis, who'd put on weight since I'd last seen him. His hair was graying at the temples.

Dr. Snow scrutinized me. His eyebrows were as black as his mustache, a stark contrast to the white of his beard.

But what I hadn't noticed before, and what I couldn't help noticing now, was that his eyes and skin were a ghostly shade of blue. Not bright blue, not like the Cookie Monster or the guys in Blue Man Group, but a dull, silvery blue that made him look like a strange, mutant robot, burnished metal through and through. The whites of his eyes were blue, and his lips were so blue they were almost purple. No wonder he wore a beard.

His expression lightened. "Roseanne—you don't like me very much, do you?"

I set down my wine. "What makes you say that?" I asked.

"Just a sense I have. But that's all right, I understand. You're being protective of your brother. I had a brother once, Grayson. He died in the nineteen-eighties of a blood cancer. We weren't close. I envy closeness between siblings. Grayson lived in Winnipeg and ran a charity providing food to local homeless shelters. Allan King made a short film about him. It's a shame he died so young."

"I didn't know about the film," Wallis said.

"Ah, yes, a documentary. Never released. I thought I told you about it, Crim."

"You didn't."

Snow's eyelids fluttered in apology: *blue blue blue.*

"Why do you call my brother 'Crim'? His name's Wallis," I said.

"Crim and I are colleagues. In academia, colleagues often refer to each other by their last names. It's a sign of respect. I call my good friend at Memorial University 'Dr. Robichaud' when we're working together. On the golf course I call him Phil."

"Dr. Snow calls me Cherry at home but 'Doctor' when I'm at work," said Charity, who was a dentist in town.

"You're calling him 'Doctor' now," I pointed out, and she laughed softly. I felt sorry for her. Every night she slept next to a blue monster.

"And what would you like me to call *you*, dear?" asked Dr. Snow.

"Just Roseanne. I don't have any titles or credentials. I'm Wallis' sister, that's all," I said.

"And a mother," he said.

I conceded this. "Yeah, obviously."

Wallis shook his head once.

"Steffi and your daughter seem to get along. But what can you tell from the first five minutes," said Charity. Her daughter, Steffi, was the girl I'd seen reading a book in the window. She and Star had gone off to watch a rerun of *Planet Earth* on the Discovery Channel.

"That's a long drive to make with such a young girl. I came east from Toronto with Steffi when she was just three. Took us five days," Charity continued.

"Fleeing the proverbial bad marriage," Dr. Snow said.

She patted his blue hand. "Oh, *fleeing's* too harsh. Relocating. I drove and she napped. Lunch and dinner in the car. My sister wired us money once we got to Halifax."

The security lights blinked on again. The two men in tank tops were searching for something out by the pond.

"Don't mind Neil and Sander. We've had some unpleasant encounters with the CRA—they're like your IRS, only less charming. They don't seem to mind the time of day either. That's who we thought you were at first," said Snow.

The men went as far as the end of the lot and came back. "Are they your bodyguards?" I asked.

"Oh, no. Neil's actually my personal chef. Sander does maintenance around the house. He's ex-military. I'm lucky to have them both."

I threw back the rest of my wine. A burp stalled in my chest.

"What'd you do, cheat on your taxes or something?" I asked as Snow refilled my glass.

Wallis spoke up. "Hey, sis-"

Snow laughed. "No, it's quite all right. You see, Roseanne... my family has done quite well for itself over the years. My father, Emmanuelle's grandfather, invested in hydroelectricity at a time when the rest of the industry was turning to nuclear power. I don't need to tell you how well that decision paid off. Still, it's hard to make any money in this country. I don't mind paying my share, of course. Unfortunately the CRA and I have different opinions about what's fair."

Before I could ask any other questions, Charity took my plate to the kitchen and Snow went off to confer with his men. Wallis and I caught a moment alone together.

"Okay, what's the deal with the blue?" I asked. No response. "The *blue*, Wallis—the man's skin is blue. Am I right or am I wrong? Am I suddenly hallucinating? Maybe I am. Maybe I'm just tired. Maybe I've been driving so long that my eyes are no longer functioning properly, and I'm seeing things. Is that possible? I don't think it is. I don't think that's the explanation for why I'm sitting here... and I'm looking... and dude is *blueberry*-fuckin'-blue."

"All right, calm down. I didn't think it was a big deal so I didn't say anything. It's called argyria. I hardly even notice it anymore. He's been like that the whole time I've known him. Don't bring it up—he doesn't like to talk about it," Wallis said.

"So I'm just supposed to ignore it. That's challenging. That's honestly going to be very hard. It's not contagious, is it? I shook his hand when we got here. Should I wash my hands?"

"It's not contagious, sis. It's actually a pretty common skin disorder. People sometimes get it from drinking this stuff called colloidal silver. It's an alternative medicine. Some people think it protects against cancer and HIV and a whole bunch of other things."

"And does it work?" I asked.

"Not really. It makes your skin blue, though."

"It sounds like you've met my father," said a voice behind me, and I turned. In the doorway stood a woman with platinum-blonde hair down to her waist and a pair of reading glasses hanging around her neck. Even in her stocking feet she looked six feet tall.

"Mandy, you remember my sister, Roseanne?" Wallis said.

Mandy leaned against the doorframe. We hadn't seen each other in ten years; my whole experience of her was based on what little I knew from Wallis. She was prettier than I'd remembered—her eyelashes were long and thick like a deer's, eyebrows tweezed, the right and left sides of her face perfectly symmetrical.

"Roseanne... wow. Look at you—the little sister. Married now? And with a crew of little ones. Three of them?" she asked.

"Four," I said.

She walked over and kissed me on the cheek.

"Welcome to the Snow Globe—that's what we call this

place. Clever, no? Otherwise known as 'Snow East.' We like to have fun with our surname."

"The puns…" Wallis groaned.

"Family fights are called snow storms. Parties are snowballs. You get the idea." She poured herself a glass of wine and joined us at the table.

"How do you feel?" Wallis asked.

"Better. I just needed some time to decompress. I don't know if Wallis told you, Roseanne, but I've been doing ER rotations at St. Clare's Mercy. I'm almost never home. I'm lucky if I get to sleep in my own bed one night a week. Cheers," she said, and we clinked glasses. "Anyway, don't let my dad creep you out. I actually like having a blue father. It's like being in a fairy tale. *My dad, king of the Blue People.* Though he's gotten more gray lately—gray isn't as much fun as blue. I liked him better when he had that really intense, primary color glow. Now he just looks sick. It's not remarkable anymore."

"Oh, *I* think it's remarkable," Wallis said.

"To an outsider, maybe. And God knows we don't meet a lot of those."

A man with snow in his beard came into the room. I'd never seen so many beards together in one place. Even the gas station attendant at the bottom of the hill had a beard. What did it mean?

"Foul conditions. There will be fog in the morning. We should all take care," he said. He spoke with a clipped rhythm, his accent strange. I would've believed anything, French, German, English.

"Sander, come have a drink and warm up," Mandy said.

The man stepped out of his shoes, conscientious about not leaving footprints on the hardwood floor. I watched his big feet in their dazzling white socks. I'm the sort of woman who believes you can tell a lot about a man by his feet. For this person I imagined callused soles and trim toenails.

"Think it'll snow much?" Mandy asked as Sander poured a shot of whiskey from the liquor cabinet.

"It's possible. These are the remnants of a system from the south. Unpredictable. Maybe as much as a hundred millimeters. I shouldn't expect more," he said.

"How much is that?" I asked.

"Four inches," he said without looking past his glass. He pounded back the shot, and his face contorted in pain. "Oh, my God. That's no good. That gives me no pleasure."

"Sander isn't much of a drinker," Mandy said.

"Alcohol is medicine. I drank Crown Royal when I served in the CF. Not to excess—two shots a day was the custom."

"Good man. Keeps the liver honest," Mandy said.

"CF… is that, like, the military?" I asked.

"Strictly speaking, I served in the Maritime division. You call it 'Navy.' Based in Halifax. The best five years of my life," Sander said.

He poured a second shot and sat with us at the table. I wondered how an ex-military man felt working for a known adulterer and tax evader like Snow.

Still hung-up on his beard, I asked, "Have you always had a beard? I mean, not 'always,' obviously… I know you weren't born with it."

"This beard? This beard is four years old. I have gone beardless for most of my adult life. I grew my first beard when I was eighteen and worked for a logging company. It did not last the summer. Beards were frowned upon in the service. One person had a beard. His name was Marshall. We shared a cabin with two other men." He sipped his drink. "This man, this Marshall, was a racist. He said things that would make me uncomfortable. He would not sit at a table next to anyone whom he suspected of being Cambodian."

"The *beard*, Phelps. She's asking about the beard," said Mandy.

"It's a good beard. I like it. It looks permanent. I don't feel like you're going to shave it off tomorrow morning," I said.

"It's not something I spend time thinking about. I had a job stacking shipping containers at the Port of Montreal. Beards were part of the culture. A select few men wore mustaches. Rarely would you see someone who was clean-shaven. At that time I had long hair and a beard and I wore an orange knit cap and rode my bicycle to work each morning, and at night I would collapse from fatigue," he said.

Star appeared, her cheeks flushed with excitement. "Mommy, come look at the TV! They're showing fishes getting killed!" She'd discarded her shoes, and her feet were pink and bare.

Wallis stayed behind as we followed her down a long, white corridor to the room where the two girls were watching *Planet Earth* on a giant plasma-screen TV. Star cheered, "They had a whale and a shark and then two whales and then one whale got killed by the other!"

The other girl didn't acknowledge us as she lay on the floor, her chin in her hands. "This show's always about animals getting killed and one animal fighting another and baby bears dying," she complained.

"It is an honest depiction of the natural world," said Sander.

On the screen a long-beaked bird, maybe a heron,

snatched up a small rodent and killed it by flinging it against the hard earth. The small rodent's broken neck dangled in world-ending slow motion.

"An egret," said Sander.

For several minutes we stood transfixed by the carnage on TV. Birds pecked at each other, a snake attacked an egg, rams clashed headfirst, an old elephant simply lay down and died. The girls watched with interest but not compassion. Steffi wondered out loud why they never showed the animals going to the bathroom.

"Maybe it's because the animals can't poo and pee when people are around," she said.

"Highly unlikely," said Sander.

"Maybe it's because it's disgusting and who wants to see it," I said.

We fell silent as a green and gray lizard with nubbed skin ventured onto a rock, its head darting around like a chicken's.

"Guess who's gonna get it," said Mandy.

Sure enough, the creature took another step when another lizard, greener and more prehistoric-looking than the first, sprang out and seized its throat in its jaws. They struggled as a female voiceover said neutral things about the mating rituals of the South American green iguana. Finally the second lizard brought its jaws together and the first's throat exploded in a burst of black, oily globules.

"Ew," said Steffi.

"Did he die?" asked Star.

"Yeah, I think he died," I said. It struck me as funny for some reason. I couldn't get enough of it—it was like eating peanuts. I wanted to watch animals killing each other all night.

The lizard's blood continued to radiate in slow motion as its body retracted into a coil. "Someone in the world masturbates to this," Mandy said.

Sander laughed grimly, and Steffi asked, "What's masturbate?"

Fortunately Charity and Dr. Snow came by to save us from answering. The other bearded man—Neil, Dr. Snow's chef—was with them. He had slow-blinking eyes and a flat-footed, solid stance. His beard implied some allegiance with Sander.

"Did you know that a primate indigenous to the Philippines will actually commit suicide when held in captivity? It will bang its head against the bars of its cage until its skull caves in. Of course, 'suicide' suggests a sophisticated awareness of cause-and-effect, so perhaps it's not the best word," said Snow.

"I *did* know that, actually. It was on my SAT," I said. Only Neil laughed.

"The natural world is a violent place. Leopards and certain species of whale kill for amusement. Eagles will kill their brothers and sisters in the nest. The crowding behavior of trees growing in the Amazon canopy can only be described as homicidal."

"This is a cheerful conversation," said Mandy.

I looked at my watch; it was too late to call Josh, not that I really wanted to. "Star, sweetie? Time to tuck in."

She peeled herself away from the TV. "Mommy? Steffi says we can go hiking tomorrow."

"Can we? I told her about Stiles Cove," Steffi asked her mother.

"Not if the weather stays like this. It might be a better day for staying indoors," said Charity.

The girls looked disappointed, so Neil said, "How about I make you two a special breakfast in the morning?"

"Andouille and spinach frittata?" asked Steffi. Star had no idea what that was, but she nodded eagerly. I was happy and relieved to see her having a good time. We were on vacation, that's all. Visiting friends and family.

Charity showed us to a guest room on the first floor. The floral sheets were clean and neat, and the room smelled of air freshener. Like the rest of the house, one wall was all glass, and we could hear the waterfall running outside.

"Thanks for letting us spend the night, Mrs. Snow. Is it Mrs. *Snow* or...?"

"Please, call me Charity. My professional name is Blaise. That was my first husband's name. I suppose I should've changed it, but... all those business cards."

I laughed like an idiot. I'd never had the need for business cards. Even my name-tag at Pier 1 just said "Rosie."

"Does the pond ever freeze?" I asked as she laid fresh towels at the foot of the bed. Star was putting on her PJs in the bathroom.

"In December, yes. The whole island freezes. We made it down to minus-twelve last year. Not what you're used to, I suppose."

"What do you mean? It gets cold in Michigan."

She gave the room a quick once-over. She seemed reluctant to leave me alone with her stuff.

"Let me know if the bed's uncomfortable. It's flame retardant. It used to be Steffi's but Steffi's allergic to polyurethane," she said.

I smiled gratefully and said good night. I couldn't

imagine Charity being a dentist, and then I could. I wondered what her fingers would feel like in my mouth.

After Star was settled in our bed—we were sharing again—I crept off and found Wallis sitting in his own room down the hall. He looked mildly startled to see me.

"You don't have to go to bed so early," he said.

"Are you kidding? I'm exhausted." The room was equipped with all the railings and raising-and-lowering devices he'd had back home. Dr. Snow had gone to some length to accommodate him. "Who helps you at night?"

"Mandy, usually, when she's not at work. I'll buzz her down in a bit."

"No. I'll do it," I said, idly fiddling with the bed's controls. The bed featured wooden crib rails and an adjustable knee break, and the console even had a button to call for help, just like in a hospital.

He steered his chair over to the window, which had its own view of the pond. Gnarled and spindly dwarf pines grew on the rocks. A quick burst of sleet slapped against the window, slashing crossways. Then nothing.

"I'm surprised to see you here," he said, stating the obvious.

"Are you mad?"

"No, just a little concerned. I feel like you're not telling me something."

I stopped tinkering with the control console and left it in the sheets. "Not really. It's been a hard year. The twins. I think I left Josh."

"You think."

"No, I *did*—I definitely did. But there's 'leave' and there's 'leave-leave.'"

"What's leave-leave?"

"I don't know. More than one 'leave?' Seriously, Wallis,

that's not why I'm here. I can handle my own situation."
He looked unconvinced. "Really, you don't think so?"

"I didn't say anything."

"You made a face."

He tensed. "I did?"

"Yes. You're still making it."

His lips parted slightly. "There. Now I'm not."

"Too late. Damage already done."

We laughed. It felt good talking to him again.

"Why are you here, then?" he asked.

"Because I'm worried about you. Maybe I just don't understand the business—research and papers and shit. But it seems strange to me that you could do all this hard work for Dr. Snow and only get one little mention at the back of the guy's book."

"Two mentions, actually. I'm in the chapter about Nuuk—that's the capital of Greenland. We stayed in Nuussuaq with a language professor from the university. Dr. Snow was busy so I interviewed the CEO of Grønlandsbanken. He said some interesting things a-"

"Wallis, I absolutely do not care. You worked *hard* on that project. It should say on the cover, 'Written by Dr. Snow and Dr. Wallis Crim,'" I said, spacing out the words with my hands.

"I'm not a doctor."

"Well, then Mr. Wallis Crim. I can't believe you're not more angry about this. I would've been *ripshit*, dude! You're wasting your life up here. You should be writing your *own* books, getting credit for shit. Think about Mom and Dad. They used to brag about you all the time. Now they don't even know what to say when people ask what you do... and they sure as fuck don't have anything good to say about me."

He unparked his chair and drifted back from the window. "Poor Rosie."

"Poor Rosie? What do you mean, 'Poor Rosie'? This isn't about me. I'm just *saying*... because I'm your sister. People take advantage of you, Wallis. You don't see that? Maybe you don't. Maybe you're that naive."

"I *am* naive. Hey-" He leaned forward. Traditionally this signaled a change of subject. "Know what I'd like right now? If I could have anything in the world? I would like a great big glass... of pink lemonade. And a Nilla wafer."

"You're being a pill. You know what? Even worse—you're being a dick."

"It doesn't have to be pink lemonade. Regular lemonade is fine too."

I gave up. "I've got to get back to Star. Let's talk in the morning."

He grinned and clacked his teeth like a crazy person. "Creepy," I said affectionately.

Wallis' mechanized bed made transferring him from the chair as easy as sliding a warm cookie from a pan to the plate. I got him situated with his pillows and extra blankets and kissed his cheek.

"You look the same," he said.

"I do? I don't look a thousand years older?"

"No. You look your age, which is a good thing when you're-"

"Twenty-six."

"Right. Do you still smoke?"

"Dude, I quit smoking years ago. What kind of mother do you think I am?"

He didn't answer. Thank God for that.

CHAPTER TWELVE

The next morning I woke to find another five messages from Josh on my cell phone. Calling back seemed risky under the circumstances. I'd once seen a movie about drug dealers where the drug dealers used disposable cell phones so their calls couldn't be traced. Maybe I'd get one of those. It sounded like the kind of thing you could buy at a drug store, or a Radio Shack.

Throwing on some clothes, I did my best to make the bed, then went off to look for the girls. The house had two floors but every room seemed to occupy its own mini-level. The ramps between rooms either pre-dated Wallis or didn't. The interior walls were all white, and not the sedate eggshell white you'd find in most homes but a bright white that stabbed the eye. Dr. Snow collected paintings, modern abstracts, many of them quite valuable according to Mandy; paintings with colors and textures as their subjects: turquoise, translucent, the paint either thickly applied like cake frosting or undetectably smooth like the surface of a photo.

Eventually I found Steffi and Star eating breakfast in the kitchen. Star wasn't quite sure what to do with her frittata and hadn't made much progress, though Steffi looked ready for another. "Where's everyone?" I asked.

"Mandy and Mom are at work and Sander drove Dr. Snow and your brother to meet with some people," Steffi said.

Neil called over from the stove, "Ma'am, tell me your name again-"

"Oh, it's uh…" Neil: clean, domestic, a white apron tied around his waist. "It's Roseanne."

"Can I make you something to eat?"

He looked die-cast with his T-shirt-stretching physique and clutched spatula. "Just coffee's fine," I said.

He smiled. "Are you sure? It's my job."

I changed my mind and ordered the frittata. As he made my breakfast, I kept an eye on the girls. Steffi ate like a nervous forty-year-old, quickly cutting her food into small bites with both knife and fork. I thought, now here's a girl who's grown up without her natural father and she's done all right. At least she seemed normal enough. She wasn't rude or anti-social.

"Why aren't you in school today?" I asked.

"It's Saturday. School's closed on Saturday. What about you, why aren't you in school?" she asked Star.

I'd completely lost track of days; I'd thought it was Wednesday. "She's too young for school. Star still goes to kindergarten," I said.

"Kindergarten's school. I'm in second grade."

I smiled thinly. "No, school starts in first grade. Kindergarten's more like pre-school."

"No, it's not. In kindergarten we wrote poems and learned about solar energy."

"I'm sure you did, but technically kindergarten isn't an 'official' part of school. You only go half-days and it's not even in the same building." I turned to Star. "How's your breakfast? Maybe the nice man has some hot sauce and you can put hot sauce on it."

Star left her fork in the mush of her food. "Can we call Daddy this morning?"

I lied, "Of course we can. In fact, I just called Daddy but he was sleeping. You can talk to Daddy and Vance and Grandma Pam. It'll be a big party." *Yeehaw*, I thought.

Neil set down my coffee and a tray of cream and sugars. I wanted to kiss his hand. "Oh, thank God. That coffee smells wonderful. What kind is it? I've been chugging Dunkin Donuts all week."

"It's Jamaican Blue Mountain. It's very expensive," he said.

"Smells it. Is it better black or with cream and sugar?"

"It's wonderful either way," he said, and we both laughed. Neil's hair and beard were two shades lighter than Sander's. They could've been brothers. Sander was dark and haunted while Neil was fair and cheerful. I imagined them boxing in the back yard after a hard day.

"How long have you been Dr. Snow's cook?" I asked.

"Not long. I don't really think of myself as a cook. I used to tend bar in L.A. but the work dried up," he said, taking down a plate from the cupboard.

"That's too bad," I said.

"Helps to have a second skill." Cutting a piece of frittata with his spatula, he garnished it with a sprig and presented it to me.

I smiled over the plate, letting the smell waft up. "Heavenly. Do you have any classical music? I feel like I should be listening to classical music," I said.

He pulled an iPod out of a drawer. "Vivaldi?"

"Anything. Is he like Mozart?" Neil frowned. "Guess

not. All I know is Mozart and Beethoven and one or two others."

"Mom…" Star groaned—I was embarrassing her.

"It's a *little* like Mozart," Neil conceded, starting the music. A familiar, trilling melody filled the room.

"Oh, I know this one! This was in that movie… with Nicholas Cage. Not Nicholas Cage—John Travolta. Not John Travolta…"

"I'm sure it's been in a lot of movies," he said, edging down the volume. "Eat while it's hot."

I took up my fork, and Steffi chirped, "Neil's a better cook than our last one. Our last cook couldn't bake."

Neil clucked in mock-horror. "Oh, dear, what on earth did you do?" To me, he said, "Stephanie's a *wee* bit spoiled."

"Am not. 'Spoiled' means you expect things because you think you're better than other people. I don't think I'm better than other people, and I don't ask for things unless I *really* really need them."

"Well… thank you for clarifying that," he chuckled. "How's the food?"

I had a bite and dropped my fork onto my plate. "Shit! I mean… wow, that's good—better than good. That's, like, *five star good*. I would pay a lot of money for that in a restaurant."

"Yes, you would," he said, pulling off his apron.

I tried not to gobble but couldn't help it, I was so hungry. At home we typically had cereal for breakfast—Special K for me and Cap'n Crunch for Josh and the kids. I was a failure as a cook and Pam wasn't much better. Our food was plain and safe: boiled vegetables, heavy starches, steaks well done.

"Where did you learn to cook like this?" I asked as Neil

poured himself a cup of coffee and sat at the kitchen counter.

"From my dad, mostly. He cooked as a hobby. Entered the Pillsbury Bake-Off every year—just him and a bunch of housewives from Quebec City."

"Your mom didn't cook?"

"You mean 'Maggie Microwave'? No... Mom wasn't much of a homemaker. She worked long hours in a textile factory and my brother and I ate alone most nights. My brother, Henri, basically lived on hot dogs and-"

"That's your brother's name, Henri?"

"*Ahn-ri.*"

"*Ahn-ri.* Very nice. So how come he's got a French name and you don't?"

The girls slid down from their chairs and left to play in another room. I yelled after Star—"Sarah! Finish your food!"—but she ignored me.

Neil picked up their plates. "I've never really thought about it. Henri was my father's name, and I guess my mom just liked the name Neil."

"That's sweet—here, you don't have to clean up after my daughter."

He scraped Star's plate into the trash. "Sit. I'm working, you're eating."

I laughed—*oh, Neil.* "I wish I could cook. I'd love to be able to make something more complicated than spaghetti. My husband... well, my *ex*-husband, soon-to-be—gave me a wok for my birthday. Don't know what he was thinking. I never used it."

Neil listened with professional courtesy. I probably didn't interest him. His life seemed so much bigger than mine; maybe it had something to do with his parents being French, or French-*Canadian.* I assumed they were dead, given his references to them in the past tense. I didn't like to think about people losing their parents. My mom and dad were sixty-three and fifty-seven and I still thought of them as having another forty years.

Wallis and Dr. Snow returned around noon; their animated talk reached me in the guest bedroom where I'd gone to stay out of Neil's way. In addition to doing the cooking, Neil cleaned and ran errands. It was some weird kind of family.

I slipped on my shoes, patted some water on my face, and wandered down two ramps and around three corners to the living room where Snow and Wallis were taking off their coats. I slowed at the edge of the room.

"I don't think these public auctions are the way to go. Attracts too much attention. We don't want people to know who we are," Wallis said.

"If anyone asks, we're in salvage and recycling. Let's not waste a lot of time negotiating a private transaction. You're still young but I'm not. I want to pay cash and be done with it," said Snow.

They saw me, and I froze. "I'm sorry, I'm just looking for Star. I think she's watching TV with Steffi."

"You're not interrupting," said Snow, though his tone didn't convince. "If you want something to do, I'm sure Sander would be happy to drive the girls into town. Steffi likes the Geo Centre."

"Oh, that's not necessary, I've got a car. We'll get out of your hair. Is there a mall around here? I need to buy some things—toiletries. Travel toiletries. Little shampoos and mouthwashes. I should've thought of it before we left."

"Sander won't mind. I'll tell him."

He went to find Sander, and I asked Wallis, "What were you guys talking about? Sounds pretty shady. '*We don't want people to know who we are.'* And where were you all morning?"

"Come on, sis, too many questions." He stopped at the coffee table and pretended to read a copy of *Architectural Digest*.

"I'm not trying to be nosy or anything... but you said 'We don't want people to know who we are' and *he* said he wanted to pay cash for it, whatever *it* is."

"*It* is a piece of property that Dr. Snow is considering buying, and he doesn't want to attract attention because he doesn't want competition. Anything else?"

"No. I'm just being a concerned sister. So that's where you were, checking out this house?"

"It's not a house. It's nothing, sis. Work-related."

I knew I wouldn't get any more out of him, so I backed off.

Sander came around with a silver Beemer and drove Steffi, Star, and me to a mall on a dismal stretch of commercial road near the airport. Sleet and gray snow stood in sloppy piles. I rode in the back with the girls on either side of me. Steffi held her thinsulated gloves in her lap while Star pointed at all the interesting new things out the window.

"Mommy, what's that?"

"It's a Honda dealership."

And later:

"What's that?"

"Come on, Star, you know what that is. It's a KFC. See? Colonel Sanders? The old guy with the funny tie?"

"I served in the Forces with a young man whose father was friends with a distant relation to this Colonel Sanders. He was a terse man, apparently—Colonel Harland Sanders. Plagued by phobias, his last name similar to my own. News of mudslides delighted him," Sander commented. It was the only thing he'd said the whole trip.

We pulled up to the mall entrance and Sander held open the car door. "I'll be back in one hour," he said.

"You're not shopping with us? Sander, come shopping with us," Steffi ordered.

"I'll buy lunch," I said. I wouldn't have minded some adult company.

Sander agreed reluctantly, and we waited curbside as he drove back out to the edge of civilization and parked the car. While he was gone we watched with amusement as a boy, maybe fifteen, played air-drums to the music being piped out over the mall's sound system.

"I don't like country music. I don't like people who like country music," Steffi complained.

"This isn't country music. This is Carly Simon. My mom used to listen to Carly Simon," I said.

"I think all the country music albums in the world should be burned and melted down and put in a box and dropped to the bottom of the ocean, and then the country music radio stations should be torn down and turned into parks for kids to play in."

Sander returned, jogging slowly and out of breath. "A man nearly hit me with his Dakota truck. Words were exchanged."

"Cool! Did you swear?" Steffi begged, but Sander remained silent. "What swear word did you say?"

"This is not a good topic. Let's move on," he said, ushering us indoors.

The girls ran ahead as we drifted into the mall's atrium. The black and white floor tiles were polished to a liquid veneer, and my eyes caught someone losing grip on their milk shake and jumping out of the way. The shake splattered, leaving a spreading puddle. The spiller made a sound like, "Hanh."

"I was in the dress section at Macy's when two women tripped at the same time. They weren't shopping together—one was browsing the markdowns and the other was digging through her purse, and they both went down: boom, boom. Or more like, 'b-boom!' I thought there'd been an earthquake. It's so scary when people trip. I tripped on the escalator at Kohls. Someone I know tripped coming out of an Arthur Treacher's and broke her thumb," I said.

"We should keep an eye on the children," Sander reminded me.

Past a Foot Locker, then an American Eagle and a Baby Gap, we let the kids run around in Lawtons Drugs while I picked up some travel shampoos. No disposable cell phones, unfortunately. Sander needed some shoelaces, and I told him to add them to my stuff.

"I can't let you buy these shoelaces," he said. It was like I'd offered to give him one of my kidneys.

"What are they—forty-five cents? Get two. What else do you want, some gum? A magazine? How about one of these hibachis?"

We finished our shopping and had lunch at a brewpub whose décor was all LP jackets tacked across the walls. We sat in a booth overlooked by copies of *Let's Dance, In Through the Out Door*, and *Diver Down*.

"All before my time," I said, peering up at the record jackets. I vaguely recognized Neil Diamond's swarthy face from my mother's CD collection. "How old do you think I am? Don't you hate it when women ask that question? Do I look twenty-six? Because that's what I am."

"Mommy, look what I can do with my straw!" Star squealed. A waitress ran by with some bread.

"You look like a young woman," Sander said diplomatically. I thanked him.

"Quick: name every David Bowie album not including live albums and compilations, in-reverse-order-go!" I said.

Star poked me with her straw. We watched her bend the straw into a triangle, securing the ends together by creasing one end and inserting it into the other. "Is that the trick?" I asked.

"I can make a ten-speed disappear," Steffi said, and we waited. "Not *now*."

Our menus were hard and huge, tri-folded, like those screens people put in their windshields to keep their cars from getting hot. "Are you going to order a beer?" I asked Sander from behind my menu.

"Not while I'm working," he said.

"You're not working. You're having lunch." I slammed down my menu and it knocked into Steffi's water, spilling it on her. She screamed like Roger Daltrey.

"Oh, honey, I'm sorry," I said, throwing some napkins at her. "The table's too crowded, that's the problem. How bad did I get you? We'll ask for some more napkins." I waved down the waitress, who brought a roll of paper towels. "Thank you—it's my fault, I hit her with my menu. These things are enormous! They're like board games."

The waitress went away with our orders and came back with Pepsis for Steffi and Star, iced tea for Sander, and a tall beer for me.

"How are you drying off over there?" I asked Steffi, who'd been sulking.

"Good," she said.

"Good. I won't spill anything else. You can spill on me, though. Nothing hot."

"Mommy, look! Now I made a square," Star said, holding up her straw.

"That's good, but can you make a circle? A perfect circle with no bends or creases. *Then* I'll be impressed."

Sander looked dazed—he wasn't used to spending this much time around children. "Kids are a trip, aren't they? Got any?" I asked.

"I have never been married," he answered.

"Good for you. Stay free. I don't know why people get married. It's unfair to everyone involved. My husband and I went to a wedding last year in St. Ignace—do you know where that is? It's in Northern Michigan—redneck country. And the bride and the groom were hanging out with other people the entire time and didn't even really kiss when the guy pronounced them man and wife. They just sort of leaned together, like *Hey.*"

Our food came up distressingly fast—my club sandwich looked compressed, the lettuce and bread the same neutral color, all earth tones. While the kids ate and amused themselves, I tried prying information out of Sander.

"My brother mentioned a piece of property—I don't think I was supposed to hear about it. You know when you walk into a room and everyone clams up? Maybe that doesn't happen to you," I said.

Sander blinked three distinct times. It was like trying to have a conversation with an ATM. "Dr. Snow is a wealthy man. He owns property all across the country. He owns a dairy farm in Manitoba. He has an apartment in downtown Montreal. I've stayed there myself. It's not uncommon for him to get involved in real estate speculation."

"Nah, this sounded different. He said he wanted to pay cash, and that he didn't want people to know who he was. That's when they clammed up."

More blinking. *Please enter your five-digit PIN number.* Star nudged me.

"Star, what is it? The adults are trying to have a conversation," I said.

"Mommy, what if a hand came out of my nachos and tried to grab me?"

Transaction cancelled. "That would be awful, honey, but it's so unlikely that it's really not worth worrying about," I said.

We finished our meals in near-silence. After lunch we drove past the airport on our way back to the Snow compound. Barbed wire, pavement, sleet and slush, a half-empty parking lot. A cop was making an arrest near the gate.

"Where were you on September 11th?" I asked. "I was looking at apartments with a girl I worked with at the time. Her name was Lisa—we lived together for a couple of years. We stopped at the bank to get a certified check for the security deposit and they had it on the TV. I'll never forget it. I remember thinking, 'At least we live in Ohio.' It kind of felt like someone else's problem."

"I was painting a wall," Sander said.

The kid being arrested had long curly hair and a mustache and was mouthing off as the cop handcuffed him over the hood of his car. "I wonder what he did," Steffi said.

"Drugs, probably," I said.

"How do you know?"

I snorted. "Oh, darlin', I know the type. Hey, look!" The girls popped up in their seats. "There's a Pier 1! Of all the places. Pull over," I told Sander.

"What's a Pier 1?" asked Steffi.

"Mommy works at Pier 1," said Star.

"*Worked.* It's a furniture store, Steffi. People like your step-dad don't shop there. They also sell bath accessories and stuff for the kitchen. That's where I worked for ten years. Me and Pier 1 go way back. I once yelled at a customer for slapping her kid. Totally went off. Another time I fell off a step stool and hairline fractured my kneecap. All sorts of famous people shopped at our store. Noah Wyle... the lead singer of Tool."

We parked and went inside. I hadn't been in a Pier 1 in months. The smells—cedar chips, floor polish, wisteria potpourri—the k.d. lang music, the splintery display crates, the sales associates in their blue aprons stocking candles and dented-brass wall sconces... it all gave me an unexpected jolt. I almost felt like grabbing an apron and pitching in.

"My store wasn't quite as big as this one. We didn't have our stemware so close to the front. That cushion pattern must be new." I showed Star the display of wicker rockers and love seats near the cash wrap. "Wow, they must sell a lot of white wicker. We couldn't give it away. It's interesting to see the little regional variations from store to store."

Star wandered off to look at the holiday decorations while I stayed behind to take it all in. I'd spent so much of my life here—how many thousands of hours? How many papasans sold, broken wine glasses damaged-out? Working at Pier 1 meant rough hands, short fingernails, a bad back. It meant finding pricetags stuck to your jeans or the bottom of your shoe when you got home from work. It meant always smelling like candles.

But it was okay. It was a place to be.

CHAPTER THIRTEEN

Back at Snow's house, I parked Star in front of the TV and re-checked my messages. One was from my mom—her voice had the formal tone and veiled hostility of a first late-payment notice. She'd heard from Pam, who was hysterical. Pam wanted to know where I was in Canada so she could send Child Protective Services after me. Various legal options were being considered, none of them favorable to me. Some of this shit I didn't learn until later on. See, you can't take a child across an international border and into parts unknown without both parents' consent. That's kind of obvious. And it's either a big deal or not, depending on whether one of the parties involved is Pam Okerfeldt. The only saving grace was that Mom didn't like Pam any better than I did, so I could probably trust her to hide my whereabouts for at least a little while longer.

Hanging up the phone, I went to find Star and got lost on the way to the TV room. I wasn't thinking clearly. I'd considered this to be a safe place, but now I wasn't sure. Between staying here and going back to Michigan, neither seemed the better alternative. If I went back, I'd have no peace. It wasn't a question of the Okerfeldts "forgiving" me. I didn't want their forgiveness. I didn't want *them*, period. We were a bad match from the beginning, and now I'd be even more on their shit-list than before. They'd always hold this over me, Pam especially. But if I stayed, the chances of a civil resolution would decrease by the week. Higher authorities would get involved. Prison time wouldn't be out of the question if the Okerfeldts decided to allege abuse, which I could totally see them doing. Add to that whatever shady dealings Wallis had going on with Dr. Snow, and things didn't look good for me.

Retracing my steps, I went left at a junction between corridors and honed in on two voices, Wallis' and Dr. Snow's, coming from a nearby room. The door to the room was cracked open. I didn't want to be accused of eavesdropping, so I barged right in.

"Sis!" Wallis said. He and Dr. Snow sat across from each other at the far end of a conference table. They had paperwork spread out, maps, two laptops. I smelled coffee and carpet freshener.

Snow leaned back in his chair. "If you're looking for the children, they're down the hall."

"I'm not. I mean, I *am*. I was. I heard voices and I..." I stood at the table. "I want to know what's going on here. There's some big secret no one's telling me about." As I came closer, Snow tilted down the screen of his laptop. "There! See? You're hiding things from me." He made a gesture of not understanding. "You did! You just moved your computer. I'm not stupid, man. Maybe I only went to one year of community college and smoked too much pot in high school, but I know when someone's giving me the runaround."

Wallis sighed loudly. "This is a private meeting, sis.

We'll hang out tonight, I promise. We'll have Sander drive us downtown and get a beer."

"No, it's all right. I don't mind her being here. She's a guest of this house. We can finish our work later," said Snow.

"That's not the point. Benoît's calling in an hour and we still don't have any hard information on the airstrip up in Gander."

After some bickering between the two, Snow finally urged me to sit. "You seem angry, Roseanne. Why is that?" he asked.

"I'm not angry. If I was angry, I'd be going off right now. I don't get like that. I know what anger can do to people. I've seen it. Work a retail job for two weeks and then let's talk," I said.

"I'm simply responding to your body language and tone of voice. But I have a sense of what's bugging you. You have some questions about your brother's role here. You feel that people haven't been forthcoming enough, and that's reasonable. The family members of gifted young people often find themselves with the same questions."

"Y-yeah. That's right," I said, still not quite trusting him.

"You want to know that he's not being exploited. Believe me, I get it. It happens all the time in academia—older colleagues taking advantage of their protégés. Perhaps we should ask him. Crim?" He smiled and turned to my brother. "Do you feel exploited?"

"Annoyed, yes, exploited, no," he said, staring at his watch. Snow had a good laugh at that. I hated his laugh. Something show-offy about it.

"So if he's not being exploited, why are you fucking him over?" I asked.

Snow's eyes narrowed. "Define your terms."

"*Fucking him over*. Wallis worked his ass off on that book. Even I know that, and I don't know anything. He gave up his future to come up here, dude. Going to grad school, being close to his family, *me*. And everything is a thousand times harder for him, don't forget. It's not just his legs. It's his whole life."

"I understand that."

"You do? Then why not give him some real credit instead of *jacking him around-*"

"Come on, sis, we've been over this," Wallis said.

Snow waved him off. "It's a fair question. Roseanne, let me be very clear. Your brother has a brilliant future ahead of him. He's a better writer than I'll ever be, for one. I'm fluent with the technical language—other specialists understand me—but Crim can take those abstract concepts and translate them into clear and simple English. I envy him. I have no doubt that he'll write a great book one day, an important book, and when that day comes I don't want to hurt his chances. You see..." He moved his laptop another six inches away from me. "The name 'Dr. Clement Snow' means different things to different people. Not everyone has a positive view of the work I do. I have personal enemies as well. It's not necessarily a good thing for people to know the extent of our collaboration. So, in lieu of giving him the full credit he deserves, I can offer financial security, a place to work, a place to live, and my loyal support. I'm afraid it's the best I can do."

"Sounds like jacking him around to me."

He finally relented and agreed to explain some of his work. I could sense him making time for me, mentally rearranging events in his busy schedule.

"Forgive me if I leave out a few details. None of it is

illegal or unethical, I assure you." Reaching for his laptop, he saved whatever he was working on and cleared the screen. "I'm not sure how much you know about my research. I'm a linguist by trade, which means I study languages—where they originate, how they evolve, and how they relate to demographic factors like economics, religion, and politics. It's a subject that's fascinated me since I was a very little boy. But language is really only the starting point. In reality we're talking about the very nature of communities; a community being defined as two or more individuals working together to reach a common goal.

"I'm especially interested in how people interact in small clusters. That's what brought me and your brother to Greenland, where settlements of a hundred or fewer are often separated by great distances—if you can imagine fifty people living in Manhattan and another fifty on the outermost tip of Cape Cod, with nothing in between but ice and rock. And yet somehow these populations manage to support themselves even in the absence of a developed economy. They produce their own food, look after their sick, and settle their disputes—not always peacefully, perhaps, but surely as well as we do in the U.S. and Canada. I believe—as does your brother—that world populations will become more and more decentralized over the next years. Technology is a certainly a factor when you consider all that a person can do without leaving his house. We work at home, shop at home... as long as the basic infrastructure is in place, we hardly have any use for each other any more."

On his laptop he pulled up a picture of what looked like a dilapidated barge in the middle of the ocean. Two giant pillars supported a massive iron platform and something that resembled a small airplane hangar. A steel crane dangled over the platform's edge.

"You're looking at the Principality of Sealand off the coast of England. The structure itself was built during World War Two as a sea fort for the military. It was abandoned by the Royal Navy in the mid-fifties and occupied in 1967 by Paddy Roy Bates, a former Major in the British Army and pirate radio operator. Though Bates' initial reason for occupying the platform was to set up an independent radio station, he later rechristened the platform 'Sealand' and declared his independence from the UK.

"Sealand still claims to be a sovereign nation, though it's not recognized as such by the world community. It has a constitution, a currency, even issues passports. At various times it's operated as a data haven, a political asylum, and a destination for adventure-seeking tourists. Go to their website and you'll find a detailed history of the country's scuffles with the English courts. It's an interesting story. I've visited Sealand myself, though I found the political climate not to my liking.

"The fact is, Sealand is only one of dozens, if not hundreds, of so-called 'micronations' scattered across the globe. There's an unusual ball-shaped house in Vienna whose owner founded the Republic of Kugelmugel after a dispute with the local building authorities. The entire country consists of the house, the front yard, and the barbed-wire fence surrounding it. The Other World Kingdom is a matriarchy on the grounds of a chateau in the Czech Republic. Women own male slaves and control the police force. They're quite popular, as you can imagine. Other micronations are non-territorial or exist in virtual space. You'll find them nearly everywhere—man-made islands, city blocks in West London. Some of these efforts are more serious than others. Some amount to little more than publicity stunts, while others represent a genuine effort to establish new societies, whether Marxist, libertarian, or what have you."

I interrupted. "So you want to start your own country, is that it?"

"I'm sorry, Roseanne, I've already said too much. I *will* say that unlike many of our forebears, our intentions are entirely serious and our motivations are completely pure. What your brother and I have in mind is a serious social experiment. We intend to establish a community of like-minded individuals who don't mind living in isolation and who have an interest in looking after their own needs. That's where the future lies, and we want to get there first."

I asked Wallis, "And what's your stake in all this? *Isolation*. I'm sorry, bro, but that ain't you. You need help with things—you more than most people. It's bad enough that you're living up here in another country, away from your family and doctors. Why do you have to make things so hard on yourself? Come back home, go to grad school, and get a normal job. Tenured college professors make a shitload."

"But sis, I'm part of the experiment. Think about it: if I can survive under these adverse conditions, anyone can," Wallis said.

"What do you mean, 'adverse conditions'? Where the hell is this place, Antarctica? It is Antarctica, isn't it? Wallis, you're *not* moving to Antarctica. Seriously, I'll kick your ass. Your wheelchair will freeze up."

They both chuckled. "It's not Antarctica, don't worry. It's no place currently in existence," Snow said.

"No place currently in existence. Well that ain't a hell of a lot better."

"Come on Roseanne, Dr. Snow answered your questions. Can we get back to work now? I'll buy you a beer down at Trapper John's. Please, just leave us alone," Wallis begged.

"I have a better idea. Let's finish up for the day and check on the kids. I'm satisfied with our progress," said Snow.

He rose from the table. I wasn't sure if I felt better knowing these things or not. Snow spoke of isolation as a physical place; it meant not having any neighbors, waking up and seeing nothing but an empty field out your window. But I knew something about isolation too: those long afternoons when Vance was a baby and Star was a toddler, Vance understanding nothing except maybe tones of voice—Mommy's angry, Mommy's sad, Mommy's being silly—Star understanding little more. *That* was isolation. I could tell Star anything: "Sarah, guess what? We're moving to Dallas and buying a house with a blue roof and ridiculous plastic awnings and I'll start my own business making those little paper cones French fries sometimes come in at restaurants, and you won't have to go to school ever, and I'll let you dye your hair glittery colors and you can even paint your face orange and black like the Cincinnati Bengals..." and she'd just nod and coo and hand me her toys as if I hadn't said anything at all. In some ways it was worse than actually being alone. When you're alone you can let down your guard; you can lie back on the couch and close your eyes and switch off for an hour. Taking care of the kids was constant, anxious work, and I never felt I had someone to share it with.

It was just me, by myself, in charge of these humming energies that existed in a dimension other than my own.

We left the room and continued down another endlessly winding corridor to the far end of the house. Snow walked fast, taking big strides: outdoor steps. Wallis and I chugged far behind.

"I hope I didn't embarrass you. What's Trapper John's? Is that a good bar? I think Star and I might've passed it when we drove in," I said. He didn't answer. "Come on, Wallis—I'm sorry, I'm just checking up on you. On behalf of the family, you know?"

"On behalf of the family," he repeated dully.

The hallway brightened and we entered through a curtain to a greenhouse filled with plants growing in long dirt troughs. The room had its own atmosphere, cool and humid. It smelled like the spring term of seventh grade science. The smell made me hungry for dirty salads.

"Wow, this house has everything," I said. Star and Steffi were playing in one of the dirt troughs, hands sunk to the wrists. Star wore a red T-shirt with a decorative slit cut up the sides. I dimly remembered being in a bad mood when I'd bought it for her.

"What are you doing, Star? Are you making a mess? Are you going to be the filthiest kid on the planet when I have to give you a bath?" I asked.

"Steffi is showing me her o-kids," Star said.

"*Orchids*. Dr. Snow, my Epidendrums are wilting," Steffi complained.

"That's because it's too cool in here," Snow said kindly.

The kids finished planting a silver-leafed sprig in a pot of gooey black dirt, then Steffi gave us a tour of her orchid collection: creamsicle-colored petals, a pornography of lewd, dewy stamens. "This one's from Venezuela. Dr. Snow got it for me for my birthday," she said.

Snow rubbed his thumb and forefinger together. "That was a day's pay. Stephanie, you should use the light filter. You don't want too much direct sun."

Star bumped into Snow's legs. "Dr. Snow, why do flowers smell so good?" she asked.

"Why? The same reason pretty women like your mother wear perfume, to attract attention. Flowers are just like people. Big people make little people—your mother and father made you. If they didn't, there'd be no more people and that would be a bad thing, wouldn't it?" he said. Star nodded. "It's the same with flowers, but flowers are different because they need help. They need birds and bees and other insects to help them make new flowers. So they give off a good smell, and that smell attracts their little helpers, and that's how they make new flowers. Do you understand?"

"Yes," I said.

"How's that 'like Mommy'?" Star asked.

Snow tittered. "I'm sure she'll tell you someday. But the sense of smell is very powerful. Some plants and flowers even emit bad smells to ward off predators."

"What kinds of bad smells?"

"Strong smells like medicine… or skunks. Smells that say, 'Don't touch me!'"

"Does Mommy do that too?"

"I'm sure she does… in her way. People are like that. We wear perfume and attractive clothes when we want people to notice us and we keep our heads down and our hands in our pockets when we want people to go away. Do you understand?"

"Yes," I said.

Star groaned. "Mommy, why do you keep saying that? He's asking me."

The girls returned to their gardening, and I followed Snow across the greenhouse. Wallis had gone off to do something else. It was the first time Snow and I had been alone together.

"You're good with kids. You should make educational DVDs. You could do one on plants and flowers and another on the solar system and another on earthquakes and volcanoes," I said.

We stopped at a table of potted cactuses, and Snow gave one of the pots a quarter-turn. "I like children. I wish I'd had more. Teachers naturally make good parents. I sometimes think of my students as my children."

I wondered if he'd felt that way about the girl he'd slept with in Ottawa. Maybe not. Maybe it was the girl's fault. Girls can be determined sometimes.

"I *try* to be a good mom. I wonder if it's possible to be a bad parent and still raise good kids."

"Oh, I think so. I think it happens all the time."

As we moved down the row of cactuses, I watched Star dig around in the dirt with a garden trowel, her jaw set in icy concentration. Snow stopped at the end of the table.

"Roseanne, you've had a lot of questions for me. Do you mind if I ask you one?"

I said sure. His blue skin intensified, aura-like. It drew on the environment.

"Why are you really here?" he asked.

CHAPTER FOURTEEN

Winter came early to Newfoundland. An outdoor thermometer hung from our bedroom window, and I got used to converting degrees Celsius to Fahrenheit: six degrees Celsius on November 15th, two degrees on the 30th. Dr. Snow wasn't happy with me sticking around; he had enough legal issues of his own without my little white trash soap opera jeopardizing the purity of his experiment. But he tolerated me for Wallis' sake.

Star celebrated her sixth birthday with Steffi at a roller rink downtown. Wallis gave me a few bucks so I could buy her presents. I got her some cute pink shoes and a picture book about seals. I must've cried a flood that day.

At times I thought about the other kids' birthdays, which were coming up: Vance's own sixth, the twins' first. Birthdays I'd probably miss. A first birthday is no big deal—I wasn't worried about Mary and Connor. With Vance, maybe I could find a way to give him a call. Vance always hated talking to me on the phone; Pam or someone would hold the receiver up to his ear, and he'd stand with his arms crossed, sulking as I told him that I loved him and would be home soon from work, and Vance wouldn't say anything, not even "I love you too," so I'd keep talking to fill the silence, not knowing if he was still there, if anyone was still listening. Maybe not a phone call, then. But I'd definitely send him a present, or have someone do it for me.

At a certain point I had to come clean to Star about her daddy. I told her that we'd decided things would be more fun if I lived in one place and Josh lived in another. That way she could do cool things with her dad in Grand Rapids and cool things with me here or wherever—as opposed to staying in one place and just doing cool things there.

Star naturally wondered why she couldn't see her father. Lying wasn't an option so I explained that her daddy was mad at me for the time being and the best thing was to just stay put until people stopped being mad.

"Why is Daddy mad at you?" she asked. It was a few days after her birthday and we were sitting on our bed in the guest room. We'd been sharing the same bed for two months now. She was a good sleeping partner, much better than Josh. Some nights I'd hear her giggling about something in her dream and I'd put my arm around her and giggle too.

"Why is he mad at me? That's a good question. See, it's complicated—it's not like when you spill pop on someone's favorite dress or kill their pet goldfish and they get mad at you for a few days and that's it."

"Did you kill something?"

"No, I didn't... it's nothing like that. You gotta understand, I wasn't much older than you when your father and I met. In the grand scheme of things. I was still pretty immature."

"What's 'immature?'"

"It means I wasn't ready to handle some of my responsibilities like being a mom and a wife and a daughter-in-law and so I just sort of went with the program because I didn't know what else to do and because I felt a lot of pressure to keep people happy and not disappoint anyone, and it worked for a while until…" She looked confused so I gave up. I wasn't sure what I wanted to say anyway.

One night in late December I was reading to her in the living room when a pair of headlights scraped across the window. I looked up, decided it was nothing, and went back to my reading. Another set of headlights parked next to the first.

Sander shot into the room, nose sniffing like a bloodhound. "Duck down! Hide in the basement and don't come out!"

I asked what was wrong but he hushed me and went to answer the door. Star and I dropped behind the sofa and scurried in a crouch down the hall to the basement. Star looked scared.

"Mommy, what's happening?" she asked.

"I don't know, sweetie," I said, though I could guess.

We waited in the basement for fifteen minutes. Dr. Snow's basement wasn't like Pam's: no twenty-year-old washer and dryer stashed in the corner, no stockpiles of dried goods and bottled water. Instead he had a special library where he only kept books and articles he'd written. The rooms were temperature and moisture controlled, and he had a sleeper sofa for overnight guests. There weren't a lot of hiding places so we opened the glass door to the wine cellar and made ourselves small behind a rack of bottles. Star shivered as I held her close. Footsteps pattered over our heads. It sounded like at least three people talking, all of them men.

"Are we in trouble?" Star whispered.

I shook my head and tried not to think. The wine bottles were brown and green, and a mellow auburn light decayed from a recessed ceiling fixture. I took out one of the bottles and read the label, which was all in French.

"Mommy?" Star asked.

"Yes?"

"Does wine cost a lot?"

I put the bottle back. "It can."

"How much?"

I could say a thousand dollars and it wouldn't mean anything to her. "Ten, twelve dollars, usually. These are more."

"Why are these more?"

"Because Dr. Snow is rich as sin and can buy whatever he likes."

Light fell upon the basement steps, and I pushed Star's head down. A man's black work boots descended a step and the door closed behind him. More footsteps—I squeezed my eyes shut. The door to the wine cellar opened and I felt warmth on my face. A hand on my shoulder made me jump.

"They're gone. Come up. We need to talk," said Sander.

Star and I went up the stairs with Sander to the conference room near the back of the house. Snow and Wallis had already gathered, along with Neil and Dr. Snow's wife. Mandy was at work.

"The girl can go," said Snow.

"No, I want her here," I said.

Snow and Wallis exchanged a wary look, and we sat at the table. No laptops this time, no charts. Snow had thrown a robe over his pajamas.

"Do you know who that was?" he asked.

I squeezed Star's hand.

"Local police. They'd received a tip that you might be here. Sander had to do some explaining, which he's good at."

I glanced back at Sander, who'd taken up his station by the door. He folded his arms.

"What did they want?" I asked.

"Your mother-in-law got this address—how, I don't know. You've got a lot of people looking for you back home. I told them you'd been here for a few days in October to visit your brother and we hadn't heard from you since. Fortunately you parked behind the house, otherwise they would've seen your car," Sander said.

I nodded. Everyone was staring at me, including my daughter. "And what did they say?"

Sander unfolded his arms. "They looked doubtful but they left. Our police aren't as persistent as yours."

"Maybe not," interrupted Snow, "but they'll be back, you can be sure of it. They'll bring the CBSA next time. They've got an office in town."

The CBSA was in charge of enforcing customs regulations and tracking down undesirables. As far as the authorities were concerned, Star and I had outstayed our welcome.

"Maybe they won't come back. Don't the police have bigger things to worry about? We're not hurting anyone. It's not like we're al-Qaeda or something," I said.

"No, but you're a U.S. citizen under suspicion of a number of potential charges, including kidnapping and child abandonment. That makes you a person of considerable interest. I'm sorry, dear. I appreciate your situation but you have to admit that you've brought most of this upon yourself. Wouldn't it be better to acknowledge your mistake, surrender, and face the consequences?"

"I can't. They'll take Star away from me," I said firmly. Next to me, Star stared straight ahead. She wasn't crying or anything. Something inside her had simply shut down.

"It's her *daughter*, Clem," said Snow's wife, Charity.

"One of several, I understand. Two daughters and two sons, is it?" Snow retorted, holding up two fingers.

I said yes.

"Four children, three of whom are living at home with their father, wondering where you are."

"I know," I said.

He paused. His robe was one of those thin, clingy things that some old men spend their whole lives in. "Let me put it this way. This isn't the first time the police have been to this house, *capiche*? Perhaps your brother has shared some of this with you. It's quite remarkable what our tax agencies feel they're entitled to. Plus there's the matter of my research, which is at a very sensitive stage." He looked around the table. "Someone help me out here. Sander, what do you think?"

Sander held his arms behind his back. "I think she's a risk," he said, clearing his throat. "Sorry," he apologized to me.

"Neil?" Snow asked.

Neil put up his hands. "I'm just the cook."

"You're more than that. Speak."

I caught Neil's eyes.

"She's not a risk if we keep an eye on her," he decided.

"If we don't let her out of the house," added Sander.

"We hardly leave the house as it is. Just give us a few more weeks. I know my mother-in-law. She doesn't like me anyway. She'll be delighted to have me out of her life. Everyone just needs a little more time," I begged.

"A few weeks is not a little more time. We can't afford—I can't afford—any more unwanted attention. You have no idea the damage you could cause just by being here. If it were to come out that I was, in essence, *harboring a fugitive*," Snow conjectured, then stopped. "Well, it could jeopardize this entire operation. Years of work—not just my own but your brother's as well. Would you do that to him?"

Before I could answer, Mandy blew into the room. "What's going on? I ran into Steffi. She said you were having a *big meeting*—her italics," she said.

Snow tapped his watch. "Home early?"

"I switched hours with someone. I thought I might change and go to the gym. Who died? You look like you swallowed a bird," she said to me.

Sander explained what had happened. Mandy took off her earrings, dropped them clattering onto the table, and sat down. Somehow I'd missed this part of being a woman: the part where you went to the gym whenever you wanted and wore professional clothes to work instead of jeans and sneakers. There'd been a woman in my creative writing group like that—Sheila or Sam or Sabrina. Mid-30s, a self-employed CPA. Always cracked her neck and did shoulder stretches before we wrote in class.

Mandy finished listening and said, "What's the big deal? Let her stay. The kids like each other. Besides, the in-laws sound like hell."

I didn't want to bad-talk the Okerfeldts in front of Star. They were her grandparents, after all.

"They're nice people," I said unconvincingly. Mandy gagged.

"Emma, dear, think rationally. We can't keep her," Snow protested. I was starting to feel like a stray dog.

Mandy smiled coolly, leaned far back in her chair, and made a tent of her fingers under her chin. "Aren't you being a little hypocritical?" she asked.

He turned an ear, as if he hadn't quite heard. "How so?"

"Well, you're always talking about the *police* and the 'goddamn government' and how bureaucracies are always interfering with everything."

"Yes, that's true. And? I fail to see the relevance."

"What's wrong with a woman making choices about her own life without the government or the border patrol or some other agency telling her what to do? From what I understand, Rosie's not the one causing trouble. It's this creep mother-in-law back in Michigan. Am I right?"

I didn't know what to say. I hadn't expected Mandy to come to my defense. "I guess," I managed.

"That's right—*she's* the one making threats. You're not trying to hurt anyone, are you? Of course not. Look, you did those people a favor. You popped out four grandkids, practically wrecked your body in the process, and now they expect you to live in the middle of a wheat field for the rest of your life and rub your husband's feet every night."

"I'm sure you're right, Emma, but isn't this a personal matter between Roseanne and her husband? I don't understand why I should get involved," Snow said.

"Dad, you're not thinking. This is exactly what Mobility's all about—people like Rosie. People in a jam."

Everyone at the table suddenly became very agitated. Snow made a signal for her to pipe down.

Mandy shook out her hair. "What? Rosie's inner circle now, isn't she? Mobility's the perfect place for her. She won't have any trouble from the Canadians or the Americans. If anyone asks, we'll just say she's with us."

"And then we all go to jail," said Wallis.

"No, because we're not breaking any laws. We're simply upholding the integrity of our national borders. Why are you laughing? This isn't me talking, this is you—your words."

"You're taking the wrong things literally," Snow said.

"Am I? That's interesting. Would you care to elaborate?" she asked. He didn't. "I don't see why you're so resistant. Is it because Rosie's problems aren't 'politically radical' or 'globally significant' enough?"

"Don't be silly. I'm as concerned about her as you are. I just…"

We watched and waited. I'd never seen the old man at a loss for words before.

"I simply worry about our motives appearing transparent," he finished.

Mandy laughed. "Well, we wouldn't want that now, would we? As opposed to opaque, I suppose."

"What's Mobility?" I asked, but no one answered.

Mandy tried again. "Dad, look at it like this—you want people to respect you, don't you? No one is going to think you're for real unless you've survived a test first." She pointed at me. "She's your test."

Snow remained speechless. As usual, I didn't know what the hell was going on.

Star asked if she could watch TV, and I reluctantly let her go. She climbed down from her chair—I remember chairs being so huge when I was her age—and trotted off. "Poor kid," I said.

"I'll sit with her," Neil volunteered and left.

I also wanted to go but Snow and Wallis' staring eyes wouldn't let me. They'd gone from wanting me to leave to wanting me to stay.

Snow said, "Fine, but there's got to be some ground rules first. You're to stay out of sight for the time being. We'll pull your car into the garage in the morning. If you need anything, Sander will drive into town and get it for you. There's no playing outside for your daughter. During the day you'll confine yourself to the back of the house, is that clear?"

I nodded. I actually liked the idea of being stuck indoors.

"You're here at my sole discretion. If I have second thoughts and ask you to leave, I don't want to hear any argument about it."

Charity said, "Oh, dear, they can't live like that forever."

"It's a temporary measure," he said.

"Temporary until what?"

He snapped, "Until things change. We'll all be gone in a few months anyway. I'll be spending more and more time in the field so I'm depending on Sander and Neil to take care of things around the house. One more visit like the one we had this evening and you're gone, madam, do you understand?"

"Gotcha, sure. Uh, thanks," I said.

Charity still looked concerned. "Shouldn't the girl be in school? She'll fall behind."

"That's her mother's problem, not mine," said Snow.

"But we ought to do something. It's not healthy for a young person to lie around the house all day watching TV. I'm busy with patients most of the week but I have Mondays off. I can help her with her reading."

"I'll see to it that she exercises every morning," Sander offered.

"Oh, no, Sander—you're busy enough. You too, Charity. Star's not your responsibility. I'll figure all that out," I said.

"She is our responsibility—for now. All of ours," Charity said, blinking at her husband. Snow ignored her.

The meeting broke up, and I looked for Star in the TV room. Being in the house felt different now. I was aware of windows, the possibility of people watching from outside. The abstract paintings seemed to conceal miniature cameras and recording devices, time-code advancing in the corner of the screen.

Star and Steffi were sitting on the floor in front of their usual nature program while Neil watched from the sofa, his legs crossed and a magazine in his lap. On the TV an angry baboon beat its chest and charged the camera.

I dropped next to Neil and peeked at his magazine. "Nice car," I said.

"Natürlich," he said.

"You like sports cars?"

"I like to dream." He turned the page. The same car from the previous page flanked a stone mansion somewhere in the country. The woman leaning against the car wore a form-fitting dress with a slit up to the thigh and silver high-heeled sandals.

"Who's prettier, the car or the girl?" I asked.

"Both are impeccable," he said, closing the magazine. The ad on the back featured another impeccable girl draped across an enormous bottle of Disaronno.

"You can keep reading," I said.

"I wasn't really reading it."

The baboon leapt on the back of a meek, four-legged mammal and began gnawing on its hide. The animal twisted in agony. Steffi moved on her elbows to be closer to the screen.

"That was German, wasn't it? The word you just said. Do you actually speak German?" I asked.

He laughed softly. "Oh, no. I was just being flippant."

Steffi said, "The baboon is mad at the antelope. The antelope makes the baboon nervous. He thinks the antelope wants something from him. The antelope wants to steal the baboon's food. They argue. The baboon slaps the antelope with his heavy paws. They are both hungry. The baboon has cancer."

A fish flopped on a hill of sand. Granules covered the fish's sticky body. Somewhere else in the world a mountain lion bit through the head of a goat.

"What's Mobility? It's okay—you probably can't tell me either," I said. Neil sniffed and rubbed his nose.

After the show ended, I called Star to bed. She wouldn't hold my hand as we walked down the long hall to our room. She was mad at me, I guess—everyone was. Things would've been better if I'd just stayed in Michigan. Been a better wife, not complained so much. Not let my mind wander.

Star changed in the bathroom and came out with her pajama top buttoned wrong.

"Would you like to watch some more TV before we fall asleep?" I asked, already in bed. The guest room had a small flat-screen TV, a stack of travel magazines, and a basket of perfumed sachets.

Star harrumphed and curled up in the chair beside the bed. "Why are you sitting there? Aren't you coming to bed?" No. "You're just going to sleep right there?" Unh-huh. "Come on, Star, that's silly. At least let me sleep in the chair and you take the bed. How's that sound? I'm the bad person, I did the bad thing, I should sleep in the chair." She didn't move, so I turned on the TV. "Okay, but let me know if you change your mind. Give me a poke, even if I'm asleep."

Minutes passed. The show was a documentary about a man who'd burned his hand badly and whose friends were trying to keep him from going into shock on their way to the hospital.

Come on, buddy. Look at me. It's Rick! Keep it elevated.

(Cut to steaming hot soup pouring onto a hand and the hand rearing back: OW!)

(Lips spelling out an address into a cell phone: We're at 8300 Woodbine.)

Come on, buddy. Look at me.

(OW!)

(Hurry, please! Blue house on the corner.)

Hot soup, steam. The hand clenching at the sudden shock of it all.

Look at me. It's Rick!

(OW!)

Keep it elevated.

"Star, honey? Don't worry. We'll get you your own room," I said.

No answer. My daughter with her ten little toes.

CHAPTER FIFTEEN

She came to bed around midnight.

CHAPTER SIXTEEN

Star and I spent most of the winter and the following spring indoors. Dr. Snow was nice and let her move into a finished room in the basement with a dresser and a couple of empty shelves for her books. I hadn't had the bed to myself in months, and I missed her. For the first few weeks I held onto my pillow for company.

As promised, Sander led her through a round of calisthenics each morning. They did sit-ups, crunches, jumping jacks. Star loved it. She'd turned into a feisty little tyke. I worked out with them two or three days a week. Sander counted our repetitions in a dispassionate monotone, correcting Star whenever she showed bad form:

"The pain is natural. The pain is logical. Let it consume you. The pain is a fire burning deep within. *Ten!* You need it. You love it. It *is* you. Be a candle. The pain does not judge. It does not lecture. *Fifteen!* The pain is the goal. You must touch it."

I asked him after one of our workouts what he meant by, "Be a candle."

"It's a particular theory of mine. The body contains stored energy that can only be released through suffering.

It's like a candle. The candle is inert until its potential is converted into energy. Burning releases that potential."

Star didn't seem to mind this kind of creepy talk. She did her sit-ups without complaint, eyes open, forehead perspiring.

In between her workouts and reading lessons with Charity, Star and I talked about our future. We'd been told a little more about Dr. Snow's plans. We knew that the entire household would be relocating in a few months. We knew that the place in question was small and isolated. And we knew that the name of this place was Mobility.

One night after reading a chapter from her *Illustrated Grimm's Fairy Tales*, Star asked, "Mom, can I bring Neil's book with us when we go?"

Neil had given her a big hardcover cookbook filled with full-color pictures of turkeys being trussed and fish fillets crackling in a skillet. Mostly she stared at the pictures, though she'd learned some new words like "simmer" and "purée."

"It depends where we're going. I don't want to get stuck lugging that big ol' thing around," I said, sitting on the edge of her bed.

"When we go to Mobility," she said, pronouncing the word primly, in four distinct syllables. "Charity says we're leaving in ten weeks."

"Oh, really? How is it that you know this and I don't? Normally adults find out things first, before kids do."

"Nunt-unh."

"Yeah, usually. Like when someone dies, they never tell the kids until all the adults have been notified. I didn't know my dad's mom died until three days later."

"You didn't?"

"Nope. I missed everything. I didn't even know when the space shuttle blew up. I was three or four when it happened. Years later I'm in sixth grade science and I'm like, 'Really?'"

"Charity's seen pictures, and Uncle Wallis and Dr. Snow have been there four times already."

I closed the fairy tale book. "Four times, huh? Somehow I doubt it. Why wouldn't they have told me any of this?"

"Maybe they didn't want to tell you."

"And why not?" She scratched her chin. "That's no answer. Come on, what else did she say?"

"Who?"

I lightly rapped her forehead. "Charity, you nitwit. Where is this place? How do we get there? How big is it? Where do we sleep? I need details, kid. I might not even want to go there. It might be horrible. It might be worse than-"

Worse than living with your father.

"Charity says it's in the middle of the ocean and looks like a big spaceship," Star said.

She looked tired, so I wished her good night—she actually let me kiss her this time—and went upstairs. By now the prickling sensation I felt in front of windows was second nature.

Charity was in the tiny study playing a board game with Steffi. Steffi got to stay up until nine-thirty, a fact that she flaunted over Star. "Isn't it your bedtime?" she'd say on the rare nights when they weren't getting along. Her attitude toward Star was that of an older sibling who'd gone off to college and had returned with a slouch and a richer vocabulary—kind of like Wallis and me when we were younger.

"Who's winning?" I asked, looking down at the game in

progress. Steffi kept her Monopoly money in neat stacks separated by denomination and tucked under the edge of the board. She also had a "Get Out Of Jail Free" card that she hadn't yet used.

"It depends what you mean by winning. Mom has more assets but all of her money's tied up in property. I'm doing better in terms of cold cash," Steffi said.

The Monopoly game proceeded in silence, money humorlessly changing hands. "So… where's this picture?" I asked.

"What picture's that, dear?" asked Charity. I envisioned myself diving elbows first into the Monopoly board, scattering money and game pieces. An evening ruined, or at least changed. Steffi was a sports car and her mother was a shoe.

"Star told me you've seen a picture of Mobility. I want to see it too."

"You'll have to ask Dr. Snow."

Steffi said, "Monopoly's more fun than Clue but less challenging. Clue takes deductive reasoning and powers of observation. Monopoly requires strategic thinking. People who prefer Clue to Monopoly are more likely to: drive standard transmission, enjoy classical music, and develop Crohn's disease in their thirties."

"Are we really leaving in ten weeks? I'm not ready. I thought we still had a lot to do," I said.

"You don't have to come with us, Roseanne. You just can't stay here. Dr. Snow's renting the house to one of his former students and his very nice wife from Ecuador. I'm sure they'd rather have the place to themselves," Charity said.

I listened for some hint of distress in her voice. My options were slim, as she well knew. Back home I was the "unbalanced mother" who'd kidnapped her own child and disappeared into Canada. There'd even been a piece about me on *America's Most Wanted*; not a full episode but twenty damning minutes. They'd called the segment "Against God and Family," and the actress in the reenactment looked like she'd been picked up for selling knock-off T-shirts at a Dave Matthews Band concert. She was supposed to be me.

"Aren't you a little uncomfortable about all this? What's Steffi going to do for school?" I asked.

"We'll teach her. There'll be other children there." Sizing up the board, Charity said, "I wish I had St. Charles Place. St. Charles Place has its own Chance Card. It's a good money-maker."

"What other children? You mean there's other people? Who?" I asked.

She smiled. "Surely you didn't think we'd be going by ourselves? Mobility is a whole community. There'll be doctors, lawyers, tradesmen... young and old. We've got twenty committed so far, and we're hoping to hear from a few more."

"But who are they? Friends of yours?"

"I know some. Most are students, young people dedicated to Dr. Snow's work. We've got a marine biologist from Victoria. There's a woman from Maine who makes her own hammered dulcimers."

"Oh, that'll come in handy," I said. The whole thing was starting to sound like a cult. We were to be the disciples of Dr. Clement Snow, willing to travel long miles to sit at the great man's feet. One day the FBI would find our dead bodies arranged in a pentagram somewhere in the jungle. "And what am I supposed to do?"

"You'll find some way to contribute. In the meantime

you'll be a good mother to Sarah." Her playing piece landed on Electric Company, which Steffi owned, and she became focused on the game. I left them to it.

Back in my room, I shadowboxed in the moonlight. The general form of my body promised a certain spunk and attitude. My ponytail looked cool bouncing around.

I confided in Neil the next morning. "Seriously, Neil, what am I going to do? I can't go home now. I'm afraid what'll happen to Star."

"You'll stay here. You'll get a divorce," he said as he served me breakfast in the kitchen.

"Easier said than done. And then when everyone leaves—you and Wallis and Sander... then I'll really be stuck. I don't know anyone else here."

"Come with us. We'll put you to work."

I held my coffee without drinking it. "Doing what?"

"You can help your brother. He'll have a lot on his hands—you know, as President."

He returned to his kitchen chores, and I rose after him. "Wait... President? Of Mobility? Why is he President?"

"Why not?"

"Why not Dr. Snow, for one? Isn't he the brains behind this whole thing?"

"Dr. Snow prefers to stay behind the scenes. He's been in a lot of scrapes in the past. Besides, he really believes in your brother. Mobility was his idea, after all."

"It was? Wallis never told me that."

He poured himself a coffee, taking the dregs at the bottom of the pot. "Wallis doesn't tell you much, does he?"

"What do you mean? Neil, talk to me. No one's giving me any straight answers. I'm all alone in the goddamn world and I'm looking for a friend. Please."

He set down his cup. "Look, Dr. Snow's a bright guy

but he's basically a businessman. He uses people, okay? It's not exploitation because they always know what they're getting into and they're always well paid. How he's treated your brother is no different from how he's treated anyone else. He paid off his first wife, he's been manipulating his daughter ever since she was a kid... he's helped me, too."

"How has he helped you?"

"Lots of ways. I used to have a problem a long time ago, and Dr. Snow paid for me to get better. I was doing some drugs that weren't very healthy, prescription pills. He sent me to a thirty-day treatment center near Calgary. A beautiful place in the Rockies. We'd go on hikes and swim in the cold water and cook up breakfast together on the beach by the lake. It was nice. Danny Bonaduce was there."

"You went to rehab with Danny Bonaduce?"

"Sure, we were in the same cabin. We talked about cars and good places to get Szechuan hot pot in L.A. He pretty much stayed in his pajamas and drank the free ice tea in the common room."

I let that sit with me. Neil's ears were round and small. They lacked earlobes. "Okay, so Wallis is President. That's fine. And what else? Does everyone have a title?"

He gave me a rundown of the posts already filled: Vice-President, Secretary of State, Chief Communications Officer. Most of the names were of people I didn't know. Mobility had a cultural attaché, an archivist, and even its own education tsar. It all seemed pretty absurd to me.

"What about you?" I asked.

"I'm head cook. I'm also in charge of immigration until we can find someone else."

Incredulous laughter seemed the obvious response,

though he gave no sign that he found any of this funny or at all out of the ordinary. "And Sander?"

"Head of Security."

"Why do we need a Head of Security?"

"You always need a Head of Security."

"But why?"

"In case of danger."

"What kind of danger? I don't like danger."

"That's why you need a Head of Security. You never know what's going to happen. Riots, lawlessness, civil disobedience. There might be brigands."

"What are brigands?"

"They're like pirates, but they..." His voice trailed off, and he made the sound of a sputtering boat engine.

I had so many other questions, but Neil looked busy. I wondered if being a cook was hard. You had to work with knives and open flames, not to mention the long hours. Neil kept a homey kitchen. The pineapple on the cutting island was decorative and had been there for weeks. It looked like a black woman with a punk hairdo.

When the house met for dinner that night, Dr. Snow raised a toast to Mobility. "I'd be surprised if we ran into another snag. The problem with a diverse portfolio is that it's so difficult when you need to consolidate funds," he advised Star, probably for no other reason than she happened to be sitting next to him.

"Father was *very* convincing at the bank today," Mandy said.

"How would you know? You weren't there," said Snow.

"I can imagine. Tell us, Sander. Wasn't Father convincing at the bank?"

Sander set down his knife and fork. "Your father was quite persuasive," he said.

Snow coughed and reached for his water glass. "I made it clear through my demeanor and the weight of my argument that the bank's policies were unacceptable, and if they couldn't accommodate my simple request, I wouldn't be using their services in the future."

"That's when Sander held down the branch manager, and you beat him with a tire iron, right?" Mandy laughed; Snow didn't. "I'm just teasing you, Dad. I'm sure you were very eloquent. So what's next? When do we get to plant the flag?"

"That's a long way off yet. No one migrates until we're sure everything's safe. We still don't have a constitution. We can't do anything without a constitution. We need a constitution and a Bill of Rights. We need a national anthem. We need an official sport. I suggested javelin but no one liked my idea. We need a defense fund and a poet laureate and a list of banned books," Wallis said.

"You need a core philosophy: *This is who we are*," Mandy added.

"We need a line of succession in case one of us dies. All of this should be spelled out in writing and posted to our website. We need a website," Wallis said.

"Relax, it'll all get done. And as for a constitution–" Snow surveyed the table. "Let me suggest keeping it short and simple. A constitution is a guide, not a rulebook—or rather it's a drawing and not a blueprint. That's better. I like my clever analogy."

"I can't do anything until I buy a new printer cartridge," Wallis said.

Snow pushed aside his food. "Here's an idea. Let's go around the table. Everyone—and that includes the two girls—gets to make one addition to the constitution. It doesn't matter what it is."

"Can't we have some time to think about it?" asked Neil.

"Just say whatever comes to mind. Think of yourselves as framers. Crim, you'll be our secretary; you can write them down. I'll start. I propose-"

Charity interrupted, "Oh, you've got one planned already. You've been thinking about it all this time. No fair, matey!"

The coals in his eyes cooled. "I *don't* have one planned. Don't be silly. In fact, it just occurred to me. I propose a 'Right to Connectivity.' Every citizen should have the same access to technology, from personal computers to handheld communications devices, all at the cost of the state. There. Sander?"

Sander lifted his chin solemnly. "I have always believed that a man should receive a tax credit for conserving utilities."

"And for composting!" Charity covered her mouth. "Oh, was it my turn? That wasn't my choice, anyway. I was going to say that the voting age should be twelve for girls and sixteen for boys."

"Why younger for girls?" Neil asked.

"Because women live longer, so their voting decisions have the potential to affect them for a longer period of time."

"Horseshit. If that's yours, I want a bill rendering discriminatory voting ages unconstitutional."

"I *liked* mom's law," Steffi moped.

"You can use yours to overrule Neil's, dear," Charity said.

Steffi thought about it but decided to use hers to establish a collective retirement fund on the model of the Illinois State Pension. The bill passed unanimously.

Other rules followed. Mandy suggested an allowance

granting physicians limited protection from malpractice suits. Wallis had something to say about term limitations for elected officials. Star wanted a law requiring people to "be happy all the time."

"What about Rosie? She hasn't gone yet," Wallis said.

"Oh, I don't need to. I'm not good at making important decisions," I said.

"Not at all. You're one of us now, so... by all means," Snow said weakly.

I finished my bite of chicken and washed it down with some ice water. The question touched on areas that made me uncomfortable. It asked me to reflect, to delve into autobiography.

Snow said, "If you can't think of anything–"

"It's not a rule, but... I don't like the way women are treated back home. Here too, I'm sure. I'm sure it's the same wherever you go. It's especially hard on young women—girls. I'd like to live in a place where things are easier for girls in their teens and early twenties. Maybe there's no rule or law, but it would be nice if girls were encouraged to gain a little life experience before settling down. Can that go into the rules, or is that too vague? For example, say a girl is nineteen or twenty or even older and she gets pregnant... because that's what happens, isn't it? You can be a hermit and stay at home and never go out with anyone, but that's not natural either. It's *natural* to want to go out with people and be admired by guys and have fun. Guys want to be admired by girls, and that's natural too. There shouldn't be a *penalty*, you know? It's the same with animals—Steffi, those shows you watch. Animals are always getting knocked up... little polar bears and giraffes and gazelles. But the difference is, a girl polar bear doesn't know any better. She's just a polar bear. She doesn't even really know she's alive. I think women—human beings—have more potential than that; it just takes time to discover it. So if there were something in the constitution that could *change all that*, I would support it."

And then, because everyone was staring, I added, "Thank you."

Ten weeks later we boarded a chartered fishing boat from St. John's Harbour and left the mainland for Mobility.

III. WHAT I DID ON MOBILITY

CHAPTER SEVENTEEN

It's night, and I'm cold as fuck. The man driving the boat hasn't spoken the entire trip. He has a broad back and a fat neck, and he likes to drive fast. Dr. Snow introduced him as Pål from Norway. He's blasting heavy metal on a cassette player that rattles around as the boat skims the waves. There are times when the boat feels airborne. Cold spray crashes all around us. Pål drives with one hand on the polished wood wheel and keeps the other in the back pocket of his jeans, thumb out. The song is all noise. I think it might be the Scorpions. It sounds before my time.

We've been out for forty-five minutes, an hour. Snow thinks we might be halfway there. The moon over the water looks bright, over-bright. Something's wrong with it. It's what the moon will look like once the earth's atmosphere has all burned off and there's nothing left to protect us. It's bright and round and fully three-dimensional—a ball, not a disc—but when the light hits the water it's giggly and girly. It's Star when I tickle her.

As for Star, she's being choked by her life vest. It's a vest instead of a jacket, so it hangs around her neck and sticks out like a crazy orange beard. The adults have life jackets that fit around the arms and snap up the front; there's status in that. My life jacket is glow-in-the-dark chartreuse. It's never been worn before, and my name's on the back in black marker. I can't imagine surviving if I fell overboard, with or without the jacket. The water is dark and cold and empty. There's nothing living in it, just dumb, building-sized mollusks, and it has no bottom.

Snow is screaming in Pål's ear, something about turning on the transducer. I know it's a transducer because there's a steel box near Pål's steering wheel marked TRANSDUCER. I don't know what it does, though. Pål takes his left hand out of his back pocket and flicks a switch on the box. I expect him to be missing at least one finger.

Star wants to pull off her life vest, and I have to tell her three times to leave it on. "It looks good on you," I say. "It makes you look like you've got a weird beard. Don't you want a weird beard?" Wallis is dozing on the floor. For safety reasons he's not in his wheelchair. If the boat flips over we'd all be at an equal disadvantage. We'd all be in the same boat, heh. Mandy is the only one of us who doesn't have her life jacket fastened all the way to the top; instead she leaves the top two fasteners open, casual-style. Her long hair is piled and tucked under a baseball cap that says "Marine Corps Devil Dogs." Her boots are black and come all the way up over her knees.

Snow returns from the front of the boat to sit near Charity. She's dressed for a snowstorm, her hair tied up in a bonnet. She's chewing gum to counteract her motion sickness. She sees me watching her and gives me a toothy smile. Then she says,"You look cold." Wind slices down over the boat and blows off her bonnet. The bonnet whips and flaps; it stays with the boat before finding its courage and peeling away.

Steffi prowls the rear of the craft analyzing weather conditions with a store-bought meteorology kit. She's got a barometer, a fistful of maps and charts. She's got the thing with the cups that spins around. Periodically she returns to report her latest findings. "The atmospheric pressure is dropping," she says urgently, thinking she's being helpful. She considers herself a full-fledged member of the team.

"Duh," I tell her. Steffi is eight years old, a year and a half older than my daughter.

"The relative humidity is at seventy percent," she says.

I cover my mouth with both hands and shudder sarcastically. "We're all going to die."

A bottle of Jameson whiskey circulates back to me. I wipe it off with my sleeve and take a drink. In addition to Pål, Snow, Mandy, Wallis, Charity, Steffi, and Star, four others are on board, two men and two women. I only know their names, and even those I've forgotten. Neil and Sander are leading the other two boats that have also departed for Mobility. We're the last wave; Sander's boat left first, followed ten minutes later by Neil's. If I squint real hard, I can just make out a tiny red light in the distance. I miss those guys. No one in our group really seems in charge.

I consider offering Star a sip of whiskey but don't. She's been nagging me for a juice box ever since we left. "We don't have juice boxes. There's not a single juice box on this boat. If you can find a juice box, you may have it," I say.

She tries flattening her life vest to her stomach but it springs back up when she moves her hand away. "It likes you," I say.

Securing the cap on the Jameson, I walk low to keep my balance and nudge Wallis with the bottle. "How can you sleep?" I ask as he blinks awake.

"I wasn't really. I'm not thirsty," he says.

"It's whiskey. You don't drink it because you're thirsty." I offer it to him again, and this time he takes it. Wallis isn't much of a drinker. I've never seen him intoxicated. Mainly he drinks ginger ale, cold tea, water.

"I have so much to do," he says. I sit next to him, my body turned to keep an eye on Star. Waves bang and roll. My last swig of whiskey feels parked behind my Adam's apple.

"You have nothing to do. We just need to get through this ride without puking. I don't want to throw up. I throw up once and then I can't stop. Constant puking for twenty-four hours," I say.

Wallis closes his eyes and moistens his lips with his tongue.

Mandy hurries to the front of the boat, a pair of binoculars swinging from her neck. I like her boots. They're tight, form-fitting.

Peering through the binoculars, she sings out, "Closer!"

"What time is it? I've lost all sense of time. My watch stopped working—I think I got water in it," I say.

Charity and Snow join Mandy up front, each taking turns with the binoculars. Snow stands between them and puts his arms around their waists. The boat seems to be slowing down. Along with pitching forward, now we're rocking from side to side. Pål isn't at the wheel anymore; he's digging through a storage chest, pulling out ropes, pulleys, and winches and setting them on the floor.

"Apparently no one is driving the boat. That's what I'm getting from this," I say, staggering to my feet for a better look. The wheelhouse—is that what they call it?—is abandoned. The wheel isn't a classic ship's wheel with long handles sticking out at all points. It's just ordinary. It does nothing special except steer the boat.

Pål returns to the wheelhouse with a coil of rope around his arm. We're getting ready to land or dock or whatever. I still can't make out our destination. The mainland disappeared long ago, with nothing that I can see to take its place, just ocean. I watch in amazement as Pål sets down his rope and actually takes the time to flip over the heavy metal cassette and press play before seizing the wheel. The music starts up again and he relaxes back into his job.

I feel a hand on my shoulder. "Want to take a gander?" Mandy asks, passing me the binoculars. They're heavy, huge. They're made for someone else's hands, not mine.

"I'm no good with binoculars. I never know where to look," I say.

She leads me to the front of the boat. I can barely stand. I don't see the point in being on a boat if it sucks so much. The water's violent—it's gnarly. Fish must hate their lives.

Mandy aims the binoculars at a distant point of shaking gray and directs me to look. All I can see inside the binoculars are my own eyelids blinking. Then I spot something. It's black and it's big and it's still so far away.

"Is that it?" I ask, handing back the binoculars.

"That's Mobility. That's your new home."

I close my eyes and can still picture it. I feel like I've seen it somewhere before. The Eiffel Tower—but an ugly Eiffel Tower. A clunky Eiffel Tower. It's steel and concrete and must be tall to loom so high over this empty patch of ocean. Where are we exactly? Think of it like this: you're on a plane en route from New York to London. You've taken off and you've been flying for an hour. The stewardesses are just coming round with their drink cart. Some passengers have already gone to sleep. You're at cruising altitude and you've leafed through the in-flight magazine twice. You're too high up to see anything out the window, just clear atmosphere. Okay: we're down there somewhere.

Star asks for the binoculars. She handles them expertly, even knows how to refocus them. Where did she learn that? Probably from Steffi.

"What do you think, kid?" I ask.

She slowly lowers the binoculars. She looks disappointed—or maybe she's just tired or not feeling well.

"Is it going to be bouncy like this?" she asks.

"What do you mean—is it going to rock back and forth like a boat? No, I don't think so. No, it's too large. It'll be like being on a big cruise ship. Not even that—it'll be like being on an island. Islands don't rock back and forth, and they're big and they're in the middle of the ocean too."

I'm just making things up. I don't know anything about Mobility. I don't know if it rocks and moves around or stays anchored in one place. I wonder how we'll get up to it, if we'll have to climb a ladder or take an elevator.

Snow pops round with a walkie-talkie. "We've just heard from Sander. The first group has arrived. One of the power generators isn't working. We'll need to fix it in the morning."

"What does that mean?" I ask. Star snuggles against my leg.

"It means we'll be running on limited capacity for a few hours. We'll get through it. We'll have flashlights, battery backup. It won't be the last hardship, I'm sure."

"Mom!" Steffi cries across the boat, and we look to see where she's pointing. The visibility's poor but a shape clarifies about a half-mile on the horizon. Suddenly it's there, solitary and huge. It seems to have no interior space, no walls, just an open network of girders like something left unfinished. The structure rises out of the water on enormous, thick piers. Coming a little closer reveals a network of criss-crossing beams, faint auburn light glowing from inside. It's ugly and awesome. I literally, physically, actually, swallow my gum.

"Don't let the appearance fool you. It's quite comfortable on the inside. Plenty of room for all of us. Sleeping quarters for eighty, not that we'll need it at first. Most of the rooms we'll be using have private bathrooms. Two mess halls, both of them

spacious. The communications center is state of the art. The medical wing needs work but it's coming along. By the end of the year we'll have a fully-equipped recreation facility up and running. There'll be a banquet hall for special events, a library, maybe even an aquarium to house some of the local fish species," Snow says. Charity kisses him on his blue cheek.

Pål slows the boat, and Snow yells at him to turn off his music. For the first time I really hear the ocean, waves applauding. The sound is big and constant, lacking contour. The waves break upon themselves.

"What time zone is this?" I ask, but no one answers. Maybe it doesn't matter. It's whatever time zone we say it is.

"Crim, come look," Snow calls back to my brother.

Getting Wallis to his feet takes three of us, Mandy, Pål, and myself. I hold him under his armpits, which are hot and perspiring. I haven't carried him in a long time. I used to be able to do it by myself, when we were kids and I was the only person he'd let near him.

We lean him up against the boat's side rail, Mandy and I holding him by the elbows. His legs dangle down like roots.

"How 'bout it?" I ask, watching his face. His first reaction is important to me.

Before he can answer, his torso buckles and Mandy and I gently set him down. He throws up on his chest, a small, brown puddle. It seems more like an emotional response than a physical one.

"Sorry," he says, "waves got to me."

We clean him up and get him positioned in a chair as the others prepare for disembarking. Mobility is no longer an object on the horizon. There is no horizon anymore; there's just this huge, multi-level contraption ahead of and above us. The support piers rise high up into the sky, and the lower deck casts *everything in shadow. Pål has switched off the engine. We're basically drifting.*

"Remember this moment," Snow speaks from the front of the boat, one foot on top of Pål's storage chest. The wind blows his beard back. "The sounds, the smells. Remember what you thought and felt. You're passing through customs. There are no forms to fill out. You're leaving your old self behind."

"I can feel it," I say. Our voices echo against the underside of the rig. The other two boats are here, tied up and bobbing. The water seems calmer. A white sea bird stands on the edge of a loading dock. It must've flown forever to get here.

Pål helps me onto the dock and goes back to assist the others. I stay out of the way as supplies are unloaded and stacked on the dock, crates labelled FRAGILE and PERISHABLE. The stacks leave a narrow path across the dock to a cargo elevator that will take us up to Deck Three. Ladders also run down from the belly of the rig. Men and women dressed in rain gear transport equipment from the three boats to the elevator. Even Star's pitching in. I should do something to help out but I don't know what.

CHAPTER EIGHTEEN

We'd been on Mobility for a full day before I really started to explore the island. The accommodations were cozy enough as promised. Our room was at least the size of my basement in the Okerfeldts' house, and it had a much better view. According to Snow, our windows faced away from the mainland, which left us with an uninterrupted vista; the whole planet might as well have been engulfed in water. The sun announced itself early, spreading shadows across the waves. From this high up—maybe a hundred feet—we could hear the wind rattling against the dirty, barred windows. I'd tried cleaning the windows with a tissue when I realized most of the grime was on the outside. Along with a couple of chairs, Star and I had a bunk bed, one dresser to store our few belongings, and a tiny bathroom with a sink, toilet, and shower. It was all we needed, really.

Our rooms didn't lock, so we just had to take it on trust that no one would break in and steal our stuff. Every third room on Deck One was unoccupied, and the main hall was silent at night. I'd said hi to a few folks, but most of the thirty-eight people who'd migrated to the island were still strangers to me.

At dinner the second night, I asked a woman who was

eating alone if Star and I could sit with her. The mess hall was a big room with tall ceilings and mint blue floor tiles. The many tables and benches could easily seat close to a hundred, but there were just a few dozen of us. Huge steel light fixtures threw down a harsh yellow light.

The woman lifted her tray and slid over. Like the rest of us, she wore a cobalt blue jumpsuit with red and gold patches that Charity had designed with help from Steffi. The jumpsuits were meant to encourage us to think as a team; we were explorers, settlers, all equal and none better than the rest. The uniforms weren't required but everyone wore them just the same. We'd also been fitted for boots.

"I'm Roseanne," I said, sitting down.

"I can see that," the woman said, eyeing the patch over my right breast. Dinner tonight was frozen fish thawed and cooked in butter. No garnish, no side dish, just rolls. Choice of milk or lemonade.

I glanced down at my name. "Oh, right, I forgot. And you're Cathy," I said, reading "Cathy Oines" from her name patch. "How do you know all these people?"

"My husband worked with Clement at the University of Ottawa. This was before Clem got in trouble with that awful girl. We've known each other for thirty-two years," she said, keeping her head down and her eyes on her food.

"Is your husband... here?" I asked.

She peered up. She had a rugged, orange complexion, long honey blonde hair, and murky blue eyes. "He's dead," she said.

"Oh, I'm sorry."

"He's been dead a long time. He committed suicide. He hung himself."

"That's awful," I said, nervously looking over at Star,

who had her head turned toward the barred, floor-to-ceiling windows and the moon-winking ocean below.

"It happened so long ago that it doesn't even bother me anymore. May 11, 1988. We'd just come to the end of the semester. We had a summer trip planned to Antibes. I found him. He'd hung himself in the basement from a beam under the stairs. I cut him down with my garden shears. He fell with a clunk. I'll never forget that clunk. It sounded like a muffled implosion."

My fish was getting cold. "I can't imagine."

"It's okay. He left a note blaming me for his depression. We owned a summer home on Lake Winnipeg. He was never a happy man. His name was Ronald Oines and he taught ethnomusicology. His students were indifferent to him. He knew this—he even cultivated it. I think in some ways he cherished their indifference."

"That's so sad. Star, eat your dinner."

Cathy smiled grimly and took a bite of her roll. "It's not, really. It happened a lifetime ago. Brian Mulroney was Prime Minister of Canada. I was thirty-seven and Ronnie was forty-one. I wrote a play about it. It was produced at the Toronto Fringe Festival. We got a good review in the *Toronto Star*. The *Globe and Mail* didn't get it."

Desperate for something else to talk about, I said, "So that's what you do? You write plays?"

"Oh, no. I've written a few. It's something I do on the side. Occasionally I've had work produced. *He Raped Me* ran for three weeks in Portland—that's where I moved after Ronnie died. No, I design and build musical instruments, hammered dulcimers mostly." She paused and stared. I had the feeling I'd said or done something wrong.

"Oh, Charity mentioned something about you. That sounds like fun," I said.

"*Fun,* no. Actually it's tedious, back-breaking work. The materials are fragile and expensive. It can take up to six weeks to fill an order. Many times I've been tempted to pack it all in. It's murder on your eyes and fingers. The measurements must be exact to within a half-millimeter." She took a small, bitter sip of her lemonade. "Plus there's the people."

"The people?"

"The handmade dulcimer community is, in general, the most close-minded, superficial, acquisitive, and culturally ignorant group of people I've ever had the 'pleasure' to work with. They're competitive, they're dishonest... there's no spirit of cooperation. And that goes for the people who make the instruments as well as those who play them. And you can't have a rational conversation with any of them because half of them are dyed-in-the-wool libertarians and the other half are so racist and misogynistic..." She shook her head, her voice never rising above a dangerous simmer. "I've had conversations. I've been called *many* things. I've been called 'that dyke.' I've been sued twice, both times without merit. A man cornered me at a convention of string instrument manufacturers in Syracuse and said if he ever saw me on the west coast, he'd 'smash my face in.'"

I'd stopped eating. Star leaned over with her fork and started picking at my fish. "And what did *you* say?" I asked.

"I don't remember but I'm sure it wasn't pleasant. I don't go to those things anymore. There's too much drinking, and the guy who's been running them for the past six years is a real jerk. I hate him." Another sip of lemonade. "I hate that man."

"Why do you still do it if it's so stressful?" I asked, wondering if everyone on the island was as strange as Cathy.

She set down her glass. "I have a responsibility to the art form. Never mind the politics, never mind the bullshit behavior. Dulcimers have been around for over two-thousand years. Without them there'd be no American folk music, no Indian music, no... Persian, Greek, Hungarian, the list goes on. It's one of the basic foundations of world culture. And *that's* why I still do it—because it's *important.*" Her hands were shaking.

The room quieted down as Snow called for attention. He and my brother had their own table near the doors to the kitchen. Neil and an assistant, a thin man with russet-colored skin, came out of the kitchen to listen.

Snow stood, looked around the room, and smoothed his beard. "A few announcements, if you don't mind. I know the past day has been pretty hectic, and the weather hasn't helped. We've got enough rations to last through the week. If you haven't met our head cook, Neil Laporte, you should introduce yourself. The man standing next to him is Gavin Baptiste, Neil's assistant. Neil needs three or four good men or women to help him catch some fish in the morning. Neil, what boat are you taking? Mandy One?"

"If the outboard's working," Neil said.

"I have made the necessary repairs," Sander answered. The other three men at Sander's table had their heads down, vigorously shoveling in food as they half-listened.

"Thank you, Sander. We appreciate the help. So if anyone's interested in being on Neil's team, meet him down at Mandy One unless that information changes," Snow said.

"We leave at sunup," Neil said, then went back into the kitchen with Gavin.

Snow continued with his announcements. The lift in Block Alpha would be out of service for another twenty-four hours. Don't use the common-area bathrooms on Deck Two until further notice. People ate and listened and sometimes raised their hands with questions.

"Yes, Cathy?" Snow asked, calling on the woman at my table.

"When's the next cargo transport back to the mainland? All of my things are still in storage," Cathy said.

Snow nodded. "Our pilot—has everyone met Benoît?" Heads turned as a smiling, bald man rose in his seat and stiffly sat back down. "Benoît knows a helipad in Mount Pearl where we can land off-hours, but it's weekdays only."

Benoît interrupted with something long-winded and entirely in French.

"Week*ends* only," Snow clarified, "between midnight and six, then the regular security takes over. It's not the most convenient but it's quicker than going by boat. Do you have a lot of stuff, Cath?"

"I have my entire workshop, all of my tools—*yes*, it's a lot of stuff. These are complicated musical instruments. I can't build them out of thin air. I need my drills, my saws... *hand* saws, coping saws," Cathy said.

"We'll make sure you get everything you need—if not this week, definitely next week. Talk to Benoît." He smiled at the rest of us. "Is there anything else?"

Mandy stood. "Just to follow up from last night, a number of people have been complaining about flu-like symptoms, coughs and runny nose and low-grade fever. We don't know if this is a virus or just seasonal allergies, but until we *do* know, protective masks are available in the medical wing on Deck Two. I'm requiring anyone with these symptoms to wear their masks until I've determined a correct course of action. This is a closed environment, people—we're all breathing the same air. By the way, Benoît will be flying in a supply of flu vaccines sometime next week. I have a sign-up sheet in my office if anyone still needs their shots."

We finished our dinners, and a few of us went into the kitchen to help Neil with the dishes. Not everyone had an assigned job yet. Our numbers included two electricians, two carpenters, a seamstress, and a handful of teachers, accountants, and mechanics. Everyone was expected to do a little bit of everything.

After dinner I tucked Star into her top bunk. I stood on the bunk bed's ladder and kissed her forehead. "You're pretty close to the ceiling," I noticed. The ceiling was steel and painted pale yellow.

"I don't mind. What're those?" she asked, pointing up.

"Those? Those are rivets. They keep the ceiling together."

Her eyes studied the rivets. She'd never really taken an interest in mechanical things before. "How long are we going to stay here?"

Her light brown hair looked gray in this light, and I brushed it out of her eyes. "I don't know. Maybe not long. Let's just try to take it one day at a time."

"I like it."

"You do? How do you know? We just got here."

"I want to stay here forever and ever."

I cringed inside. "What about Daddy? Don't you want to see your daddy again?" She shrugged, and I withdrew my hand. "What do you mean? I'm sure he wants to see you."

Her lips tightened. I sensed her not wanting to upset me, or at least not hurt my feelings. "Do you know how deep the water is here? Twelve hundred feet. It's even deeper farther out. Sander told me. He also said there are places where the ocean floor drops away thousands of feet all at once."

I shivered. "I could've done without that information, kid. I didn't even like swimming in the big kids' pool back home in Milner. Anyway, I'll be right back. I think I need a Motrin or a Tylenol or something."

I left her in bed and walked down the hall to get something for my headache. What I really needed was a chardonnay. The infirmary looked closed, so I tried the kitchen where Neil was busy organizing supplies in the pantry. He'd unzipped his jumpsuit, and I could see his white T-shirt and a thin gold chain around his neck.

"Don't you have to get up early tomorrow?" I asked, gazing at the steel counters and white tile walls. Boxes marked COFFEE and POWDERED MILK lined the pantry, while others still hadn't been put away: OATMEAL, SALT. No FRANZIA WHITE MERLOT, unfortunately.

He rested a heavy-looking box on the counter. "I do, but I also have to get this kitchen up and running. We can't always wing it like we did tonight."

"I liked my fish," I lied.

He smiled like he didn't believe me and lugged the box the rest of the way to the pantry, heaving as he set it down. "Why are bread crumbs so heavy? They're like bowling balls. They look innocuous enough. I mean, *one* bread crumb is nothing. A hundred. A thousand. At some point they turn into iron pellets."

"I can help," I offered.

He set the box on the shelf so that the label, RYE BREAD CRUMBS, faced out. "I'm okay. This is why I stay in shape. Were you looking for something?"

I asked about the Tylenol. "I can't decide if I have a headache or not. I think I do."

"If it's here, I haven't unearthed it yet. Maybe you just need some fresh air."

Helping myself to a packet of saltines, I complained, "Where am I going to find that?"

He pointed up. "Haven't you been above deck? Plenty of fresh air there."

I hadn't even thought to go outside. For some reason I'd thought the top level was off limits.

"Here," he said, zipping up his jumpsuit, "I'll go with you. I could use a break."

He led me down the hall to the elevator and hit the button for the top floor. The elevator was more of a steel cage than an actual compartment. It surged and stopped, surged and stopped, ancient parts groaning. A single light flickered and dimmed. "I've been in worse, believe it or not. Try the Radisson on Huron Road in downtown Cleveland," he said.

Finally the doors opened on the top deck, and a strong gust blew us back. Neil yelled, "Over here," and we ran behind an observation shed that kept some of the wind at bay. We sat with our backs to the corrugated steel wall.

"Pretty impressive, isn't it?" he said.

"I just hope we don't blow off," I said. The helipad looked wide and long enough to land a commercial plane, and a tall crane loomed on the other side. The ocean churned far below us, matching the color if not the texture of the night sky. A pair of red and white lights blinked in the distance.

"What're those lights?" I asked.

"Probably a ship. I don't think it's the mainland."

The blinking wasn't rapid but steady enough to pick up a rhythm. "So we're not *completely* isolated," I said.

"No, not completely. There's always an escape hatch if you need it. Talk to Benoît and he'll have you back in St. John's by morning. I'll bet a third of us won't last the month."

"Me included?"

He nodded, and we both laughed. "You're probably right," I said. "I'm not really the 'last-one-standing' type. But you never know, I might surprise myself. And Star likes it here, so I owe it to her to try. I've done so much to fuck up her life. She could be at home with Josh and her grandparents, going to school in Grand Rapids, playing soccer with her friends. That's what I did when I was her age, played soccer... before I got into other things."

Neil wedged his hands between his legs to keep them warm. "Were you any good at it?"

"Not really. I don't even remember if I scored any points. I just liked taking the ball away from the other girls."

Something moved near the crane, and a figure emerged swinging a flashlight. "There's Sander. He must be on patrol," Neil said, waving to get Sander's attention.

"He sure takes this security thing seriously, doesn't he?" I asked.

"That's good. We really don't know what to expect out here. It's a dangerous environment. Always best to assume the worst."

"And what's the worst?"

"The same problems facing any new country. Internal collapse, threats from the outside. There's a lot of valuable equipment on this rig. Someone might want to steal it."

Sander crossed the helipad and drew back the hood of his rough weather parka. He had a gun strapped to his hip.

"I have secured the perimeter. I don't anticipate any trouble tonight," he said.

Neil offered him some chewing gum, which Sander took. "We were wondering what those lights were," Neil said.

Sander assessed the lights on the horizon. "It's probably a freighter from Sweden or the Netherlands. Pirates tend to travel in darkness. We're fortunate; we don't have the problems other countries like Somalia face. We'll be safe as long as no one knows we're here."

"Where'd you get the gun?" I asked. I'd never held a gun or even seen one fired except on TV.

"The munitions shed in Block Delta. Neil, you should arm yourself as well. Take Pål with you when you go out in the morning. I have spoken with him. His English is limited but he has experience in the Norwegian Special Forces." He stopped chewing and frowned. "What is this gum?"

"Doublemint," Neil said innocently.

Sander accepted this answer and went back on patrol. Neil and I watched him pace out to the edge of the deck and come back. "Does Sander have any brothers or sisters?" I asked.

"I don't know much about him. He's hard to have a conversation with. Everything comes out stilted. He once gave me a gift basket from Hickory Farms for Christmas. He's a good guy. I like him."

"I like him too. I don't like guns, though. Have you ever shot a gun?"

"Only recreationally—target practice. I don't hunt."

"Good. Ugh. My husband hunts—my soon-to-be-ex. I like eating meat but I don't like killing."

"You're like most people, then."

The wind reached around the observation shed, and I scooted a few inches on my butt to sit closer to him. "Sorry," I laughed, "am I cramping your style?"

"It's fine. Close quarters."

I thought it might be nice if he put his arm around me, just as a friendly gesture. We'd known each other for nearly a year now. I'd been eating his cooking for months. What would be the harm? It didn't mean I had to sleep with him. But then I changed my mind. I'd been through all that before—you're sitting close to a guy and pretty soon your hand's on his leg and he's brushing a lock of your hair behind your ear and telling you how much you look like Sandra Bullock. It was nice but not for me.

"I need to get back to my daughter," I said.

Neil rose first and helped me stand. "Thanks for the break."

"Any time. I'd go fishing with you tomorrow but I don't want to leave Star behind."

"Good excuse," he said, following me into the elevator. The carriage rode smoother on the way down. We both got off on Deck One, and I realized that he was walking me back to my room.

"She's probably asleep. Where's your room?" I asked, peering down the hall. We were whispering; it felt like being in a hotel.

"Down on Two," he said. We'd paused next to my open door.

"Oh, that's so far away! No, it isn't. But I suppose it's closer to your work." We snickered, and I covered my mouth. "Listen to us—we sound like we just moved to a new town. Do you have any roommates?" He shook his head. "Lucky. Not that Star's a roommate. What're you going to do with all that extra space?"

"Whatever I want. That's why we're here, isn't it? To do whatever we want." His beard smiled. It needed a pet name, like Horst.

"I guess. It depends who you ask."

I had my back to the door, and he rested his open palm on the wall near my head. "And why are *you* here?" he asked.

Because I don't know where else to go. "A little adventure," I said randomly. In my mind I looked sexy and confident.

A moment later he was apologizing for kissing me. The cold had gone from my cheeks, and I could still feel his beard on my lips.

"I have a daughter," I said.

"I know." His eyes were troubled chocolate.

"A daughter who's nearly seven." I kissed him again. "I'm just saying it's a bad idea."

"Columbus was a bad idea. The law of gravity was a bad idea," he said.

"No they weren't. They weren't even ideas. They were just... things that happened." One more kiss. Kissing a beard was like being kissed a thousand extra times. "I'm sorry, I'm stupid. I'm, I'm—are we tipping? Is the building shaking?" I clutched the wall. "No, I'm imagining things. I'm just tired. I still don't have my—what's it called? When you're not used to being on a boat?" I snapped my fingers twice.

He looked confused. "Sea legs?"

"That's it. I don't have my sea legs yet."

"But we're not on a boat. That's different."

"Is it? *Is* it now? *Very* interesting. Ah-ha." Seizing his head, I kissed him and pushed him so forcefully away that he stumbled back on his heels. "You're not thinking carefully, Neil. You're going to wake up a different person."

I went into my room, leaving him out in the hall. My first thought was to check on Star. Creeping to the bunk ladder, I stood on the second rung and placed my hand on her mattress. Nothing stirred. Good, I thought. Just to make sure, I climbed another step and peered over the edge. The room seemed darker near the ceiling. I couldn't see much, just brown darkness. The blankets rose in folds and piles. I reached out to touch her pillow.

"Star... Star?" Nothing under the pillow either. The bed was empty.

I called across the room. No Star. She wasn't hiding out by the windows and she wasn't sitting in one of the chairs and she wasn't stuck to the ceiling for whatever weird reason.

I nearly fell hurrying down from the ladder, banging into the dresser with my hip. The bathroom door was open. The lights were off and I turned them on. My reflected face and hair were a terror in the mirror.

Whirling around, I smashed into something hard, a chair. With my arms out, I raced toward the door. Neil had made it about twenty yards down the hall.

"Neil!"

He turned and held his arms open, like *what?* I ran into him.

"Star's gone, she was in the bed when I went out and now she's gone."

"She can't have gone far. Maybe she's looking for you," he said.

"No," I answered categorically.

"Why not?"

Heads stuck out of doorways to investigate the commotion in the hall.

"I don't know why not. *No*, though. Someone's taken her. One of those pirates Sander was talking about. It's my fault, I let it happen, *I* dragged her out here."

A man with a sleepy head leaned out of his room. "Should we raise the alert status to Code Yellow?" he asked.

"Are you kidding? My daughter is *missing*. That's not Code Yellow, that's Code Red."

"There is no Code Red," the man said.

"Are you sure? There's always a Code Red."

The man touched his cheek, his lips, his forehead. "I don't believe there is a Code Red."

"Well no offense, but you don't look like you know what you're talking about."

"We're not raising the alert status to anything. Let's check the other levels first," Neil said.

We ran off down the hall, taking the stairs to Deck Two. I called out, "Star? Sarah?" as more people came out of their rooms, some still wearing their jumpsuits, others in regulation Mobility blue-and-red PJs. In my panic I recognized Pål, Benoît, and one of the married couples from the boat.

Cathy Oines, the hammered dulcimer lady, waddled up in her bare feet. I asked if she'd seen my daughter.

"Which one's your daughter?" she asked.

"We were sitting with you at dinner. Little girl, six years old, light brown hair. She sat right next to you. You were telling us about your play and your husband and the guy from Syracuse who punched you in the mouth. Nothing, huh? *That* forgettable?"

"He didn't punch me in the mouth. He threatened to. I would've kicked him in the balls otherwise."

In halting English, Benoît suggested, "You might try... the control bridge. A possibility? I saw your brother there an hour ago."

I nodded vigorously. Any idea sounded like a good idea to me. "Where is it? I don't know where anything is around here."

"I know where it is," Neil said, starting back up the hall. Benoît and I came along. Benoît looked nearly naked in his thin, loose-fitting pajamas.

"I had a dream this would happen. I have the gift of prophecy. It's nothing—it's more an annoyance than anything else," he said.

We turned left down a sub-corridor, Neil in the lead. "If you have the gift of prophecy, you should be able to tell me where my daughter is," I said.

"It doesn't work like that. It's not exactly prophecy, more like vivid dreaming. I dreamed the attack on the World Trade Center five years before it happened. Usually the information in my dreams is so vague as to be entirely unhelpful. Women screaming, women weeping. A man doubled-over in pain... but this could mean anything."

A ramp continued down the sub-corridor. I couldn't

imagine Star coming this far on her own. The floors were steel mesh, and I could see straight through to the deck below us.

"Why would she wander off like this?" I asked.

"Curiosity. She's a young girl. She wants to explore," Neil said.

The corridor swung around again at the bottom of the ramp and emptied into a dark, broad room. Tall, hulking racks of computer equipment stood in rows, some with red lights blinking. Cooling fans made a low rumble.

"I think we've found our princess," said Neil, moving toward the sound of voices. I wasn't scared anymore. Now I was just angry.

Snow's blue voice greeted us: "Hello Roseanne. Your daughter couldn't sleep so we're showing her how to change the temperature settings on Deck One."

He waved us over to where he sat with Star, Mandy, and my brother in front of a bank of computers. The moonlight outside the barred windows was slug gray.

Star barely acknowledged me. They'd given her a baseball cap with 'Mobility' on it. "Hi Mom," she said.

"Hi Mom nothing. You scared me to death. Take off that hat and let's go back to bed. Why are you playing with those buttons? You'll break something and then we'll all be sorry."

"I'm not *playing* with them, I'm monitoring stuff."

"Oh, what stuff."

"Important stuff. Dr. Snow and Mandy and Uncle Wallis showed me. Besides, it's your fault because you left and didn't come back and I waited for like forever because I wanted to tell you something but you didn't come back and I couldn't fall asleep and so I came here and that's what happened."

"Do you know what you sound like when you whine like that? Like a jerk."

"No I don't."

"You sound like an unpleasant person. I don't want you ever coming in here again—at least not without telling me first. *Ask*, not tell. You ask and then I'll say yes or no."

Mandy playfully tugged at the brim of Star's hat. "Sounds like Mom knows best."

"Yes I do! Not always. Sometimes I'm wrong but this time I'm right. What are you guys drinking? Is that wine? Is that white wine? Where'd you get white wine?"

"Would you like some wine, Roseanne?" Smiling, Mandy set down her plastic cup and opened a small refrigerator at her feet. Snow had a glass as well. Star was drinking what looked like soda water.

"Not right now. Well, maybe half a glass. I'll take a small glass but then we're going." As Star sulked, Mandy poured me a glass of wine. The wine was sweet and thin but it soothed my nerves. "What else have you got stashed up here?"

"We're not hiding anything. There's wine and some good cheese and liver pâté from home. Help yourself. No one owns anything on Mobility," Snow said expansively.

I glanced inside the refrigerator. "It doesn't look like there's enough to share with everyone."

"Oh... probably not," he said in a humoring tone, and I thought about the milk and lukewarm lemonade we'd had with dinner.

Lights on a computer console flashed, and a calm bell sounded.

"What's happening?" I asked.

Snow tapped a button to switch off the alarm. "Marine radar. It'll eventually be able to tell us when there's a boat in the area. It needs fine-tuning, though. The system's not able to distinguish between large shapes. That signal might be a fishing vessel or a chunk of ice or even a big shark or a whale."

"Cool!" Star said.

I sipped my wine. "It's not a shark," I said.

Finishing my drink, I hustled Star out of the room, letting her keep her baseball cap as a souvenir. Neil came with us. I thought about our kiss in the hall. I hadn't kissed anyone other than Josh in many, many years. I liked Neil—his neat hairiness. I wanted to French kiss him in a dark closet, to feel him inside me, to write a screenplay together.

"What kind of name is Benoît?" I asked as we climbed the stairs to Deck One.

"French. Actually, Benoît's from Belgium. He's part of Snow's old crew. I think they might date back to Toronto. Snow used to be more involved in managing his investments, and Benoît worked for him for a time. He'd fly Snow to meetings, drive his cars, keep the gas tanks filled. Kind of like Sander, but with less personality," said Neil.

"And with E.S.P. Didn't he tell you? He's got 'the gift of prophecy.' He predicted 9/11."

"He did? I guess I missed that part."

Star pushed open the door at the top of the stairs and charged ahead with a raucous cheer. I hissed after her, "Star! There are people *sleeping*."

She pulled up short midway down the hall and dragged her feet. Neil and I followed at our slower, adult pace. "She's just excited," he said.

We walked in tired silence, two pairs of black boots. I bumped into him and apologized. "I have trouble walking in a straight line. It's an inner ear thing. Also, one of my legs is slightly shorter than the other."

"I have occasional tinnitus," he said.

"You do? I had eczema growing up."

"I have an overactive hair follicle on my right shoulder."

"That's not so bad. I have ugly feet. My *feet* are okay, it's the ankles. They're fat. They're *almost* fankles."

Star reached the door to our room, gave me a mopey look, and went in. I stopped Neil with my hand. "Hey, thanks for putting up with me tonight. I'm always in the middle of some big mess. But it was nice hanging out with you and taking a tour of the place. I feel like I've seen about ten percent of it," I said.

"You're not missing much. It's just a bunch of halls and stairways."

I looked around and overhead: walls and ceilings with exposed plumbing, the gray paint slopped on. "It's got potential, I guess. I've seen worse."

"You belong here," he suggested.

"We all do."

His arms dropped around my waist, and he asked what I was thinking.

"Oh, I just worry," I said, "about my brother, mostly. I still can't figure it out. I mean, here we are, and Wallis is supposed to be our president, and it seems like Snow's the one who calls all the shots."

"That's how it always is, isn't it? You're American, you know that. Bush and Cheney... what's another example?"

We both thought about it. We couldn't think of another example.

"Bush and Cheney, though," I said encouragingly.

"That's right. There's the guy out front and the one behind the scenes."

"But doesn't the guy out front usually get shot?"

"Bush didn't."

"No, but JFK did. Who was *his* Dick Cheney?" I asked.

Neil chewed on his lip. His beard between his teeth made a little rustling noise, like *tthhhzzzpp*.

"You know what? I really don't know anything about U.S. history," he admitted.

We kissed sloppy for about three minutes, maybe less. Long enough to hear almost any Beatles song once. Then we said good night.

"I'm gonna get it when I get home," I said.

Back in my room, I took one last peek at Star to make sure she was still there. She was—asleep, or pretending to. The rivets inches above her head seemed to support an immense weight. I slept in my boots that night.

CHAPTER NINETEEN

As those first days passed, I tried giving Star a little more freedom. I let her watch as Snow and his technical advisors worked on getting the island's communications system online. New words started to creep into her vocabulary, like "interface" and "override." Each morning I dropped her off at the control bridge and picked her up again around four to play with her friends. Two other kids lived on Mobility in addition to Star and Steffi: a girl named Ada, who was eight, and a fourteen-year-old boy with the geriatric-sounding name of Walter Sachs. All the parents were either separated, divorced, or (in Charity's case) divorced and remarried.

Charity and I met with the other two mothers in the mess hall one afternoon to talk about setting up some kind of organized school for the kids. Neil was out fishing with his team, so we made our own coffees and sat at one of the cafeteria tables in the high-ceilinged room.

"Walter's a quick learner," said his mother, Beverly. Her son was pale, quiet, and small, unlike Beverly herself, who was a beanpole with red hair. "English is his weak subject. Mainly he's mechanically inclined—but that's okay, I don't push him to do well in everything. That was part of the problem with his father, why we divorced. There's nothing wrong with being one-dimensional."

"Oh, God, no. I think it's healthy. I wish my Stephanie were more one-dimensional," said Charity.

"*I'm* not one-dimensional. Women frequently aren't. Walter was at the top of his class in physics and trigonometry before I pulled him out of school—and that's the end of my bragging."

We laughed. Ada's mother, Paulette, hadn't done much but glance around the room and grin irrelevantly whenever the conversation perked up.

"Why'd you take him out of school?" I asked.

"Because of the public schools in Nashua. Walter got bullied a lot—this whole family of horrible kids, the Dietzes. Johnny Dietz, Bobby Dietz, Ronnie Dietz. Even the girl, Joan, was awful. Bobby's in jail now."

"There are no Dietzes here, so don't worry about that," said Charity.

"And that's when you met Dr. Snow?" I asked.

"Oh, no. Clem was my teacher back in college. Life-changing class. My second favorite professor, though no one could touch Mrs. Lane. I had her for 'Theater of the Absurd'. *She* was phenomenal. She had an aura. She owned race cars and had a black belt and knew Warren Beatty and then she died of complications from MS," Beverly said.

"What's 'Theater of the Absurd'?" asked Paulette.

Beverly gritted her teeth. "You know, Beckett, Ionesco, Jean Genet. Those guys. It's not worth talking about."

"I knew someone who had MS. Horrible. But it's not as bad as some things," said Charity.

"It's bad enough. What's worse than fatal? I've been lucky, I've never been sick. My mother died of throat cancer and my father had three heart attacks between the ages of fifty-seven and seventy-three before the last one killed him." Beverly took another sip of coffee and spilled some of it setting the cup back down. "Anyway, we're here and I'm happy, and I'm very happy for our children who won't have to worry about things like bullies or peer pressure or Ronnie Dietz pulling you off your bike and *spitting* on you and then telling everyone in the sixth grade that you went to the bathroom in your pants-"

"He didn't," said Charity.

"-and when we went to the principal about it, he told us, '*Weh-ull*, you shouldn't associate with those people, and what are you doing talking to Ronnie Dietz anyway, you're just asking for trouble.'"

"That's helpful," I said, somehow knowing that all future conversations with Beverly Sachs would involve her mentioning the Dietz brothers at least once.

The discussion gradually turned to gossip, with the four of us comparing notes on the island's other inhabitants. We all agreed that Pål seemed the most likely person to lose his temper. Beverly didn't especially trust Yvonne Baker, our IT expert, though she couldn't say why. Paulette had already disagreed with Cathy Oines about the common area on Deck One.

"She wants to turn it into a music studio. I think we should use it as a research library. I'm going to have to say something to Dr. Snow about it," Paulette said.

"Cathy is a brilliant woman—a brilliant playwright and a brilliant musician... but yes, hard to get along with," Charity said diplomatically.

"What about the men?" asked Beverly.

"What about them? I'm not interested in men. I came here to get away from *all that*," said Paulette.

"All what? We're just talking. Besides, if we're really serious about building a new life here, someone's got to..." Beverly made a lewd hand gesture.

"What's that mean? Does that mean sex?" Charity asked as Beverly just smiled.

"Yes, Charity, she means sex. Though I'm happy to leave that to the married couples. How old are the Fosters? They look like they're still in their thirties," said Paulette.

"Curtis is thirty-eight, Wendy is a little older," said Charity.

"Young enough," Beverly said.

Paulette turned to me. "What about you, Rosie? You're one of the youngest ones here."

The others stared. Of the three, only Charity knew about my other kids back home.

"Not me. I've already done my damage," I said.

The clock over the kitchen door clicked to indicate the top of the hour. Charity gathered our empty cups. "I expect Neil and the boys will be back soon. Good talk, girls. Let's include the kids next time. It's *their* school, they should help with the planning."

The meeting dispersed, and I headed straight for the bridge. It was early to fetch Star but I had nothing else to do for the next hour and no one to talk to. Mid-afternoons were always quiet on Mobility, with most of the islanders busy at their self-assigned tasks. I missed Neil. We hadn't progressed much since that night in the hallway. In between his fishing trips on Mandy One and the daily chore of cooking for thirty-eight people, we hardly saw each other, which was fine. Our few conversations had been friendly, short, and in the presence of at least two other people.

Down the sub-corridor, I descended the by-now-familiar ramp to the bridge. The usual five people were there: Snow, Wallis, Benoît, Yvonne Baker, and Star. The room looked neater, which suggested progress. Fewer cables littered the floor, and three giant storage cabinets had completed their weeklong journey from one end of the room to the other.

Wallis sat at the main computer console holding a ringed binder in his lap. Looking up from his work, he reached for a steaming mug. "Is it four yet?"

"Three. I'm a little early. Looks like you've been rearranging furniture," I said.

"Oh, that..." He glanced at the storage cabinets. "Sander did that this morning."

I joined him at the console, careful not to disturb Star who was having something on a computer explained to her by Snow. "What are you drinking? Is that beef boullion? That's not all you've had to eat today, is it?" I asked.

"No, I've had other things," Wallis said.

"What else?"

"Well... for breakfast I had some oatmeal, and then for lunch I enjoyed a little cup of pudding. Vanilla pudding. It was good. The consistency was firm and silky. I ate it all up."

"Asshole. At least have a real dinner."

Benoît, who'd been working with some tools deep inside the guts of the room's electrical wiring, stuck his head out of a wall panel. "I have fixed the splice. You should be able to power it up again."

"That's what you said last time," said Yvonne. She was a thin, athletic woman with short hair and gangly limbs; high-energy, constantly jazzed-up about one thing or another; always head-banging or playing air-bass to the music inside her head.

Emerging from the wall, Benoît stood aside to show her his handiwork. She peered at the wiring, nodded once with satisfaction, then tickled his armpits.

"Ow! I hate when you do that!" he screamed.

"Yeah? You do, do you? You don't like this? You don't like this?"

The tickling continued as Benoît laughed and squirmed and backed against the wall. "Please, no! Stop tickling me! Stop tickling me! I *hate* it!"

"You don't look like you hate it to me," she said, working her hands deeper under his arms as he bucked and screeched and thrashed about. Finally he managed to extract himself and fled to the middle of the room. Wallis sipped his boullion.

Breathing heavily, Benoît said to Yvonne, "It's really intolerable. Do not ever do that again. This is an assault on my dignity, and it's unprofessional, and I will not stand for it any longer."

She giggled lightly and clapped her hands. "Benoît, you're awesome. Seriously, really good work. Okay, people, let's power up bank two and see what happens."

"Excuse me, you're not listening. Clem, Wallis, am I right? This is the third—*fourth* time today. Twice in one *hour*. It's just not acceptable. Never was I treated like this... in Antwerp... at University of Ghent."

"Yvonne, stop tickling Benoît. He obviously doesn't like it," Wallis said.

"Aw, it's affectionate! Benoît, I'm sorry, I won't do it again. Come on back, buddy," promised Yvonne.

Not budging at first, he reluctantly hobbled back to the group, stopping a few feet short.

"I will remain here," he said.

"No prob. Like I say, kudos on the patch job. What kind of a splice did you use there?"

He swallowed. "I used a braided-"

She jumped at him, jabbing and thrusting and lifting him off his feet. "You used a what? What was that?"

He wept with laughter as he fended her off. "Please... you can't... you can't..."

"I can't what? I can't do this?"

Benoît squealed in falsetto. "I hate it, you hell-fucking... *Ow!*"

Wallis said, "Come on, Yvonne. Not cool, okay?"

The tickling subsided, and Benoît stormed out of the room. "He'll be back. It's near quittin' time anyway," Yvonne said.

"Don't piss him off. We need Benoît. He's the only one who can fly the helicopter, for one thing," Wallis said.

Yvonne flicked a switch on the console, and a row of computer screens lit up. "Praise be," she said.

"Are we back online?" Snow asked.

"Let's find out." She settled in front of one of the computers and entered a flurry of commands. The screen responded with data vomit before going dark.

"Come on, bitch," she said, cracking her knuckles. A browser window opened, and she punched the air with her fist. "That's what I'm talking about! Benoît, you're a genius."

Snow drew closer in his chair. "Is the cloaking activated?"

"Let me see." A few more keystrokes. "Looks it. We're in stealth mode."

Wallis tested the new system as Yvonne leaned back in

her chair, air-bass-ing and singing the chorus to "Paradise City" by Guns N' Roses.

"What's stealth mode?" I asked.

"It's means we're untraceable. As long as the cloak is up, we can use the Net without giving our location away," said Wallis.

"And why is that a good thing?"

Wallis typed and stared, typed and stared.

"It's just a temporary precaution. We'll be able to relax our outgoing communications once we've better established ourselves on the island," said Snow.

"Once we've finalized our constitution, once we've..." Wallis looked away from the screen. "Yvonne, can you stop singing that song *right in my ear?*"

"You don't like my Guns? Aw, my Guns are my babies." She mimed unplugging her air-bass and threw it to Star, who caught it.

"So I'd be able to email my family... my mom and dad... and let them know we're okay?" I asked.

"Of course, Roseanne. Go right ahead," Snow said, pointing me toward an available computer.

I sat in front of the screen for a while, thinking what to write. It'd been weeks since I'd been in touch with my parents. As far as they knew, we were still in St. John's living with Wallis and hiding out from Pam. I certainly couldn't tell them the truth about Mobility—they'd freak. Mom had always encouraged me, even when I was very little, to tell the truth, but then she'd get mad at me for telling. She didn't want the truth, really. She just wanted the truth to be different.

Not bothering to check the sixty gazillion messages in my Inbox, I wrote:

"Dear Mom and Dad, it's Roseanne. I hope you're both

well. Sarah's here and we're staying with Wallis, who says hi. Everyone is safe and healthy. You have nothing to worry about. Sarah's going to an alternative school where she's learning all sorts of interesting things. Her vocabulary is insane! Anyway, thanks for being so patient and understanding, and for being on my side." The last part was mainly wishful thinking.

I clicked 'Send,' not knowing what I expected by way of response; just to hear that everyone was alive and doing well, and people weren't mad anymore. I wanted to know my dad was still walking to church every Sunday.

When it was time to leave, I collected Star and waited at the door as she said her goodbyes to Snow, Wallis, and Yvonne. On our way upstairs, I asked what she'd learned today. "Miss Baker and Dr. Snow taught me how to read a sonar screen," she said.

"They did? And that's going to come in handy… when?"

She stared up into her bangs, so I tried a different approach.

"What do you think about this Yvonne person?" I asked.

"She's nice. She's smart."

"Yeah, but is she cool?"

"I guess. Why?"

"I don't know. I just want to know what cool is."

We reached our room, and I sat on my bunk to take off my boots. Star went straight up to her bed and flumped down on the mattress.

"Hey," I said, "listen to what *I* did today. I had a very important meeting. You remember Mrs. Sachs? And Ada's mom, Paulette—the one with the fuzzy hair? Well, she and I and Mrs. Sachs and Mrs. Blaise talked about it, and we're going to set up a little school for you and Steffi and Ada and that boy, Walter. What do you think about that?"

"I don't want to go to school."

"Oh? Why don't you want to go to school?"

"I already go to school—with Uncle Wallis and Miss Baker and Dr. Snow."

I lay back in bed. "That's not really *school*, Star."

"Why not?"

"Well, you don't learn anything, that's why."

"I learn tons of things. Ask Uncle Wallis. He and Benoît and Dr. Snow are teaching me all about computers. I know how to reboot the mainframe if the power goes down."

"That's great, but it's different from having a well-rounded education. There are other things you've gotta know. You gotta know math, you gotta know English, you gotta know how chemistry works and physics and Earth Science."

"Who's gonna teach me that?"

"*I* will. Me and Mrs. Sachs and the other women. There are some pretty smart ladies on this island, Star. Don't be such a snob." I kicked the bottom of her bed. "You're gonna get a real education here, I promise. Good as you would back home. We're going to do long division and algebra and read *Animal Farm* and *A Tale of Two Cities* and a collection of Kurt Vonnegut short stories... and we'll even do plays! Aw, that's a great idea. We'll start a theater group. I did theater when I was a girl... older than you. I was just on the stage crew but we did *The Sound of Music* and *You're a Good Man, Charlie Brown* and a bunch of other shows. You could be Snoopy. You wanna be Snoopy? Snoopy's a good part. I don't think you're right for Lucy."

More moping silence. "I don't want to go to school."

I sighed and turned toward the wall. "Well, I got news

for you, kid: no one wants to go to school at your age. I sure as heck didn't. I was a smart girl just like *you*, but I was a punk and a troublemaker and didn't care about anyone or anything but myself. You wanna be like that? You wanna be like your miserable old mom?" She didn't answer, so I nudged her bed again. "What are you doing up there? You're not saying anything."

"I'm listening," she yelled.

"All right. Don't yell."

"I'm yelling because you're yelling."

"Okay, I'm not yelling anymore. And I don't think I was yelling before. I just don't see what's wrong with going to school during the day, and then you can spend as much time as you'd like with Uncle Wallis and the rest. Fair enough?"

Her voice came muffled through a pillow. "Fine."

She sounded like she wanted to be alone, so I rested my eyes for a minute, then went down to dinner by myself. The people on the island ate in shifts, the first group at five and the other at six-thirty. As a first-shifter, I always tried to clean up after myself. Nothing worse than sitting down to a bunch of crumbs.

I arrived early to find Neil wiping off the table tops from the late lunch.

"Do you want me to wait outside?" I asked, standing in the doorway.

He wadded up his dishrag and threw it into a bucket. "Uh, *yeah*, Roseanne, I want you to wait outside. Don't be silly. The door's always open."

I paused at the first aid poster on the wall. A prone figure illustrated what to do in the event of a choking. "Have you ever seen a person choke?" I asked.

"No, thank God."

"Me neither. How would you go on eating? That's what I don't get. You're in a restaurant and someone chokes and it's awful and everyone's screaming—and even if the person doesn't *die*, then what? Do they close the restaurant?"

"I doubt it. Why would they?"

"Because it's so upsetting. *I* wouldn't be able to eat. I think I'd just sit there with my head in my hands and ask for the check."

"You never know. Maybe you wouldn't. And I can tell you from experience that it takes a lot to close down a restaurant. I was working at an Asian fusion restaurant on September 11th. We stayed open that whole week, and people still came in."

"Not me. I would've been too upset," I said, drifting away from the poster on the wall.

"They *were* upset. But people need to eat. We even tried turning off the TV in the lounge but the customers made us switch it back on again. They wanted to see."

"While eating."

"While eating, while drinking at the bar… sure. Why not?"

We sat at a table. "I guess my stomach's just super-sensitive to things like that. What's Asian fusion?"

He explained it to me, and it made a kind of abstract sense.

"So you've worked in a lot of restaurants?" I asked.

"Over the years. Everywhere from Pizza Hut to the steakhouse in the Park Hyatt Toronto. But I've done other things too. I've pretty much always had a job."

"Good for you. It must be nice to have a useful skill. I've only ever worked retail. I should open a store here, like a consignment shop. I need something to do during the days. Everyone's busy except me."

"Sounds like a good idea."

I looked down and saw that we were holding hands. The backs of his wrists had a faint covering of sandy brown hair. I liked it, the masculinity of hair on wrists.

"What's for dinner?" I asked.

"Oh shoot, that's right—I need to look in on my fish chowder. It's the same thing we had two nights ago. Benoît also flew in some fresh veggies if you're sick to death of fish."

"I don't mind fish. It's healthy. It's good for your eyes."

He squinted and I laughed.

"Hey," I said as he stood to check on dinner, "what are you doing later?"

"Tonight? Working until nine—but we brought in a good haul of salmon this afternoon, so I don't have to get up early."

"Does that mean you're free?"

He slid his hands into the pockets of his jumpsuit. "Yeah, I guess I'm free."

We made plans to meet up after I put Star down to bed. I liked that we were both wearing jumpsuits. It was kind of like being naked together.

At dinner I sat next to Cathy Oines and told her my idea to open a consignment shop on Mobility. "It'd be like a little boutique. People could bring in things they don't want anymore and trade them in for a store credit. We'd also sell new items from the mainland like toiletries and books and personal electronics."

She left her spoon in her bowl of fish chowder. "Why don't you just go back to Canada and open a store there?"

"I'm not from Canada. I'm from the U.S.—Ohio."

"So open a store in Ohio."

"I don't want to open a store in Ohio. I want to open one here. I've worked retail for ten years—I know what I'm doing. I can design merchandise displays and keep track of inventory and I'm really good with customer service."

"What 'merchandise'? This is Mobility. There's no capitalism here."

People at another table were listening in, so I lowered my voice. "I'm just trying to help out. I can't *do* anything else. I can't fix computers or cook or fly a helicopter. Everyone on this island has some sort of useful skill. I can't even do what *you* do—build mandolins or glass harmonicas or whatever."

"Hammered dulcimers. Not even remotely close to glass harmonicas."

"You know what I mean. Musical instruments. You build musical instruments."

"No, I don't build musical instruments. I build a very specific musical instrument. Hammered dulcimers require a skill set that is *absolutely unique* in the world of handmade instrument building. There are only about six or seven craftsmen in the world who have the talent and the technical ability to construct authentic, guild-approved dulcimers, and I'm one of them."

My shoulders sagged. Cathy and I clearly had nothing to talk about.

Scarfing down the rest of my dinner, I borrowed a Tupperware from the kitchen to bring some chowder back to Star. On my way I stopped off at the control bridge to see if my mom had answered my email. Most of the lights were off except for a lone florescent hanging above the middle of the room. Wallis was alone in the dark.

"Don't you normally eat first shift?" I asked, hitting a switch to turn on a few more lights. He shook his head as if I'd woken him up.

"Hm? What time is it?" He looked out the window, where the moon had already risen over the water.

"It gets dark early in this part of the world," I said, taking a seat next to him. "Early and quickly. Do you want this soup? I was going to give it to Star, but I can go back for more."

"I'm not hungry. I started reading and then I guess I took a nap." He yawned, pulling on his cheeks.

I put the soup on the counter. It smelled good, like warm milk.

"How was dinner?" he asked.

"Oh, fine. I just had an annoying conversation with Cathy Oines. I don't think she likes me. I don't think she thinks I'm very smart."

"Probably not."

I slugged his arm. "What do you mean, 'probably not'?"

"I mean from her perspective. She can be pretty myopic when it comes to other people."

"Define 'myopic'," I said, logging onto my email.

"Myopic, it means... oh, I don't know exactly. But it means she has her one way of looking at things and that's it."

I mouthed the word: my-o-pic. I still had Wallis' dictionary with me, one of the few things I'd brought along from the mainland. Over the years the cover had torn and I'd spilled coffee and red wine on the pages. I rarely used it except as a step stool. But it still meant something to me.

"Here's a note from Mom," I said. She'd changed the subject line of my email from "Hi there" to "Where are you?" I hesitated. Seeing my mother's name brought back a number of associations, not all of them good: how she'd get mad and swear when the car windows were slow to defrost on cold mornings; the bitchy way she'd talk to phone solicitors instead of just saying "No thank you" and hanging up; the time she burned her hand on a pot and yelled at my father because he didn't seem concerned enough. But there were good memories as well: the warm, soft, impossibly deep cavern between her breasts where I liked to put my face when I was three or four; some of the fun nicknames she gave me when I was little, like "Hot Stuff" and "Kooky Pants"; going out to lunch with her when I was older, the two of us drinking white wine and laughing about my father. One memory in particular—where were we? when was it? what occasion?—summertime, hot day, an outdoor table, the waiter in a vest and black bow-tie... tangy cold wine and a salad with shaved parmesan...

Wallis peered over my shoulder. "Good to see the network's working."

"Hey, can I read my own emails in private? God *damn*, I know these are close quarters but *Jesus*..."

He went back to his book and I opened the email. The words looked tense, angry:

"Roseanne, will pass all this on to your father. Your father very worried about you and Wallis. We trust Wallis to be more responsible at least. Hearing from Pam Okerfeldt on a near daily basis. Getting to be too much. Your husband has questions, wants you to make contact. Your children being cared for though the situation is not ideal and things could get worse the longer you stay away.

Please think. I'm not angry just very concerned and I have to say a little hurt and disappointed. Police in Michigan and others in Canada want to speak with you, worried about Sarah's safety. You've been on TV several times though less in recent weeks. Jail time avoidable but you have to decide. The police in Canada think you've left the country—is this true? Hard to get updates. You must come home with Sarah and face the consequences of your actions. Is Wallis with you? We've heard nothing from him in four months. That's long even by your brother's standards. Roseanne I'm sorry that you and I have had our disagreements in the past but your father and I are getting older now and we need to cherish the time we have left."

There was more but I couldn't read it. Believe it or not, I'm not a heartless person. I didn't like the idea of causing Mom or anyone else so much pain. But what could I do? I didn't *want* to face the consequences of my actions. The consequences of my actions were bullshit.

I kissed Wallis goodnight and went back upstairs to bring Star her soup, which she ate at the small desk in our room. The desk always felt cold to the touch, just like the rest of our furniture. Even things that weren't metal felt like metal.

We played a few rounds of cards after dinner. Steffi had taught her a full range of games like Hearts and Euchre but I only knew plain ol' Go Fish.

"You're holding your cards wrong," she accused me during one round.

"I am? No. How am I holding my cards?"

"You're holding them stupid."

"I don't know what holding them stupid means. Can you show me?"

She held her cards in a way that to me didn't seem any different from how she'd been holding them before.

"What's wrong with holding them like that?" I asked. She didn't answer, so we kept playing.

After a while she asked, "Mom? What kind of music did you listen to when you were younger?"

"Oh, all sorts of things. A lot of rock music, like Black Crowes. Do you know Black Crowes?" She shook her head. "*The* Black Crowes, sorry. And Stone Temple Pilots. I went to their concert once. But I also listened to classical music. I used to play this one Mozart piano concerto on my headphones."

"What about rap?"

"Sure, a little."

"What about gangster rap?"

"*Gangsta* rap? Uh, no, not too much. Why are you interested?"

"I want to listen to gangsta rap."

I couldn't tell if she was being serious. Star sometimes said things just to say them. "Well, maybe. You can listen to some of it, but some of it isn't appropriate."

"Why not?"

"Because it's about things that aren't very nice, and there are words that you shouldn't be using. Why are we talking about this? Let's play cards."

We attended to the game for a few more hands. The game was something physical we did together, without pleasure—a task, like stacking bricks.

"What about country music?" she asked.

"Do I like country music? No I don't, now that you mention it. And I don't like folk music either, so don't ask. Though country music and folk music are two entirely different things." I gathered the cards and reshuffled them. "Do *you* like country music?"

"Maybe."

"Can't be maybe. Either you do or you don't."

We talked and played cards until it was time for her to go to bed. I made sure she got into her pajamas, then I stood on the bunk ladder to say goodnight.

"I'm going out for a little while, hon. You sleep," I said.

"Where are you going?"

"I've got an appointment with Neil. Won't be long. You'll be asleep when I get back."

"What kind of appointment?"

"A meeting. We're going to meet. Meet and talk, that sort of thing. Typical meeting stuff."

"Is Neil your boyfriend now?" she asked, staring up at the ceiling rivets.

I smiled gently. "Oh, honey… no. Where'd you get that idea? Neil and I are just good friends. It's okay for me to have a friend, isn't it?"

"Do you kiss?"

"No."

"Do you hold hands?"

"No, we don't kiss and we don't hold hands… and *someone's* being very nosy." Leaning over, I rubbed her nose with mine. She looked serious when I pulled back, thoughtful.

Leaving her there, I went downstairs to meet Neil in his room. He'd washed up; the sultry warmth and soapy smell of the recently-used shower rolled out of his private bath. Under his desk he'd lined up two pairs of boots and a single pair of slippers. One of the two ceiling lights had burned out, and part of the room was absolutely dark.

"Do you ever think about the people who used to live

here?" I asked, sitting on his bed. "I keep picturing these Norwegian guys with big beards and greasy hair."

"You're probably not far off," he said, pouring us both a cup of the cheap white wine that he'd taken from the stash on the bridge.

"I can't imagine working on an oil rig. Sounds pretty hardcore. When I was a kid I thought I wanted to be a nurse."

"Talk about hardcore."

I laughed. "I guess everything's hard when you don't know how to do it."

We drank our wine, neither of us saying much until he stood to shut the door, pushing a chair against it to keep it closed. "Door swings open," he explained.

"Stupid door."

He sat on the bed, setting our cups aside. We kissed—not serious at first. A joke kiss. A peck. But then our lips relaxed and it was the night in the hallway all over again. I shivered when he grazed the side of my neck with his fingers.

"How'd you know that was my secret spot?" I said.

He smiled blandly, almost dumbly: a vacant man, brain removed.

"You smell great," he said. Then, in a low, fiery voice: "You're too goddamn sexy."

"Oh. More," I said, letting him kiss and chew on my neck.

"You're the sexiest woman in the world."

"More, more."

I pushed him back onto the bed, straddling him, our jumpsuits rustling. Neil's beard was a little animal with sharp fur scampering all over the mattress. "I should take off my boots," I said.

"You should. You should take everything off."

I sat up. There was no way to just pull them off so I had to take the time to unlace each boot. Neil rubbed my back as he watched. "Sorry," I said.

"It's okay. I like watching you do it."

"You like watching me take off my boots? Wow, you're an easy please."

I finally got them off and fell back onto him. His heat-seeking hands found my breasts, squeezing them, testing them for size and firmness. "You wanna see?" I asked, already shrugging out of my jumpsuit.

He nodded, almost trembling, ready to be blown away.

I popped off my bra and tossed it over my shoulder. Instantly his mouth attached itself to my right breast.

"You sure that door's good and closed?" I asked.

"It's fine."

"Because we don't want Cathy Oines walking in on us."

His teeth released my nipple. "Oh, don't talk about her," he groaned.

"You're right, I'm sorry. It's like talking about baby shoes." He looked like he wanted to say something, so I filled his mouth with my other nipple. "This one's jealous."

It was hard to do with Neil on my chest but I managed to kick off the rest of my jumpsuit, using my toes to pry off first one sock then the other. He began to steam up visibly, hot breath exhaling through twin nostrils. Fingering off my panties, he said, "You've got a beautiful body."

"I want to see yours."

"You got it."

He undressed swiftly, as if hurrying through an inspection. Inevitably I wound up comparing him to Josh.

Neil had more of a built-up body, whereas Josh was scrawny when I'd first met him and medium-pudgy later on. Neil's chest was hairless, his stomach taut. His penis was a big, crooked finger, a witch's finger. It stood straight out but seemed interested in the floor.

For a while we just touched each other, enjoying being naked together, the newness of it. I held the shaft of his penis in the cradle of my fingers as he kissed my throat.

"Wait." He hurried over to the dresser, pulled a condom out of the top drawer, and ripped it open.

"Where'd you get that?" I asked.

He smirked, fitting the condom in place. "Infirmary. There's a big box of 'em. Whoop-" He took the condom off, flipped it over, and tried again. "I always get it backwards."

The condom made me a little sad, as condoms often do—I don't know what it is. They're downers. They're like being reminded that you can't really fly.

He kneeled between my legs and together we worked at getting the right angle—it was nice and something we did as a couple, looking down at ourselves, getting it wrong and getting it wrong and then with a sudden easy push getting it right.

"You're strong," I said. He ruffed like a happy dog.

Neil and I had great sex that first time. I came twice (always a good thing), and he handled me gently but with a forceful, almost gruff authority. He spread his kisses everywhere, my fingers and toes and both breasts. I felt respected, appreciated, adored. He didn't retreat back into his own world as men sometimes do. Instead he kept his eyes open—I don't think he blinked once—soaking up whatever it was that he saw in me.

Toward the end, when I could tell he wanted to come, I said, "I want to make you feel good."

His eyes opened wider and he blurted out my name. It sounded like he'd been punched in the stomach. I held onto the backs of his shoulders and stared up but mainly just gave him his space. He deserved it. His orgasm was the one I'd been picturing when I'd thought about sex as a teenager: a man's sweet face, smooth and bronze, actively dreaming through the center of his head. Then he softly came crashing back down and lay sweating and breathing hard against my chest. I hummed a little as I stroked his ear.

"Wow, you're really hot when you come," I said finally.

He lifted his head and smiled. "I should probably take care of this," he said, reaching down to guide himself out of me.

I made a pouty face. "Don't go."

He kissed me sharply on the mouth. "I'll be back." With the condom off, he rolled out of bed, found the wrapper, and discarded it in the basket by his desk. "Let's get under the covers," he said.

I raised the sheets and he slid in, his arm finding a comfortable space around me. "I can't stay long. I should get back to Star," I said.

"Spend the night with me," he said, kissing my ear, his leg around my waist.

"Oh, I wish."

"I want to make love to you all night."

"You know I can't." I felt under the sheets. "God, are you hard again? What are you, sixteen? I think *I* need a break."

He chuckled and raised up on an elbow. "I'll lay off," he said, love-tapping me on the chin.

"No, it's fine. You're just… amazing. You have *incredible* orgasms, you know that? You're like a porn star," I said.

He looked pleased and embarrassed. "No, I'm not."

"You are. You're like a female porn star. You could do pay-per-view. I'm serious! There should be a neil-laporte.com."

"That's okay, I'll pass," he said warmly.

I tugged on the sheets to wrap them tighter around us. I wanted to be as close to him as possible. "Hey, I'm glad we did this. I mean it. Sometimes I do things without thinking about them first. It's a problem of mine. But this was a lot of fun. I'm gonna have good dreams tonight."

He smiled; maybe he thought I wasn't being serious.

I stayed another hour—we finished the wine and killed off another condom—before I got dressed, kissed him goodnight at the door in full view of the empty hall, and crept back upstairs to my sleeping daughter. Boots in hand.

CHAPTER TWENTY

Months passed on the island. The thirty-eight inhabitants of Mobility survived a rough winter and a stormy spring, and by the time the summer of '11 rolled around, we'd hardened into a crack outfit. Our weekly emergency drills went off with wordless, grim-faced precision, and all of us—minus the very youngest children—knew how to handle a firearm, spear fish, and repair a simple motor. I'd built up my arms and shoulders, my stomach was toned, and my legs and butt were commando-lean, all thanks to the group calisthenics that Sander led in the gym every morning at ten. Having crazy sex with Neil three nights a week didn't hurt either.

Despite the muted objections of a few on board, I opened my store in late August of that year. It had taken most of the spring and early summer to clean up the all-purpose room on Deck Three and to assemble the merchandise displays, which Benoît flew over from the mainland in six covert shipments. We featured a modest selection at first—toiletries, clothing repair kits, etc. Because Mobility hadn't yet established a currency, most items were sold on an exchange basis; people would bring in their used paperbacks and trade them for mittens or sunglasses. I offered an assortment of compact discs and movies on DVD, which people could check out as they would from a library. Our hours varied from week to week and depended on whenever I could get away from my other responsibilities. In addition to running the store, I worked four hours a week in the laundry and another four hours doing security patrols with Sander. Star also helped out in the store after school.

One afternoon Pål stopped by to browse the DVDs. We had about twenty different movies in stock, though I was always trying to feature more new releases. Our most popular title was *Casino* with Robert De Niro.

Pål looked up from the DVD box in his hands and asked, "What is *Tootsie?*"

He'd been working on his English but still sounded like a thug from the Norwegian mafia. He'd shaved his head and had a jagged scar, like recent surgery, running down the side of his skull.

"It's with Dustin Hoffman. It's an old movie, a comedy. Dustin Hoffman plays an out of work actor who pretends to be a woman in order to get a part on a TV show. And then he falls in love with a woman on the show, only *she* thinks *he's* a woman too," I explained.

"Is make me cry?" he asked.

"No, Pål, it's a comedy. No cry. Laughing."

He thought this over, his arched right eyebrow rippling. "Do the two women make love?"

"I don't think so. It's a PG rated movie, so I doubt it."

He looked disappointed and set the box down. "Do you have..." I nodded, eager to help. "...*porno* movie?"

"Oh... no, we don't carry those kinds of movies. I can try to get some."

He frowned, shaking his head, clarifying, "...is, *jack off?*"

"Yeah—no, I know what you mean. Sorry, though."

He eyed *Tootsie* on the DVD rack. "Is jack off with *Tootsie?*"

"I don't know. Maybe. You could try jacking off to *Tootsie*. Jessica Lange's in it—she's pretty. And Teri Garr. That's what the pause button's for."

Pål decided to go with my recommendation and left with *Tootsie* and a package of Dr. Scholl's boot inserts. He'd been my only customer all day. Business was kind of slow most afternoons—two or three people stopping by to pick up shoelaces or a writing tablet. I'd sit by the counter, getting up on occasion to carpet-sweep and re-straighten the merchandise. Typical Pier 1 stuff.

That day I closed up early and had a quick dinner with Star before joining Wallis, Dr. Snow, Sander, Neil, and Mandy on the bridge. The island's first anniversary was fast approaching, and Wallis had called a planning committee meeting with those he considered his closest advisors. One of the long work tables had a red tablecloth thrown over it, and Mandy had set out cookies and red punch.

"Is that Kool-Aid? I didn't know we had Kool-Aid," I said, pouring myself a cup.

"It's in very short supply, so take only what you want," said Wallis.

I held up my cup. "Am I allowed to have this much, or should I pour some of it back?"

"I don't care how much you have as long as you drink it. You can have five cups if you'd like."

"Just don't *waste* it, he's saying," said Mandy, bringing her punch and cookies to her seat.

"I have no intention of wasting it." Helping myself to three butter cookies, I sat opposite Neil. I didn't know how many people knew we were dating and I no longer cared. Neil was so busy in the kitchen that the only time we really saw each other was in bed.

"It's not actually Kool-Aid. It's a no-name generic. Taste how it's a little flat? You don't get that flatness with Kool-Aid. Kool-Aid has more of a citrus kick," said Neil.

"It depends how much you use. It probably also depends on the pH of the water," said Snow. His blue skin had lightened over the past year. It wasn't really sensationally blue anymore. He'd faded like a book in a storefront.

Calling the meeting to order, Wallis said, "I'd like to talk a little about our plans for our one-year celebration—Mandy, I know you've got some ideas—but I also want to focus on the next year or two... where we're going, where we'd like to be in 2012, 2013."

"I'd like a gas fryer that actually works," said Neil.

"We can look into it. We'll need to talk to Benoît," Wallis said.

"Medical is short on wound dressings and we've been asking for two months," said Mandy.

"Check with Benoît, but I think they're on the next shipment. That's not really what I mean. I'm talking about our long-term plans. From my perspective, our first year has been an unqualified success. We've had no defections, no major incidents, and the community seems healthy and relatively happy. It's a good start. I'm worried about some things, though. Our finances could be in better shape. We're surviving but we're not creating any revenue. If we want to attract newcomers to the island, and if we want to generate enough income to buy the things we need—like wound dressings and a gas fryer for Neil—we've got to raise our profile in the international community. Our neighbors in the U.S. and Canada need to know that Mobility is for real, we're not going anywhere, and we're a country they can do business with."

"What kind of business? We don't produce anything," Sander said.

"Not yet, we don't. We have to look at what we have to offer. Obviously, we don't really boast any natural resources to speak of."

"Fishing," Neil suggested.

"I wish. You've got enough to do simply keeping everyone on the island well-fed, Neil. No, what I have in mind is something on a smaller scale, but I think it suits our needs." We listened eagerly. Wallis seemed to rise an inch or two in his seat. "Novelty items—in other words: T-shirts, shot glasses, souvenir billfolds, um... what's something else you'd find in a gift store?"

Blank stares. It felt more like half of a question than the whole thing.

"Do you mean, like, knickknacks?" I asked.

"Yeah, but specifically," said Wallis.

More blinking computation. I tapped my teeth with my fingernails.

"Baby onesies," tried Mandy.

"What're those?" asked Wallis.

"Newborns wear them. You know, the little one-piece suits that snap up between the legs?"

"Okay, baby onesies. What else?"

Neil rattled off, "Calendars, playing cards, stuffed animals, baseball caps..."

"Good, *good.*"

"...snow globes, posters, stickers and decals, souvenir photos, souvenir coasters..."

"Excellent suggestions."

"...travel mugs, men's and women's underwear, socks,

souvenir sunglasses—like wacky glasses, like those plastic glasses…"

"Okay, *stop*. And I'm appreciative of the ideas, Neil, it's just right now I'm mainly interested in outlining a general sense of the thing."

"So these novelty items," Snow asked, frowning darkly, puzzling it out, "they would somehow *feature* Mobility—is that it?" Wallis nodded. "But who will buy them?"

"That's why we need to go public. We need to appoint a full-time Director of Marketing. I nominate my sister, if no one objects."

"Me? Why on earth me?" I asked.

"Because you're the only one of us with any retail experience. You and Yvonne Baker can put together a website. I'm also putting you in charge of designing the product. Use your imagination. It's your job to get people excited enough about Mobility to want to own a piece of it. We'll fabricate everything on the mainland—Benoît can take care of that."

I gulped my punch. "This sounds hard. Hard and complicated."

"Come on, sis, you've been looking for something to do. It'd be a big help. Mostly we're talking about online sales, which can be fully automated. We'll keep the money in Canadian funds and draw on it whenever we need it. If all goes well, you can even sell direct to customers right here on Mobility—that's once our tourism picks up."

"Tourism? Who said anything about tourism?" Snow demanded.

"That's phase two. I figure people will spend a lot of money to fly out to Bermuda for the week. Why not Mobility?"

"Because Bermuda has white beaches and perfect weather eleven months out of the year. Mobility is a pile of concrete and steel in the middle of the North Atlantic. Big difference," said Mandy.

"True, but Mobility has a lot going for it as well. It's unique, for one thing. And the views are incredible. We just need to sell ourselves a little."

"Sell ourselves," Snow muttered.

"Play up our strengths. The uniqueness, the strangeness factor."

"What's 'the strangeness factor'?" Snow asked, looking peeved.

"We don't think it's strange, but other people might, and that's okay. You've just got to have a sense of humor."

"I'm not interested in what 'other people' think, and I'm certainly not interested in making myself or anyone else on this island look ridiculous for any reason, financial or otherwise. It degrades the purity of what we've created."

"Not if we do it right. Think about the Statue of Liberty—what could be purer than that? And yet I've seen Statue of Liberty T-shirts with the Statue of Liberty wearing dark glasses or a mohawk or a Yankees jersey, and it doesn't degrade anything."

"You don't think so?" Snow challenged.

"No, I don't. We're not making fun of ourselves, Clem. We're selling. We're trying to keep our heads above water, which isn't easy when you're surrounded by it."

Sander raised his hand. "I'm afraid I have to agree with the doctor. It's not just our integrity, it's also a matter of national security. One of the reasons we've been able to survive here for a year is our low profile. If we start advertising our presence, it will embolden those who would do us harm. Make no mistake, these are dangerous waters."

"That's why we have you, Sander, to keep us safe—and more money will let us build a new defense arsenal. You'd like that, wouldn't you?" Wallis asked.

Sander nodded curtly. "Our current munitions are deficient in some ways, yes."

Wallis turned back to Snow. "At least give it a chance. I promise we won't do anything to degrade the purity of the island."

"T-shirts…" Snow said, tapping the side of his nose.

"It will be very tasteful."

The older man took another moment to think about it. "I suppose it's worth a try… if it's tasteful, like you say."

Wallis beamed relief. "Excellent! I mean… thank you—I mean… motion passed."

From there the discussion moved on to a few other items of business—the weird smell in Block Delta, cleaning the bird crap off the helipad—before adjourning for the night. Sander and I were the last to leave. He looked concerned as we stepped out of the bridge room and into the corridor.

"This sets a bad precedent. Your brother is sincere in his intentions, but he lacks a clear vision. What is required is real commitment. The kind of commitment that literally inspires a man to set himself on fire for a cause greater than narcissism."

His words scared me. "Oh, I don't know about that…"

"For example, there is the case of Thích Quang Duc, the Vietnamese monk who lit himself on fire to protest the treatment of Buddhists by President Diem. Or Ryszard Siwiec, who burned himself to death at a public event in Warsaw as a critique against the Soviet invasion of

Czechoslovakia. History abounds with instances of people who have self-immolated to call attention to a political cause or a case of injustice. Wait, I must tie my shoe."

I waited as he cinched up the whip-like laces of his right boot. "Wow, you sure know a lot about this," I said.

"It's an interest of mine, I admit. Since the early nineteen-sixties, dozens of men and women from countries like Greece, Spain, and even Canada have burned themselves to death in support of an idea or in non-support of an injustice, and in every case what motivated them was something solemn, grim, and community-minded. Not trivial. Not T-shirts."

We continued down the hall. "I can't fathom doing something like that to myself, even if I wanted to. I once burned my finger on the stove. It was one of those smooth top ranges, where you can't really tell if it's on or not. We were making soup. That was some of the worst pain ever," I said.

"The pain of being burned alive is intolerable. Fortunately it is short-lived for most people. More typically the victim will succumb to smoke inhalation within the first few seconds. At the same time, the specialized neurons that communicate pain messages to the brain, called nociceptors, are damaged by exposure to extreme heat. This numbs the affected area, at which point the victim experiences acute headache and nausea before losing consciousness entirely. The human body ignites when heated to fourteen-hundred degrees Fahrenheit. This is nearly twice the temperature of the surface of Venus."

"Stop. Actually... you know what? You're going to give

me nightmares. Let's talk about something else. La la la... cookies, cupcakes, creamsicles."

We stopped in front of his room. "It's not something that will ever happen to you, Roseanne. You are one of those people who will live a long life and die peacefully in a quiet room with flowers." He made a face, as if a taste in his mouth disagreed with him. Then he left me there.

The next day I met with Yvonne Baker to work on setting up an online store. We were alone on the bridge. Star was at school and half the island was either out fishing with Neil or attending a technology seminar with Benoît in the mess hall.

"I got into computers by accident," she explained as we took a break. "My ex-husband and I ran a couple of businesses together. We owned a Subway franchise but got rid of it because it was too much work. Then we decided—or he decided and I went along with it—to give day trading a shot, which was a good way to blow through four-hundred thousand dollars in about six months. Yep. So I said fuck that. But that's me—I've never really settled on any one thing. I used to be part-owner of a Gold's Gym in Scottsdale, Arizona. I've done limo services, Porta-Potty, wedding photography. I worked as a message courier back in college... I'd fly out to Tokyo once a month, stay for two days, and come back. Workin', workin', makin' money.... makin' money and havin' fun. My ex-husband was the guy who took over that insurance claims office in Atlanta back in '07 and shot and killed three people."

The smile died on my face. "Oh, that's—"

"We weren't married anymore. He was married to his second wife who was a Filipina woman named Mae or Rae or some shit. I saw it on TV. Turned on CNN and

I thought fuck if that ain't Garry. He shot his shift supervisor in the back and then went on a rampage and killed two other people before his mother got him on the phone and talked him down. It was terrible. We were married for eight years. We hooked up when I was nineteen and Garry was twenty-seven. How's that for a recipe for disaster? Wha'bout you?"

I told her about Josh and our four kids, how I'd settled in western Michigan without any friends or life of my own, how one day I couldn't take it anymore and left with Star to see my brother in Canada. The short version didn't sound so bad.

We got back to work, and Yvonne and I had fun brainstorming ideas for little trinkets to sell. Lighters, guitar picks. (We snickered to ourselves.) Placemats, napkin rings. We tittered and stamped our feet.

Later that week the entire population of Mobility gathered to celebrate our first year on the island. It was a decent party. We had a dance in the mess hall, and Neil made a big cake shaped like a football. I asked him about the significance of it.

"No significance. It's the only cake mold in the kitchen. The Departed left it there," he said.

"The Departed" was our local slang for the people who'd lived on the island before us. They were the cause of any number of woes—bad plumbing, faulty wiring, weird sounds in the elevators.

"It's kind of appropriate, I guess," I said. We stood at the edge of the party watching Yvonne play D.J. with the dozen or so CDs she'd brought from the mainland. The music skewed heavily toward late-eighties hard rock.

"No, it's not," he said, "but you're nice."

The song broke off, and Wallis dinged a fork against his

glass to make an announcement. "Some news, everyone, and this just came in. We're going to have a visitor in a couple of weeks. Her name is Cassia Samuel-Jones, and she's the host of a TV show—what's the name of it?"

"*Positive I.D.*," said Mandy, standing behind and to the right of him. Dr. Snow flanked him on the other side, the others all gathered around.

"It's a weekly newsmagazine. It's a bit like *20/20* but it's not as… something."

"It's not as hard news," she said.

Snow disagreed. "Oh, no, I think it's harder news. It's not as hard news as *60 Minutes*. It's more like *Dateline* but with more of an emphasis on human interest than true crime."

"It's on Wednesday nights at ten," said Mandy.

"She's doing a segment on us—just on our little community and what we've been through over the past year. It's an opportunity for us to introduce ourselves and to let people from around the world know about our values and our way of life," Wallis said.

"How did she find out about us?" Sander asked, sitting at a table with Pål and Benoît.

"I reached out to her. I've been reaching out for some time now, and I was fortunate to catch her and her producers' attention."

"They're not going to slam us, are they?" asked Cathy Oines. Some of the other women also looked concerned.

"Oh, no, it's not one of those programs. I'm sure they'll ask some hard questions, but this isn't a 'gotcha' kind of thing."

"I know that show. I used to watch it when it was on Mondays at nine. They're always slamming people."

"We're not going to get slammed, Cathy. I've traded

several emails with Ms. Samuel-Jones, and she's excited to tell the story of Mobility through the eyes of the people who live here."

"They did a segment on this family in the Dallas area and tried to imply that the father was the head of a sex-traffic cartel smuggling underaged girls across the U.S.-Mexican border even though he'd been twice exonerated in federal court."

"I don't know anything about that, Cathy, but I can tell you that she's very articulate and personable and has absolutely impeccable journalistic credentials. Dr. Snow and I both checked it out."

Pål raised his hand and asked with great difficulty, "Is she... good-looking, you know. Is she... hot? Like Diane Sawyer?"

Wallis waved his hand, trying to get onto something else. "I don't know, Pål, but the point is-"

"Is she... *fuckable,* you know... can you *fuck* her?"

Cathy, Paulette and Beverly hissed, and Pål blinked innocently.

Wallis said to the women, "It's a language thing, I think. We all know what Pål is trying to say. He's asking, is she approachable, is she a friendly person..."

Pål nodded eagerly, as if that explained it exactly. "Yes, is true. Is she... *anal?* You know... sixty-nine? This is how you say?"

"No, no..."

"What is in English... cumblast? *Cum in face, cum in mouth?* This is idiomatic?"

Wallis suffered through a few more of these questions before giving up. The buzz in the room continued, now with this new information added.

Benoît whispered to me, "This is an exciting

development. I'm not sure what it portends. Visions are murky."

"I just hope it doesn't cause a lot of problems," I said.

He squinted at something vague circling in the near distance. "I see… a woman—*that's* clear. She's screaming or laughing or just has her mouth open. And *warmth*… a mild warmth. Temperate. Men with shoes, men wearing jackets. I'm tentatively aware of kneecaps. No odor. The quality of light is unremarkable." He sighed, releasing the tension in his neck. "It's gone now."

"It's a start, though," said Neil.

"Perhaps, but… to interpret…"

"It's better than not knowing anything at all."

Benoît tried again. "I see a beige something…"

"It's better than having no clue and resorting to sheer guesswork."

I pinched Neil's butt.

Later in bed, I said to Neil, "I'm starting to panic, hon. Everyone back home is going to see me on TV. I *know* Pam, she watches this kind of junk all the time. She'll send people after me. I'll lose Star, you, everything."

Neil held me, and I buried my face in his chest. "I suppose it's smart in the long run… if it can bring us some recognition, some attention from the international press."

I was nearly in tears. "Yeah, but what happens to *me?*"

"You'll be fine. Technically we're giving you asylum here. You and Star are our little treasures." He hugged me tighter. "Now don't worry about it. You've got T-shirts to sell."

I tried. For the rest of the week I made a semi-conscious effort not to think at all, in fact to deny the existence of an inner life. Daydreams were banished, as were feelings, personal reflections of any kind. I worked,

I ate, I shat. I had no name. I was merely a representative of my species. I wanted to be like those animals Steffi watched on TV: doomed, but too dumb to know it.

By the time Ms. Cassia Samuel-Jones arrived two weeks later, the Mobility online store was officially open for business. So far we'd received one order for a Mobility coffee mug, which I later learned was my brother testing the website.

I was on the bridge checking orders when Star cried from the hall, "Hey, Ma, the lady from the TV show is here!"

I zipped up my jumpsuit and followed Star and the rest of us down one of the cargo elevators to the loading docks. The water was choppy that day, and Mandy Two bobbed as it approached and tied up to a pier. Cutting the motor, Sander brought a pair of red leather suitcases onto the dock before helping a woman in a furry snow parka step up from the boat. This was Ms. Samuel-Jones. A cameraman with a dark handlebar mustache wore a navy watch cap and a reindeer sweater with a high turtleneck.

Ms. Samuel-Jones wavered a few steps in her moon boots. Nearly all of Mobility had turned out to welcome her, Wallis and Dr. Snow in the lead. I stood near the back with the other moms from school.

"She's pretty. How old would you say she is?" asked Paulette.

"She's probably older than she looks. It takes a long time to work your way up in that business. I'd say thirty, thirty-five," said Beverly Sachs.

"Oh, no… she's not a day over twenty-eight."

Ms. Samuel-Jones pulled off her snow goggles and gloves. She seemed uncertain whose hand to shake first.

Wallis reached up. "I'm Wallis Crim. Welcome to Mobility."

She took his hand in both of hers. "*You're* Wallis. I thought *you* were Wallis," she said, pointing at Dr. Snow, "I don't know why."

"No, I'm Dr. Clement Snow, I'm President Crim's technical advisor. We've been looking forward to meeting you."

She smiled, trying to decide what seemed odd about Dr. Snow. "It sure is another world out here. It's like floating in the middle of the ocean. It's literally like floating in the middle of the ocean." She glanced over the edge of the dock. "I suppose I'd sink straight to the bottom if I fell in, wouldn't I?"

Star pushed forward in the crowd and I followed. Noticing us, Wallis said, "This is my sister, Roseanne. She's our Director of Marketing and Public Relations."

Her eyebrow raised at "Public Relations." "I majored in Public Relations at Temple before I switched over to the J-School at Columbia. Couldn't hack it though. Where did you go?"

"Oh, just Montclair Community College. It's a little school in Ohio," I said.

She nodded sympathetically, as if I'd shared something personal. "We did a piece on community colleges last season. I co-produced. Not many people know the rich history of community colleges in America. Some famous and important people have gone to them. I can't remember a single one off the top of my head but I remember doing the research."

We filed indoors, leaving Sander to carry Ms. Samuel-Jones' bags. Riding in the elevator, she said, "So this is an actual elevator?"

"One of four on board," said Wallis.

"Amazing, when you think of the work involved... bringing it all here, and the construction." She signaled to her cameraman to start taping. "We're not actually wired for sound. We could be talking about anything and it wouldn't matter. Who wants to say something rude on national TV? Anyone, anyone?"

We laughed politely. Ms. Samuel-Jones seemed a foot taller than the rest of us. I stared at her pierced ears. Her honey-brown hair suggested a smell without actually having one.

The elevator doors opened on Deck Three, and Wallis led a tour down the hall, stopping to show her the rec room, the library, some of the sleeping quarters. She listened, her face reacting, her default expression one of interest and concern. Occasionally she'd interrupt to point out something of note to her cameraman.

"What's impressive is the austerity. Everything's so stripped-down. What do you do when someone breaks a law? Are there rules, or does literally anything go?"

"A lot of Mobility is a work-in-progress. We've only been on the island for a year. Fortunately nothing untoward has happened," said Snow.

The tour continued up to the top deck, where the wind was fierce. Sander took us along his patrol route, skirting the eastern perimeter of the helipad, past the munitions shed and the weather station that Benoît had built over the summer.

"We're well equipped with two Colt M4 Carbines, a half-dozen Beretta M9s, a Smith & Wesson Model 500, an AA-12 shotgun, a Remington bolt-action, plus a stockpile of M67 fragmentation hand grenades," he said.

"Wow, those are some serious weapons. What sort of trouble are you expecting?" asked Ms. Samuel-Jones.

"We just like to be safe. We think of it as an elaborate home-security system. We also have a VTS that can detect any maritime traffic in the area," said Wallis.

Ms. Samuel-Jones tapped her lips. "Isn't it all a bit paranoid?"

"Not really. There's no such thing as being overly-cautious in the North Atlantic. Even our boats come equipped with their own radar systems and self-defense kits in case of trouble."

"And your people are trained to handle all this?"

"We run weekly security drills, yes. Our Head of Security, Sander Phelps, brings many years of experience from his time in the Canadian Forces."

"It's rather like a para-military outfit, isn't it?" she asked as we went back inside.

"I wouldn't say that. We're simply a small group of rugged individuals trying to survive under difficult circumstances, like the early American settlers."

The tour concluded in the mess hall, where Neil had prepared a special meal for our guest. Ms. Samuel-Jones sat at my table for dinner.

"Your brother is really a remarkable person," she said, digging into her fish. "Does he ever talk about the wheelchair?"

"Sure, I guess, if you ask him," I said, wondering why she'd want to sit with me and not Wallis or Snow or someone more important.

"I wasn't sure if it was taboo. Was it an accident?" I nodded, and she let out a breath. "Oh my God, and what that must've done to you as a sister."

"Yeah, it sucked," I said.

She left her fork on her plate while I kept eating. "You're a tough woman, aren't you?" she asked.

"What makes you say that?"

"It's your body language, the way you sit there with your arms folded."

"My arms aren't folded."

"Not now—they were folded a few minutes ago. I'm not saying it's wrong. I have a strong intuition about people. Body language tells us a great deal. When someone folds their arms, it's a defensive posture. It means, 'Don't talk to me.'"

"Not always," I said.

"No, not always. But it means something, you see? Everything means something. For instance, I yawn a lot. Even when I'm doing an interview—and it doesn't matter if I'm tired. I cover my mouth, of course."

"I haven't noticed."

"That's because I'm very subtle about it. Sometimes I can actually swallow the yawn, which makes it virtually undetectable. Generally speaking, a person yawns when he's tired or bored or distracted or not interested in talking—and yet that's rarely true of me. I like talking, otherwise I wouldn't have gone into this profession. I like meeting new people. So why do I yawn all the time? Maybe it's my body telling me something. Maybe I do bore easily, maybe I'm not interested in what other people have to say. Maybe I don't know myself as well as I think I do. It's like you when you fold your arms."

"I'm not-"

"Everyone has a mannerism that reveals a deeper psychological or emotional truth. Take my ex-husband—'ex-fiancé,' really. Whenever he got angry—I mean angry enough to throw a punch at someone—he'd go up and spit in their face. Right in the eye if he could. And always that—no shoving, no cursing. Isn't that something? Now there's another example of a mannerism pointing out, however obliquely, a deeper psychological truth." She stared at me.

"What?" I asked.

Her face drew closer, and I folded my arms. "Roseanne, why are you here?" she asked.

I gave her a discouraging look, or tried to. "Oh, because of my brother. We've always watched out for each other."

"And what about your children?"

Now I knew why she'd picked my table. "Star's here—that's my daughter, Sarah. She's around somewhere. She likes to eat with her friends."

"I meant the other three." We looked at each other flatly, and I went back to eating.

"It's okay," she said, "I'm not trying to get you in trouble. I did a little research before coming here. Your married name's Okerfeldt, isn't it?"

I pushed the heel of my fork into my fish fillet, bringing up juice. "Yes."

"And your other children are Connor, Mary, and Vance. Vance is seven and the twins have got to be almost three. What's your husband's name? John, Josh?"

"It's Josh," I admitted.

"And has he been in contact with you?"

I found myself wanting to tell her. Slowly finishing my bite of fish, I said, "He doesn't know where I am. No one does."

"They will now, right?"

I kept still.

"Listen, this could be a good thing for you. You have a side of the story. What happened to you happens to a lot of women. They get pregnant young and wind up married to someone they hardly know, and it's overwhelming. Sorry, one moment-"

She yawned like a cat, and I waited for her to finish. Her eyes stayed open through the yawn—wild, calm, and straining.

"I see what you mean about the yawning," I said.

She covered her mouth. "Oh, that wasn't a yawn. That's something else I do. I have this thing where my jaw stiffens up and I need to work it loose otherwise it gets stuck wide open and I end up in the hospital. Comes from too much caffeine."

Neil popped out of the kitchen to ask how she liked her fish. This was something he never did, inquire about the food.

"It's actually... sensational. I'm sorry, I don't mean to sound surprised." She laughed, and he smiled down at his chest. "It's just that I wasn't expecting such a fine meal. I was expecting military grub. You should have seen the food in Kandahar. I've never eaten so many whipped potatoes."

He thanked her and went back into the kitchen. Watching him go, she fanned herself with her napkin.

"And he cooks too. Must be popular with the locals, no?" she asked.

I didn't know what to say. What could I say? Not only am I a bad wife and mom, I'm also sleeping with the cook? "Neil's a nice guy," I said.

"He's delish…. though I think the most handsome man I've ever met would have to be the former French Ambassador to Japan. The most attractive was Johnny Depp. I only met him in passing, but he had an aura about him that one could actually measure with the right equipment. I'm not exaggerating—my wristwatch literally stopped working for twenty minutes."

She seemed to have forgotten our earlier conversation, which was fine with me. We spent the rest of dinner talking about wine, river tours in Spain, and the perks of flying first class on Virgin Atlantic. Mostly I just listened.

CHAPTER TWENTY-ONE

The real problems began three nights later, and they had to do with Pål. Since Ms. Samuel-Jones had arrived with her cameraman, she'd interviewed everyone from Dr. Snow to Benoît to Yvonne Baker, gathering scenes—what they called "B-roll footage"—of the island's daily activities. She'd more-or-less learned to blend in with the general population, and I'd even sold her some Chapstick from the store. She was a nice enough person—at least I wouldn't change the channel if I saw her on TV. I couldn't tell if her English accent was real or not.

That night I woke around eleven o'clock to the sound of male/female commotion in the hall. One voice I recognized as Ms. Samuel-Jones'; the other was low and mostly garbled.

When I stuck my head out, I saw Ms. Samuel-Jones retreating from her room wearing a towel, her hair hanging wet around her bare shoulders. She looked angry at whoever or whatever was inside her room.

Catching up to her, I noticed a person standing in the dark near her bed. A male person—I could tell that much at a glance, fumbling to put his pants back on.

"I was taking a shower," Ms. Samuel-Jones explained,

out of breath, "and I thought I heard a sound, and when I came out to look, *he... he...*"

I switched on her lights, and Pål blinked at us. He was shirtless and had his fly wide open. He covered himself with his hands.

"Pål, what the fuck are you doing in Ms. Samuel-Jones' room?" I asked.

He looked less embarrassed than annoyed at me for interrupting. "It's just... I try to be nice..."

"Well you're *not* being nice. It's not nice to sneak up on people in the shower. Where did you learn that?"

"It's okay, Roseanne. I would just like him out of here," she said.

A few others stopped by, sticking their heads in and exclaiming at the half-naked Pål. Ms. Samuel-Jones hurried off to finish getting dressed in the bathroom. Pål started to leave but Sander, who'd just arrived, pushed him back onto the bed.

"You stay here," he said.

Pål became more agitated at seeing the crowd increase in size. I'd always been a little afraid of him myself. He was a cornered bull, puffing with stupid outrage.

"I act nice... she like it," he said.

"She obviously didn't like it, otherwise she wouldn't have gotten upset. Wendy," Sander said to Wendy Foster, one of the married women who lived down the hall, "will you knock on Ms. Samuel-Jones' bathroom door and make sure she's all right?"

Wendy went to check on her as Pål continued to plead his case. "I see it... in movies. The man is *hard-on*. This is very popular sometimes. The man *always* hard-on in these movies."

"In the movies, Pål, the movies," said Neil, who'd

entered the room with Sander. I found him in the group and took his hand.

"No! You no understand. More than once, I saw. I have no woman—in fifteen months! Only jerk-off. I spank to *Tootsie*? No good. This is your fault," he said, pointing at me.

Neil stepped between us. "Lay off her," he warned.

"I spank to Sharon Stone in *Casino*—this is okay, if timing right. There is one scene in *Harry Met Sally* movie... but hair is bad. For fifteen months, this happens—and no one will fuck me!"

"No one's feeling sorry for you, buddy," said Neil.

Pål shifted his appeal to Sander. "Sander, my friend, you know these movies. Everyone like. The girl in movies always suck dick, and no one say no. Is very popular."

Beverly Sachs whispered to me, "Amazing. His whole frame of reference comes from porn. It's almost sad."

Dr. Snow arrived as if officially summoned, and Ms. Samuel-Jones eventually came out of the bathroom in a shirt and slacks, her hair combed straight back. Sander told Snow what had happened.

Pål spoke up, "I hurt no one. Always the girl decide when to fuck—I no force. Miss Jones is beautiful woman. I have great pleasure to meet her. We have sex... maybe," he shrugged.

Snow snapped, "That's quite enough!" Ms. Samuel-Jones looked thin and pale.

"*Or...* maybe not. Is okay. I no force. I am happy with kissing and touching and shared nudity." He turned to her, his eyes wet. "Miss Jones, *please*, I believe... in my heart of hearts. You and I are good friends. We take shower together. I, maybe, am sexy for you."

Hissing at him to shut up, Snow addressed Ms. Samuel-Jones. "I am so sorry... on behalf of the entire island..."

"It's fine—I'm better now. He didn't touch me," she said dully.

"It's not fine, and it won't go unpunished."

Pål stood and yanked up his fly. "You know what I think? I think you men is all faggots. Oh yeah! Butt-fuckers! You know it..."

Neil and Sander shouted him down as Snow continued his apology to Ms. Samuel-Jones in private. By now a good third of the island had assembled out in the hall.

I suggested we give her her room back and discuss this elsewhere, and Snow agreed. "Sander, you're in charge of Pål. Consider him under arrest for the time being," he said.

"Can we do that?" Neil asked. He and Sander stood on either side of Pål, each holding an arm.

"It's just a temporary measure. Stow him in the kitchen or something—and keep an eye on him. We'll figure out what to do with him in the morning."

Neil and Sander dragged Pål out of the room, leaving the rest of us in a daze. Beverly handed Ms. Samuel-Jones a tissue.

"It's the strangest thing—I had a dream that something like this would happen. Not literally this. I was in Northern Africa and I was traveling with a photojournalist I knew from grad school... we were on assignment with a group of humanitarians from Lausanne. And all the while I had this strange sense of foreboding. It was uncanny, really," she said.

Snow patted her hand. "I hope this won't change your feelings about us."

She had a distant look in her eyes. "Oh, no... quite the

opposite. This is part of it, isn't it? Life on the frontier. Men and violence, men and sex... sex and violence."

Beverly and I stayed with her as Snow went down to interrogate Pål. I offered to spend the night in her room but she said it wasn't necessary. "I didn't even get to finish my shower," she complained.

"Go on and finish it. We'll wait," Beverly said.

"Oh, it's all right. My hair's washed. I was just looking forward to a nice long soak. I probably shouldn't waste your water anyway."

We hugged at her door. It was about as awkward as you'd expect. "I'm down the hall if you need me," I said.

Before going back to bed, I followed my curiosity downstairs and found Neil, Sander, and Dr. Snow in the kitchen with Pål. They'd tied him to a folding chair with some rope from one of the boats.

"Should we wake my brother?" I asked.

"No, we'll brief him tomorrow. Someone needs to be well-rested and thinking clearly." Snow paced in front of Pål's chair, his face growing purple with rage. "You idiot! Do you know what you've done? That woman could've been a big help to us. We don't need this kind of bad publicity."

"I don't care about you," Pål grumbled. His lower lip was bloody—there'd been a scuffle on the way downstairs. "I work hard, seven days a week. Always I work. No pay? 'Pål fix this, Pål fix that.' Fix my dick. In Oslo I make seventy thousand Euros a year. Switch box, home and commercial wiring. I have my own business. Hookers fuck me. Bartender buys me drinks."

"Go the hell back to Oslo then," Neil said.

"I will! You pay me what you owe, I go tomorrow."

"We don't owe you anything," Snow said. "As a citizen

of Mobility, you enjoyed the benefits of living on the island in exchange for work, just like everyone else."

"What benefits? Every night I sleep on a cot. I own, what—three T-shirts, three pairs of socks? Breaded whitefish for dinner every Tuesday and Thursday."

"That's not true. I haven't made that recipe in two months," Neil huffed.

Snow turned to Sander, always the calmest person in the room. "What do you think we should do?" he asked. Even Pål stopped to listen.

"It will be tricky. Mobility has no system of justice as such. There's no precedent for dealing with lawbreakers," Sander said.

"We don't even have any laws, do we?" I asked. The men fidgeted as Pål grew listless.

Snow said, "I started working on them, but…"

"You got busy," Neil suggested.

"We have a few laws. We definitely have some laws. But none of them really apply to a situation like this."

Pål looked ready to nod off in his chair. Neil went to the pantry and returned with a half-empty bottle of Jack Daniels and some shot glasses. "I don't know about you guys," he said.

"Perhaps a small one," agreed Sander.

Neil poured three glasses of whiskey for himself, Sander, and Snow. "Roseanne?" he asked.

"I'm good," I said. Pål snored as he slept.

"I hope this doesn't mean our segment's getting cancelled," Snow said. The men threw back their drinks. "I'll have to speak with Ms. Samuel-Jones in the morning. The outside world has to know that this sort of behavior will not be tolerated on Mobility."

"We have standards. We have a code of conduct," said Neil.

Snow waved his glass for a refill. "That's right, we do. Not an actual code of conduct. Nothing on a piece of paper."

"It's an unspoken understanding. A pact between men—and women. *This isn't done here. You can do 'A' but you can't do 'B'*."

Neil poured the second round. I wanted one too but felt I'd missed my chance.

"She'll see," Snow said, his nose in his glass. "Maybe it'll be good for us in the long run—to have our collective will tested like this."

"It legitimizes us," said Sander.

"Shows we're not just a bunch of clowns," said Neil.

I broke in, "What about that poor woman upstairs? Doesn't anyone care about her? She could've been raped tonight!" They just stared. "I'll tell you what we *should* do—put locks on some of these doors. That should've been done a year ago. We need to start thinking about people's safety first. There are children living here—*my* daughter."

Snow looked wary of me. I was taking something simple and making it overly complicated.

"Roseanne, please... calm down. I'll issue a formal apology tomorrow. I'll write it myself. What else can I do? She seemed to be handling it quite well, to be honest. In fact-"

"Oh, how would you know?" I swept them up in my dark gaze, Neil included. All men looked the same to me. I wanted to head-butt one of them and not get hurt.

Everyone on the island knew about the Pål incident by morning, and Wallis called an open meeting for 10 a.m.

The mess hall was picked as the meeting site because of its size and proximity to the kitchen, which served as a makeshift holding cell. Pål was led out by Neil and Sander, who were both armed. Pål's legs and wrists were bound with rope, and he looked like he hadn't slept much overnight.

Wallis updated the islanders before turning to the prisoner. "Pål, you know the charges against you. Do you deny them?"

Pål kept his eyes on Ms. Samuel-Jones in the front row. "I do nothing."

"Pål, we have witnesses. My sister saw you."

Pål smirked at my brother. "You no understand because your dick no work. My dick tell me! Miss Jones and I have an instant connection."

"So that gives you permission to confront her in her bathroom?" Wallis asked. Ms. Samuel-Jones hung her head.

Pål lit up, "Ask her! We have flirtations happening." He struggled with his ropes, and Neil and Sander brought their weapons closer.

"Oh, when?" Ms. Samuel-Jones asked drily.

"Three times, on three occasions. Once, two days ago in laundry room when you say I have nice hands—these hands!" He held up a puffy hand, evidence A. "Second, when you smile at joke I make about old woman and the giant fish. See, you smile now—it's a funny joke! Third-"

"I don't want to hear the third one. I'm sure it's just as irrelevant as the first two. The point is, you committed a crime last night, and the people of this island have a duty to pursue justice," Wallis said.

Pål tried crossing his arms but the ropes wouldn't allow

it. "Crime? What crime? There's no crime here. Who are you to say what is crime. I no see it written down."

Getting impatient, Wallis asked the room, "Okay, let's make this quick. Who here thinks Pål is guilty of assaulting Ms. Samuel-Jones and should be punished for it?"

Absolutely everyone thundered back, "Yes!"

Pål looked dumbfounded, searching from face to face. "Is bullshit! I do nothing. Benoît, my friend, remember when I fix altimeter—I work for three days? And Miss Baker, when I carry all those boxes for you—sixty, seventy boxes I carry, and then stacking, and then taking the boxes back down, so many boxes, my hands hurt from carrying such heavy boxes."

Wallis spoke over his protests, "The question now is punishment. I'm not proposing we go overboard-"

"Cut his balls off!" Cathy Oines yelled from the back of the room.

"No, no... I'm looking for serious suggestions-"

"Cut off his dick and rape him with it!"

"No... Cathy. Please, the language."

"Hold him down and fuck his ass with a red hot piece of metal and then take his dick and-"

"Cathy! Come on!" Wallis shouted.

The whole room stared at Cathy Oines, who looked grim and unrepentant. Sander raised his hand, and Wallis gratefully called on him. "I speak only for myself when I say behavior such as this hurts us all. Pål has embarrassed us in front of our guest, and the punishment should be severe."

"What are you recommending?" asked Wallis.

"Exile, Mr. President. Effective immediately."

Pål leapt to his feet, and Neil and Sander shoved him

back down. "You'll have a chance to speak once we've finished. Now be quiet!" Wallis ordered.

The rest of the trial proceeded swiftly, with arrangements made for Pål to be transferred off the island at nightfall. Pål listened, by turns enraged and resigned. I almost felt sorry for him, the poor, dumb ox.

Finally Wallis asked if he had anything he'd like to say. The room hushed as Pål stood up between his guards. "First, I no do what you say. Miss Jones know. All I do: I go into her room, take off my clothes, and show her my penis—that's it!"

"But Pål," Wallis said, "that *is* what we said you did. That's why we're here, because you did all that."

Pål ignored him. "Other thing—and this you don't know. I come from very small town in Norwegian country. People are poor. Hills... rocks fall. *Very* hard to walk. My father lost his hand when he was fourteen. But this is what we do in Norway. All of us. You come there, you see."

"People in Norway like to expose themselves to women, that's what you're saying? This is normal?" Wallis asked.

"Is very normal. The men are naked all the time. The women not so much. In Norway we have tradition—is called ekstreme offentlige mannlig kjønnsorgan. Is where the men who are healthy and of adult age go on public bus or tram and make jizzing on women's shoes and purses. I do it myself five, six times. And this go back many years. Everyone like it!"

Wallis put a quick end to the trial and told Neil to prepare Mandy Two for a night departure. I didn't like the idea of Neil riding in a boat with Pål all the way back to the mainland, but I felt better knowing Sander would be with him. The two of them together could handle pretty much anything.

After Neil and Sander led Pål back to his room, I asked Ms. Samuel-Jones how she was doing. "Better. Maybe it's best if I get back to New York," she said.

"Are you going to tell anyone about... you know?"

We wandered out of the mess hall and into the corridor, along with the rest of the adjourned meeting. "I probably should. I don't want to make trouble for you people, though. One ugly incident aside, I quite enjoyed myself on Mobility."

"And what about..." I almost didn't want to ask. *What about me?*

We hung back as the others continued down the hall.

"Ah, yes... my other big scoop. As far as I'm concerned, the real story here is the island itself. I think I've already got enough material to fill thirty minutes." She squeezed my hand. "You did me a good turn, Roseanne. One deserves another."

We hugged, and I smelled the rose blossom perfume in the soft of her neck.

The islanders assembled at eight p.m. to watch Neil and Sander leave with Pål on Mandy Two. We stood on the loading dock, braving the wind and the cold ocean spray to see them off.

Wallis officially pronounced Pål's sentence. "Sorry it didn't work out, Pål. Maybe it just wasn't a good match."

Pål glowered, first at Wallis, then at the rest of us standing in a row of blue jumpsuits. "I'll be back. You wait. I have friends. I get what you owe me."

Neil grabbed him by the collar and ushered him toward the boat. "Come on, we've got a long ride ahead of us."

Pål sat with Sander in the back of the boat as Neil

cranked up the motor. As a parting shot, Pål flipped us off and yelled, "You no like *my* friends! That's right, baby! *Cra-zy boys!* Freedom forever! Rolling Stones, Who, Led Zeppelin. Shit." Then he started to rap.

The boat pulled away and we watched until the lights on board Mandy Two winked out of sight. Then we went back into the rig where it was warm.

Neil and Sander returned around midnight. Pål still seemed present somehow; the feeling gave me the creeps.

I was waiting for Neil in his bed. "Make love to me," I said, pulling him down.

He kissed my mouth and chin. "Can I take a shower first?"

I laughed. "If you hurry."

The sound of the shower in the dark was like someone frying a steak.

After his shower, after we'd finished making love, I asked how things had gone with Pål. "He's an idiot. We dropped him off a mile away from the Harbour Authority."

"And where will he go next?"

"It's a big world. He'll find something to do. He's lucky—he would've been in a lot more trouble if this had happened on the mainland. Personally I don't care if the dude drops dead."

That didn't sound like my Neil talking. I suddenly wished we were someplace else—Detroit, or Buffalo. A Ramada Inn in Buffalo next to a Chili's and a Bugaboo Creek Steak House, a blizzard outside and the roads all jammed up.

CHAPTER TWENTY-TWO

After a quiet Christmas, Ms. Samuel-Jones' Mobility story ran on TV in early 2012. The thirty-seven remaining islanders gathered on the bridge to watch it stream live. The segment mostly featured interviews with Dr. Snow, plus footage of Neil fishing on Mandy One, Benoît landing the helicopter, and Cathy Oines playing her hammered dulcimer. No mention of the Pål incident, nor any direct reference to me or Star. I only appeared once in passing, standing in the chow line for breakfast. Star never appeared, nor did any of the other children. On balance it was a fair piece of journalism; the producers didn't try to put us down or make us look strange.

During the commercial, Snow said, "Well, *I'm* pleased. I was expecting more sarcasm."

"It's a little sarcastic," said Wallis. For snacks Neil had made popcorn that dated back to the time of the Departed.

"When was it sarcastic?" Snow asked.

"Oh, the crack about Benoît. The 'power of prophecy' part. I could've done without that."

Benoît looked affronted. "I merely answered the woman's question. I certainly don't go around advertising my abilities, if that's what you're implying."

"I know, but… 'soothsayer.' That's a little weird. And the thing with the hands."

"I can't help 'the thing with the hands' as you put it, and soothsayer is actually the proper term."

Yvonne Baker chuckled. "A sayer of sooth."

"Yes, a sayer of sooth, from the Old English *sooth*, meaning 'reality' or 'truth.'"

"Okay, everyone," said Mandy, "it's coming back on."

Cathy Oines grumbled, "The audio could've been better. You could hardly hear the dulcimer, the attack of the hammers, the full punch and nuance of the-"

Wallis shushed her, and we watched the second half. A shirtless Neil and Sander doing chin-ups in the weight room got a cheer from the ladies. More about Mobility's history, our funding, our connections to the mainland. Then it was over.

The room applauded, and Dr. Snow reached to close out the computer screen. "Well, I think we can safely say-"

Yvonne jumped up. "Wait, is that Mick Mars? Aw, dude, leave it, leave it! I think they're doin' a piece on Mötley Crüe."

Snow sagged back into his seat. "-that the next few weeks should…"

His voice got lost in Yvonne's explaining to Benoît, "Mick Mars, he's the guitarist of Mötley Crüe. I saw them in '86 at the Palladium. Mick's my buddy. He's been sick."

Benoît, who detested Yvonne, said, "I neither care nor appreciate-"

"He's got this thing where his bones are all fucked up," she said, shifting her attention to Charity, who was sitting on the other side of her. "Like, his bones don't work anymore, the joints and shit. They all froze up."

"Oh that's too bad," Charity said, leaning forward, trying to listen to her husband.

"...we'll see if there's any response from the U.S. or Canada. Now that they know we're here, they'll probably send out an emissary," Snow said.

"He still tours with the band, though. I don't know how he does it. Dude weighs, like, sixty pounds. I guess he can still move his fingers." Yvonne gawked at the band performing in their mid-eighties heyday; whirling pyrotechnics, mid-air jump-kicks. "Yo, turn it up! *Where my rednecks at?* Fu-uck, look at Vince!"

"...have to risk it," Wallis added, "but at least with the increase in web traffic..."

Yvonne had her air-bass out, which she plucked at waist-level inches from Benoît's granite, non-responding face. "*I'm on my way... jes' set m'free...*"

Benoît was saying, "...this kind of harassment. I'm serious, Clem. You and I have spoken of this before..."

"...something we'll have to watch out for," Snow said, agreeing with Wallis, "but in the meantime the increased revenue should help us stabilize..."

Doing pelvic thrusts now, grinding her crotch in Benoît's face, forcing his stiff and resisting head back with each blast of the chorus: "*Home... Sweet... Home!*"

Finally Benoît shot out of his chair and threw her off. Yvonne sailed back and crashed butt-first into Charity and Curtis Foster, who spilled his coffee.

Benoît turned to Snow and Wallis, his chest heaving. "That's it—Clem, Mr. President, I'm leaving. I've had it with this woman and her inane chatter."

Picking herself off the floor, Yvonne said, "Hey, man, you hurt my wrist. My wrist really fucking hurts right now!"

"Calm down, both of you," Wallis said as Snow switched off the program. Yvonne cradled her wrist in pain.

"I'm perfectly calm. I've been very patient over the past months. You know this, Clem. I'm not a complainer. But I can't go on like this anymore. I'm sorry," Benoît said, starting toward the door. "I wish you all the best. Sander, you may keep the bottle of Dauvissat that's in my footlocker."

"You can't leave, Benoît. No one else knows how to fly the helicopter," Wallis pleaded.

"I'm afraid that's not my problem. Either she goes," he said, nodding at Yvonne, "or I do."

"But we need her, too. We need both of you. Yvonne's our IT person. She's the only one who knows how all this stuff works."

Holding her wrist to her chest, Yvonne said, "You better not have broken my wrist, asshole, or else I'm gonna fuck you up hard. I already broke this wrist once, man. I fell comin' out of a Steak & Lube. It felt just like this."

"You can send the bill to my local address in Antwerp. President Crim, Dr. Snow…" Benoît bowed to the rest of us.

Wallis tried one last time. "Please, Benoît, you're part of the team here. The whole island will fall apart without you. Tell me what you want and I'll give it to you. You want a bigger room? You want to move up to Deck One? Just name it. Here-" He took off his watch. "Take my watch. Seriously. This is a great watch. I got this watch in Hong Kong six years ago. It's a Luminox. You can go diving with this. You can take it down to six hundred feet. I don't need it."

Benoît smiled benignly. "Keep your watch, Mr. President. And don't worry about the island. You'll do quite well without me. I saw it once... in a vision..." His eyes went cloudy as his jaw stiffened and trembled. "It's coming back to me now... the pattern's assembling—lines and shapes and colors. Energy in motion. The air is not humid, or rather it lacks humidity." Sharpness returned to his eyes, and his shoulders sagged. "And then it fades... always on the verge, I'm afraid. My friends."

He left, and Mandy went with Yvonne to the medical wing to look at her wrist. I picked up the chair that Yvonne had knocked over. "He'll change his mind," Wallis said, still holding his watch.

Benoît didn't change his mind, and in the morning Sander took him back to the mainland on Mandy Two. As with Pål, the island gathered on the landing dock to see him off. The only notable absence was Yvonne, who'd suffered a mild wrist sprain and was pouting in her room.

The next few weeks were busy and anxious. Because I was in charge of media relations, I spent a lot of time monitoring our press coverage on TV. CNN carried our story online, as well as Fox and MSNBC, though buried in the Human Interest section; we weren't "news" per se. Sales of T-shirts and other merchandise also jumped by two-hundred percent, which was good for our economy.

Along with the increased attention, more ships had started coming into the area. Our on-board radar was pretty much always beeping with visitors large and small. Some times a cargo ship from Sweden or Great Britain would buzz us in the middle of the night; if you were standing on the landing dock, you could see the wake slap against the piers. Occasionally a brave little boat would even tie up for a visit—adventure seekers who'd heard about us from somewhere. We'd give them a quick tour, feed them, and send them on their way with a bag of free T-shirts.

Early that summer Sander held a security briefing on the control bridge. The thirty-six of us in our folding chairs looked like the audience for a badly-attended play. We had meetings like this every week; generally they lasted ten minutes and consisted of Sander rehashing the same three or four points about the need for more training. Tonight was different.

"What we are looking at," he said, gesturing at the big screen above the main bank of computers, "is a compressed time loop captured this morning. As you can see, the green blips on the radar correspond to ships in the area—the usual array of commercial fleet and privately-owned vessels, nothing special there. The numbers refer to the registration number of the vehicle. From these we can identify each ship, its country of origin, and the owner on-record. Mobility constantly monitors this information—I myself compile the time loops and study them for irregularities. Here-"

He zoomed in on a particular blip lurking a few inches on the screen from the larger, stationary blip designated as Mobility.

"You see in this case there is no registration number, just a blip to indicate the presence of a 'Zero Status Event.' Under most circumstances, not a cause for concern—our radar systems are so sensitive that they will sometimes pick up pieces of drifting debris, even large marine life such as whales or sharks. What bothers me is the pattern. This same unknown object has appeared regularly for the past two weeks, always following the same path of approach and withdrawal."

"It's watching us," said Snow.

"I think so. The timing is identical from day to day. Every morning it appears at these coordinates-" He pointed at the screen. "-and exits roughly thirty minutes later."

"That's some smart whale," joked Beverly Sachs. We laughed uncomfortably.

"What do you think it is?" asked Mandy.

"Our first thought must always be pirates. It is as I feared—once our presence became known, the number of potential threats would increase, as we can now see."

"What kind of pirates?" asked Neil.

"We won't know until we conduct more reconnaissance of our own. I will be going out in Mandy One tomorrow to see if I can get a better look. But make no mistake—the pirates that roam the North Atlantic are dangerous and sophisticated. We are not talking about the pirates of yore. No eyepatch, no spy glass. No 'Yo ho ho.' This is not the series of popular movies starring Johnny Depp."

"But what do they want from *us*?" asked Cathy Oines.

"Any number of things. They might be interested in stealing some of our equipment."

"Yeah, but they'd have to know what's up here. They hardly showed five seconds of the control bridge on TV. They'd need inside information," said Curtis Foster.

We looked at each other, all of us thinking the same thing. *Pål.*

"It could be simple harassment. These pirates believe they own these waters. Perhaps they mean to extract protection money," Sander explained.

"Fuck them!" brayed Cathy. A few nodded their heads in agreement.

"Or it might be something else entirely. The first thing is to determine who they are, and then what they want."

Steffi Blaise, who'd grown into a precocious ten-year-old, raised her hand. "Sander, are we going to be okay?"

Sander's normally stern features softened. "Stephanie, of course we are. From my time in the CF I can tell you that a lot of this is posturing. These men are, by and large, poor tacticians. Besides, we have several advantages. We are well-armed, well-trained, and we own the high ground. We are like a fortress here. The important thing is vigilance. We can't let our enemies gain a time advantage. That's why I'm recommending we increase the number of daily security patrols from three to six. Mr. President, I trust that won't be a problem."

"Approved," Wallis said.

"I will be available after our meeting to take volunteers. If not enough people sign up, I shall have to impose a mandatory service." Several boos from the audience. "The easy solution, if you do not like the idea of enforced service, is to encourage the strongest and most capable of us to step up and serve their country. We will be able to scale back the number of patrols once the danger has passed. These pirates will grow tired of us once they encounter resistance. You have to remember, these are thugs. They're the maritime equivalent of street criminals, interested only in the quick and easy score. We, on the other hand, have principles. Our nation's honor is at stake."

The next morning, Sander and two other men left to inspect the mysterious object on our radar screens. Neil kept monitoring Sander's whereabouts via radio, and when the crew came back, most of us were on the landing deck to greet them.

Stepping up from the boat, Sander shook water from his beard and unzipped his rough-weather parka. "At least a half-dozen men, all heavily armed. Mixed descent—two blacks, another man who looked Spanish or Peruvian. There may have been more belowdecks."

"Was it a big ship?" asked Neil.

"A good size trawler, perhaps sixty feet. Clearly someone is backing them. More typically you would expect a smaller skiff, but these waters are too choppy. I was able to spot their on-board radar, which suggests they can intercept our communications. We should keep our radio transmissions to a minimum. Can I have a glass of water or some tea with ice in it?"

"Sure." Neil called up the row of people on the dock, "Can someone get him a glass of water? Here-" He took Sander's arm. "Let's go inside. Did you notice any unusual markings, a flag?"

"No flag. One man wore a bandana, red and black. Sunglasses, a gray beard. Another looked young... a boy in shorts and a windbreaker. Lanky, the word comes to me. I know I'm not describing it well."

We shuffled into the cargo elevator, and Sander squeezed more water out of his hair. "What weapons did you see?" asked Snow.

"Mostly AK-47's. We can assume a full array of semi-automatic handguns. Based on the evidence I would say an attack is imminent. They are probably waiting for nightfall. I would suggest test-firing the grenade launcher this afternoon. At the very least it might serve as a deterrent. All non-essential personnel should confine themselves to their quarters until further notice."

The rest of the day was spent watching the radar and preparing ourselves for battle. Sander was busy but I managed to corner him in the hallway and pressed him for details.

"So… on a scale of one to ten, what are we talking about here? If ten's full-out nuclear war and one's just a little skirmish where no one gets hurt," I said.

He looked distracted. I'd caught him between errands. "It's hard to put a number value on it. I'm hoping that most of the violence can be averted. Sometimes in warfare it takes a gesture on the part of an individual to quell the momentum."

"So would that be a five, a six? Maybe a five-point-six?"

"I truly believe that the will of the individual is stronger than any army. This is what officers in the military speak of when they say, 'Lead by example.' It took the act of one man to bring about the start of World War Two. Ultimately it took the decision of another to end it."

"I think I'd be happy with anything less than a six. Once you get up past six, that's when I start panicking."

The floors shook, and we grabbed onto the walls for support. Down the corridor, people stuck their heads out of their rooms. I yelled at Star to stay indoors and followed the others up to the top deck where Neil was already handing out guns. Past the helipad and about three hundred yards out to sea, a boat similar to the one Sander had described was trolling our waters. Gritty black smoke rose from the far corner of the rig.

"I don't know what happened. They must have a rocket launcher or something. They blew up two of our storage sheds. At least they missed the armory," Neil said.

Sander instructed three men who worked with Neil in the kitchen to see to the damage. "Have we returned fire?" he asked.

"This just happened! We need to remount the M203

or else we're not going to be able to reach them at this distance." Surprised to see me, he asked, "What are you doing here? Get downstairs. Soon they'll be close enough to hit us with anything short range."

I nodded but couldn't move. All around me people retrieved weapons from the munitions shed. "What's the strategy?" asked Snow.

Sander ordered, "Yvonne, join President Crim on the control bridge and try to establish contact with the ship. For now, the rest of us will assume a defensive posture. I don't want to escalate the situation until we know what their immediate intentions are."

Yvonne ran off, and Neil and Curtis got to work positioning a big gun on a tripod. Mandy said, "I'll be down in sick bay in case anyone gets hurt."

Across the helipad, the sheds smoldered as we turned our hoses on them. The smoke blew straight at us, and we coughed and blinked. The gun seemed to take forever to assemble. Three times Neil put the gun on the tripod only to take it off and set it down on the floor.

"What the hell's wrong with this shit?" he said, struggling with the gun and a wrench and a pair of bulky gloves. Curtis Foster took off his baseball cap and wiped his forehead on his sleeve.

More anxious minutes passed. The boat wasn't getting any closer, nor was it moving away. I'd assigned myself the task of watching the fire-fighters; it seemed important, vital even, that their efforts go observed.

My attention became diverted away from the fire. Neil and Curtis were arguing about the gun, Curtis now taking his turn with the wrench. "It's the wrong panel!" he shouted as Neil spat at the ground. I saw despair in both of their faces. "Panel" was a hopeless word. It suggested a permanent obstacle, something rooted and fundamental.

Sander unhooked his walkie-talkie from his belt. "Phelps here. Have you gotten through to them?"

Yvonne's voice came back. "We're still trying. What the hell's going on up there? We can see smoke blowing across the window."

He hung up on her. The fire had mostly gone out—what was left of the smoke was changing over to steam. The smell of the smoke quickly dissipated. White birds circled and dove overhead. They looked irritated—we were annoying them.

Sander's walkie-talkie buzzed. "Phelps," he said.

"Yeah, they finally answered back. These guys ain't going away. They want permission to board or else they're gonna hit us again," Yvonne said.

"Yes, and...? How did you respond?"

"How do you think I responded? I said, 'I don't give a *fuck* what you do, motherfu-'"

Another small explosion rocked the surface of the helipad. The chopper took part of the hit and tipped onto its side. The guys who'd extinguished the first fire shot back at the boat. A popping of bullets.

"Stay sharp, everyone! They're weaker than they look. We're stronger and more numerous," Sander said, though he sounded less confident now. Across the helipad someone's pant leg had caught fire; he shook it and it went out.

"...back! Back!" a voice cried. Someone else was saying, "It's... fuh. Right? No. Did you get it?"

Sander and Curtis had the gun back on its tripod. Curtis had lost his baseball cap somewhere. He turned the wrench with his whole body.

Training a pair of binoculars on the boat, Cathy said, "Son of a bitch... hey, guys! Listen up! He's there."

"Who?" I asked.

"That Scandinavian piece of shit. Probably led 'em to us. Shoot to fuckin' kill, baby."

Moments later Yvonne confirmed on Sander's walkie-talkie that the bridge had also spotted Pål on the boat with the rest of the pirates. "I don't know if you guys have noticed, but they're getting closer. Any last minute action-hero moves, now's the time to bust 'em out," she said.

"Neil, how long until the M203 is back in service?" Sander asked.

Neil answered over his shoulder, "We've almost got the mount fixed. The hand crank's all fucked up. We need at least a couple minutes to stabilize and rearm."

Meanwhile the boat had turned to face us, its speed increasing. Pål stood near the front, doing pelvic thrusts and flipping us off with both hands.

Sander passed Curtis the walkie-talkie. "You keep in touch with the bridge. I will be right back," he said, hurrying across the helipad and into the smoke.

Feeling useless, I asked Neil what I could do to help. He snapped, "You can let me concentrate so I can tighten these attachments. No, wait—go into my kit bag and get me a rag and the half-inch torque wrench—it's the one with the orange handle."

I went to Neil's kit bag and pulled out a rag and something with a long orange grip. It had a lurching, sloppy weight in my hand. "Here you go," I said.

He dropped one tool and picked up the other. "These old fucking tools ain't grabbing. Son of a bitch and fuck me with a spare rib."

Another rocket-propelled grenade missed the rig by a few yards and blew up as it slipped into the water. Shots fired upward bore slim chance of reaching our men on the top deck; and yet Pål had already hit us twice.

"Where's Sander?" asked Beverly. With a gun in both hands and an ammo chain around her shoulder, she looked like a kid wearing a costume.

"Oh, he's..." I waved at the downed chopper. The fire crew had dragged the hose to the helipad and was busy putting out the second fire with seawater.

"We *need* Sander. We need instruction. *I* need to know what I should be doing right now," Beverly said.

"He'll be back. He said he would." Looking away from Beverly, I watched Neil let the wrench slip with a clank. A 'V' of perspiration bled through the back of his jumpsuit.

"I got no time, I got *no* time! My hands are shaking and I can't set this fucking focus," he ranted. "This is so much harder to do in an actual combat situation!"

Curtis held the walkie-talkie away from his ear. "Neil, bridge wants a time check."

"Tell 'em they can bite my balls and I'll let 'em know," Neil said, not looking up from his work.

After relaying this message back to Yvonne, Curtis said, "They don't actually know what that means."

"It means thirty seconds, a minute, I got no idea."

"They're lining up again," warned Cathy. The boat had closed to where we could clearly see twenty or so men, each waving guns. I thought about them coming on board, terrorizing our halls, looting and smashing, grabbing the women. I thought about Star.

"Neil!" I screamed as a third grenade exploded on deck, and some shrapnel from the impact caught his right forearm. He winced, a circle of blood seeping through his clothes, no bigger than a dime.

"Almost there," he said, still clutching the grenade launcher.

"Neil, you've got to get out of there!" Curtis yelled. Neil dropped to his knees to heave the ammo into the firing chamber. Indistinct voices, male, barked across the deck.

"What the hell are they looking at?" asked Beverly. The rest of us peered out at the boat. Both the driver of the boat and the other men were no longer staring back at us but at something off to one side.

"*Now*, Neil!" Curtis shouted.

Neil slid closed the firing chamber, aimed, and launched a missile at the boat. It streamed up in the air and came down in a shrieking arc. Before the pirates could react, the missile slammed into their vessel and exploded on impact. The sound and heat from the explosion blew us back all the way up on the top deck. The boat was a sinking ball of flame as men on fire fell or jumped into the water. The debris field was dark with floating blood, here and there punctuated with islands of burning fiberglass.

"Fuck yeah, baby!" cheered Cathy.

Yvonne roared over the walkie-talkie, "Great fuckin' shot, dude! You blew 'em right out of the water!"

I ran to Neil and looked at his arm. "We need to get you down to sick bay."

"I'm all right," he said, his hands cut and bleeding.

Curtis beamed; he'd even found his baseball cap. "Where the hell's Sander? Hey, *Sander*! Neil hit 'em with a dead shot."

I patted Neil on the back. He seemed a bit stunned. "I

was in a hurry and I... I thought I missed. I've never shot one of these things before."

"You did great," I said.

"I thought I'd left it short. I didn't think it was going to come out hot like that. Isn't that funny?"

Amid the celebrations, Beverly hushed us. "Listen!" she said.

A sound rose from the other side of the munitions shed, low and unhappy. Leaving the grenade launcher on its side, we rushed around the shed and came upon the fire crew struggling to lug the hose across the helipad. The fires from all three explosions had been put out; now a new, smaller fire burned at the edge of the tarmac.

One of the fire crew ran at us and grabbed Curtis' sleeve. "We've lost water pressure! We need buckets from downstairs... the hoses aren't working."

The charred ground felt warm through our boots as we slunk closer to the spot of the blast. Someone ran ahead with a fire blanket and used it to cover a body lying on the tarmac. The fire whipped out.

The guy from the fire crew explained, "There was a fireball from the last explosion. You must've felt it. Sander was trying to draw attention away from your position. It was bad timing, that's all. No one saw it coming."

"Sander!" Neil cried, but Curtis held him back.

"He's gone," he said, looking down at Sander's body. Charred boots stuck out from under the blanket's edge.

I bent over and vomited. With my head down, I heard Neil shouting and crying, boots running hard, a patter of activity. Finally Curtis and the other guy, Rich, grabbed Neil by the arms and dragged him to a safe distance. Neil's face was wild, all wide eyes and stretched mouth. His eyes ranged over the rest of us.

"We were fine! I mean… it's. Luh. It's. But I got it off in time, right? I mean, that's what I did. I had 'em all lined up and I… I remember. I saw it. That's what happened. *I didn't know what the fuck I was doing and then I did it.* But then I thought-"

Curtis took off his hat, as did the other men. Cathy and Beverly had their arms around each other, and I just stood there by myself.

"-I thought, no, it's cool. It's cool, I got 'em, I got this, I'm good. I'm cool, I'm on it, I'm whatever. I didn't *need*, I mean—I didn't need-"

"Deep breath, buddy," said Curtis.

"*I didn't need any help!*"

I couldn't watch, so I stared down at Sander's boots. I've always said you can tell a lot about a man by looking at his feet: whether he works sitting down or standing up, takes care of himself or doesn't typically bother to groom. You can get a sense of his general character just from his feet. Soft or hard, dirty or clean.

CHAPTER TWENTY-THREE

We told Star that Sander had gone back to Canada.

CHAPTER TWENTY-FOUR

The next day everyone pretty much kept to themselves. I spent my time in the store filling out orders for T-shirts online. It was dull work but kept my mind off things. We typically sold to about twelve customers per day: some person in San Antonio, someone else in Duluth, Minnesota—they'd hear about us on TV or read about us in a blog and it would pique their interest. A few videos had turned up on YouTube purporting to show Mobility from one passing boat or another, but half the time it didn't look like us. I imagined people back home probably talked about us, made jokes, speculated. We were one of those weird stories, I guess.

Two days after Sander's death I ran into Neil coming out of the infirmary. We hadn't seen each other much since the attack. He needed some time to himself and I was happy to give it to him. I thought I was being a good girlfriend.

"How's the arm?" I asked. He wore a tank top that showed off his bandage. Through the door to the infirmary I saw Mandy in her white coat, her back to me.

He closed the door behind him. "Hurts. I just took a painkiller. Should feel better in a few minutes."

I took his hand and he winced. "Does your hand hurt too?" I asked, letting it go.

"Everything hurts," he said.

We continued on toward his room. His bandage looked clean and fresh. "It's been so quiet around here. I heard Cathy playing her instrument-thingy last night and I actually liked it," I said.

He laughed politely. He hadn't combed his hair—*bed-head*—and I wondered what that meant. *Grooming*, I thought again. A well-groomed man. Grooming meant tweezers and toenail clippers.

"Is Mandy a good doctor?" I asked. We weren't exactly walking together.

"Why?"

"Oh, just curious. I've never gone to her for more than a headache. One time I thought I had Lyme disease, but I always think I have Lyme disease. What is Lyme disease? It's just like being really tired, isn't it?"

"You don't have Lyme disease."

We stopped just outside his room. I had laundry duty in an hour. Most people hated doing the laundry but I didn't mind it really. Usually I'd sit on the dryers and pass the time reading a dumb book.

"We can talk about it, you know," I said.

"Talk about what?"

"Everything that's probably going through your mind right now. I know what it's like. My brother... when he got hurt. My parents sent me to a psychiatrist for a year. Her name was Dr. Graham and she was this big, bosomy black woman... I just wanted to put my head between her breasts and cry. And then I-"

"Roseanne, if you don't mind... I'm really tired and these antibiotics are making me loopy and I need to get to bed early because we're all out of food for dinner tomorrow and that means getting up at five and... I just need some rest."

"Sure." I nodded. "Okay."

"I need ten to twelve hours of hardcore sleep and then I'll be better. And then we can talk. Really."

He sank back into his room and I blew him a quick kiss. The room was dark and looked cold. "You want me to close the door?"

"I'll get it in a bit," he said. The room hummed with brittle alertness.

I left him there and went back to my room for an hour before going to work. The laundry was on the lowest level of the rig—what we sometimes called "the basement"—behind the main boiler that serviced the entire island. The windowless room was always warm and smelled of wet lint. Low-hanging pipes and fluorescent lights meant you had to bend down to avoid smacking your head.

Charity was just getting off-shift when I joined her. "I'll leave you the whites—I did the colors," she said pleasantly. I liked Charity. She rarely said anything edgy or controversial, unlike some of the other women on board.

"Laundry's still got to get done, I guess," I said.

"There'll be less of it now," she said, loading her bundle of clean laundry onto a pushcart, "with Wendy and Curtis leaving."

I leaned against one of the washing machines. "Wait—Wendy and Curtis are leaving? When did this happen?"

"They decided this morning. Wendy finally put her foot down. They're going back to the States. They're lucky, they held onto their place in North Carolina. And they're not the only ones—the young man from Lebanon?"

"Rafiq?"

"Yes... he's Lebanese, isn't he? He's going back home too."

"So that makes it..." I counted on my fingers. "...thirty-three-"

"Thirty-two. You're forgetting Sander, the dear."

We said nothing. Charity patted the back of her hair, which she always wore up.

"Don't look so sad, Roseanne. People die, relationships end... you know that. I knew the day I married my first husband that it wouldn't last. I remember standing in my grandmother's dress in front of the Presbyterian church in Hamilton and thinking, 'We'll have a couple of good years, we'll have children,'—we only had one—'and then you'll decide I'm not exciting enough for you and wind up having numerous affairs and then blame me for breaking up the marriage.'"

"Why did you marry him, then?"

She smiled. "I wanted to. I *liked* him. Hans was a nice guy. We had similar interests. We both enjoyed the symphony. That's how we met. We were at a concert of Grieg and Brahms and spoke during the intermission. He was very knowledgeable about late nineteenth century romantic music."

"And did he wind up cheating on you?"

"*Oh* yes—many times. He actually had a long-term affair with a Lithuanian woman and got her pregnant twice while we were still married—I learned all this after the fact, of course."

I wondered if she knew her current husband, Dr. Snow,

had cheated on his first wife too. "You don't think more people are going to leave, do you?" I asked.

"They might. Beverly Sachs sounded uncertain the last I spoke with her—I know she's concerned about her son. I wouldn't worry about it, though. As long as Clement stays—and your brother—there'll always be a Mobility."

She went back upstairs, leaving me in the rumbling semi-dark.

Dr. Snow and Wallis called a meeting a few days later to address the latest wave of departures. Along with Wendy and Curtis Foster and the Lebanese guy, Rafiq, three others had left the island, bringing our numbers down to twenty-nine. We'd lost nearly a quarter of our initial population in a matter of months.

"It's like a giant tidal wave coming along and wiping out the entire eastern seaboard," Snow speculated. The only people not present in the mess hall were the children and Neil who, from what I could tell, simply didn't want to come.

"It's worse than that. It's like a meteor striking the planet, leaving an impact crater the size of France," said Wallis.

Cathy, Yvonne and Beverly groaned and said "ooo."

"That's maybe an exaggeration," said Snow, "but there's no saying it won't get that bad if something isn't done to keep people from leaving the island."

Beverly raised her hand. "See, I don't like the sound of that. We're all here on our own free will—you, me, all of us. No one can keep us here."

Snow fielded similar protests from others in the room. "You're absolutely right. That's always been true since the day we arrived. Anyone who wants to leave, can. Have I ever suggested otherwise?" Voices reluctantly admitted no. "Has our president ever suggested otherwise? President Crim? Of course not. The people who left us have all made a choice. Benoît made a choice, Rafiq made a choice... even Pål, in his own way, made a choice."

Gavin Baptiste called out, "What about Sander?"

The room chattered, inspired.

"Yes, Sander Phelps made a choice too. And it was a selfless choice and an act of great courage and this nation shall forever remain grateful to him for it," Snow said.

"It wasn't no choice. I mean, he *chose*—he choose whatever."

"That's what I'm say-"

"What he choose is some bullshit," said Gavin.

Snow frowned and tugged on his ear. "How's that?"

"It's some bullshit. I mean, we on here—how long? Two years, not quite. Since forever. And you get to where you don't think clearly. See the same people, eat the same damn—fried fish, fish 'n' chips, French fry. I have for breakfast this morning-"

"If there's a problem with the food-"

Gavin's eyes flared. "You damn right there's a problem with the food."

"I want to hear what Gavin has to say!" screamed Cathy.

Everyone quieted down, and Snow gave the floor to Gavin. "There's a problem with the food, there's a problem with... everything! Everything, man, I tell you. Here we are, me and Neil and Richard, and we are expected to work seventy, eighty hours a week, hard physical labor, and for breakfast I have—the most little piece of stale, not even good tasting-"

"You'd like better breakfasts, is that it?" asked Snow.

"I can verify what Gavin is saying. The breakfast this

morning was cold by the time the second shift made it downstairs," said Beverly.

"The kitchen has been under pressure lately, as I'm sure you'll understand," said Snow.

"It's not the kitchen! I work in that kitchen, man. I have been peeling potatoes, slicing potatoes... all morning, since six in the morning, and no one give a fuck-all. We work hard in that kitchen," Gavin said, thumping his chest. Cathy nodded on the bench next to him.

"We're all aware of it, and it's deeply appreciated," insisted Snow.

"No, it's not deeply a—if you deeply appreciate, then why I gotta eat the same fish 'n' chips, the same spaghetti with no meat in it, the same..."

"I think what Gavin is saying is that it's unrealistic to expect people to work long hours if they're not getting the proper support," translated Beverly. Gavin threw his head back, done listening.

"That's fine, and I *agree* with you, but these are things we can work on. This is why we have these meetings, so we can fine tune and make adjustments. But we gotta be on the same team. Sander wouldn't want to see us fighting like this," said Snow.

Cathy said, "We don't know what Sander would want. That's the point. No one knows. We're all emotional right now and we've been though a lot and what some of us are looking for is reassurance-"

"I'm trying to re-"

"-but substantive, meaningful-"

"I am, I'm trying. I've always been straight with you, Cathy—and you too, Gavin, and you Bev. God knows I have. I wouldn't have brought you here if I didn't believe in you, and that means each and every one of you—Gavin and Dan and-"

"I'm Rich," said Rich.

"Rich, of course—I was looking at you but I was pointing at Dan—Rich and Dan and Yvonne and every other man, woman, and child on this island. We've bled together, we've cried together. I can't tell you the sleep I've lost worrying about you, and all the hard work I've put in to make this thing happen... you know that, don't you?"

We do, we said.

"Haven't I worked hard for you? Haven't I done all I can?"

"No one's doubting you, Clem," said Cathy, "but you're the one who's sitting in that control room all day. You have information we don't have. I think what most of us are concerned about is the possibility of another attack like the one we had last week."

Wallis spoke up. "Clem, can I take that one? As far as that goes—and it's impossible to know definitively—we don't have any reason to believe Pål's group was in any way involved with a larger network of-"

"They're not," Snow said. His eyes were closed and he shook his head as if thinking or praying.

"-no talk over the shortwave, at least not that we were able to intercept, no suspicious behavior, nothing on radar-"

"They're gone and they're not coming back. They're not coming back, people, okay? Cathy, weren't you there? Didn't you see it? There was a skirmish. We all know what happened. There was a skirmish and the enemy took out two of our storage sheds and we lost one of our men but that's all over and it's not gonna happen again. It's just not. Those folks are gone, dead, finished."

"But Clem," asked Cathy, "what proof do we have that it won't happen again? It seems to me you're just asking us to take your word for it."

"That's exactly what I'm asking, Cath. Take my word for it. I've never lied to you and I'm not lying now. I'd lay down my life for each and every one of you in a heartbeat and goddamn you know that's true as sure as I'm standing here talking to you. What do I have to do to prove it to you people? Why are you constantly questioning me when you know I've done everything I can to keep you safe and happy?"

We know! we shouted, and *You have!*

"It's so easy. It's as easy as saying a little prayer. Do you remember when you were a kid and you'd kneel at the edge of your bed and fold your hands and say, 'God, my name is Cathy'—or Dan or Gavin—and you'd talk to God for five or ten minutes and it always made you feel better? That's what I need from you now. I need you to not ask questions, just get on board and hold on because good things are happening."

"But isn't that blind faith?" asked Cathy. The whole room turned to look at her.

"Explain that to me," said Snow.

"Well, if this is a free and open society—and that's something we all agreed on when we first came here-"

"Can I say...?"

"Just wait now." Snow sighed and rubbed his eyes as Cathy went on. "Sure, we all have our roles, but when it comes to making the big decisions, it's the group-"

"But what defines the group?"

"All of us! We're the group. The free citizens of the

independent island nation of Mobility." A few cheered groggily. "But now you're saying no. You're saying-"

"Cathy, you're making me sad right now. You're breaking my heart—you of all people. Every nation, just like every religion, is built on *faith*. Faith in *me*, faith in God or whatever. Our old friend Benoît lacked that faith, and that's why he's no longer with us. Same with Curtis and Wendy and..." Over murmurs of disagreement, he said, "Hey, look, I'm not saying they're bad people. Am I saying that?"

"You're saying they betrayed us," said Cathy.

Snow held his fists up to his mouth, preaching now. "I'm saying they lacked faith! Jesus *Christ*—Cathy, I'm not saying they betrayed us. That's your trip, that's your thing—that's you, not me. I loved that man. I loved Benoît. There's not a day that goes by when I don't think of him."

"You treated him like shit," said Gavin.

Snow looked stung. "No. When? I never-"

"I was right there! Last January, we were working outside and you blew up at him, man. You got right in his face. You called him a fuck."

"No, I didn't."

"You did! You called him a fuck and then you grabbed him and screamed, 'You stupid fucking asshole...'"

"I'm sure I was responding to something specific."

"'...I kick your fucking ass,' you said... and then you *spit*, man. You spit right in his face!"

"No, now... come on, that's pure folklore. Paulette, you've had your hand up. Get in here and join the discussion."

Ada's mother, Paulette, said, "No one has mentioned the children. What are we doing to protect them? My daughter is only ten years old, Beverly's son is still in his teens. Roseanne, how old is Sarah?"

"Eight," I said.

"Ten and eight. We're talking about very young people, and we have an obligation-"

Having failed to find an ally in Paulette, Snow said, "Paulette... you know... I'll say what I said to Cathy, and what I'm saying to all of you right now. Those people who attacked us last week? Those folks who shot at us and destroyed our property and spilled our blood? Those folks are gone, gone, gone, and I'm talking D-A-D dead. D-*E*-A-D. Let me put it like this: you know how life throws you challenges? People get sick or lose a lot of money or... Yvonne, like when your ex-husband freaked out and killed all those people down in Atlanta? It happens, man. It's a part of life. What happened to us last week was a challenge big-time, and we met that challenge and persevered and I'm damn proud of every last one of us. That's a valuable lesson for the kids on board, too, and I wish Steffi and Sarah and Walter and Ada were here with us. Where are they?"

"Downstairs," said Beverly.

"What are they doing there?"

"We didn't want to upset them," she answered back evenly, and Snow wisely let it go.

"I'm not asking you to do anything new. Keep the energy coming and keep thinking positive. Everything I'm saying here comes straight from the heart. You all know me. I've been a father to you and I've been a friend." Gavin had his hand up, and Snow reluctantly called on him.

"Yes. Thank you for recognizing me on the floor. My point is this: you tell us to think positive. You say, 'Pray, have faith. There is no need to be asking these questions.' But if we're to pray, who do we pray to—you?"

"No, not me, obviously," Snow grumbled.

"Because I don't pray to any man. I got to tell you right now."

"That's not what I'm talking about at *all*. Don't be a hothead," Snow said, finally losing his temper.

Gavin jumped out of his chair. "Oh, a hothead? I'll show you a motherfuckin' hothead... blue ass motherfucker."

He came charging at Snow, and Dan and Richard held him back. Others shrank away from the tangle of struggling men.

"Get his head, get his head!" someone shouted.

"I'm not gonna touch the man," said Gavin, "I just wanna-"

"...a civilized discussion, if we can't have a civilized discussion..."

"Everyone just *stop* it!" Cathy screeched. Some of the struggle had lessened, and the men let go of Gavin's arms.

Gavin jumped in place, working his neck in a cocky circle. "I control myself. I know who I am. My mother raised me right."

"...no place for that in a civilized conversation. I'm answering your questions, I'm trying to answer your questions, if you don't like the answers..." Snow said.

"Keep it together, people," Yvonne advised.

"I don't get on my knees for no man. You ain't lord and master. You just an old man with a lot of money," said Gavin.

"Not a lot, Gavin, I can tell you. Now can we resume our discussion? Can we finally, like grown human beings...?"

Gavin sat back down, guarded more closely by Dan

and Richard. Snow wiped his sweating forehead. His eyes were flaming hot and his hand was trembling.

"Jesus Christ, folks... is anyone hurt? Are we all all right together? Can we get all right? Good God up above... I am so sad about what has happened today. I think I need a glass of water. Can someone get me a... Bev?" Beverly ran off into the kitchen and came back with a glass of water for Snow, who drank it. "We all just need to cool down. Gavin, people... we can't do this to ourselves. We can't go there. Richard, what happened to your shirt? Did you tear your shirt? Do you want a new one?"

"I'm fine," Rich said.

Snow finished his water and set it down. "It's time to take a big step back. Can you do this with me? Everyone take a big step back and let's remember what brought us here."

"Everyone listen to Dr. Snow and show him some respect!" shouted Yvonne.

"Listen to *yourselves*, listen to yourselves." Snow looked to Wallis for help, but Wallis just shook his head. "We can't turn on each other like this. We've worked too hard... I've worked too hard. Think about how far we've come together. We've grasped the unknown. All of us, from the youngest on up. And that's a beautiful thing. I mean, think about it—we're pioneers! We're more than pioneers, we're space explorers. This is outer space! And sometimes space is a scary place. There's meteors and asteroids and... space monsters. We call them monsters, they're not really monsters. They're just creatures who've adapted to their environments. Do you ever wonder why people on Earth have two eyes and two ears and a full set of lungs and kidneys? Because of our environment. If we lived on Saturn, we'd be different. We probably wouldn't need lungs because there'd be nothing to breathe. First of all, Saturn is a gas planet, so we'd have to cope with that. But we'd figure it out. That's the thing about space: everything looks scary but nothing actually is."

"Saturn is a gas planet?" asked Beverly.

"Yeah. There's no real surface to the planet. It's just down and down and down." More sad, puzzled silence. Heads were bowed around the room, and I could sense everyone thinking.

Snow said, "Brothers and sisters, I wish I could make last week go away. I'd cut off my right hand to bring Sander back, I really would. But it doesn't work like that. The duty of the survivors is to honor the memory of the dead, and that's what we're doing... and that's what we'll *keep* doing, God willing. I just need your help. I'm only one man—one very mortal man. God knows I have my limitations. Jesus was different—Jesus was a man, but he also had divine properties... so he had that to fall back on. I don't have any divine properties... or if I do, they're the same divine properties we all have. We're all equally divine or not-divine, take your pick. All I have is a vision—I call it prismatic vision. Prismatic vision is the ability to take that which is inherently obscure and to make it even more obscure. So if I'm the prism, every one of us is a beam of colored light." He knew he was losing his audience, so he said, "Think of it like this: if I'm a prism, Jesus was a magnifying glass. And Buddha, Buddha was a... bowl full of water. With a goldfish swimming in it. Two goldfish. No, just one goldfish."

The meeting concluded with all of us streaming out of the mess hall in a daze. The group brain had divided; we'd gone back to being individuals with separate destinies.

You could almost hear people making travel plans in their heads.

IV. WHAT I DID IN LIMBO

CHAPTER TWENTY-FIVE

They leave one at a time. Two over the course of one week, five more the next. Sometimes they leave in pairs. Neil takes them wherever they want to go. It's his main occupation—it gets him out of the house. A few leave angry; most don't. Most just leave. They give us a day or two warning and have their bags packed early.

Cathy Oines stands on the loading dock as Neil stows her things aboard Mandy Two. She's wearing nice clothes for some reason, black pointy shoes. Maybe she's meeting someone for dinner. "I won't miss the smell. I'm a very sense-oriented person. I can't stand the smell of oranges. Anything citrus. It never bothered me until I met my husband. He loved oranges—but Ronnie was strange. He had a reputation for being effeminate amongst the faculty at the University of Ottawa. I never thought of him as effeminate. He had certain expressions and mannerisms that some might consider effeminate."

People change after deciding to quit the island. They walk with a lighter step. They actually seem to get bigger, taller. They're getting bigger and the rest of us are shrinking. There's less laundry to do, fewer people to talk to in the mess hall.

Beverly Sachs and her son Walter watch Neil prepare for the two hour trip back to the mainland. The loading dock is gray and wet; waves reach up to snatch at our ankles. I'm there too—I'm always there. I say goodbye to everyone.

"I feel like I'm forgetting something. I packed three times. I haven't packed a suitcase in two years," she says.

Walter is pacing behind his mother. He looks like he wants the world to shut up.

"We're staying with my brother in New Hampshire until we get our bearings. He's got a ranch in Meredith. It's not much. He and his wife own a steakhouse on Lake Winnipesaukee. You should stop by if you're ever in the area. It's not just a steakhouse. The prime rib is actually the worst thing on the menu."

Walter stops pacing and glares at his mother's ear. I want to ask him something but don't know what. I used to date boys his age—hard to imagine.

The halls and stairwells are empty. Somewhere there's the sound of a metal sheet banging. Abandoned bedrooms are left open, the covers stripped. I look out one barred window and see a blue-black ocean. A fresh smell comes up to me, wide open wind.

Yvonne Baker throws her duffel bag at Neil, who catches it and puts it on the boat. "I'll be back on my feet in a week, two weeks tops. I never have any problems finding work. It helps when you know how to do shit. I ran concessions for Kiss back in '07—point-of-sale, your basic touch-screen interface. Gene and I hung out. We went to Europe, South America... fuckin' Latvia. Dude makes killer barbecue."

The next day it's someone else: a guy named Adam, another guy named Lance. People I still barely know.

"The Swedish word for goodbye is Adjö. In Gaelic it's Slán agat. In Farsi, Khoda hafaz. Fir milaan ge means 'See you again' in Punjabi." The man looks up from his spiral notebook.

Behind him, Neil starts the engine on Mandy One. "Guess what country speaks Urdu. Do you know? It's not Guatemala. Guess. It's not Vietnam."

In the laundry room I wash my own socks and underwear. I sit on top of the dryer and read an old paperback. It's a science fiction book about Captain Kirk. Captain Kirk and Uhura seem to like each other. They're on a planet where everyone dresses like Roman senators. The dryer hums and bumps. I look at my wrist where years ago I used to wear a watch. I open the dryer door and feel around but my clothes are still damp.

Paulette calls to her daughter Ada across the loading dock: "Don't waste time, now. I want to leave before dark. Where are your glasses? Hold onto 'em—those glasses were expensive. I got a million things to do when we get back. I gotta call your uncle. I gotta see if that money's still in savings. Should be six thousand dollars last time I checked. What'd you do with your jacket? You're gonna need it, baby, trust me."

The weight room is a cold, quiet tomb. Twenty pound barbell plates lie stacked on the floor, and there's a towel thrown over the saddle of a stationary bike. I move the towel and sit down, pedaling slowly. I'm not working out, I'm just moving the pedals. The speedometer tells me I'm not even going one mile-per-hour. The pedals offer resistance at such a slow speed. My heart rate is seventy-five beats-per-minute. I'm not sweating. Eventually the display shuts itself off.

A woman named Penny and a man named Ted wait for Neil to prep the boat. They came to the island separately but they're leaving together.

"Ted and I are going into business. I've got an accounting degree and Ted knows how to drive a truck," says Penny.

"I can do a lot more than that. I can fix transmissions. I'm licensed to work on BMWs. I used to know how to pour concrete.

I haven't done it in a while but I can pick it right back up. I can pour foundations. Pouring foundations is simple if you've got the technical knowhow," Ted says.

Couples with plans—it sounds romantic but I'm not sure it is. Some of these people are just faces to me. Penny has short brown hair and deep temples that pulse like gills. Ted once told a joke about Danica Patrick that no one liked.

"I can do surveying. I worked as a surveyor for the town of Carmel for three years. I also know how to windsurf. I'm not saying all of these are marketable skills. I've got a box of baseball cards in storage. I've got a full set of '68 Topps that's probably worth about three thousand dollars," he says.

Neil tosses up a pair of life jackets, which both Penny and Ted fail to catch. One of the jackets skitters across the loading dock and slides into the water.

A few people leave without much fanfare. As our numbers dwindle there's less fanfare to be had—a handshake, a quick hug. They chew gum to counteract the effects of motion sickness. Most look relieved: a guy named Jack, a woman named Michelle.

"You'll be fine without us. Fewer mouths to feed. We should've made better use of our human resources. That's my only regret."

"We should've spent more time worrying about our civil defense."

"We should've had more meetings."

"We should've started a church."

Everyone sighs; the ones still here and the ones about to leave and the ones who've already left.

CHAPTER TWENTY-SIX

After Sander's death, Gavin Baptiste more-or-less took over his old duties, which meant handling most of the island's physical labor by himself. We turned to him whenever we needed something fixed or moved from one floor to the next. We were a small crew now, just nine people, and Gavin was in charge of shutting down Deck Three and bringing everything up to the top two floors. He resented the job and complained about it constantly.

"I've said it before, and now I'm saying again... I am not anyone's bitch, okay? I have been moving furniture all morning. You see this cut on my hand? I have cuts and bruises all over," he said. We were relocating boxes of cleaning supplies to a utility closet on Deck Two, and Snow had stopped by to watch.

"I made no such insinuation. I merely asked if it would be possible to stack the floor wax along one wall so that there could be more room for the extra linens over here," Snow said, using gestures to accompany his explanation.

Gavin leaned back against the wall of the closet. "Hm. Interesting. I hadn't thought of that. Stack these drums four-high all the way up to the ceiling, is that what you're saying? That's interesting. It could be possible. I would have to be an orangutan or a gorilla or some such... or maybe a human forklift."

"Fine, don't do it then."

"No, I think it would be something... if I were a human forklift and had metal arms that could raise thirty-gallon steel containers over my head—I should try this."

Snow stomped off, and Gavin complained to me, "He's no different from any other foreman. They have no regard for basic humanity. Simple things, such as: a man must stop and rest every few hours or else his arms will fall off. This is one. Eating is important. I work fourteen months at a fruit packing plant in Port-au-Prince. Mangos, cantaloupe, bananas, breadfruit. The foreman was a man from the United States by the name of Henry Evans. I can still remember his face. One day this man drove his jeep into a crowd of workers on their lunch break. Three killed, four more badly injured—and still the American government refused to prosecute. This is my life."

"Why did they refuse to prosecute?" I asked, handing him a small box up from the floor.

"The magistrate claimed that one of the men eating his lunch had provoked the man in the jeep. Do you believe this? I saw it myself! There was no provocation. We were eating our lunches on the beach, and the man named Henry Evans climbed into his jeep, pulled out of his parking spot, and drove at a high speed directly into a group of men at a picnic table. I was not fifty feet away!" Gavin pointed at his own throbbing eyes. "Men were screaming, begging Henry Evans to stop what he was doing, but the man just threw the jeep into reverse and ran them over a second time."

"God. Why?"

"There is no reason! Never is there a reason. We are not human to them. We are specks of dust. I would've been killed too had I not chosen to eat my sandwich near the riprap. The beach was soaked with blood. The blood of my friends, my coworkers... and to this day Henry Evans is a free man in America with a good job at Morley Foods."

We finished reorganizing the utility closet and went on to our next task, moving Star's things out of our room and down one flight to Deck Two. She was old enough to have her own room, though I would've preferred she stay and keep me company. I guess I'm just one of those women who likes to know there's someone else there at night.

"You really don't need to help us, Gavin. It's just a couple of bags," I said once we got upstairs.

He threw both bags of clothes onto his back. "It's okay. I will be crippled in the morning anyway. Where is this going?"

Star answered, "The Fosters' old room."

I stood in the door to our quarters. "Oh, no, Star. Didn't I tell you I wanted you to stay in Block Alpha?"

"What's the difference? It's only one floor away, and the Fosters have a double bed. I'm tired of sleeping in a stupid bunk bed," she grumbled.

We argued about it until I finally gave in, saying, "Be good, though. Just because you're living in Delta doesn't mean you get to hang out on the bridge all night."

Gavin hauled the bags downstairs and dropped them off in Star's new room. I had to prod her to thank him before he left.

"Can I try out your bed?" I asked.

She stood aside, and I flumped down on the Fosters' old mattress. Here they'd slept for two years, probably made love a hundred times—although maybe not. You never knew about other people's sex lives.

"It's going to be quiet upstairs without you," I said. "Let me see, there's just me and Gavin... and Charity and Dr. Snow. That's four. Who's left? You and Mandy..."

She zipped open one of her bags. "And Uncle Wallis."

"Right... and Steffi's down here too. That's eight."

"Don't forget Neil," she said, tossing some socks and underwear onto the bed. I moved my leg.

"Right, Neil. But he's all the way down the hall, so he doesn't count."

"Why not?"

"Star, honey, Neil's almost on the other end of the island. I bet he could scream at the top of his lungs and you wouldn't even hear it."

"Nunt-unh."

"At the top of his lungs. Seriously, it's like a half mile away."

"I'd hear it—and it's not a half mile. The whole island's only three hundred feet across."

I squinted at her wadded-up clothes, little lumps of thin, faded cotton. "Really? That seems small. I would've thought a quarter mile at least. Where'd you get three hundred feet?"

"I looked it up. Steffi and I found a bunch of old blueprints in the basement. You should check it out. There's a lot of junk down there—pictures of people. The Departed," she said, nodding solemnly. The Departed meant more to her than they did to me. To her they were like mythical figures, ghosts. Their absence was profound.

She finished unpacking her things and stood at the window. The shaggy haircut I'd given her two months ago had grown back to her shoulders. "I can see the mainland," she said.

"You can? What does it look like?"

"A line. Do you think they can see us?"

"Probably, if they're looking."

She gripped the protective bars over the window. "What do you think we look like to them?"

"I don't know. You ask such good questions. A dot, maybe?" Rolling off the bed, I stood next to her. The island made a gray shadow across the water. I couldn't see a line out there, just the horizon. "Do you miss it?"

A shrug. "What's to miss?"

"The world. America. Cities and towns and mountains. Movie theaters. Restaurants. Billions of people. Maybe even more than billions. There's football stadiums and car washes and people playing basketball. All sorts of stuff."

Still no sign of land; our eyes told us different things.

Heading back to my room, I bumped into Neil coming out of the infirmary with Mandy. We'd sort of broken up; "sort of" because there'd been no discussion, just this awkward distance between us. Sander's death had sent him into seclusion. He cooked but rarely ate with the rest of us. Whenever I looked for him, someone would tell me he'd gone out on one of the boats.

Mandy and Neil stopped talking when they saw me. Mandy's hair was a mess, and one of the long laces of her boots had come undone.

"Roseanne, what are you doing here?" she asked.

I glanced down both ends of the empty corridor. "Shouldn't I be?"

"Don't be silly. I guess I just didn't expect, I mean—I saw you and then I..."

"...right..."

"Brain fart."

"It happens."

Neil stood tall above us. He had a small cut over his right eye, which could've been from anything.

"Hey, your birthday's coming up, isn't it?" she asked suddenly. Her eyes pulsed wide. They almost seemed to be sweating.

"Not really," I said.

"It isn't? Why did I think it was? That's dumb of me. Oh well, I suppose it doesn't matter. Listen, we need to have a team meeting soon, all nine of us. I got so mad at Gavin the other day, I almost threw my soup in his face."

She gave Neil's sleeve a quick tug and went back into her office. I didn't mind the tug. She'd known Neil a lot longer than I had. She'd probably tugged on his sleeve a thousand times before.

Neil started down the hall, and I hurried after him. "Why were you in the infirmary? Don't you feel good?" I asked.

"I feel fine," he said, his eyes on the door to the staircase at the end of the hall.

"Just hanging out with Mandy, then?"

He either didn't catch the sarcasm in my voice or didn't care. I grabbed his arm, and we stopped in front of one of the empty bedrooms.

"Please, Roseanne, I've got things to do. I've got to fix the outboard on Mandy One, there's about a million boxes of inventory to unpack, and I need to thaw some fish for dinner."

"How long does it take to thaw fish? You bring it out of the freezer and throw it in the sink. Can't you take a little break? We haven't talked in three months."

"Not that long."

"I mean *really* talked. Hey, believe me, I understand—I've been dumped before, but can we at least be civil to one another? I feel like you're mad at me and I don't know why."

He hesitated before pulling me into the bedroom. I couldn't remember who'd occupied it last. The stripped bed and gray metal furniture said nothing about the previous tenant.

"What'd you do to your eye?" I asked.

He felt the cut above his eyebrow. "Hit my head."

"You hit your head? How'd you do that?"

"Just... bending down."

"You whacked it on something?"

He folded his arms. "Yeah."

I deliberately didn't ask for any more details, not wanting to seem overly concerned. "So that's why you went to the infirmary, to put something on it?"

He kicked out a chair from behind a little writing desk and sat down. "Look, Rosie, I don't mean to be a dick... I like you and all, and we had a lot of fun together, but I've been in a pretty dark place lately and there are just some things I don't feel comfortable talking to you about." He rubbed his nose and sighed at the ceiling. "I guess I'm looking for someone who 'gets' me a bit more."

"Gets you."

"Yeah. Where I'm at—mentally, physically, emotionally."

I concentrated on standing firm on both of my feet. I wanted to look strong, immobile. "Okay. Fine."

"And the other thing is... you're *married*, you know? I mean, I know that's all over, but you're still technically with the guy and... it just weirds me out. I don't feel comfortable with it anymore."

"But you knew when you-"

"I know I did. I know! It's fucked up." He laughed for some hard-to-fathom reason. "I should've thought about it more carefully, but you were there and you seemed interested and I was like 'why not?'... not that I regret it, because I don't. I'll always remember hanging out. I'll always remember the time we made love outside in the rain."

"We did?"

"Yeah... or took a shower together. That's how I think of it—water, being together in the water. Being naked with the water rushing all around." He smiled tentatively, as if he was worried about breaking his teeth. "I just need to be with someone who doesn't already have so much going on in her life."

"And who might that be?" I asked. Seconds passed, steady and countable. "Oh," I said.

"It would be nice if you could be happy for us."

I moved over to the bed and sat on my hands. Mandy's loose bootlace suddenly made sense. "When did this start?"

"Not long ago. A few weeks. I started seeing her about my arm and... she was very helpful. We talked about Sander and our childhoods and where we wanted to be in five or ten years. They were some of the deepest, most intimate conversations I've ever had in my life. And then..." He stretched and cracked his back; I almost expected him to cross to the bathroom and start flossing his teeth. "One sort of intimacy led to another, I guess. Neither of us knew what was happening. I mean, we'd hooked up before—once or twice, way back when."

My hands popped out from under my legs. "Wait, wait. You and Mandy? When was this?"

"Oh, ages ago. Long before you came around." His eyes lost their focus as he pictured something funny from his past. "But that was just sex. That was Mandy being a kid and acting out against her dad, and me being horny and in my twenties. We used to laugh about it. We'd get together once a year for old time's sake."

"And have sex?" I asked, but his eyes were still stuck in 2002. "I thought you said you only hooked up 'once or twice'?"

He blinked. "Yeah. Those were the initial hook-ups. And then we'd get together once a year-"

"-for old time's sake and hook up again, Neil. What's the difference?"

He seemed to think about it. Neil wasn't particularly good with rhetorical questions. "We used condoms?" he tried.

"Nice."

"Well we did! Jesus Christ—why are you being so hostile about things that happened three or four or nine or ten or seven or eight years ago? Maybe you've never been in a relationship like that, where it's just sex and that's it."

"Don't assume anything about me, Neil. You obviously don't have a clue."

He clammed up for a while. I wouldn't have minded sitting like that for hours, making him suffer. But what good would it have done?

"Are you mad?" he asked finally. My look could aptly be described as "withering." "That's not what I meant. I *know* you're mad, obviously, and I don't blame you. I'd be, like, so fucking pissed off."

"I'm not pissed off, Neil, I'm just a little hurt."

"I know, and I'm sorry. I should've been more honest

and up front from the get-go. I mean it. This is me apologizing. I'm an asshole, I'm a shit, I'm the biggest prick ever."

"No, you're not," I said, but he shook his head vigorously.

"I am. This is what assholes do. They lie to people—not that I lied to you per se, because I didn't... not in the sense of saying something that wasn't true. Maybe I emotionally lied a little."

I frowned. "What's 'emotionally lied'?"

"It means I... oh, I don't know. *Emotionally lied*, I can't put it any better than that."

"That's not very helpful. I don't know what 'emotionally lied' means. Does it mean you didn't have any real feelings for me when we were together?"

"No, it doesn't mean that."

"Then what does it mean?"

He shifted impatiently. "I don't know! It's just something I said because I had to say something and that's what came out. It doesn't mean anything, okay? Just forget it. Why are you busting my ass on these little subtle nuances of word choice-"

"Because you said 'emotionally lied' and I'm trying to understand what that means."

"It means I... I..." He gave up—neither of us cared anymore. "Look, never mind. That's in the past. Right now I need to know you're going to be okay with this. Mandy and I both do."

"Why does it matter? It's none of my business who you're sleeping with."

He paused. "It matters because Mandy's pregnant, see, and we're going to have a baby. That's right. That's what we've decided. Mandy doesn't want to get married but she wants to keep it and I'm okay with that too."

His eyes sought approval in mine. Boring news, I thought, not interesting. What else did I have to do today? Eat lunch. Eat a big fucking lunch. I felt like defrosting the one steak on the island and eating it in my room.

"It's crazy," he said, "but I never thought I'd be a dad. I don't know why not. I like kids okay. I did Big Brothers Big Sisters when I was younger. I worked with this fifteen-year-old from St. Catharines named Sean. He was cool. I'd take him to the skate park every Thursday night and we'd-"

"Does her dad know?" I interrupted. I liked stepping on his sentences. It was like stepping on his toes.

"We told him yesterday. He's very happy for us, though I think he's more excited by what it means for Mobility."

"And what *does* it mean for Mobility?"

"Oh, you know—no one's ever been born on the island before. That's kind of cool. It's... what's the word? Historic. It'll be like George Washington, when George Washington was born in the United States. That was cool too."

"George Washington was the first President of the United States, Neil. He wasn't the first person born there."

He glared suspiciously—I was being annoying again. "So? So this'll be even better. Do you not want to talk about this? Because everything I say-"

"No, I'm-"

"-there's this little sarcastic-"

"I'm fine, Neil. I'm not trying to be sarcastic. I'm just a bit stunned by all this—you and Mandy... and now you're having a baby..." I said, mad at myself for getting emotional.

"Roseanne, I'm so sorry." He held his hands in his lap, palms up, to show how sorry he was.

"No," I said, pushing the tears back, "these are happy tears. For you and Mandy. I'm sure you'll be good parents together. Mandy's very organized. You need to be when you're a parent. And you're patient and kind. Where will you be having this baby?"

"What do you mean?"

I shrugged at the gray walls around us. "Not here, I assume."

"We were planning on it. Both Mandy and Charity are doctors."

I laughed, almost relieved, glad these weren't my problems. "A.) I think Mandy's going to be busy enough as it is, and B.) Charity isn't a doctor, she's a dentist."

"Yeah, but in dentist school you have to take all these basic classes where they teach you that kind of stuff."

"They teach you to be an OB/GYN... as preparation... for being a dentist..."

"Yeah! That's what Charity said. She said she took classes. She took a class where they watched a woman give birth and learned all about the proper positioning of the head and how the head has to come out first."

"There's so much more to it than that, I don't even know where to begin."

He gave me another of those looks that told me I was being difficult. "Obviously. Charity's not a moron, you know. She's a very smart woman who cares about Mandy's well-being. She's going to be delivering her own step-grandchild, for God's sake. How do you think most people have babies? Not everyone has the luxury of going to the hospital and having a team of doctors looking after them 24/7. There are some places in the world where the women just push it out."

I decided not to waste my breath. These were crazy people making their own crazy decisions. At least I'd had the excuse of being young and naive when I'd had my first child, whereas Neil and Mandy were both well into their thirties. Still, I felt sorry for the kid. There ought to be a better way of coming into the world than this.

"I hope you know what you're doing," I said.

CHAPTER TWENTY-SEVEN

I spent a lot of time by myself in those days. It was the summer of 2013, and the weather on Mobility was beautiful. We enjoyed fairly pristine conditions four months out of the year. The air was mild with a near constant skimming breeze that raked over the top deck. I'd lie out in my shorts and tank-top and take in the sun before heading back inside to help Star with her afternoon studies. Sometimes Charity would join me for twenty minutes or a half hour. The wreck of the disabled helicopter provided strips of shade that passed over my eyelids as the sun drew across the sky.

I was tanning on the top deck one morning when a shadow touched my face. I'd heard Wallis' chair approach from the other side of the helipad. His battery was running low and the motor sounded labored.

I opened my eyes. "Gonna catch some rays?"

His chair buzzed to a stop. Sweat stains bled through the underarms of his blue jumpsuit. "I couldn't find you downstairs so I decided to try up here."

Raising up on one arm, I asked, "Aren't you boiling hot in that thing?"

"I don't plan on staying long." He wrinkled his nose. "It smells like sunscreen. Where did you get the sunscreen?"

"There's a whole box in the infirmary," I said. I'd grabbed a bottle when I knew Mandy was out of her office. We generally avoided each other, which wasn't too hard. Now in her second trimester, she spent her entire days relaxing on the bridge with her feet up, watching YouTube videos about natural childbirth. She clearly planned on doing as little work as possible between now and her due date.

"You should put some on your face and forehead," I said, offering him the bottle. He frowned it away.

"Nah, I don't like that stuff. I don't like having creams and ointments on my skin."

"You'd make a lousy woman then."

He smiled and, changing his mind, held out his hand for the bottle. "I'd make a lousy woman anyway. I like the smell of suntan lotion, I just don't like the feel of it. It's too greasy."

"This isn't greasy."

"Yes, it is."

"Wallis, it isn't."

"It is. You're lying to me. You're a lying woman." After examining the bottle, he set it back down by his feet. "Anyway, how do you feel about being in charge of the island for a few days?"

The breeze was picking up, and I wrapped a shirt around my legs. "Me? Why?"

"Because it's either you or Charity or Mandy or Gavin or one of the girls, and Gavin can't do it because I need him to fix the air conditioning in Block Delta, and both Charity and Mandy already said no."

I counted the names in my head. It had become a compulsion lately, counting the names of the people who still lived on the island, wanting the number to total something other than nine.

"What about Neil? What about Dr. Snow?" I asked.

"They're coming with me. Snow and I are meeting a guy in St. John's about transferring some of our bank accounts overseas. It's getting to be too much of a hassle dealing with the Canadians every time we want to touch our money. We won't be gone long. This guy has a house south of town where we can lie low and do our business. He's pro-Mobility and Clem's known him for twenty years."

I swung my legs over the side of my deck chair. "Can't you do it over the phone? Oh, right, we don't have phones. What about online?"

"We're trying to minimize the paper trail, sis. Don't worry, it'll be easy. Just keep an eye on the VTS and let Gavin know if something strange pops up. Neil's got a butt-load of fish sticks in the freezer and they should get you through the weekend. They're good—I had some for breakfast."

"But what if something breaks? You know I can't fix anything. What if there's a fire or Gavin goes psycho like he did last month?"

"He won't. You shouldn't have any problems with the weather either. Just be sure to pull Mandy One out of the water if the wind picks up."

"I don't know how to do that. I can't *do* anything. I'm dumb," I said.

He lifted an invisible remote control and hit the fast-forward button. It was a gesture I'd learned to interpret from years of being his sister.

"Yeah, yeah. We're not back in Ohio anymore,

Roseanne. No one thinks you're dumb. That's Milner talking, not Mobility," he said.

I finally said okay, mainly just to get rid of him. The thought of subbing for Dr. Snow and Wallis freaked me out—I'm good at fucking things up, if you haven't noticed—though a small part of me liked the idea of calling the shots. I suppose I'm better at giving orders than receiving them, which was why I'd made a good assistant manager at Pier 1. At Pier 1 I normally worked the closing shift, so I got to supervise the evening clean-up and count down the drawers before locking up for the night. I wouldn't exactly call it "fun" but I liked the routine of straightening pillows and throw-rugs, assigning girls to stand at the registers while I inspected the sales floor for merchandise left out or cleaning supplies not put away. We'd stay a half hour past close, trading the usual k.d. lang for some loud hip-hop to keep us awake as we pushed the broom around. Girls would kick off their shoes and talk about their plans for after work. Sometimes they'd use the store phone to call their boyfriends, which I didn't mind. In some ways I felt more responsible to my coworkers than I did to my own kids, sad as that sounds. I felt like less of a failure at work, less squeezed.

The next morning Neil, Dr. Snow, and my brother left in Mandy Two for the mainland, and I gathered the remaining six of us on the bridge for a meeting. Mandy wasn't feeling well and wanted to end early.

"This'll just take a minute. Wallis left a few notes he asked me to go over," I said.

She came back from the door and plopped down in a chair. Her baby bump wasn't much; you could hardly see it under her jumpsuit. "Can we keep this short? I've been throwing up all morning," she sighed.

"Yes, like I said, it'll only take a minute."

"*One* minute," she emphasized.

"I can't promise exactly one minute. It might take two or three or even five."

She frowned uncooperatively but kept her mouth shut. Charity sat next to her. She'd brought her breakfast to the meeting: a bowl of oatmeal, which she held in her lap.

"Thank you. Again, Wallis left a few notes... it's nothing important. Just a reminder about the A/C in Block Delta..."

"Girl, that oatmeal smells so good!" said Gavin. I stopped and closed my mouth.

"Would you like some?" Charity asked.

"No, you enjoy it. It smells like... maple syrup!" He smiled at the bowl. The others also took a moment to appreciate the smell.

"I added a little sugar to it," she explained.

"Mmm, goodness gracious. Makes my mouth water just looking at it."

I set down my notes for the meeting. Charity said to Gavin, "Really, you can have a bite."

He waved her off with his big, leather-brown hand. "No, I've already had my plain white toast with imitation butter and watered-down instant coffee served at lukewarm temperature in a cup that has not been washed properly. Let me see that bowl." He leaned over Mandy for a better look. "This is not the same oatmeal I have been eating for breakfast all these years."

"It is, it is!" Charity said as he continued to tease.

"No, this is different oatmeal. My oatmeal tastes like porridge or gruel or some sort of suet-like-mixture that one might feed to livestock or barnyard animals for the purpose of keeping them alive."

I raised my hand. "Guys? Trying to run a meeting here..."

"What's suet?" Star asked.

Steffi answered, "It's like the stuff they use to make candles. Birds eat it. It's gross."

"I just added some sugar... and a pinch of cinnamon," Charity said.

"I don't believe you. There is favoritism on this island—you see, you see? I will start a revolution this afternoon," said Gavin. Everyone laughed except me.

"Come on, people, let's be serious. I think we're annoying Rosie," said Mandy.

"You're not annoying me. If you guys don't care, that's fine. I've got other things to do," I said.

"Rose*anne*, we're sorry!" said Charity. The others quieted down, and I snatched up my notes with a huff.

"As I was trying to say, Wallis wanted me to remind you about the problem with the air conditioning in Block Delta, and he was hoping that you, Gavin, would be able to fix it before he returns." Gavin saluted. "Also, Neil noticed some mouse droppings in the boiler room last week. We need to make sure we're inspecting the boats throughly for mice and other pests whenever we come back from the mainland."

"Ain't got to tell me. I'm not the one who drives them boats, that's Neil," said Gavin.

"I know, but... just as a general announcement. It's not directed at any one person."

"Those mice have been here since forever. I see them... four, five times. Eating dust, eating old pieces of insulation."

"Mice eat dust?" asked Star.

"Mice will eat anything—dust, lint, bacteria. A hungry mouse will eat right through your arm."

"Not if you swat it away," Steffi said.

"No, Miss Smart, but if you were unable to do so…"

"If someone held you down," Mandy conjectured.

"Ew. I don't want to think about it," said Charity, stirring her oatmeal. I folded my notes and put them away.

After the meeting I stayed behind for another hour to monitor the VTS. Just the usual shipping traffic, none of it passing closer than a couple of miles. No one took much interest in us anymore. The green blips on the radar screen pulsed and drifted with nothing apparently on their minds. It was like we weren't even there.

For the rest of the day I stayed in my room and wrote in my journal, occasionally bringing out Wallis' dictionary to take a break from staring at my own handwriting. There were times when the dictionary seemed like the least interesting book ever written. Each definition ran on for lines and lines, and the bulk of it went over my head. I wondered how many different words I used over the course of a typical day, not counting repeats. Five thousand? Probably not even five thousand. There were so many things I wanted to know about myself, so many concrete, quantifiable things.

At five o'clock I went back downstairs to prepare dinner for the crew. I couldn't remember the last time I'd actually cooked for a group of people. The homey practicality of it appealed to me—wearing an oven mitt, using a timer, guesstimating the seasonings.

Star helped me carry the food from the kitchen to the dining room. Everyone on the island ate at the same time now that there were so few of us. With Neil, Snow, and Wallis gone, we all fit around the same small table.

Gavin reached for a second helping of cod sticks. "I like what you did with the fish, Roseanne. Neil overcooks it," he said.

"Thanks, Gavin," I said. It was nice to know I could cook fish better than Neil.

"Neil doesn't overcook anything. It's just hard to make dinner for a lot of people at once," Mandy said. She'd taken only one fish stick, heaping the rest of her plate with reconstituted mashed potatoes.

"Nine people is not a lot of people. Try cooking for three hundred. That's what we did when I was a line chef in the Haitian army. Three hundred hungry soldiers, and we'd serve them beans and toast and on Fridays Sloppy Joe sandwiches. I was in the kitchen from four in the morning until eleven at night," Gavin said.

"Aren't you cool?" said Mandy. Steffi, who thrived on adult conflict, laughed cheerfully.

"There are worse jobs. Try being a mom," I said, kicking Star under the table to show I was kidding. The girls chewed their fish sticks with their little beaks open.

"Tough yet rewarding," Charity agreed. Gavin breathed heavily as he ate, drowning in it. It was noisy, strenuous eating.

Mandy put down her fork. "What do you mean, 'There are worse jobs'?"

"'Harder,' not 'worse.' I meant to say harder," I said.

"No, you said worse. You said 'There are worse jobs.'"

"I know but I meant to say harder. You know... 'there are harder jobs.' Being a mom's a hard job, that's all."

Mandy stared. "You know what? You can be a real jerk sometimes, Rosie."

Gavin, Charity and the girls all stopped eating to watch. "What are you talking about?" I asked.

"Saying 'there are worse jobs' and I'm sitting right here."

"I meant harder. Good lord, Mandy... relax, okay? I just misspoke."

She looked like she wanted to cry. "I'm gonna be a mom, you know. In a few short weeks."

"I know you are. Why are you getting upset? I don't even know how we started on this."

"Because you said 'There are worse jobs, try being a mom-'"

"...*harder*, harder..."

"-and what kind of a mom are you? Tell me. Come on, you're sitting there... 'There are worse jobs,' and you just-"

"I fucking meant to say harder!"

"-you haven't even *seen* three of your kids in however many fucking years."

"The language, dears," Charity begged softly.

"Oh, yeah? I haven't seen 'em, huh? I haven't seen 'em. Okay. I know that. I know it. I haven't seen 'em! What does that-"

"You have no right to sit there while I'm at the same table and say 'There are worse jobs than being a mom...'"

"I didn't say-"

"-or there are worse jobs, try being a mom."

"I didn't say that either. I mean I did—I said it but I meant to say-"

Gavin cut in with his deeper voice, "Ladies, why are we fighting? There's no need for all of this anger. This is a simple misunderstanding."

Mandy pushed her mostly untouched food aside. "Look

at yourself, Roseanne. Do you ever do that? Do you ever take a moment to just-"

"All the time," I said.

"I mean, here you are... and Star's a great kid. She's great. But that's as much due to the other women on this island as you. We've raised that girl together, just like we've all raised Steffi—no offense, Charity. And as far as your other kids go-"

"You better shut up now," I warned.

"...what are their names? I don't even know their names."

My eyes flared. "Their names are Vance and Mary and..."

"Right."

"... and Connor—what? Those are their names. You asked me their names and I told you."

"After some thought and hesitation."

"No, I didn't. That's crazy. Did I hesitate?" I asked Charity, who literally shrank away from me. "You asked and I said Vance and Mary and Connor, just like that."

"That time, fine," said Mandy.

"That time fine, the other time fine too. What's your point, anyway? Why are you picking on me? Really, seriously, I'm asking. What did I ever do to you? Have I ever criticized you or made little comments?"

"Ladies, will you please stop this infernal female bickering?" Gavin demanded, wanting to enjoy his fish sticks, resenting not being able to.

Mandy spoke acidly, "The point is this, Roseanne. You do what you want. Hey, I don't care, whatever. But I'll tell you one thing. You haven't earned the right to talk about being a mom. Charity has. Other women have."

"Oh, and you have?" I said.

"I will. And when I do-"

Out of nowhere, Star yelled, "My mom is a good mom!"

That silenced us. Star never raised her voice except maybe to complain about something. I stared, probably more shocked than anyone else. "Thank you, honey," I said.

She jumped up and ran out of the mess hall, Steffi calling after her, "Star!"

"She'll be all right. Everyone just needed to let off some steam. Finish your dinner," said Charity.

"I'm not hungry," Mandy said, taking her plate into the kitchen. We heard the sink run and a sharp bang on the counter. Gavin whistled once, quietly and to himself. Then Mandy popped back through the swinging double doors and left without speaking.

"Someone's being a little hormonal," Charity said.

"Damn girl is crazy," said Gavin.

"I was like that when I was pregnant with Steffi. I wouldn't get angry, just terribly depressed. So depressed I'd sit in an empty bathtub for an hour and cry. And then the next day I'd be fine."

"I don't ever want to have kids," said Steffi, who was eleven.

"You don't have to, dear," her mother said.

After two more bites, I finally said, "I guess I'm not that hungry anymore either."

"Someone gotta eat these fish sticks," Gavin said, throwing a few more onto his pile.

I brought my plate and silverware into the kitchen and washed them at the sink. Mandy had made a point of leaving her cleaned-and-dried plate on the counter where I could see it.

Saying goodnight to the others, I searched for and

found Star sitting by herself on the bridge. The room was dark except for the blue glow of the computers by the observation window. She was playing a video game on one of them, and I sat next to her.

"Thanks for sticking up for me back there," I said.

She shrugged, more focused on her game. It looked violent, with a lot of shooting and heads blowing up.

"Do you want to be alone?" I asked gently.

Another shrug. Her player expired in a hail of bullets, and she brought her hands to her lap.

"Look," I said, "I can understand if you want to go back to your brothers and sis-"

"They're not my brothers. I don't have any brothers and I don't have a sister," she said.

"Aw, come on, you know you do. Maybe you just don't remember them very well."

"I don't like Vance. He hit me once."

"I'm sure he didn't mean anything by it. Vance was just a baby."

"He bit me too, right on my hand." She rubbed the soft part between her thumb and forefinger, as if it still hurt. "Why is Mandy always so mean to you? You didn't say anything wrong. You just made a little joke."

"It's hard to explain. We're two very different people, Mandy and I. She's smart and I'm not. She's beautiful and I'm, well…"

"You're beautiful," Star said.

"I am?"

"You're *pretty*," she clarified.

"Oh. Well, thanks anyway. I'll take pretty."

"You're smart too. You just don't think you are."

Star amazed me sometimes. It was like she'd been

around my whole life, known me as a kid. "Oh, Star... how can you be only nine and already know so much?"

"I'm not nine, I'm twelve. Steffi and I worked it out. We decided that a year on Mobility equals two years on the mainland. That's because you learn so much here and you have to grow up quicker. So... we came here when I was six—three years ago—three times two is six, six plus six is twelve."

"Sounds complicated. I'll stick with the old system."

She gave up explaining and put her head on my shoulder. Strands of hair tickled my nose and mouth. "You should punch Mandy the next time she says something nasty to you."

"Hey, that's not even funny. That's a pregnant woman there. Both she and the baby could get really hurt."

"Something else then. You could spit in her dinner when she isn't looking."

"No, no... she hardly eats anyway. I think I'd rather just avoid her."

"Here? Good luck with that."

I glanced around the room. Someone, probably one of the men, had left his denim work jacket on the back of the chair next to mine. "Good point, kid," I said.

I spent most of the next day lying in bed, writing in my journal. Every now and then I could hear Gavin's loud voice echoing down the halls, talking to himself. Occasional sounds reached me from the other floors: noises in the elevator shaft, the muffled cough of a toilet flushing.

Charity stopped by once to ask if I had any laundry. "The world misses you," she said. I thanked her.

It wasn't until the third day that Wallis, Neil, and Snow returned on Mandy Two. I was happy to see them, even

Neil, and I kissed Wallis as soon as he got off the boat. "We're still here," I said.

"How's the A/C?" he asked. Neil had already gone ahead to the elevator with his bags.

"I had to ask Gavin five times but it's finally working."

"Good," Snow said absently. His blue face had a greenish tint to it, possibly from the ride back. "We should gather the others. We have a lot to talk about."

Minutes later all nine of us minus the kids had assembled on the bridge to hear Wallis and Snow's report. Neil sat with his arm around Mandy, his beard and hair still wet from the boat. I chose to stand.

"Sorry we took so long. Our host wanted to introduce us to some people from the U.S. who couldn't come up until last night. Business folks. They want to pay us to advertise their mail order concern on our website. We're still undecided. Clem thinks it's a bad idea," said Wallis.

"I didn't say that. I simply said we ought to wait until we see their proposal in writing," insisted Snow.

"Agreed. It was a nice dinner at any rate. I'm also happy to announce our partnership with EFC Bank in Geneva, which means it should be easier to tap into our finances from now on."

"Though let's not forget what we talked about. Mobility needs its own currency, its own system of banks—by 2015 at the absolute latest," added Snow.

"Of course. The two aren't mutually exclusive, but… we can discuss that later."

Wallis and Snow seemed to be talking at cross-purposes, which they did a lot back then.

"It sounds like everything went well," said Charity.

Wallis hesitated, and Snow said, "Not everything. We had a quick drink with Manuel Andrade and his wife before we left. Manuel's been looking after our place in St. John's," he explained to those of us who didn't know.

"Nothing wrong with the house, I hope?" asked Charity.

"The house is fine. We didn't stop by, obviously. We didn't even go near the city."

Wallis' eyes were on me, and I felt my cheeks redden. "What? Why are you looking at me like that?" I asked.

"Don't get worked up. It could be that Manuel's being overly cautious. His wife in particular tends to exaggerate," Snow replied.

"Why would I get worked up? You haven't told me what's happening yet," I said, hearing the anxiety rise in my own voice.

"Manuel thinks some people in town have been looking for you. He's had one visit from immigration and another from the national police over the last month. We've told him what to say, but the Mounties seem to know more than they're letting on."

"We don't know if that means they know you're here—in which case we need to act now—or they're still tracking down leads and haven't yet traced you to Mobility," said Wallis.

"It's a constitutional crisis," said Snow.

"In either case it's probably just a matter of time before someone from the CBSA shows up, probably with a lot of friends. It could get ugly for both you and Star. We need to come up with a plan."

"It's a constitutional crisis," Snow repeated. His skin thrummed violet.

"How so?" Wallis asked.

"It calls into question our very existence here. The Americans can't take your sister from us and neither can the Canadians. They don't have the right. We define our own laws, defend our own borders, and protect our own citizens regardless of their legal problems in other countries."

He spoke with passion, though I doubted he had any real concern for me as a person. I represented something big and theoretical in his mind.

"Did this Manuel guy mention someone by the name of Pam Okerfeldt?" I asked.

No one answered. Gavin looked like he'd fallen asleep.

"We should curtail our number of trips to the mainland, at least until the heat dies down. Roseanne, both you and Star need to stay out of sight. Avoid the top deck or any place where you can be spotted outdoors," said Wallis.

"I can't do that to Star. She's a growing girl. She needs fresh air," I said.

"That's what open windows are for," said Mandy.

I laughed. My eyes were ice cannons. Then I told her to shut up.

"It's only temporary, sis. I've instructed Manuel to let us know if anything changes over the next few days," Wallis said.

"Nothing's temporary, everything's permanent," I muttered. I could feel my sanity slipping away, what was left of it. I was a woman with skin and hair and teeth that filled my mouth.

"We're not gonna let you hang out to dry. You're one of us. You're a Mobilian," Wallis said.

Just then Star and Steffi came bursting in from the corridor, Steffi in the lead as always. My chest inflated—everyone's did.

"Mom, Star and I caught a mouse in the basement! We killed it with a pipe," Steffi said.

"I hope you didn't touch it," said Charity.

"We didn't touch it. We left it there. Star saw it and I grabbed a pipe and hit it—bam!—like that, and then its head broke open and all its brains came out."

The adults received this with something like awed silence. Gavin nodded himself back awake.

"The poor thing," said Charity.

"It almost got away. I hit it twice. The first time I think I just stunned it a little, and then I hit it again and its whole head exploded."

"Mm, lord..." Gavin sighed, rubbing one flat palm down his face. He snickered, eyes half-closed. He looked delighted by something that was happening in a parallel stream of awareness.

"Do you want to see it?" Steffi asked us. Star stood behind the older girl, mimicking Steffi's posture. The two together looked threatening, like a girls' gang.

"Just leave it there and someone will dispose of it later," Snow said.

They started to leave but didn't. Star's jumpsuit was dirty and she needed a new pair of boots.

"What are you guys talking about?" asked Steffi.

Wallis, Snow, and I glanced at each other. "Oh, nothing. We're just having a meeting," I said.

"You look serious."

"We're not."

"You look it."

"We're not. It's actually a very lighthearted meeting."

They seemed unconvinced. We'd raised them to be suspicious, to think of adults as clowns. Hand signals were exchanged, and they wandered off. The meeting broke up soon after.

CHAPTER TWENTY-EIGHT

Summer passed into fall, and soon it was too cold out for sunbathing anyway. For weeks we heard nothing from the mainland, and I grew annoyed at Manuel and his overreacting wife for worrying us to begin with. Mobility stood in quivering limbo, a jelly mirage. Virtually the only things we had to occupy our time and thoughts were our chores, which were many, and Mandy's pregnancy, which was now reaching its term.

Mandy was in her seventh month when we held our annual Christmas party in the mess hall. She couldn't drink but the rest of us passed around a few bottles of champagne. Alcohol was a rare commodity on the island so it didn't take much to get us buzzed. Instead of presents we read poems that we'd written about each other. This year it was my turn to compose an ode to Steffi. It went:

Stephanie, my friend, years younger than I
How I admire your physical strength and intelligence
Not to mention your great sense of humor
Which I used to experience as sarcasm
But now I don't

Everyone clapped, and Steffi said, "Thanks, Roseanne."

"Sorry. I wanted to make it rhyme," I said.

The party thinned out early, with Mandy going off to rest her big belly, and by ten o'clock the only ones left were Neil, Gavin, and myself. Gavin was hammered.

"Look, you two… look…" He leaned toward the door, taking a bottle with him. "This is what I tell you… all the time. People don't know. They say, 'Christmas is a religious holiday.' But I say: bullshit!"

Neil and I laughed to see him so drunk. "Bullshit, man," Neil said, egging him on.

"I say bullshit! Don't tell me about Santa Claus. I'll tell you about Santa Claus. The myth of Santa Claus has been around as long as the myth of Jesus Christ—the factual myth of Jesus Christ."

"Oh I know," I said.

"They are the same! Historically they are one and the same. Both represent the same loving expression of kindness. And this is true the world over—in North Africa, in Bolivia."

"Especially in Bolivia," said Neil.

Gavin swung his head high and low, agreeing adamantly. "There are fossil records. You can see them on display in many fine museums. Even the names are synonymous. Christ. Claus."

"Both start with 'C's."

"You see? This is what I tell people. I tell them *no*. I tell them bullshit."

He finally bumbled off, and Neil and I shared an awkward chuckle. "Do you think he'll be all right?" I asked.

"He'll probably sleep it off in the infirmary. I wouldn't worry about Gavin. He's been in trickier spots before."

I nodded—*yes*—and glanced around the room at the disarray. "I think I'll pick up."

He put his hand on my arm, and I looked up at him. "What?" I asked.

"I miss you," he said.

He didn't have a tight hold on me. I could've twisted away if I'd wanted to. "What are you talking about?"

"I'm sorry, I know I shouldn't." He leaned down to kiss me, and I pulled free.

"Neil!"

"I'm sorry. Things are hard with Mandy. There's no closeness. We haven't had sex in two months."

"She's pregnant, Neil. Give her a break."

"It's not just that. There's no emotional closeness. I lie next to her at night and I can't stop thinking about you."

He looked like he wanted to take my arm again, so I hid it behind my back. "Are you sure you're not just horny?"

His neck blushed. "You don't understand. I want you. I want to make love again. Right now."

"We can't. I'm not that kind of person. I won't mess around with someone's boyfriend, particularly when she's about to have his baby. I've done a lot of rotten things in my life, but I won't do that."

"Why not? This is Mobility, Roseanne. We can do whatever we want."

"Good, then I'm cleaning up and going to bed."

"That's not what I meant. I mean there's nothing stopping us. We can be together—it doesn't matter about Mandy. We can have a baby too."

I folded my arms. "Ha! That's crazy. *You're* crazy."

"Am I?" He grabbed me around the waist, mashing my arms against his chest. "Let's go somewhere and get naked."

"You're drunk."

"I'm not drunk. Think about it. This is what's cool. It's what being free is all about."

I shook him off. "Nah, that's dumb. Just shut up. Leave me alone. I'm not interested in you anymore. You're ugly, you smell bad, I hate your beard. You sound like a girl when you come. Get the picture?"

The words took a moment to register. He looked stung. "Are you trying to hurt my feelings?"

I didn't say anything, just waited until he finally gave up and shuffled away. My heart thumped in my chest. It was too bad: a part of me wouldn't have minded having sex with him again, if only for purely physical reasons.

I slept well that night, and in the morning I got dressed and bumped into Wallis on his way to the bridge. He looked slightly worse for wear, though he'd only had one glass of champagne at the party.

"Can you do me a favor? I don't want to go back upstairs and I've got to send a message to our guy at EFC before the banks close in Europe. Take this up to Snow," he said, handing me a thin stack of paperwork. It looked like a money ledger, numbers in columns. "He's in his room. Tell him October looks good and I'm working on November."

"What is it?" I asked.

"It's our record of operating expenses. I got behind a month." He continued onto the bridge, calling over his shoulder, "Tell him I hope he feels better."

I tucked the paperwork under my arm and walked back to the stairs, hurrying past the mess hall to avoid running into Neil. Once upstairs, I smiled at Charity coming out of her room.

"He's not feeling too good today," she said.

I peered into the room, which was dark; some lumps

under the bed covers. Lowering my voice to a whisper, I said, "Wallis wanted me to give him this paperwork."

"Just set it on the bureau. I'm going to fetch him some tea."

She slipped away, and I quietly stepped inside. The air smelled dusty. Snow spied me from the bed and invited me to come closer.

"From Wallis," I said, offering him the pages.

His head shook in the pillow, showing disinterest. "I'll look at it this afternoon."

I left the stack next to his watch and some tubes of Charity's makeup; the same things you'd find on any bureau anywhere in the world.

"One too many last night?" I asked. I never knew what to say to him.

"It's not my head, it's my chest. I get like this sometimes. It's nothing to be worried about. Oh, while you're here-" He pointed at the bureau. "Would you bring me my pills? I forgot to ask Charity. It's the bottle with the yellow stripe on the label."

I brought him the pills. "I can get you a new glass of water if that one's stale."

"That's not necessary." He tried opening the bottle but gave up. "If you could just... do this for me."

"Adult-proof, huh?" I took it from him, noticing that he looked out-of-breath. "Are you sure you're all right? Maybe I should get Mandy."

"No, really. It's part of my condition. It's frustrating—I thought the salt air might help. It has, I suppose. I haven't had a bad day in six months."

It occurred to me that the whole reason we'd come here—maybe the only reason Mobility existed—was to give Dr. Snow a place to clear his lungs. But that couldn't be it.

"It must be a drag, being sick like that. I'm lucky, I've always been healthy... although being pregnant's a lot like being sick," I said, watching him take his pills. He seemed to want me to stay, so I did.

"Don't feel sorry for me. It's my own fault. I was stubborn, I didn't want to believe the warnings. In those days, not quite so much was known about the hazards of drinking colloidal silver, though I should've been more skeptical as a scientist."

"Hey, you didn't know. I've done things like that. I smoked halfway through my first pregnancy, which was dumb. I'm lucky Star turned out okay."

"Yes, you are," he said, not unkindly, and offered me a seat next to his bed. "In my case, a colleague recommended the treatment to me. I traveled a lot back then, often to undeveloped countries, and I thought drinking silver might boost my immune system." He laughed at himself. "Was I wrong—I nearly died of blood poisoning, in fact. But we can't punish ourselves for our past mistakes. The future matters, only that—not the past, not even the present."

He gave me a penetrating look. I felt like he was telling me something with his eyes. "Well, that's good to know," I said.

"What's your future, Roseanne?" he asked suddenly.

I stared at my hands. Snow was probably the person I least knew on the island, which might've been why I found myself confiding in him. "I don't feel like I have a future. I don't want to stay here, I don't want to go back home. I can't go back home. And Star likes it here. I'm just... stuck."

"Sometimes being stuck is better than drifting. I drifted for many years after my divorce. I lived in Thailand for six months. Spent another year just traveling, teaching for two weeks in Paris, another week in Beirut."

"See, but at least that's exciting."

"It can be. It can also be extremely tedious and lonely. Before I came to St. John's I didn't even have a permanent mailing address. I didn't find out my brother had died until a week after the funeral. That's when I realized something important about life: you need a home base. It doesn't matter where it is. I wish I'd learned it earlier."

His eyes became distant, and I wondered what he was thinking about. "How old was Mandy when you and her mom split up?"

"Oh… quite young. She'd hardly started school. It was fortunate in a way—it spared her some of the details. She found everything out years later, of course."

"Was she pissed?"

He chuckled weakly. "You'd have to ask her. I think I told her by phone. By then the girl was long out of the picture."

"The…?"

"Yes. Surely she's told you about this?" I nodded. "Then you know what happened."

"I just knew there was a girl. Mandy didn't-"

"No, of course not. Emma's not a gossip," he said lightly. I couldn't tell whether these memories pained or amused him. "There was a girl, a student of mine. Olive. What a name, eh?"

I didn't say anything. I probably looked a little sick.

"Olive LeClair, from Victoriaville. She was a good student too. She's on the faculty now at McGill."

I let out a sigh of relief. I'd been expecting him to say

that she'd killed herself or something. "Do you still keep in touch?"

"Oh, no, no... professionally, yes. I haven't seen Olive in twenty years. I know she's married and has two children. We're both members of the ILA. No, I'm afraid I did poor Olive no favors. We even tried living together for a few months after Emma's mother found out about us, but... we were from such different worlds."

"How young was she again?"

"Too young. Call it nineteen."

"Nineteen. That's how old I was when I got pregnant with Star."

"Hm," he said, and I suppressed a mild urge to slap him. "She always seemed much older to me. She was a musician, knew her modern composers. She knew more about the atonalists than I did. Well-traveled, spoke a number of languages, and not just the usual French and German. She could cook... some things. Had a wonderful laugh. I almost loved her."

"So what happened?"

He hesitated. "I want to say she grew tired of me... but perhaps that's not quite it. Regardless, our affair died a mercifully quick death, and I like to believe no one suffered any permanent damage."

"Well... your wife probably did, and your daughter. I'm sure the girl herself had a tough time of it."

"Maybe. Don't be so certain though. In my experience, young women are not as fragile as we make them out to be. What do you think?"

We let the question hang. It's still hanging around here somewhere.

After Charity returned with the tea, I left and went back to write in my room until lunchtime. Writing was getting easier the more I did it. I worked in blue ballpoint on lined pages that became stiff and crispy as the words piled up. In one paragraph I wrote "angry" five times, then crossed out one of the "angrys" and changed it to "pissed."

Neil and I were cool to each other at lunch; he was finishing up just as I was coming in. The only other person in the mess hall was Gavin. I made myself a sandwich and asked if I could join him.

"God damn it, I'm hungry. Why am I so hungry? I had a muffin for breakfast," I said. I took a big bite and the sandwich went straight to my stomach.

"I can't eat. I had a terrible dream last night. It woke me up. My eyes were hot and my heart was racing. I thought a ghost was in the room," Gavin said.

"This is a fuckin' good sandwich, man. I might make another. Would that be weird, if I had two sandwiches?"

"So much of this dream has stayed with me, even hours later. I believe it is a message, perhaps even a warning. An omen? Yes, it is."

"Maybe I'll just have another half-sandwich. I should probably finish this one first and then decide."

"Roseanne, please listen." His tone stopped me, and I set down my lunch. "In this dream, I foresaw the demise of the island. I swear to you this is real. The rooms and hallways were abandoned, the exterior covered in ice. Only one inhabitant remained, and that person was you."

I laughed nervously, wanting to get back to my sandwich. "Hey, come on… I don't believe in that sorta-"

"No, there is more. That was only the beginning. There was a middle section as well."

"A middle section."

"Yes. Even more disturbing than the first."

"I don't want to hear it then."

He tapped a finger to his lips. "Okay, I'll skip that part. But the ending is important. This you must hear. It is what woke me up: a voice speaking in my ear—a man's voice. Maybe Jewish? I don't know. But what it said I will never forget."

"What did it say?"

Gavin looked toward the kitchen to make sure no one was there, then whispered, "*Gravy Gallagher.*"

CHAPTER TWENTY-NINE

Obviously I'd told him about Gravy. Obviously I'd mentioned Josh's old cat to Gavin—it could've been months ago—and he'd kept it in his subconscious until the name finally popped out in the form of a twisted dream. I knew it. These things didn't just happen. But it bothered me all the same. Too many signs pointed in the same bad direction: first Manuel, now this. I felt surrounded by emptiness, by nothing.

Limbo.

Gravy Gallagher, though—whew. I could still picture that dumb cat, the way it thundered down the basement stairs to sleep in the laundry room. (What kind of detergent did Pam use? *All.* In the big fucking blue bottle.) Gravy Gallagher farting under the dining table, reposing at the foot of the TV, lying with its nose in Pam's lap. Gravy Gallagher, the cat who never went outside, who liked to swat and nip. Almost certainly dead by now.

Mandy gave birth to Sander Clement Laporte in February, 2014. I was hiding out on the bridge at the time. I didn't want to get involved: not my business, not my problem. For an hour I updated Mobility's website; we had a new line of travel mugs and beer coolers that needed putting online. Then I watched the start of an old

Julia Roberts movie, one of her first. Nineteen-eighty-something. She had curly hair back then, copper-colored ringlets. Great, great jeans, form-fitting, tight on the ass.

Sometime in the afternoon, Neil poked his head in. "It's a boy!"

"Good for you," I said, still watching the movie: Julia Roberts flirting with a man in a mom-and-pop grocery store, holding a basket of fresh looking vegetables, big carrots with bushy green stems.

"A healthy baby boy with ten fingers and ten toes. We're naming him Sander."

"Nice."

"I was in the room the whole time. I can't believe it—I'm actually a father. He smiled at me too! Charity handed him to me, and he looked up and he smiled. Isn't that nuts? What baby does that?"

"Wow, that's, yeah."

The next scene cut to Julia Roberts in fall outerwear driving a pickup down a country road. *She looks concerned. She stops the truck and leans out of the window. A tree is down in the road.*

"I think Sander would be happy. I wish he was here to see this. Damn, I miss that guy."

"Good... you know what? This is a really good movie and I'm right at the important part. Can you come back in, like, forty-five minutes?"

I had my back to him, but I could sense his disappointment. The movie was starting to look familiar. Julia and a wild-eyed old man were arguing near the fallen tree. Julia stood mutely indignant as the old man called her an interfering nuisance for meddling with local politics. Then Neil left.

That evening everyone took turns visiting the new

mom and her baby in the infirmary. I stuck my head in after dinner. "Hey, congratulations," I said.

Mandy looked tired and hot in her hospital gown. The kid was asleep in a bassinet next to her bed. "Thanks, Roseanne," she said.

"That him?" I asked, pointing at the bassinet. Mandy nodded, and I went over to it. The baby had a reddish complexion, like a boiled lobster. I began to giggle.

"Why are you laughing?" Mandy asked.

"Oh, I'm not. He's just so cute. Poor thing, he's had a hard day. Where's Neil?"

Mandy pulled her bed sheet up to her chin. "He's resting."

"He's resting? Why is he resting? You're the one who needs a nap." I gave the baby a second glance, asked Mandy if she needed anything, and continued on my way.

Over the next few weeks the halls were filled with baby Sander's plaintive mewlings. He'd been born with a mild case of thrush, and Mandy worried about him constantly. There was talk of making an appointment with a pediatrician on the mainland. At meetings she speculated at great length about her other medical concerns: pinkeye, ringworm, the croup. The kid looked fine to me but I stayed out of it.

Some days I'd see Neil or Mandy bumbling around the halls in an exhausted fog and I'd smile to myself. I didn't envy either one of them. I was happy to retire to my room every night knowing that the only thing that might get me out of bed before seven in the morning would be a full bladder. I could keep to my own schedule without having to worry about things like feedings or diapers or naps. Oh, I helped out whenever I could; we all did, including Gavin. I'd sit with the baby for an hour so

Mandy could get some rest, no problem. But it wasn't the same as having those responsibilities full-time.

As I watched Mandy struggle with her newborn, I kept thinking about those nature programs that Steffi used to watch back in St. John's. What is the bond between parent and child? There should be love, first and foremost. Animals express love by lying on top of each other. They cuddle and rub noses and sleep in a heap. Mama birds let their babies feed straight out of their beaks. They lean over the baby's beak and spit out their chewed-up worm juice. And then, once the kid is old enough to fly, that's what they do, fly. And the mom kicks back and chills.

And makes more. If she survives the winter.

Is it crazy of me to keep thinking of people as if they were animals? Maybe that's crazy of me. That sounds like something a crazy person would think. What's the word—dissociative? Probably not. Whatever word there is to describe me, I don't know it yet.

Mandy looked particularly tired one night at dinner. The grind of motherhood was finally wearing her down. I knew for a fact that she didn't like breast-feeding, but what choice did she have? The nearest baby formula was twenty miles away over choppy seas.

As we finished our meals, she said, "Neil and I have been thinking. Well, I have. I've been thinking and Neil… he's not sure. We're still discussing it. Nothing's been decided."

"What do you mean, dear?" asked Charity.

"About our life here on the island. It's just hard. It's harder than I thought. All you guys have been great, but every single night I lay awake and think… what if the baby gets sick? Or what if there's another incident like what happened with Pål?"

Snow looked up. He appeared old, his face carved out of bluish driftwood. She continued, "And I know we're supposed to be self-sufficient and blah blah—but we're not, not really. I'm not. A child like Sander needs a certain level of care that just isn't available here."

"Everything's available here," Snow said, "and if it isn't, we'll get it for you. You know that, Emma. What do you need? I'll have Roseanne order it from the mainland."

"It's not one thing, it's a million things. God, Dad, don't you see? Don't you see how... I don't know... fucked up this is?"

"No, I don't."

"Well it is! I'm really scared, you know? Not for me—I don't care about me. I'm scared that the baby is going to get sick or hurt and I won't be able to do anything for him with my little rinky-dink MASH unit down the hall."

"Don't underestimate yourself. You're a perfectly capable doctor."

Gavin pulled his baseball cap down over his eyes as Star and Steffi gawked at the adults.

"You always say that and it drives me crazy every time. It's got nothing to do with me being a capable doctor. It's about having the resources available in case something unexpected comes up. This is why people don't do this..." she said, pointing all around.

"Don't do what?"

"What we're doing. Living like this. It's not natural. You can't just cut yourself off from the rest of the world and expect to survive."

"But isn't that what we've been doing?"

"Survive? Barely... and we've had a lot of luck. I don't want to take that chance with my baby. He deserves a safer environment."

She looked to the rest of us for support. No one spoke, not even Neil. My mind was racing, doing the math. I knew we couldn't afford to take another loss. Assuming Mandy left the island, obviously Neil would join her. That would leave seven people: me, Star, Steffi, Gavin, Wallis, Charity, and Snow. I couldn't imagine Snow lasting long without his daughter. Without Snow, there'd be no Steffi or Charity, and Gavin didn't have enough personally invested in Mobility to stick around after that. Wallis, Star, and I certainly couldn't manage on our own. We'd have to go home. And going home meant facing the Okerfeldts and the cops and the possibility of losing Star.

In other words, it couldn't happen. Mandy couldn't leave the island. It was as simple as that.

After dinner I tracked her down in the infirmary. Charity was babysitting Sander and Neil was working in the kitchen.

"Hey, you look wiped. I can take Sander in my room tonight if you want to get some real sleep. It's quiet upstairs. Not so much wind on my side of the island," I said.

She eyed me suspiciously. It was true, I didn't frequently offer to help with the baby, but I thought she might see things differently after a good night's rest.

"You don't have to, Roseanne. Sander's my responsibility," she said as she straightened paperwork in her office. She looked like she wanted to be alone, but I pushed ahead.

"I remember when Star was born. She wasn't a good sleeper at first. Fortunately I had people to help out. Not sleeping is the worst. I started to hallucinate... I kept seeing things move in the dark. And my husband and I would fight."

She paused in her work. "Neil and I don't fight."

"No, I'm sure you don't, but we did. Most of it was my fault. I wasn't always very nice to Josh." She wasn't listening, so I glanced around the room. Tongue depressors, cotton balls. Her medical degree read: *Emmanuelle Catherine Snow.* "Well, it looks like I got what I deserved. Hey, I didn't know your middle name was Catherine. That's nice."

"Roseanne, do you want something? Because I haven't had a moment to myself all day and I really would like to get this room tidied up."

I stood at her desk. "I just don't want you to leave, that's all."

She smiled coldly. "But you don't even like me."

"That's not true."

"You've never liked me. You didn't like me the day we met."

I couldn't argue with that, so I didn't. "Just think about it. Wait a year or two and see what happens. You've just had a baby, for God's sake. It's natural to feel tired and frustrated."

"I'm not frustrated, I'm concerned for my child. There's a difference. Surely you can understand that," she said with as little warmth as possible.

"I know you're concerned. Hey, I get it. I'm a mom just like you. I worry about Star all the time. I worry she's going to fall off the edge of the loading dock or break her leg doing something stupid in the basement. Whatever, the situation's not perfect. But there are some good things about living on the island too."

"Like what?"

"Like a ton of things. Ask Star, ask Steffi. They both

love it here. Every day's an adventure to those kids. They're learning about the world."

"They're not learning about the world, they're learning what it looks like inside one old man's sick brain."

"That's not true. I was just talking to Star yesterday. She says she wants to be a marine biologist—I'm sure that comes from living near the water and having Neil take her out on the boat," I said, more or less fabricating the whole thing.

"If she wants to be a marine biologist, she should go back home, finish grade school, finish junior high, finish high school, go to college, go to grad school-"

"She will, she will."

"Here?"

"Sure. Part of it. I'm homeschooling her, Mandy."

"And you're going to teach her all she needs to know about being a marine biologist."

I gave up—it was a dumb lie to begin with and not worth the effort. "Look, forget I even mentioned it. Kids are always saying they want to be things when they grow up and then the next week it's something different. Weren't you like that as a kid?"

"No," she said.

"You always knew what you wanted to be when you grew up?"

She didn't say anything. It felt more like a silent no than a silent yes.

"The point is," I said, "Mobility is what Star needs right now."

"So? Stay."

"We can't stay here by ourselves. We need you."

"What on earth for? You're an adult."

"I'm not a doctor, though."

She reached into her supply cabinet and pulled out a box of Band-Aids. "Here," she said, "knock yourself out."

I took the box and set it back on her desk. "I'm not kidding, Mandy. You can't just leave. Everyone'll go if you go. I'm the only one who's stuck here—me and Star. You can't do that to us."

"Oh? What am I doing to you?"

I had to be careful not to lose my temper. "It's like your father always says… about community, and people needing each other." Mandy tapped her foot. I thought, I can be smart about this too. "In societies, where you get a bunch of people together, with their own roles and functions, and everyone has their own shit to do."

She smiled thinly, like a bitch. "I certainly don't need you. And yes, I'm familiar with my father's work. Have you read *Harsh Climates, Harsh Minds*? I copyedited it for him. Of course, Schumacher would probably disagree-"

Her attitude finally got to me. "Hey, you're not talking over my head, honey. I'm not a moron. I went to school too. Maybe not a real college, but I did my fuckin' time."

"Is this about Neil? Because if it is-"

"Ha! Don't make me laugh."

"Look, I'm sorry he's not your boyfriend but-"

"I don't give a shit what he is. He's nothing. He's shit," I said, furious at her for even mentioning Neil. I'd wanted to fight about something else, not about the guy we'd both happened to fuck.

"Oh, really? That's the father of my child you're talking about."

"No kidding. You know what? I didn't know that. Thanks for telling me."

"I'll tell you something else. Do you know what he said? About you, listen-"

"I don't care. I don't believe you anyway."

"No, this is interesting. He said that you kept after him for weeks to go to bed with him even though he'd told you repeatedly that he didn't want to get involved because you were still married-"

"Nope. Absolutely not."

"Yes, and that you begged and begged for sex until eventually you lied to him about getting a divorce from Star's father, and when he finally said okay-"

"Lying, lying."

"You're lying! When he finally said okay, you lied about your period because you wanted to get pregnant-"

"That absolutely didn't happen," I said, so angry that I almost couldn't see straight.

"Oh yes it did—more than once, he said—and then you lied again and said you were pregnant, but of course that wasn't true, you were just trying to-"

"He's lying to you, Mandy!"

"-get attention for yourself like you always do. You've always been the needy little sister. You're pathetic. You turn my stomach. One day you're gonna get what's coming to you and I'm going to laugh, laugh…"

"Okay, fine, but do you want to know about Neil? 'The father of your whatever.' Let me tell you-"

"What did you say?" she shouted.

"No, listen, just wait—because this is your problem now."

"What did you call my baby? A 'whatever'?"

I stumbled back toward the door as she pushed at me. "-about Neil's drug problem and how he spent a month in rehab with Danny Bonaduce-"

"Get out of my office!"

"-and slept with a million different women when he

lived in L.A. and how he, he, how he's an asshole and a bad person who fucks people over."

She swung at me with her open right hand and I dodged out of the way. Both of us tumbled into a shelf of books, the heel of her hand wedged under my chin, pushing up. I shook my head as our weight and momentum brought us slumping to the floor. Her hand slipped and she fell on top of me.

"Well that's what he did!" I screamed. Her wild teeth snipped at my eyes. I grabbed her elbows to keep her from swinging at me again and we rolled into the bookshelf, winding up with me on top of her and my knee between her legs.

"Stop, stop, you're choking me," she said, but I didn't even have my hands on her neck. Just then I felt a tug under my arms and a rough force yanking me up off Mandy and setting me on my feet. Gavin's voice thundered behind me, "Ladies, please!"

Mandy scooted away on her butt, pulling her knees to her chest. "Just get out now," she said quietly.

Gavin stared at both of us. "Ladies, please!" he repeated, as if it was the only thing a man could say to two women in such a situation. "We do not have time for this. Roseanne-" His fear settled on me. "For you. Visitors."

CHAPTER THIRTY

Terry Okerfeldt sat in the mess hall with a cup of coffee. He'd arrived with another man who was now somewhere on Deck One taking a shower. Gavin didn't know Terry and so didn't recognize him when his boat tied up to the island, and it wasn't until Terry had worked his charms that Gavin agreed to let him inside. Terry had a manner that served him well behind the pulpit, a kind of robust charisma that rubbed off on others.

"How did you find me?" I asked after I'd gotten over my initial shock. He looked thinner than I remembered, his cheekbones more prominent. His skin had lost its ruddy luster, and he'd stopped trimming the flyaway hairs growing out of his ears.

"It wasn't easy. We'd given up for a long time, figured you were dead. It's been hard these past years." He blew on his coffee and sipped. "Pam doesn't know I'm here, and neither does Josh. They think I'm at a minister's convention in Montreal."

"Why didn't you tell them?" I asked, hanging back near the first aid poster on the wall. It felt odd to be talking about these people after all this time.

"Pam is so angry with you that I didn't want her to come, to be honest. She's not a violent person—I don't think she's ever been in a fight, even when she was a kid—but I didn't want to take the chance. There are other things that need to happen first before Pam can get involved."

I see, I thought. "And Josh?"

His non-response told me it was none of my business. "I hope you don't mind us showing up late like this. There's a storm moving in tomorrow morning, and Ross and I didn't want to wait another day."

"Who's Ross?"

"Ross Putnam. He's my traveling companion, one of the elders from my church. Ross used to be in the Navy and knows more about navigation than I do. He's seaworthy." Smiling, he indicated for me to join him at the table.

I did, shakily feeling for the bench behind me. "Are you hungry?" I asked, otherwise at a loss.

"Oh, no. I don't want to impose. I'm sure food supplies are hard enough to come by around here."

"Not at all, we've got tons of food. I can make you something. What do you want to eat? We've got fish, fish cakes, fish sticks. We eat a lot of fish."

Again he declined. "We won't stay long. I'm assuming you have two extra rooms where we can spend the night."

"Of course. Crash anywhere. The beds are pretty comfortable. Guys used to stay on the island for months at a time when this was a working oil rig. Oh—that's what we call this place."

"The island."

"Yep," I said, realizing how dumb it sounded.

He listened without much expression, good, bad, or otherwise. "May I ask who's in charge here?"

"We all are, I guess. Wallis is our 'president,' so-called.

I'm the Director of... look, don't make me talk about it. It's embarrassing."

"Why is it embarrassing?"

I started to explain but he looked so sincere that I stopped. In church Terry would sometimes lapse into silences that could last ten seconds or longer. The silences were always an invitation to pause and reflect.

"So let me guess, I'm going to wake up tomorrow morning and the whole island's gonna be surrounded by cops in boats, right?" I said.

"Not that I'm aware of."

"You're not trying to set me up?"

"I doubt I could even if I wanted to. No, I'd really just like to talk and say hello to my granddaughter."

His calmness unnerved me, and I looked toward a window. The sky outside was starless and moonless. "How's everyone back home?" I asked, possibly the lamest question ever.

"They're very upset. Pam has had some health problems, and Josh has his hands full with the children." I heard him reach inside his jacket, and I knew what was coming next. "Here, I brought some pictures," he said.

The stack of pictures hit the table. They buzzed in my peripheral vision. "Oh, that's nice," I said.

"Would you like to see them?" There was no anger in his voice, just soft inquiry.

I reached for the pictures, keeping them covered with my hand. They felt slick, never-before-touched. Printed just for me.

"Sarah will enjoy looking at these," I managed.

"Why don't you look at them, Roseanne?"

I couldn't put it off any longer, so I lifted my hand and peeked. The man in the first picture was Josh—in his thirties now, thin, with a long neck and preoccupied smile. I didn't recognize his glasses but they suited the shape of his face. Our children were there too. The oldest boy looked about ready for the third grade; a jock, friendly and dependable. The twins, whom I'd always known to be exactly alike, had diverged down the opposite paths of gender. The boy had a buzz cut and an alert, arrested expression on his face, as if he'd recently been scolded by a parent. The girl was me when I was five.

Terry explained, "We took this at Christmas last year. Vance had a sinus cold, which is why his nose is all red. And this one's from last August. We're up north—those are the Painted Rocks in the background. Josh took the kids for a cruise up and down the Superior coast. There's a little tour boat that runs during the summer. The boys loved it, but Mary had a hard time sitting still. She's got some very minor behavioral problems. She's not unintelligent but..." He hesitated. The girl in the picture was hanging from Josh's shoulders, unaware of her weight, not caring. A *spitfire.* "Anyway, she's young and we love her."

More pictures—holidays, vacations. No candid shots, just posed photos in front of landmarks or seasonal paraphernalia; very "Okerfeldt." Getting through the stack was exhausting. It literally filled my stomach.

"They look like nice kids," I said softly.

Terry spread the pictures so I could see a few of them at once: the twins grinning over a chocolate birthday cake, Vance at karate class, Josh and Vance about to board a train.

"We're lucky to have them. They're very sweet children," he said.

Mary sitting in her father's lap. Connor with a baseball

bat. Vance dressed for church in a red tie, blue shirt, and corduroy pants.

"Do they miss me?" I asked. I'd expected a quick and unequivocal yes—*Of course, your children obviously miss their mother*—but he didn't speak right away.

"It's hard to tell. Vance talks about you more than the others. Mainly he misses his sister. Connor and Mary ask questions on rare occasion."

I wiped my eyes. Crying always pissed me off. Was the damage already done, I wondered? Had the worst already happened? How long does it take to cause irreparable harm to your child?

"I hate myself," I said, feeling like I'd been condemned for a handful of split-second bad decisions.

Terry gathered the pictures and replaced them in an envelope from a CVS photo center. "Don't hate yourself. God still loves you and the children are fine. They're healthy and they've got a good home."

I laughed miserably, not believing him. "Poor Josh."

"And don't worry about Josh either. Josh has help."

"What do you mean?"

A blush rose in his cheeks and forehead. "Help. He has friends who help. Friends from work, friends from church. One very nice young lady in particular."

I stopped crying—it was getting to be annoying. "Oh? A nice young lady."

"Very nice."

"*Very* nice. Not just nice but very nice. Okay." Politeness required a certain tone, calm and unfazed. "What's this person's name?" I asked, not knowing why it mattered to me. It didn't.

"The young lady? Oh, it's-"

"You keep saying 'young lady' and it's… what's that?

Two, three times—young lady, young lady, young lady. What is that?"

He looked confused, scared even. I was the nut-job at the end of his quest.

I sighed. "Never mind. Name?"

"Oh, uh… Jen, it's… Jen."

I barked out a laugh, startling him. "No, it's nothing. I'm just… processing all this. *Jen*. It's perfect. *Jen. Jen.*" I tried it out in a bunch of different voices—deep like a man's, high and girly.

"We call her Jen. It's short for Jennifer," he said.

"Oh, you know her too? She's a friend of the family?" He kept still. "She goes to your church, obviously. I mean, that's obvious. She goes to church, she's a member of the church, she's big in the church. Obviously, right? Hey, that's cool. What's her last name?" His silence deepened. My questions seemed rhetorical to him. "She got a last name?"

"It's Decker."

"Okay, just askin'. Jen Decker. Jendecker. It's one of those names, right? It's never just 'Jen,' it's always 'Jendecker Jendecker Jendecker Jendecker.'" The name became a train gathering speed. "My name's not like that. Your name's not like that. But people just call you Reverend Terry anyway."

The old man cleared his throat and told me that Jen and Josh were hoping to get married if I would be willing to grant Josh a divorce. It didn't bother me. Hey, I didn't love Josh. This was just some funny, funny stuff happening a thousand miles away.

"What do my children think of Jen? Do they like her?"

He barely whispered, "Yes." Every word carried toxic potential.

"And are they planning on having children of their own?"

His voice gained strength. "Well, Jen's still only twenty-five, so… yes, they are."

"Sure. Gotta keep popping 'em out. I was twenty when I had my first one. That's younger than twenty-five. That's, like, five years younger."

No response. I'd made him uncomfortable.

"I want to hear more about Jen. What's she like? What's she look like? Is she pretty?"

Terry fidgeted. "I suppose she is. Josh thinks so."

"Blonde, brunette? What does she do for a living?"

"She works in a bank."

I bobbed my head—*groovy, man*. "So she's a bank teller. She cashes people's checks for them. That's nice. Not my kind of thing but I respect it. Does she have any hobbies or interests or does she just work at the bank and then go home and crash?"

His eyes lowered modestly. I might as well have asked him if Jen made a lot of noise in bed. "She and Josh belong to a movie club with a few of the other couples from church. They get together once a week and watch a movie at someone's house."

"With the other couples? That's interesting. Weird but whatever. How does it work? Do they talk about the movie after it's finished or… and how do they all agree on the same film?"

"I don't know how it works."

"Hey, do you know what movie I want to see? *The Hangover*. But maybe that's too R-rated."

"She's *raising your children*, Roseanne," he said. His anger was fact-based, neutral.

I stopped clowning. Once again, Terry's silence invited

me to pause and reflect. Whenever I thought about those kids, Vance and Mary and Connor—and I did think of them, every day—I imagined myself saying to them: Look guys, I'm sorry. I fucked up, and it's my fault. I'm sorry it didn't work out. But you're alive, right? You've got life. And there are people who are better equipped to take care of you than me.

I thought, maybe if I just love Star. If I just love that one kid. But the idea never took hold.

Terry was anxious to see Star, so we went upstairs and searched the floor, looking for both girls. "They might be on the top deck. The kids like to watch the freighters pass at night. It's real pretty up there—wanna see?" I asked.

He zipped up his jacket and we rode the elevator one floor to the top deck. It was a warm night in mid-Spring, the air unusually still. Seabirds gathered on the helipad and roosted under the remains of the chopper that lay on its side, its blades touching the ground. Time had turned it into a tree. The birds didn't scatter at our approach—they were used to us by now. Past the helipad we heard voices and found the two girls sitting with their backs to the supply shed. They didn't notice us at first.

I cleared my throat. The girls whispered and laughed, their words a slippery code.

"Star," I said, then, louder: "Sarah."

They stopped. Star looked up and, seeing a stranger with me, jumped to her feet.

"Sarah, there's someone here to meet you," I said.

Both girls were standing now—the older girl, taller, lurking protectively at Star's side.

"Why are you calling me that?" Star asked.

Terry came forward, crouching instinctively, the way one might bend down to speak to a very young child. "Hi

Sarah. I haven't seen you since you were a little girl. I'm your grandpa, Terry."

I nodded reassuringly. She asked, "What are you doing here?"

"It's okay, Sarah. Say hi to Grandpa Terry," I said.

"My name's not Sarah, it's Star," she said, staring at Terry, then angrily at me.

He stayed put, not coming closer than a few feet. "My word, how you've grown. You're already so tall. Don't you remember me? Grandma Pam and Grandpa Terry? We remember you."

"She remembers. Star, give your grandpa a hug. He came a long way to see you," I said.

"It's okay, she's just shy. Sarah, I have some things for you—pictures of your daddy and your brothers Vance and Connor and your sister Mary. Pictures of Grandma and Grandpa too. Would you like to see them?" he asked.

She shook her head, though I saw curiosity in her eyes. "Star, why don't you give Grandpa Terry a tour of the island? I'm sure he'd like to see where you live now," I said, laying emphasis on these last words.

"You've certainly got a beautiful view," he joked, looking over the water. "I think I can see dry land from here."

She watched him study the horizon. Terry had a faint scar on the side of his neck, maybe from having a mole removed.

Finally her posture relaxed. "You're looking the wrong way. Canada's over there." She nodded over her right shoulder, like a gas station attendant giving directions.

"Oh, I-"

"You won't be able to see it anyway. Not without some good binoculars."

"Maybe you can show him in the morning," I suggested. Star gave me a hateful look. She seemed to be more receptive to her grandfather than to me.

"You're staying here?" she asked him.

"Just for the night. I need to get back home. I've got a sermon to prepare and a wedding on Saturday," he said.

She frowned at "Saturday." It wasn't a word that meant much around here. "You're not going to make me go back with you?"

"Not if you don't want to. It's your choice, Sarah. I just thought you might like to see what your family looks like now."

Drawing closer to Steffi, she said, "This is my family."

He smiled faintly. "I believe you."

"You do?"

I couldn't tell if he was being sincere or if this was all some strategy for getting Star off the island. "Of course. A family can be many things. Jesus' disciples were a family. They came from all quarters and walks of life, but they shared a purpose and a view of humanity, and that's what kept them together."

Her eyes drew inward, wanting to make sense of this. There was a message here, or a lesson, and she knew it to be true without understanding a word of it.

The girls led us across the top deck, past the munitions shed and the lookout station where Sander once had sat all day watching for threats that generally never materialized. Passing the hulk of the crippled helicopter, Terry asked, "What happened here?"

"Oh, yeah, uh… it broke, kinda. Sucks. Never got around to fixing it. Watch the bird shit." I covered my mouth. "Whoop—I mean poop. Poop, poop. Watch the bird poop."

Terry was tired after his long trip, so Star and I showed him to his room. Before Star could leave, Terry took the envelope from the CVS photo center and pressed it into her hand. "These are for you," he said.

She held the envelope but didn't open it. "What's CVS?"

Terry and I looked at each other. The answer seemed dark, adult, something to be withheld from children. It was like talking to your kid about pubic hair.

"It's a drug store chain. You know, like Rite Aid? There's one near your old house. You threw up there once," I said.

She took the pictures back to her room, and I made up Terry's bed. This had been Cathy Oines' room back in the day. She'd left a pair of nail clippers on the bureau.

"Don't worry if you hear this incredibly loud shrieking siren in the middle of the night that goes on for twenty minutes and then shuts itself off. We're aware of the problem. Not a biggie."

"I'll try not to get alarmed," he said.

I checked to make sure he had everything he needed, but something kept me from leaving. Not enough had been said between us. I didn't want to wait until morning to know where I stood.

"What's going to happen to me?" I asked.

"What do you mean?"

"I mean… you're here, and obviously you're going to tell Pam and Josh, and… and then what? How toast am I? Are we talking life-in-jail toast? Because if we are, I ain't going."

"It's up to you, Roseanne."

"How is it up to me? How has anything ever been up to me?"

He smiled. Maybe he even liked me a little. "It's always been up to you. That's God's promise to us—we're the shapers of our own destinies. You might consider prayer, though. It's worked for me in the past."

"Talking to God, huh? Oh, boy... that's next," I said, slumping in the doorway. "Prayer" was one of those churchy words that always made me roll my eyes, like "wholesome" or "fellowship." I hadn't really prayed since I was a little girl, and then it was just something I did to please my father. Prayer was part of the nighttime routine, like brushing your teeth before going to bed.

"Prayer is more than just talking to God. It's a way of spending time with yourself, slowing down your thoughts, sorting through your worries one step at a time. God can't fix all of your problems for you. Sometimes I think we expect too much of God, to tell you the truth. That's why there are so many disbelievers in the world. We're impatient, and we're too results-oriented. Prayer can't make you think, it can't make you reflect. You have to do those things for yourself."

I tried to say something intelligent but gave up. "You're good at this, Terry, you know that? You should do it for a living."

He smiled patiently. "Do you understand?"

I nodded, patting my damp cheeks. "I understand that I'm screwed—no offense and pardon the language."

"There will need to be some consequences, if that's what you mean," he admitted.

"But why? Look, I'm sorry—I know I shouldn't have run off with Sarah like that. I wasn't thinking. Why can't anyone understand? I was under a lot of pressure. I freaked out and split and then time went by and I got scared, okay? Is that so unforgivable?"

"Of course not, and if you're serious about asking for

God's forgiveness, it's a very good sign. It shows a contrite heart."

"God's forgiveness? God's forgiveness? Who cares about God's forgiveness? I'm sorry, I know that's your thing and I'm not disrespecting it, but I'm dealing with some real problems here, Terry. I know it's important to pray and seek forgiveness, and if God wants to give it to me, that's great. But look at me. I'm stuck here, dude. I'm fuckin' stuck. I'm sorry about the bad language but I gotta tell you... I'm gonna lose my mind if I have to spend another year on this rig."

"You can always leave," he said.

"Right—and then what? Will you forgive me?"

"Sure," he said, though not very convincingly.

"Will Pam? Will Josh? Those three kids? How about the courts in Michigan who want to fry my ass? Any forgiveness there?" He was quiet; he'd gone back to being afraid of me. "That's what I thought. Great—God'll forgive me but no one else will. I'll tell you what, I can't think of a more useless thing in the world than God's forgiveness—in terms of actual, practical value. I don't need forgiveness, I need help. Can you help me?"

"I can't promise you anything but God's salvation if you come to Him with a willing heart," he said.

"Then you don't forgive me."

"I do. I just said I did," he said with even less conviction than before.

"You've got a weird way of showing it. I know what you people are gonna do. You're gonna take away my daughter and march me up in front of a magistrate—it'll probably be on CNN or one of those channels—and everyone'll go 'Oh, my God, what a terrible woman...' and no one'll ever take a moment to consider what it's actually like to be me. A mom at twenty, still a kid myself. Not one person. That's what you're gonna do."

I turned to leave, but his voice stopped me. "If you won't pray, at least let me pray for you," he said.

He sounded so earnest that I shambled back. "Why would you want to do that?"

"I don't hate you, Roseanne, despite what you might think. You're the mother of my grandchildren. There must be something good in you."

He knelt beside his bed and waited until I reluctantly did the same. The floor was poured concrete with a raked texture. I felt it through the knees of my jumpsuit.

"Lord," he began once I'd settled down, "I come to you on behalf of a lost sheep. One who's sinned many times, as we all have. And this lost sheep is so lost, she doesn't even know it. She thinks she's still in the pen with the other animals, the sheep and goats and... the donkeys. The holy creatures of the Earth. And that's because her pain has caused her mind to conjure visions of things that aren't really there. Please heal her pain, Lord. Help her deny the false evidence of her senses. Bring to her the wisdom that experience has not. Suffering on Earth is but a fleeting hardship compared to the eternal grief of the imprisoned soul." Speaking as a grandfather now, he added, "And bring our precious Sarah home to us, oh Lord, in whose name we pray. Amen."

We stood, and he walked me to the door. "Have you ever prayed for something stupid, like a car or a new kitchen?" I asked. It was more of my endless nervous prattle—a bad habit of mine, if you haven't noticed—but he regarded me seriously.

"I've done a lot of foolish things in my time. The first

twenty years of my life were basically a mistake," he said. I recoiled inside.

Up in my room I spent an hour writing before going to bed. My handwriting looked sloppy, childish. It was a part of me that had never grown up.

The siren went off around two in the morning with a computerized, male-sounding voice announcing: "Emergency! Emergency! Threat level: SEVERE! Threat level: SEVERE! Evacuate IMMEDIATELY! Evacuate IMMEDIATELY!" I rolled over in bed and went back to sleep.

CHAPTER THIRTY-ONE

Star brought the pictures to breakfast the next morning.

CHAPTER THIRTY-TWO

That same morning I met Terry's traveling companion, Ross Putnam, in the mess hall. Ross looked about forty-five, tall, well-built, with a long face and mutton-chop sideburns. I figured he probably didn't think too much of me, based on what he'd heard from the Okerfeldts. All during breakfast he eyed me malevolently across the table where we sat with Terry, Star, Steffi, Charity, Snow, and Wallis. Gavin was outside lashing down some of the free-standing equipment on the top deck in anticipation of the storm that was due to arrive that morning. Mandy was still pissed at me and hadn't left her room. I didn't know where Neil was, nor did I care.

Charity asked Ross what he did for a living. He croaked, "Been out of work twenty-one months. Used to stock vending machines for Coca-Cola. Did that for a while. Then I messed up my foot."

I could see that Wallis was trying not to laugh; it was Ross' hangdog face more than anything else. I stared down at my food to keep from catching the giggles.

"Oh, that's too bad. What'd you do to your foot?" asked Charity.

"It's pretty gruesome, ma'am. You probably don't want to hear about it at the breakfast table."

Wallis barked out a cough, and I locked my eyes shut.

"Tell us, tell us," Star and Steffi both said.

"Girls, don't be rude," said Charity. "If Mr. Putnam doesn't want to-"

"No offense taken, ma'am. It doesn't upset me to talk about it, I just don't want to spoil anyone's appetite. Little things happen to people all the time. I've learned to move on with my life."

"Were you in an accident?" Steffi asked. More coughing from Wallis.

"Not as such, though accidental in nature. It could've been far worse had I not been so quick to react." After some more prodding from the girls, he said, "I was attacked, really. What it was, I was sitting in front of my house in my bare feet because it was summer time, and I heard a noise, and when I looked up to investigate, all of a sudden I feel something gnawing on my foot there."

Wallis snorted. I opened my eyes a crack, saw tears, closed them again.

"What was it?" asked Star.

"Didn't know at the time—come to find out a possum of sorts had gotten mixed up in my trash... something set it off, and next thing I know I got possum fangs sinking into my foot an inch deep."

The girls oo'ed in appreciation as Snow asked, "Do possums typically attack people?"

"It wasn't a pure-possum, sir. It was more like a half-possum, half-raccoon, which might've been why its mind went haywire like that. Coroner offered an opinion but it was pretty inconclusive."

"Did you kill it?" asked Steffi, by now utterly in awe of him. My neck, my sides, my stomach—everything ached.

"Inadvertently, yes I did. It wasn't my intention, but the

longer the animal stayed hooked onto my foot, the more irate it became, so eventually I had no choice but to beat it to death with the-"

I howled. Ross stopped talking and stared, as did everyone else. The only other person smiling was Wallis.

"I'm sorry, I'm just picturing you with this... thing on your foot, and... I'll stop," I said.

"I was three days in the hospital, ma'am," Ross said.

"I know, I'm s-... I'll stop. I'm okay. Phew," I said, fanning myself.

Charity told Ross, "That sounds awful. You're lucky you didn't lose a limb."

Terry clapped his hand on Ross' shoulder. "It takes a lot to knock this guy out of action. Ross is a decorated war veteran. He's the lifeblood of our community."

"Good for you," Charity said.

"Did you have to get any shots?" asked Steffi.

Ross nodded. "Sixteen. Counted every single one of 'em too. Then I had to go back three times a week to get a-"

I shrieked, spitting out a bite of pancake. "I'm sorry, I'm not laughing at you. I just didn't get enough sleep. The siren... y'all hear the siren go off last night? We gotta get that thing fixed."

Ross didn't look offended so much as bemused. Maybe he'd never seen my type before.

"Mom, you're being weird," Star said.

I didn't want to embarrass her so I excused myself and brought my plate to the kitchen. Once the doors swung shut, I staggered over to the sink, dropped my plate onto the counter, and laughed hysterically at my blurry reflection in the stainless steel cabinets. Spasms wrenched my body. It was the best release I'd had in years.

The storm rolled in around ten o'clock, and some of

us gathered on the bridge to watch. Storms were always pretty spectacular on Mobility. The wind would swirl like a hurricane, coming at us from all sides. Sometimes fishing boats would tie up and we'd let their crews dry out in the mess hall. This particular storm was just a squall. Ross and Terry would be able to go home after lunch if they wanted to.

Neil came onto the bridge. "Has anyone seen my Rangers cap? I thought I left it in Delta but I can't-"

"I need to talk to you." Yanking him out of the room, I dragged him by the wrist down the hall.

"Hey, that hurts. Your ring's cutting into my hand," he said.

"Good," I said, pulling him into a nearby stairwell. The door shut, and I gave him a good hard shake.

"What are you doing? Ow! I bit my damn tongue!" he said, clamping his hands over his mouth, looking small and weak and ridiculous.

I folded my arms. "What the fuck did you tell Mandy about us?"

"I think I'm bleeding. Ow." He frowned at his hand. "Nope. How can I not be bleeding?"

"You're gonna be bleeding in a minute. I want to know exactly what you said to her."

"Wh-when? What? Roseanne, my hand and tongue kill."

Backing him into the door, I said, "I'm gonna kick your bitch ass if you don't start talking right now. Did you really tell Mandy I tried tricking you into getting me pregnant?"

"What? No! I mean-"

"And that I lied to you and said I was pregnant when I wasn't?"

"No, look, what I said—what I said—let me tell you

what I said." Fluttering one eye, he sucked his tongue. "Oh, I think I need stitches."

I punched him—not slapped, not swatted. I closed my fingers into a fist, aimed at his face with the engagement ring that Josh Okerfeldt had given me back in 2003 (yep, still wearing it), and decked him right in the beard. And yes, it probably hurt me more than it hurt him.

"Jesus Christ, Roseanne! You're crazy, you're fucking crazy," he screeched.

I shook out my hand. The throbbing pain goaded me on. "You don't know crazy, bitch! I'll throw you down these fucking stairs, baby, just you watch. You wanna push me? You wanna push me?"

He shielded his face with his arms, his elbows actually trembling. "I didn't tell her anything. I mean, I did. We talked about it."

"Talked about what? Put your goddamn hands down."

He did. "About our relationship and how I felt weird hanging out with you because of your husband."

"My husband has absolutely nothing to do with who I am or my life or the decisions I make. You got that? And I certainly didn't beg you for sex—don't even talk right now," I snapped, and he closed his mouth. "I talk, you listen. I don't beg for sex. Never have, never will. I do what I want, when I want. And the last thing I want is a child with a drug addict motherfucker who treats women like shit."

My courage ran out, and I caught my breath. Neil looked petrified.

"How's your tongue?" I asked. He twitched, too nervous to speak. "I thought you hurt your tongue. No? Oh, that's good. I'm glad you didn't really hurt yourself. I'm glad that was just some bullshit you made up. Sorry about your balls, though."

"H-"

"-fuckin' bitch!" I said, finishing the job.

Leaving Neil crumpled in the stairwell, I rejoined the others on the bridge. Terry asked if everything was all right.

"Everything's great. Wow, it's really coming down out there," I said.

Rain pelted the windows, though miles in the distance the sky was already starting to clear. Across the room Wallis and Snow were showing Ross something on one of the computers.

"What's wrong with your hand?" Terry asked.

I realized I was clenching my left hand. "Oh, yeah. I hurt it a little. It's okay—I don't think anything's broken. It already feels ten times better. Do you know where the kids are?"

He glanced around, still unsure of his bearings. "I believe they're downstairs helping the African-American gentleman whose name I can't remember."

"Gavin? What are they doing with Gavin?"

Wallis overheard and said, "Power's out in Block Delta again. Gavin's gonna hook up the new generator to see if there's an easier solution than shutting down the whole system for repairs."

"Gee, that'd be nice." I explained to Terry, "Gavin's not actually African-American. He's from Haiti or something."

Terry stepped closer to the windows. He seemed to have a lot on his mind, and I certainly didn't blame him. "Sarah sounds like she's interested in mechanical things, working with tools. It's unusual for a girl."

"Maybe it's unusual in Grand Rapids but not here," I said kindly. "Sarah can do a lot of things that most kids can't. She can weld, she can switch out a light socket."

"And all that's safe?" he asked, pressing the fingers of one hand to the window.

"I wouldn't let her if it wasn't."

He smiled faintly and took his hand from the glass. "No, I'm sure you wouldn't. I'm sorry for my questions. It's just so…" he said, searching for the word, "…strange here."

"Strange good or strange bad? Or strange you-don't-know?"

He kept his eyes on the window, as if the sky could feed him answers. "Strange different."

By the time the storm blew off to the east, Gavin and the girls had finished restoring the power in Block Delta. Terry and Ross wanted to leave in the early afternoon so they could be back in St. John's in time for dinner.

I found Terry in his room packing his bags. He'd stripped his sheets and had left them neatly folded at the foot of the bed. "So, what happens next?" I asked.

"That's up to you. I'm satisfied that Sarah is in no immediate harm."

"She can stay here? You won't tell anyone you saw me?"

"I can grant you some time, that's all. Sarah belongs with Josh and her brothers and sister. At some point you need to accept the responsibility for the pain you've caused others."

"But why?" I asked, nearly begging him. I still couldn't figure Terry out. His heart never seemed to stay in the same place.

"Because there can be no salvation without it."

"I don't need salvation, I need a break. Look, I love

Sarah. I know I messed up. I know she doesn't belong here—but I can't just give her back."

"You can. You must. Think of what our Lord sacrificed. The pain of the Cross, the-"

"But that's not me, okay? I'm not God, I'm not Jesus. I can't compete with those guys. I did what I did and I'm sorry. Why can't that be good enough?"

"Because you don't mean it," he said. With Terry it wasn't a matter of expressing an opinion; he spoke as if he could actually look into my heart and pry out the truth.

The men returned to the mainland that afternoon, a light sprinkle still in the air. Their rented boat bobbed in its slip between Mandy One and Mandy Two. Ross boarded first as Terry stayed behind to say goodbye.

Star hugged her grandfather, and he held onto her for a long time. "We'll see you soon," he said.

I could tell she was getting embarrassed, and she finally squirmed away. "Thanks for the pictures," she said.

"Oh, you're very welcome, my dear." He looked like he wanted to say something else but didn't. Maybe he figured he'd already done enough for one visit.

He gave me a kiss, much briefer and without the hug, then moved quickly to the boat. The outboard motor started up, and he called back, "Remember what I told you."

"I will. Have a safe trip home," I said, trying to keep the tone light.

The boat left the dock, puttering backwards. Terry kept a rigid neck, as if his moral integrity depended on not moving his head. I thought about waving but couldn't quite bring my hand up. Then Ross gunned the motor and the men snarled away.

I sought out Star in her room later that afternoon. She'd spread the pictures across her bed and was looking at one of Vance in his swimsuit.

"So what'd you think of your grandpa?" I asked, sitting next to her.

"He's okay," she said.

"What'd you guys talk about this morning? You were already up when I came down for breakfast."

"Nothing. Not much."

"Yeah but besides that."

"Mom, nothing. He told me about how he and his wife went out to dinner for their anniversary and he accidentally ordered a two-hundred dollar bottle of wine."

"He did? That's weird. How do you accidentally order a bottle of wine?"

"Ma, I don't know. Maybe he pronounced it wrong or he pointed at the wrong thing on the menu. Whatever, who cares."

"Strange. So that's what you talked about, going out to dinner and ordering the wrong bottle of wine?"

"We talked about other things too. I didn't memorize the conversation. I'm not a human tape recorder."

"You're not? Gee, and all this time that's what I thought you were, a human tape recorder."

"Do you want something?"

"I'm kidding. No, I just wanted to know how it went."

"It went fine, I told you."

"Fine's good. Fine's better than bad. Do you think you'd like to see him again?"

"When?"

"Whenever. I can arrange for another visit."

"Would Dad come too?"

"I don't know—I don't know what's possible but I can ask. Do you want me to ask? Because I will. I definitely will if that's what you want. But if you don't then I won't."

"Fine."

"Fine what? Fine yes or fine no?"

"Fine I don't know."

———

A few days later I was sitting on the top deck with my notebook and the dictionary that Wallis had given me for graduation. I'd been writing all morning, writing and crying. Being around the water all the time has a way of making everything seem so fluid and temporary. I'd been on the island for nearly four years but I realized I could leave tomorrow and it would've been like I'd never been there. And then I thought about the phrase "watery grave" and it scared me. I pictured a glass, coffin-shaped box filled with water and me in it. I thought of drowning versus dying-by-fire and of Sander who'd lost his own life just a few yards away. I wrote a sentence in my notebook—"You've never really been to a place until you've died there"—and immediately crossed it out. Clear as day I could see myself jumping over the side of the deck, falling in a straight line or an arc and smashing into the cold water below. And these were silly thoughts, silly, morbid, adolescent thoughts. But at the same time the thought of drifting in and out of Mobility without leaving a trace of myself scared me just as much. Going back to my notebook, I re-wrote the sentence—"You've never really been to a place until you've died there"—and left it this time. It looked good. It looked like a—what's the word?—an epitaph. And then, because I couldn't die, not yet, because I had a child to raise and responsibilities to face, I picked up my dictionary, walked across the deck, and threw it over the side. The heavy book dropped quickly, smacking into the water and sinking in a hurry. "Thanks, bro," I said.

Of course I'm still here. *We're* still here. Wallis is still here, and Charity and Neil and Dr. Snow, and Gavin's still here, and baby Sander and Mandy and Steffi, and Star's still here too. We're all still here. For now, anyway.

Things have been tense on the island. Neil and I basically don't talk to each other anymore. I think he's scared of me, which is how I like it. Mandy's scared of me too. Somehow she's decided I'm a bad influence on her son, even though the kid's only eight months old. It usually takes at least a few years for my bad influence to sink in.

A week doesn't go by without Mandy threatening to take Sander back to the mainland. I've pretty much resigned myself to it happening eventually. She'll go, and so will Neil, and then the rest of the human dominoes will fall. Dr. Snow might not even make it that long. His health has worsened—he's got pneumonia or something—and nowadays he rarely leaves his room. Charity looks tired. We're all feeling pretty bummed out.

I've received a number of emails from Terry requesting updates, maybe twenty in total. Some I've answered, others I've ignored. Sometimes he includes questions from the rest of the family, though so far he's kept his promise and told no one that he knows I'm here. Josh keeps asking for a divorce so he can marry this Jen person, but I've been putting it off. The thought of taking action—any action—frightens me.

Other than Star, the person I talk to the most is my brother. Thank God we still get along. No matter what happens, I'm staying put as long as Wallis is still here. Everyone else can leave, but I'm not going anywhere without him. I don't care if the entire rig falls into the ocean and all that's left is a cement post sticking out of the water. I'll be standing on top of it with Wallis, holding onto his chair.

He's why I came here, you know.

What do we talk about? Everything. Growing up in Milner, the time those two kids got in a fight on our front lawn and it scared the shit out of our mom, the night a small plane crashed in a field a mile from our house and the pilot turned out to be the uncle of a girl in our school. We talk about Hayes Park and Montclair Gardens and that stupid car commercial that used to come on all the time with the guy from the dealership who looked like Satan.

Sometimes we talk about the accident, but not often. Wallis still claims not to remember anything from that day, and I hope to God that's true.

Of course we talk about our parents. I'd love to be able to sneak off for a visit someday. I'd wear a disguise—a bright blonde wig, or maybe I'd stick my hair up into a hat and slap on a mustache. It'd be fun to walk to church with my dad again—if he still goes. Maybe his experience with me has soured him on the whole God thing.

As much as I miss my folks, it's really the town I need to see again. Milner, Ohio. The place where I was born, where I grew up. A town like so many other suburban locales in that part of Ohio where you can live for eighteen years without seeing a hungry face except on TV, where the slightest act of violence makes the front page of the local paper: HOUSE ON SALEM STREET BURGLARIZED; NOTHING TAKEN. We hated it when we were kids. We dreamed about escaping to Chicago or Minneapolis and getting an apartment right in the center of downtown where the vestibule smelled like piss and there was always a stack of takeout menus by the door. *Dude, I'm gettin' the Moo Shu Pork!* Where you could work at the Starbucks down the street and openly hate your customers and still not get fired. That's what we wanted—that spark, that grit and stink. But most of us never left, either in body or in spirit. Because the bottom line, despite what we thought when we were fourteen or fifteen, is that little towns like Milner are nice. The silence at night, only the sound of cars driving under the speed limit past your bedroom window. Going out for pizza with your family and seeing other kids from your school eating out with their parents too. (Thirteen speciality pizzas on the menu, each one named after a different street in town: the Morningside, the Audubon, the St. Patrick.) Homecoming, Prom, streamers stuck to your shoe. Nice place. The mayor was an old toad named Harold Paulson whose wife died in a house fire. Standup comedy night in the basement of the community center. *You know what I don't get? Those automated checkout lanes at the grocery store.* (Heh.) *I mean, what's the deal with that?* (Ha ha.) *What genius came up with that one?* All those local bands, man—The Watch, The Lake Effect, Julie's Drastic

Haircut—kids from my school like Danny Carter and Timmy "Dorkbreath" Newton who could barely hold a guitar playing dumbed-down covers of Neil Young and CCR. Milner, Ohio—my town. That's what I miss. That's why I want to go back. I want to see Milner again because it's where I came from—it's what made me the charmer I am today, for better or for worse. There has to be a clue there, some insight into my character that I'd previously overlooked. An explanation: X plus Y equals Rosie.

Break it down for me, Milner. Tell me why I'm me. Because I'm lost on my own.

ACKNOWLEDGMENTS

My most effusive thanks to my editor, Mink Choi, who along with being a funny, generous, and unbelievably hard-working person, is a symbol for and an embodiment of why those of us who traffic in letters should take hope, and heart. Thanks to my close friends, Joshua Furst, Gordon Haber, and Joseph McElroy, for all the usual reasons, but specifically in this case for their editorial insights into this book. Thanks to J.E. Reich, for putting me in touch with Mink. Thanks to Will Hess, for trying to help (and trying is helping). Thanks to my wife, especially for her support during the difficult times that accompanied the relatively easy writing of this book, and to my daughter, for being a good napper.

ABOUT THE AUTHOR

Mike Heppner is the author of the novels *The Egg Code* and *Pike's Folly*, two collections of short fiction, *The Man Talking Project* and *This Can Be Easy or Hard*, and a novella, *Nada*. His writing has appeared in *Poets & Writers*, *The New Guard*, *The Good Men Project*, and *Golden Handcuffs Review*. He lives in Arlington, MA.

Thought Catalog
It's a website.
www.thoughtcatalog.com

Social
facebook.com/thoughtcatalog
twitter.com/thoughtcatalog
tumblr.com/thoughtcatalog
instagram.com/thoughtcatalog

Corporate
www.thought.is